Goddesses

& Other Stories

Goddesses

& Other Stories

Linda Nagata

Mythic Island Press LLC
Kula, Hawaii

This is a work of fiction. All the characters and events portrayed in this story collection are fictitious or are used fictitiously.

Goddesses & Other Stories

ISBN 978-1-937197-11-7

First Electronic Edition November 2011
First Print Edition July 2012

PUBLISHING HISTORY:
Spectral Expectations Copyright © 1987 by Linda Nagata.
First published in *Analog Science Fiction & Fact*, April 1987

Career Decision Copyright © 1988 by Linda Nagata.
First published in *Analog Science Fiction & Fact*, October 1988.

In the Tide Copyright © 1989 by Linda Nagata.
First published in *Analog Science Fiction & Fact*, September 1989.

Small Victories Copyright © 1993 by Linda Nagata.
First published in *Analog Science Fiction & Fact*, September 1993.

Liberator Copyright © 1993 by Linda Nagata.
First published in *The Magazine of Fantasy & Science Fiction*, June 1993.

Old Mother Copyright © 1995 by Linda Nagata.
First published in *The Magazine of Fantasy & Science Fiction*, April 1995.

The Bird Catcher's Children Copyright © 1997 by Linda Nagata.
First published in *The Magazine of Fantasy & Science Fiction*, January 1997.

Hooks, Nets, and Time Copyright © 1997 by Linda Nagata.
First published in *The Magazine of Fantasy & Science Fiction*, August 1997.

The Flood Copyright © 1998 by Linda Nagata.
First published in *More Amazing Stories*, 1998.

Goddesses Copyright © 2000 by Linda Nagata.
First published online by Sci-Fi.com, July-August 2000.
Mythic Island Press LLC electronic edition of *Goddesses & Other Stories*, November 2011.

Mythic Island Press LLC
PO Box 1293
Kula, HI 96790-1293
MythicIslandPress.com

Contents

Preface
7

Spectral Expectations
9

Career Decision
25

In the Tide
51

Small Victories
73

Liberator
109

Old Mother
151

The Bird Catcher's Children
173

Hooks, Nets, and Time
197

The Flood
223

Goddesses
233

Author's Preface

Like many writers in the science fiction genre, my first publishing successes came in the form of short stories, but unfortunately for me, I've always found short stories very hard to write. This collection contains every piece of my short fiction published between 1987 and 2000—all ten of them.

I use the term "short fiction" liberally, to mean anything under novel length. There are only two truly short stories here. The Science Fiction & Fantasy Writers of America defines a short story as 7,500 words or less, while a novelette is 7,500 to 17,500 words, and a novella is up to 40,000 words. I tend to write short novelettes or long short stories—five of the stories in this collection are between seven and eight thousand words. Two are long novelettes, and one, the Nebula Award winning *Goddesses*, is a hefty novella of 32,000 words.

I freely confess I'm a novelist by nature. *Goddesses* was the last "short" fiction I attempted until this fall, when I surprised myself by writing . . . well, another novelette.

Thanks for giving *Goddesses & Other Stories* a try. I hope you find it to your liking.

Linda Nagata
November 11, 2011

Spectral Expectations

It was raining when I landed on Maui, a heavy downpour that pounded the runway and pulled the terminal lights into long, watery reflections. I disembarked, threading my way past bewildered tourists and lei-bearing, professional greeters dressed in authentic Polynesiana.

A sleepy clerk at the rent-a-car booth examined my Hertz card. "Mr. Kyle Fisher," he mumbled, then turned to his terminal and called up my reservation.

Not much had changed at Kahului airport since I'd last come through, some years back—but elsewhere . . . the industrialized world was in flower. The controversy over lunar mining rights had been settled with minimal loss of life and the ensuing land rush had fostered a global economic spiral-up. The first generation of factory stations in lunar and Earth orbits were already producing more of their own kind. Multi-billion dollar investments were common, because returns came back on the same scale. Projects that would have seemed frivolous two decades ago were suddenly being drawn up in detailed plan—a sure sign of good times. Everybody had a thumb in the pie.

Even me. I'd won a position as sector boss on K.B.—my own sweet slice of glory.

"How long is this storm supposed to last?" I asked.

"Two days."

Wonderful. I only had two days of leave left.

For three weeks I'd been moving around the country, sort of a peregrination I guess, saying goodbye to old friends and family, some of whom I didn't expect to see again. K.B.—Kasorsky Biological Station—was in assembly over Venus and I was bound there, scheduled for a shuttle flight on the 31st—the first leg of a very long journey. I wouldn't be home for at least seven years.

"Are you here for business or on vacation, sir?" the clerk asked, remembering to be friendly.

"Visiting an old friend."

"Ah."

Derek and I had been college buddies, and I'd spent more than a few vacations at his folks' place, trying to lose some of the tensions built up during the University of Hawaii's long semesters. Graduate school and a few years of honest employment had passed since I'd last visited the Chun farm. I hoped that not too much had changed.

"Hitchhiking's illegal and you have to wear your seatbelt," the clerk warned. "And no smoking in the car. Have a great vacation."

"I will."

The rain had slacked off to a drizzle by the time I turned onto an unpaved road bordering a prosperous macadamia nut plantation. As I downshifted and leaned on the accelerator, the car skidded in the mud, back wheels fishtailing while the headlights swept crazily across stark, regimented rows of trees. The road climbed for a quarter mile, then split, one branch diving down to cross a gully, the other, narrower, steering a level course. I took that one, forded a long puddle, and pulled up in front of a farmhouse now nearly eighty years old.

"Shit, Derek."

The house was dark. Derek had warned me his folks would be out, but I'd thought he at least would be there. Leaving the car lights on, I switched off the engine and made a dash for the covered lanai. An old shepherd dog was lying on a mat by the front door. He got up on stiff limbs and walked over to sniff me, his rheumy eyes friendly.

"Hey, Hoku. You still alive?"

The front door was unlocked so I stuck my head in and yelled. No answer. I found the light switch and hit it. Dim yellow porch lights threw their shadows across the cement floor. I went back to the car to retrieve my bag and turn off the headlights. Derek would show up eventually.

The farm—more of a hobby than a business—belonged to all of the Chun family, though the day-to-day work was done by Derek's folks. Mostly they grew taro, a semi-aquatic plant that thrives in flooded terraces called lo`i. Taro had been a staple in ancient Hawaii; prepared as poi, it was still a popular food.

I went through the house, but found no one; returned to the lanai to wait.

Some kind of pet bird was roosting on a perch set up in a sheltered corner of the lanai. A bit of sennit bound its leg to the wood. It ruffled its feathers and made an odd, throaty sound as I approached. The bird was beautiful—somewhat larger than a mockingbird and black, with a long tail and tufts of yellow feathers on its wings, on the sides of its head, and at the base of its tail. Its dark brown eyes swept across me, a calculating look.

I turned, as a distant engine revved. Headlights flashed somewhere down the road, bouncing in and out of sight until at last a covered jeep rounded the final curve and pulled up behind my muddy rental. The rain had almost stopped.

"Kyle!" a woman's voice called.

"Terri? Hey Terri! I didn't know you'd be here. Alright! Man, it's been years."

She hopped out of the jeep and hugged me, then Derek came around and we shook hands, grinning like idiots. "You look good," she told me.

"You too." And it was true. Terri was Hawaiian/ Chinese/ French/ German; tall, thin, and strong as the earth. She still wore her hair long and straight, still gazed right inside me with those wide, dark, honest eyes. For five years she'd been the manager of the Manawainui Preserve, a tract of rainforest high up on the eastern slopes of Haleakala, one of the two volcanoes that made up the island of Maui.

"I thought you were supposed to be at a conference in New Zealand," I said.

"Busy. Couldn't make it."

"Things have been jumping around here," Derek said. "That's why we were late. Hey, grab a seat." He went inside, came out again, with a bottle of wine, a box of crackers and three plastic tumblers. "Did you see my latest creation?" he asked, and nodded towards the bird.

I glanced at it. It was wide-awake now, its dark eyes gazing coldly at a moth that fluttered around a near-by light.

"I was wondering if that was one of yours. It looks a little . . . primeval."

"It's called an o`o," Derek explained. "*Moho bishopi*, or Molokai O`o, if you prefer. A delicate species, territorial in habit . . . extinct for over a hundred years."

"Lovely."

Derek was a creationist. That is, he was a geneticist who specialized in re-creating extinct life forms. Just raid a museum, give him a few tissue samples from the preserved carcass of some extinct organism, set him down in the lab facilities at U. of

Washington and wait. Within a few months he'd have a transcript of the creature's DNA code, compiled from information still surviving in the ancient cells. Give him a few more weeks and he'd hand you the assembled chromosomes, ready for propagation. For the past three years he'd been working for the Hui Aloha Aina, a powerful preservationist group devoted to the Manawainui Preserve.

Terri walked over to the bird and encouraged it to hop up on her curled fingers. "Hawaiian bird catchers, the *kia manu* who collected feathers for the nobility's ceremonial capes, were supposed to have kept o`o as pets. We thought we'd try."

"It's illegal for us to have it," Derek said. "Wildlife laws and all—so keep your mouth shut."

Terri moved her hand slowly up and down until the bird spread its wings for balance. It really was beautiful. Then she let it step back onto its perch. "You know that there were no native land mammals in Hawaii before people came here."

"Sure." I had a minor in natural history from my U.H. days.

"No reptiles or amphibians either. It seems odd, but except for *pueo*, the owl, and *io*, the hawk, these beauties were the ultimate predators in their ecosystem."

"Eating bugs."

"Yes, fierce carnivores—when they weren't drinking nectar."

Eden on Earth, I thought, and remembered a lecture I'd heard once by a professor of exobiology who was adept at drawing parallels:

Imagine a generational starship, self-sufficient for a million years, never calling at any port, creeping through space, through the deep, a tiny world to itself where change runs at the slow, slow pace of genes. With no in-migrations to throw the ecosystem off-balance, it can adapt to itself. Competition becomes more theoretical than real. Low reproductive rates become the norm; plants and insects lose their toxins and their thorns, their bites and stings, their ability to disperse . . . No longer are defenses necessary, because everything is in balance. There is predation, yes, a natural function of any system, but finely tuned, with a minimum of waste. The ecosystem begins to function almost as a single organism . . .

We already have an analog of this imaginary ship: the isolated islands of the Hawaiian archipelago.

Except that 'had' would have been the correct verb form. Fifteen hundred years ago the ancestors of the Hawaiian people found these islands. They arrived in great double-hulled canoes, bringing pigs, dogs, rats (by accident!) and plants of their own, clearing land and changing the look of the coastlines. After them, the Europeans came. In the two hundred and fifty years since Captain James Cook made landfall on Kauai, introduced plants, introduced animals—especially cattle, goats, pigs, deer—and introduced disease have destroyed or displaced millennia of evolution. A few pockets of native forest still survive in the rugged mountains, but in a state far from pristine.

Derek pulled out some rickety old chairs and we sat down at a small card table.

"How are things at the preserve?" I asked.

"Bad," he said. "Real bad."

"We can't keep up with it," Terri said. She shook her head sadly. "I don't care how many people we have, we can't keep foreign plants and animals from invading the preserve. The system's just too sensitive. Our very presence there has an adverse effect on the forest."

"Damn shame."

"Damn waste," Derek said. He reached for the bottle and topped off everyone's glass, a good cabernet from a Maui vineyard. "A living laboratory of evolution, as they say, gone to Hell."

Sheet lightning flickered in a cloud bank somewhere off the coast and we turned to watch.

Talk wandered onto other subjects. They asked me questions about Kasorsky Biological Station and I tried to answer. K.B. was one of those New World projects, the end result of the vogue in long-term planning we'd enjoyed for the past few years. Her end-goal was the terraforming of Venus. In the intervening centuries—or at least for the remainder of this one—she would conduct research on various Earth eco-systems, evaluating their relative merits against the eventual needs of the large orbiting colonies we all believed would be built one day. Opponents argued her only purpose was to amuse malnourished evolutionists and ecologists. That, of course, is not true.

Terri tipped her chair back, so that it balanced on two legs. "Remember when we were kids?", she asked, giving me a hazy, nostalgic smile. "And our parents would take us night fishing at Mokuleia?"

"Sure. Afterwards, we'd make a bonfire on the beach, and tell ghost stories. You always thought the stories were real, especially the one's your mother told." Terri's mother had been one-half Hawaiian and I swear she knew every hair-raising story ever devised about the akua: the ghosts and the gods of ancient Hawaii. Some fears are irrational and deeply ingrained. I shivered then, just thinking about her tales.

"I still believe them. Now, more than ever . . . And I've got one for you."

"Yeah?"

There was a loud splash in the nearest lo`i; probably a toad.

Derek shot a look over his shoulder and laughed nervously—the perfect accomplice. Terri kept her eyes on me.

"Been having trouble with ghosts?" I asked, trying to be funny.

She nodded. "In the preserve."

"Oh." I didn't glance at the dark and the rain beyond the dimly-lit lanai . . . though I wanted to. I wasn't going to let her scare me . . . though it was the perfect night for her to try.

"We released the o`o last spring," Terri said, speaking in a low, clear voice as if she were giving testimony at a criminal trial. "Twelve individuals, all mature. I went back, about a month later and released four more."

"Great."

"Yes. They seemed to be doing well. Then I broke my leg trying to get down a waterlogged trail at Ahulili. I was laid up all summer; the preserve went on hold. Nobody was up there that I know of, from June to early September. So nobody felt the change."

The rain picked up again, a steady drumming on the roof; Derek stared at the table, his fingers laced in a tight weave. Very softly he said, "Apparently the birds had started breeding."

Terri nodded. "It was an experiment, trying to put the forest back together. And as with any complex experiment, there were . . . unexpected side effects. It seems that things stranger than birds and flowers were lost when the forests were destroyed."

Derek pushed his chair around so that his back was to the house, not The Night. The chair legs made an awful scraping sound on the cement. He said, "The world used to abound with gods. Maybe they were more than imagination."

I laughed at him.

Terri smiled. "It was late afternoon," she said, "when a helicopter dropped me off in the Kuiki grasslands. We went hiking there once, Kyle, remember?"

"Sure I do." The "grasslands" were an eroded planeze 6,000 feet above sea level on the windward slopes of Haleakala. Once the tract had been fertile, but a hundred and fifty years of browsing by introduced goats and pigs had stripped it of its vegetation. The subsequent erosion had removed up to six feet of soil in some places. Only a few gnarled ohia trees survived there, amidst a patchwork of bare lava and non-native grasses. The goats were gone now, removed in the late eighties by the National Park Service, but the land would need centuries to recover—if it ever did. Terri's preserve, with its dense forests, was on the lower slopes, where rainfall was higher and less damage had been done.

"I walked down to the forest," Terri said. "And set up camp where I always do, in a small patch of moss and ferns between the trees.

"A full moon rose around eight o'clock that night. It cast a grey light across the forest and washed out all but the brightest stars. I watched it for awhile, then crawled into the tent and fell asleep.

"But about midnight a gust of wind blew through camp, banging together the aluminum dishes I'd hung on a tree to dry and waking me with a start. I listened, and heard strange yippings—like lost puppies crying. It was the call of ua`u, the seabird that nests in burrows in the cliffs above Kipahulu Valley. Strange, I thought, that they'd be stirring. They're birds of the twilight, flying in to shore at dusk, and out to sea again before the sun rises. In the middle night they're quiet. So something had disturbed them.

"I sat up in my sleeping bag, trying to be silent . . . but the tent floor crackled as I moved. The outer door was partially unzipped. I leaned over and peered through the screened slit.

"The gust of wind that woke me had passed. The camp was quiet again. But there were groaning sounds in the forest. A loud *crack!* wrenched the air, followed by a rush of twigs being torn apart as a tree branch fell. "The wind came again then, this time in a flurry of gusts that shook the tree-tops and blew dark clouds across the moonlit sky. I wriggled out of my sleeping bag, unzipped the tent and hurried to quiet the clatter of the pans. With two pots and an aluminum cup clutched in my hands, I paused to listen.

"There was the sound of wind soughing through the trees; the lonely moans of branches as they scraped against each other . . . and on the edge of hearing a low-pitched trilling . . . as if the wind had made a flute of some beetle-drilled bough and was playing it in minor key.

"'Imagination, Terri,' I told myself, holding my breath to hear. But the breeze was gaining strength, and the sound—if it had ever existed at all—was lost in its roar."

She let a few seconds of silence fall there. Her eyes grew distant, her gaze wandered away from mine, restless, shifting to the attentive bird, to Derek, then finally resting on the dark that surrounded our little light. A chill walked with insect legs up and down my spine.

"It says something of the strangeness of the night," Terri said, "that I could sleep at all, but I did. For a while.

"At three o'clock I awoke again. I checked my watch: the liquid crystal figures said 3:00 AM exactly. The wind had died, but there'd been rain, and water was still dripping from the trees onto leaves, onto my tent, splashing with a sharp, slapping sound—*pock!* The forest seemed to be moving around me.

"Inside my tent, the darkness was impenetrable. I lay still, eyes open on nothingness, waiting. There was no humming, no drumming—only the quiet drip-drip of stray raindrops falling on the tent. Yet I felt a presence all around me." Her eyes closed, and she smiled, peaceful. "Its aura was cool," she said, "like leaves under moonlight, humus on the forest floor, tumbling mountain streams. Vast, like the roots of volcanoes. And old—yet younger than the sea. It seemed to permeate the life forms of the forest: the plants, the birds, the snails, the insects and—*me*."

Her eyes flew open. "Kyle, it was in me.

"Oh, my thoughts still moved in their own channels, but at the same time I could feel traces of the other. Something that breathed in diurnal rhythms, echoing the slow flux of energies in the day/night/day/night cycle. It wasn't evil, no; but not beneficent either. Only existing. *In me*. I trembled when I realized *that*. I didn't dare look to either side."

She steepled her hands, pressed the tips of her fingers against her chin, eyes fixed on the table. "Yet even in that moment, I'm not sure I wanted it gone. *Who?*, I thought, and maybe I formed the question with my lips. *What are you?* And immediately the presence began to withdraw. It was a spirit, seeping out of my nose and mouth. I stopped breathing, hoping to catch it, but it slipped away. The wind rustled briefly, then silence."

Derek let out a long breath. I swallowed. "Good story," I said. And tried to laugh.

Terri looked up and caught me with her remarkable eyes. "But Kyle, it isn't finished yet."

"Oh."

"I wondered: *what could it be?*"

"The spirit of an old kahuna," I suggested. "A Hawaiian priest."

She shook her head. "No. I could tell it was not human, it was too strange, I could sense that much. And . . . it was a timeless thing as well. It couldn't conceive of past and future as we do; for it, only the present was real. My questions had disturbed it you see, because to ask a question implies expectation and expectation demands a future.

"So dawn came—a bright morning—and I decided to stay, against all nocturnal intentions. Maybe I was enchanted even then, I don't know . . . but I wasn't afraid anymore. And there was work to do.

"In the preserve, even routine observations are fun. I watched a community of apapane—little red-feathered, black-winged birds—hunt nectar in the ohi`a trees. I saw an i`iwi and a crested honeycreeper. Then I sighted a pair of our o`o and followed them around, making notes and taking pictures; they seemed to have a nest somewhere nearby.

"But it wasn't long before the birds finished their morning foraging, and fell silent. I turned to my transect lines after that, vegetational surveys that allow us to track changes in the preserve. As the morning passed, clouds built up over the slopes, and by noon the rain began. I kept on. It was past two o' clock when I clambered across a shallow gully, water streaming in my eyes, and paused to rest.

"In the cloud-wrapped forest everything was grey except for the occasional blooms: red lehua or purple ohawai. It was a separate world—so isolated—an island of timeless past. I leaned against a fern-encrusted tree to catch my breath, listening to the stillness around me. I was the only animate creature anywhere to be seen. For a moment I felt as if I'd slipped in time and space to a jungle that had never known humankind. I felt small, like a nervous cricket crouching under a leaf, shivering in the rain.

"It was then that the sense of *presence* returned to me. It came slowly, so that I didn't notice it until it had been with me for a time. Then a dark shadow flitted across the edge of my vision. I turned instantly—but all I saw were rain-wet leaves and moss-laden branches. Yet the awareness was there, as strong as last night, in me, in the forest, in every nearby living thing.

"Until then, I had almost convinced myself that the incidents of the night had been a dream. But I wasn't sleeping now. '*E kala mai*,' I said softly. 'Go on, akua. Leave me alone. Please.'

"I didn't run, though I wanted to. I kept to a walk, concentrating on building up false images in my mind: I wasn't really alone and far from home; no, friends were waiting around the corner; food and warmth were only a few minutes away.

"In an hour I'd made it back to camp. I stripped off my wet gear and dove into the tent, burrowing into the sleeping bag and pulling it up over my head. By the time evening came around, I was almost calm again. But the presence hadn't left me. It stayed with me, the whole time I was there."

Terri sighed. "I got used to it, Kyle—that's the scary part. I learned to live within it; I *liked* being part of it—for awhile.

I stayed for days and while I was there, I suffered no human doubts, no human expectations. It was wonderful. Especially late at night, when I was only half-awake. Then it was like a drug haze, a tremendous sense of inevitability and changelessness. This akua, this forest spirit had learned during fifteen hundred years of Hawaiian occupation all about human needs. It knew mine perfectly.

"My food ran out eventually. Other than that, I'm not sure I would have left."

Derek stirred. "I went back with her later," he said. "And everything she says is true."

"Except that the sense was weaker . . . in company. Synchronicity. It was harder to forget our human selves when we were both there to remind each other of what we were. It's a true story, Kyle. Do you believe me?"

I blinked. *Are you kidding, my dear?* "No."

"But it's true."

"Sorry."

"Well. That's good, I guess."

"Huh?"

She looked at Derek. I followed her gaze and saw him nod. "We wondered what it was," she said. "And where it came from . . . because it hadn't been there before. What had changed?, we asked ourselves. What? Except that life had been returned to the forest. Organisms once extinct were again part of the community. An *ancient* community: whole, balanced . . . functioning as a unit. Could this be the answer? Could the akua be a byproduct of a finely tuned ecosystem? Even as the mind is a byproduct of that organic system we call the brain?"

"You've had too much wine," I said. "You always talk too much when you've had too much wine."

"Kyle," she chided. "Just think about it for a minute, please. What is an organism, except a collection of discrete cells existing together in a fixed yet flexible pattern that allows the free exchange of information? Substitute discrete organisms for cells, design a method of communication between the parts involving a high number of associational paths . . . why should a superorganism *not* exist?"

"By 'communication' you mean telepathy, psionics."

A tiny smile flickered across her lips. She knew that subject was a sore point with me. "Telepathy might work—"

"Uh-uh." I shook my head. "Never has; never will."

"—until you consider that most of the organisms involved don't possess enough neuronal matter to constitute a brain."

Derek spoke up. "Of course we could postulate auras, intuition. Psychic phenomena that don't require higher brain function. Some people will tell you that all life forms have a latent awareness of other life forms—an expanded Gaia hypothesis."

"And the world is carried on the back of a turtle," I snapped.

Terri laid a soothing hand on mine. "There are more mundane forms of communication that might work too," she said. "The human mind may be nothing more than an intricate set of chemical reactions, yet apparently that's enough to produce thought, civilization, K.B. station. Suppose in the eco-organism, pheromones serve as an analog of the mind's chemical messengers. Communication by airborne scent would be slow compared to the electrical impulse generated in a nerve cell, but a pheromone has the advantage in range. Insects can detect certain substances over a distance of two kilometers."

"Humans don't possess the analytical chemistry equipment of insects."

"So far as we know."

"Neither do snails or o`o. Or trees."

She laughed softly. "Maybe. Maybe not. There's a lot we don't know about communication—or about the brain; the mind. But maybe *you'll* have a chance to find out."

Inexplicably, I felt my chest go tight. "Me? What's that supposed to mean?"

She held up her hand. "In a minute. First, there's one more thing you should know."

I waited, wary.

"We—Derek and I—believe that if it can, this akua will assimilate all life forms into itself, into a single superorganism—the forest. It must do this to survive. Alien forms like you and me can't coexist with it for long because we disrupt the pattern in which it finds its existence. So it *must* guide us towards a state of compatibility."

"But Terri, *how?*"

"Remember the drug haze, Kyle? The ability to induce an effect like that would be a wonderful adaptation for disarming a dangerous intruder. And don't forget: human, o`o, or snail, we're all Earth organisms. We share the same biochemical pathways. It's not as if a new communications system would have to be devised every time a strange creature entered the woods." She drew in a deep breath. "So. Either we change and are absorbed by the akua . . . or we die."

"Or it dies," Derek said. "More likely."

Terri grunted an agreement. Apparently that was not the option she preferred.

"Be careful next time you're in the preserve," I suggested. I didn't say it nicely.

"I will. And I want you to be careful on K.B. station."

My eyebrows rose.

Derek said: "You know Mackenzie's been collecting ecosystems for K.B."

"Sure. That's why the station exists."

"She had a Costa Rican rainforest scheduled for the third deck of sector three, but that fell through. Wars, she said. Too many biologists killed trying to collect specimens. So she gave that deck to us."

"To you? Mackenzie didn't say anything to me—"

"You've been on the road for weeks; she couldn't catch up with you to let you know."

"A true story, Kyle," Terri said . . . as if it cost her. "I wish it weren't, but I had to tell you before you go. In the void . . . it's always night, isn't it?"

There aren't many people in the huge vaults of K.B. station. From horizon to upcurving horizon, only jungle. It can make a man feel very small. On the third deck of sector three the Manawainui Experimental Forest is thriving; has been, for nearly five years. Soon, it'll be time to introduce the birds—honeycreepers, parrotbills, and of course the o`o—and then the system will be complete.

Lately, I've started thinking about Terri again. I try to remember a time during our long childhood when she played a prank on me. I can't. Terri never joked. I told her story to some friends on K.B. station. I make sure I'm never alone.

Spectral Expectations was my first published fiction. It appeared in Analog Science Fiction & Fact, in April 1987. Yes, a ghost story in Analog. Ironic, isn't it?

Career Decision

Tomahoff couldn't shake the conviction that he'd been the last person in a position to stop the war—and that he'd failed.

Observe; don't interfere. Those had been his orders. And he'd followed them to the letter. Every time he screwed up, it was because he insisted on following orders. This time, too many people had paid for his mistake.

He climbed the long, concrete ramp of a subterranean parking garage up from under the superheated ruins of the Schonhausen police station. An empty munitions vault in a basement three stories underground had saved him from the fire. He still carried with him a half-empty oxygen tank. Around his neck his radio phones hung, their tiny speakers jabbering high-pitched German: *Shop at Harrah's in Schonhausen for the best in foreign fashions; Visit Restaurant Yoshitsune, featuring live lobsters, oysters, crabs and clams; Protect yourself and your unborn baby . . .* Advertisements, broadcast by an automated radio station: the only intact facility in the area. Programming should have arrived over the satellite. Not today.

Reaching the middle of the deserted street, Tomahoff paused to survey the results of the Russians' surgical strike against the West German border town. Beds of embers marked the remains of the police station and a nearby supermarket. Gingerbread-laden buildings huddled between, their paint scorched and their windows shattered by the repeated blasts. The town itself had been abandoned. Only one vehicle was left on the street: an old IVECO truck, its hood up and its front windshield a frosty span of broken glass. Turning a slow circle, Tomahoff counted nine other columns of smoke climbing on the still evening air. Those would be communications facilities and food warehouses. Beyond the jagged line of Bavarian rooftops, a huge red sun sank in melodramatic splendor.

What a fuck up, he thought. He hefted the oxygen bottle, testing its weight. Then with a roar, he heaved it through a storefront.

A few more fragments of glass tinkled bitterly to the ground.

If only he'd known . . .

The pulse-beat lament that had pounded in his head all day as he crouched in the oven-dry heat of the munitions vault, came back to him now.

If only he'd known that peace depended on the timeliness of Shamsher Rajid's forced 'defection' to the Soviet Union, he could have intervened, pointed the KGB agents towards their quarry. He hadn't known. He hadn't thought the situation through. He'd only followed orders: *observe; don't interfere*.

Shamsher Rajid had come to Schonhausen as a participant in the European Enhanced Intelligence Conference. He'd delivered a scheduled speech to the assembly, then promptly dropped out of sight along with his five year old son, Pieter.

Not out of Tomahoff's sight, to be sure. Tomahoff had been more careful than the Russians. A twelve hour bug nestled like an epithelial cell against the American scientist's right forearm sang his whereabouts at three second intervals. But Tomahoff hadn't shared that data with the Soviets.

His lips curled back in voiceless rage. *I should have exposed him to the KGB!*

Now it was too late.

The gray men had finally caught up with Rajid in the morning, when he surfaced at a local train station with Pieter. But the Kremlin generals, suspecting betrayal, had already opted for war. Even as Rajid was being forced into the back of a black sedan, the first bombs fell on Schonhausen.

Tomahoff looked down at his heat-blistered hands. How had Rajid known he was to be sacrificed? And how had he known when to set Pieter loose so the boy could escape into the early morning crowds of office workers? During the long hours underground, he'd explored those questions again and again, coming up always with the same answer: the seer had warned him.

He ran his injured fingers through his long, dark hair, taking penance from the pain of his burns. Then he took out his pocket phone and punched in a number. Silence rang in his ear for over a minute. *How many satellites have been knocked out? Has the war gone nuclear yet?* Closing his eyes, he muttered into the open line: "Secret agent James Tomahoff reporting for duty. Sir."

Behind him, a child giggled.

"Pieter?" Slowly, he turned around.

Orders hadn't covered the moment when the boy fled. So Tomahoff made up his own mind and pursued him in a crosstown chase that culminated in the Schonhausen police station, where they both sought refuge from the attack. It was Pieter who found the firedoor leading down to the basement. Tomahoff followed him underground, but lost sight of the elusive child just moments before an incendiary bomb ignited the upper floors.

Now Pieter had chosen to reappear. Half-hidden in the evening light, he crouched near the mouth of an alley, just behind a long wooden flower bed whose seared blooms had collapsed into a tangled brown mat. His wide eyes studied Tomahoff, while his child fingers picked nervously at a peel of scorched white paint. "Don't run away again, Pieter. Please."

Pieter Rajid's black skin reflected his Bengali heritage, but his hair had been styled in line with the latest American fashion: short everywhere except for the skinny French braid that ran from the crest of his skull to the nape of his neck. The already muted colors of his shirt and pants had been eclipsed by smoke stains; he'd lost his jacket with the red reflector stripes.

Slowly, Tomahoff dropped into a crouch, bringing himself down to the boy's level. Pieter struck him as a strange kid. Remote. Disconnected somehow from the real world. The depth of his eyes hinted at an age older than five years. "Hey, Pieter. Do you think we can help each other get out of this mess?"

The boy cocked his head as if listening to some faint sound. Oddly, he seemed more curious than scared . . . as if he had the situation in hand.

"When you disappeared in that basement, Pieter," Tomahoff went on, speaking swiftly as the boy began to edge away, "I thought you'd gotten lost. Wandered back to the upper levels maybe and that would have been it. I'm glad you made it through."

A pebble skittered across hot asphalt as Pieter scampered into the dusky shadows of the alley. Tomahoff swore silently. "Pieter—" he began.

The boy's small voice interrupted him: "You have a new assignment, Jim. She's coming to tell you about it. She wants you to meet her. On the east edge of town. By the highway, that's right."

A rivulet of superstitious fear trickled through Tomahoff's gut. "Who wants to meet me, Pieter?" Distant movement caught his eye. He glanced up. Three blocks away, a dog had emerged into the ruddy light. It paused when it saw him and wagged its tail hopefully. Turning back to Pieter, he asked: “Who is she?”

No answer.

When he checked the alley, the boy was gone. With a sigh, Tomahoff began walking towards the east, wondering how Pieter had learned his name.

Dinner was gleaned from an employee lunch room: sandwiches, cookies and a six pack of Coke. The dog was waiting for him when he returned to the street. It had followed him across town, though he hadn’t said a word to encourage it. He set off again in an easterly direction. The dog fell into step ten meters behind him.

Tomahoff’s thoughts wandered back (only a week!) to the first time he’d seen Rajid. It had been at the American embassy in Bonn. The psychologist had stopped there on his way to the Enhanced Intelligence Conference. Talk among the resident reporters suggested that he was directing a revolutionary artificial intelligence program, possibly under the auspices of the National Security Agency. Predictive analysis. That was the term that had been tossed about, apparently referring to a new generation seer computer, designed to foretell the course of near-future events.

Tomahoff paused to sniff suspiciously at an egg sandwich. From the rumors, he’d assumed the computer was still in the planning stage. Only when he received his orders did he realize it must have already been built, and—he took a bite out of the sandwich, forcing himself to swallow against the sudden tension in his throat—it must have worked. Why else would Rajid have been sacrificed to the Soviet Union? A functioning seer would destabilize the delicate balance between east and west. Russia would assume the device was to be used to plan a first strike against her. With the nascent revolution in Czechoslovakia already feeding Soviet anxiety, NATO command must have seen war as inevitable . . . unless they made a peace offering. What better gift than the designer of the seer? (*Learn all about our system! Build one of your very own!*)

Darkness slowly filled the street as he finished the egg sandwich. A chill breeze sprang up out of the east. The dog's nostrils flared in the wind; then it growled.

Tomahoff stared at the animal. It was looking past him, at something farther down the street. No movement there that he could see. Suddenly, a short, high-pitched human cry cut the evening air. Moments later, there came another call, much closer. Instinctively, Tomahoff dropped back into the shadows of the building.

Shadows won't hide you from night vision!

He looked for better shelter; saw a sporting goods store only a few meters away. Glass from its broken window had spilled across the sidewalk. He edged towards it. He'd almost reached it when, less than a block away, a man-sized stick figure materialized in the middle of the street, its body drawn in luminescent green strips. "*Sind sie ein soldat?*" Are you a soldier? The soft voice carried easily in the twilight.

"I'm *lost*," Tomahoff said. He recognized the apparition from news clips he'd seen. A Party of Angels commando, for sure. High-tech terrorists schooled in psychological warfare. *Mindfucking*: his lips shaped the word. Angels were supposed to be non-violent. "I'm no soldier. Just lost." He wondered if the man in the electric suit had infrared goggles.

"We're all lost," the soft voice answered. "The powers that be have led us to the edge of the abyss. Turn back now. There's still time to turn back."

Tomahoff leaned against the brick building, drew a deep breath, then reached into the store's display shelf, searching blindly for a shard of glass. His eyes never strayed from the figure in the street.

"Don't take up weapons, soldier. Peace is the answer. We'll all die unless we disarm." When he didn't answer, the stick figure sighed and switched itself off. Tomahoff was blind in the sudden darkness. "You should have gone out with the evacuation," the disembodied voice warned. "This is the central front. The war will sweep through here again. Stay, and you'll be dead by morning."

He waited, barely breathing, keeping one eye on the dog. It stared intently into the shadows for nearly a minute, its ears twitching as it tracked something he couldn't see. Only when it finally relaxed, did he drop the shard of glass. "Asshole," he said. He called the dog to him, scratched it behind the ear and fed it half a sandwich. Then he backtracked a block before starting east again down another street.

The last of the sun's light had faded by the time he found the highway leading out of town. Pieter wasn't there, so he sat on a stone wall next to the road to wait. In the north, artillery thumped like an off-balance engine. The clouds burned red.

An hour passed. He looked at the dog. "What the hell am I doing here?" The animal rolled its eyes. *I'm following orders again, aren't I?* Pieter's orders. Why had the boy been so sure of himself?

At 20:07 he thought he heard the fluttering of wind against canvas. The dog pricked up its ears. "Somebody new coming on stage, girl?" He scanned the cloudy skies, but didn't see the chute.

At 20:15 someone started playing with holograms in the stubble field on the other side of the highway. The display was typical Angel art: a quartet of radiation-rotted corpses dressed in Soviet army uniforms. The faceless light artist sent his phantoms hobbling slowly towards the highway.

The dog whined, and a moment later Tomahoff heard the sound too: the deep throated purr of tanks coming up the road from Czechoslovakia. He dropped behind the wall into a low stand of brush, ceding the highway to the Angels' grisly reception committee.

"*Jim!*"

The whispered voice was a goad that sent the dog charging, teeth bared. Tomahoff caught it by the ruff of its neck. "Come on in, Pieter," he hissed over the rumbling tanks. "If that's you."

A child-sized shadow detached itself from the brush and moved forward into the faint red light cast by the northern battle. "I hope you're tired of running, Pieter, because I'm damn tired of chasing you across half—" He stopped in midsentence and blinked hard. Beyond the boy's right shoulder, suspended more than five feet above the ground, a girl face in red-glowing wraparound glasses stared at him.

"She's here, Jim," Pieter said quietly, as he bent down to pet the dog.

For a moment, Tomahoff could see no body at all. Then she moved, and the silver glow of a pending moonrise slurred across her figure. He swallowed against a dry throat. "Camouflage chill suit, isn't it?" he asked.

"That's right." Her voice was low and liquid, tinged with the petulance of adolescence.

"I've never seen one before . . . though I've heard rumors." He reached out to touch her. The holographic skin felt cold and glassy across her thigh. As she moved, embedded microprocessors analyzed and mimicked the shifting colors and temperatures of surrounding objects, camouflaging her even in infrared light. She'd pulled the hood back; that's why he'd seen her face first.

"Here, I've brought one for you." She twisted, and Tomahoff's vision seemed to blur. He heard the purr of a zipper. Was there a pouch built into the back of the suit? Apparently so. A package appeared out of nowhere and thumped to the ground. "Please put it on."

Tomahoff glanced at it. "Your goggles are reflecting the light," he said. "You'd better get down."

The face bobbed halfway to the ground; the glowing lens turned dark. "Better?"

"Switch the display off, would you? Just for a minute."

"Sure." Opaque shadow replaced the shimmering imagery; he saw that she was kneeling. Under the taut skin of her suit she wore a cylindrical backpack; hard, tubular pockets rode on each thigh. She reached into one of these and withdrew a narrow bag. "Water?"

"Sure." She broke the seal and passed it to him. He accepted gratefully, studying her as he drank. She was young—sixteen or seventeen, he guessed—but with a rangy build that promised to be over six feet when she finished growing. Capping the bottle, he passed it back to her. "Who the hell are you, anyway?"

"Elise."

"That's all?"

"It's enough. You're James Tomahoff, a spy working for the American government—"

"I'm not a spy," he interrupted. "I'm an observer. Everything I do is legal."

She shrugged. "As you like." She sat crosslegged on the ground and began to recite his identification number, code name, birth and EOD dates.

"You're trying to tell me we're on the same side?" he interrupted impatiently.

An amused look flickered across her face. "Yes."

The last of the tanks had passed. Across the road the Angels were whistling to each other to regroup. "So, let's hear it," he said. "What's my assignment? How can I stop the war and save the world?"

"You can't. That's for others to do . . . this time."

He cocked an eyebrow. Whoever Elise was, she came cloaked

in a supreme self-confidence. He liked that. It was something he'd always missed in himself. Shrugging, he sat down beside her.

She said: "You were in Schonhausen to observe the kidnapping of Dr. Shamsher Rajid."

"*Defection,*" he corrected.

"Defection. Of course. But now the war has brought a change in command. A previous mistake must be corrected. Your new assignment is to get Dr. Rajid back."

He grinned. "No way."

Pieter stirred. "Why not, Jim?" he asked.

"Because he's in Moscow by now, Pieter. Out of our reach."

"No he's not. He's just across the border."

The boy was so certain! A cold finger of suspicion began to scratch at the back of Tomahoff's mind. "How do you know that?"

"I've been watching him."

"How?"

Elise waved a gloved hand in dismissal. "No more questions. You have no need to know the specifics."

"Oh no?" He scowled. "I think maybe I do. I've suspended judgement this far, but maybe I don't know either one of you at all. Maybe I think you're just two kids on a wild joyride, or Angels trying to put a kink in the war. Sorry, Pieter, but the powers had good reason to send Rajid over. They *needed* the Soviets to have access to that new—" he hesitated; looked questioningly at Elise "—slick brain?"

She glanced at Pieter, nodded, then raised her eyes until they met his again. "A seer computer, yes. That's what Rajid was working on."

His scowl deepened; he chewed a thumbnail. "It's real then?"

"Oh yes."

"*Damn!*" If only he'd gotten Rajid across to the other side in time!

In time to do what? he wondered. Stop the war? Had that really been within his power? Another thought occurred to him: If the seer worked, then Rajid must have known this war was coming. Why had he done nothing to prevent it?

Elise answered his unspoken question. "Don't think ill of Doctor Rajid. This engagement was necessary, and it should be limited in its scope—that's an eighty-five percent probability. Believe me, the alternative was much worse."

He massaged his forehead with the heels of his hands. Engagement? Probability? These words didn't belong in a child's mouth. "I'll ask you again, Elise: who are you?"

"I told you."

"You told me a name. *What* are you? Some kind of whiz kid? A computer freak? A math freak? A mind freak? NSA isn't in the habit of hiring teens. Why are you here?"

She paused, as if listening. After a few seconds, Pieter whispered something, but so quietly, Tomahoff was certain she couldn't have heard. At last she looked at him, a smile on her lips. "It's agreed we should tell you. I *am* the computer. Or at least a minor module of it."

She explained it to him as the moon rose over a distant stand of trees. "I have a slick in my head; a network of biochips that augments my neuronal connections. The human brain is the most compact computer ever invented . . . it's just not very efficient. When I was six my brain was re-wired to overcome that deficiency. It's changed me, Jim; I'm not like you. Not only do I have immediate access to data bases around the world, but I can think and reason and extrapolate faster than any human mind that existed before me. With the help of slicks—and the other, human, modules that compose the seer—I can analyze and organize more data in a few seconds than most minds encounter in a lifetime. It's a causal world, Jim. The present determines the future. I understand the present; therefore, I can predict the future.

"But I'm slow; almost retarded by the standards of the new generation." Her gaze drifted to Pieter, who sat against the wall, half-listening, playing absently with the dog's ears. She nodded towards him. "Nearly a hundred individuals are part of the seer, but Pieter's the first of us to wear a chip since infancy; he's the best to come out of the system so far."

"And we tried to give him away," Tomahoff said.

She shrugged. "He was to be a sample module, the basis of the Soviet system. It was no security risk—" she smiled at that peculiar statement "—with his access codes deactivated he'd be cut out of our system. It's true the seer would be damaged by his absence, but not irreparably. There are other young minds in training. No, Jim, giving Pieter and Dr. Rajid away was not a bad decision; it simply wasn't the best."

"And you've come to set things straight?"

She nodded. "The Soviets can't be allowed to construct another seer."

"Hell, why not? If it'll bring peace . . . "

"It won't, Jim. Not in the long run."

"It'll mess everything up," Pieter said.

"A Soviet seer would be an opposing force. It would neutralize us—increase the resistance in the field lines of the future so we couldn't manipulate them."

"Manipulate?" The implications of that word angered him. "You *determine* the future?"

"We all determine the future, every time we make a decision . . . or refuse to decide."

"Except that *you* see the consequences before you act." Somehow that made all the difference. He gazed up at the silver-edged clouds. "What *do* you see, Elise? One future? Or many?"

"Many," she said. "Millions. Old possibilities are eliminated and new ones created each time a decision is made. It's impossible to track all the variations of course. But possibilities are regulated by statistics, and we understand how to manipulate those. We can fix a general goal and track a course towards it through the eddies of probability and chance, refining our options as time advances. Not every imaginable future is open to us, but every possible one is."

"And what are the possibilities of my living to see another sunset?"

She smiled. "Good, I'd say. Excellent. But that's just a hunch. The perturbations of individual lives are fine grained; I can't follow them."

He raised an eyebrow. "Maybe Pieter can do better?"

"No."

A jet screamed somewhere far overhead. Pieter got up, opened the package Elise had dropped on the ground and pulled out a large, glassy-gray coverall. "You should put it on, Jim."

Tomahoff looked at it uneasily, then turned back to Elise. "Tell me about the war—this 'engagement' of yours. What's happening out there?"

"It hasn't gone nuclear yet. There's a forty five percent chance it'll still be limited to Germany by the time a peace treaty is signed. Sixty five percent that it won't go beyond Europe."

He blanched. "Those odds stink."

"They're acceptable."

"To whom?"

Her eyes flashed angrily. "The seer is doing the best it can with lousy material, Tomahoff. *We* didn't bring the world to the brink. And please believe me, we're working all the time to pull it back. Now will you put your chill suit on—*please*? Armed commandos who wouldn't be averse to taking a shot at an unidentified figure have just entered this area."

"The war's already passed over this sector," he scoffed. "The only commandos I've seen around here are Angels, and they won't—"

"Get down!"

He saw the next few moments clearly only when he played them back in his head: the smooth arc of her hand as she hit a switch on her suit and disappeared. The smeared suggestion of motion as she dove across the space between them. The concussion that knocked his breath away. He was pinned beneath an invisible weight, pressed up against the wall while her calm voice whispered in his ear: "*Be still.*"

He pitched her off and scrambled away.

"Jim!"

"Elise, don't—!" He raised a palm to stop her, but she hit him again, tumbling him against a half-buried field stone. "You can't hide me," he groaned. "You're making yourself a target. My image will be projected right through the suit!"

"No! I've got a ground image frozen in the display."

"What?" Pieter was humming a pop tune from inside the voluminous shelter of the other chill suit.

"An image of bare ground," Elise hissed.

"But it won't match the terrain . . . discontinuities—"

"Not significant. Don't worry. I've got full control through the chip. Now hush. Pieter, you too."

He lay still and waited. A breeze soughed softly through distant trees, but there was no other sound. "What's out there?" he whispered.

"Hush! He can hear you talking."

"Who? How far can you see?"

"Jim, *please*."

He saw it then. A single delta wing glider, cutting like a dark arrow across the smoky sky. The lens of an infrared camera gleamed dully in the red light. A plastic composite rifle would be slaved to the pilot's video screen. *Soviet sky sniper.*

The wing came around again, its cables buzzing angrily in the wind. A flare burst. Eyes clenched shut, he held Elise against him, thankful that she was so close to his own height.

They lay like that for a long time, listening, until at last Elise spoke. "He's moved on. We're all right for now." As she rolled away, a spatter of high-powered rifle shots erupted to the north. "That'll be the Angels," she said. "Some of them must have been caught in the open."

"They're unarmed."

"Yes."

Pieter crawled out from under his magic blanket, looked around, and grinned. "Close call, huh Jim?"

From somewhere nearby, Elise growled, "Shut up, Pieter." He felt her hand cool against his shoulder. "And turn off that suit before you lose it."

Tomahoff got shakily to his feet. "How did you know that sniper was coming?"

She switched off her suit and pointed at the sky. "A stealth drone at 12,000 feet. I can access the camera data. And I've scattered a few ground-based eyes along the road as well. Do you believe me now?"

"Maybe." He looked away. "Thanks for covering me, Elise. I would have been dead without you."

She sighed. "You may still be, Jim. You see, we're crossing the border in the company of Russian soldiers."

The suit felt like a cool gel spread across his skin. When he stretched, the material flexed with him. "Perfect fit," he noted.

"I checked your size before I came. Use this toggle to activate it."

He pressed the switch and watched the holographic skin flicker to life . . . watched himself fade away. And he sensed it: that feeling of inevitability that had dogged him all his adult life, waiting for him like some anonymous salesman at every turning point in his existence. Once again, a situation was evolving around him that he wanted no part of, yet already he couldn't bring himself to turn away from Elise. She'd touched him; a rare event in his memory. He liked her. He wanted to believe her, and not because she'd saved his life. There was something special about Elise.

He watched her as she picked up his discarded jacket. "May I use this?" she asked.

"Sure."

Pieter stood up; Elise helped him slip the jacket on. She rolled up the sleeves for him, then zipped up the front.

Strange, how they seldom talk to each other. Then he remembered: the implant. No need for archaic conversation when you could communicate at the speed of light.

"How well do you know the past?" he asked suddenly.

Elise seemed mildly surprised. "Better than you think."

He hesitated. She'd claimed to be only a minor and outdated module of the seer, yet he sensed her influence transcended the obsolete technology in her head. As young as she was, she possessed the aura of a progenitor, an elder . . . a *leader*. Was there a social structure within the seer? Who controlled the beast? He pulled an energy bar out of the pile Pieter had dumped on the ground and ripped the wrapper open. "Know why I'm here?"

She smiled. "Tell me your version."

"It was a perverse desire to be different. In school, it seemed like just about everybody was into computers, business, engineering, medicine. Not me. I wanted to be original, esoteric. I wanted to piss my old man off. So I got my degree in Russian studies." He stripped off the wrapper and flung it away.

"Obstinate, huh?" Elise said. "That fits your dossier."

He grinned. "I never guessed there'd be a demand for my services. Shit, I was practically drafted by the state department."

"They offered you a lot of money?"

"More than I ever expected to make without having to stab someone in the back." He sighed. "I still haven't had to do that, thank God. But then I've never done anything worthwhile, either."

"We need people like you."

"Sure, we gather the data your system needs to run on. But what are we getting in return?" His gaze wandered to the fiery northern skies. "Not security, that's for sure."

She settled on the ground next to Pieter, her arm resting protectively around his shoulders. "Things are in bad shape now," she agreed.

"You know the funniest part of it all? I spent my youth protesting the government, the CIA, the whole concept of covert and overt intelligence. And now I'm it. What does my dossier say about that?"

"Just what you might think. It says you see yourself as a rebel; a man who follows his own mind. You habitually berate the government that pays you; you mock state policy; you indulge in verbal cynicism at every opportunity. Yet you always toe the line." She leaned forward, her eyes flashing a challenge. "Why is that? *Are* you a rebel, Jim? Or are you just talk?"

That threw him. He tried to pass it off with a laugh but failed, because the salesman on the corner was eyeing him again, barking the same old blunt and irresistible pitch: *Sell out, Tomahoff. Play it straight, march to the company tune and I'll give you the best deal you can get.* "Whew, you like to hit a guy hard, don't you Elise?"

She raised her eyebrows mockingly. "So? Which is it?"

He winced, embarrassed and intrigued that anyone should know so much about him. She was playing him, of course. He knew that. But he could play games too. "A *faux* rebel," he announced, in a pinch nosed accent that made her laugh. "Dime a dozen next to the real kind. All talk, and no substance."

"Still true to form, huh, Jim?"

He grinned sheepishly and took a bite out of the energy bar. It occurred to him: people like himself must make predictive analysis easy—smart enough to discern the logical choice; bland enough to choose it. He chewed thoughtfully on the coarse oat grains. "So what's the plan?"

"Rest, for now. We'll be getting started in about three hours."

She woke him near midnight. When he rolled over to stretch the aches out of his body, he noticed the chill suit was active; he hadn't left it that way. "Why the camo?"

"Troops passed us twice," Elise said. "They picked up Pieter and the dog on IR. I thought it better if they didn't see us."

Pieter huddled in the shadow of the wall, his arms around the dog's neck, face buried in its thick fur. Tomahoff realized with a start that the boy was crying—whimpering softly like a . . . lost and frightened child. Tomahoff stared at him; it was the last thing he'd expected Pieter to do.

"Don't worry about him," Elise said. "He's just tired." Her chill suit was active. Tomahoff followed her voice as she walked to Pieter's side. He thought she crouched, a barely perceptible blur beside the wall. "Come on, love. Time to go."

"No!" he sobbed. "I can't see! And it's empty. There's nobody left."

"Hush, sweetheart," she murmured. "They're still out there; I can see them. Everything's going to be all right." She stole a glance at Tomahoff. "But be quiet for now. And open your eyes! That's right. Come on, I'll hold your hand."

Pieter was nervous, constantly questioning Elise as they moved east along the road. Tomahoff followed a few paces behind them. It was a strange sight: the boy, with the dog trotting at his side, demanding answers of an indefinite companion.

"Are they coming, Elise? Can you still see them?"

"Yes."

"Where are they?"

"In the forest."

"How many? Two? Or three?"

"Pieter! Quiet, my love. You know the meeting's all arranged."

Something about this continuing exchange bothered Tomahoff; after a few minutes he realized what it was: *Pieter should already know the answers to these questions!* He had access to the same information as Elise. Didn't he? Or had something changed?

Ahead, a steel and concrete bridge spanned a small, boulder-choked stream. The cultivated fields ended abruptly at the crossing. Forest began on the eastern shore—young, healthy trees crowding each other for space beneath the scraggly remnants of a previous generation withered by acid rain. On the bridge a band of Angels waited, three figures dressed in brown camouflage fatigues.

Tomahoff halted abruptly. "Do you know those clowns?"

"Sure," Elise said. "Pieter's going to stay with them until we get back."

"But you can't trust those bastards. They'll mess with his head!"

"Elise?" Pieter asked uncertainly, reaching out for the ghost of her hand.

"It's all right, love. You know how they operate. You've seen all their tricks before." She rumpled his hair. "Now go on." She beckoned to Tomahoff to wait with her while Pieter went ahead.

They watched in silence as he approached the bridge, the dog still at his side. "Peace," one of the Angels said in greeting. Pieter echoed the wish. A few more soft words were exchanged before they all disappeared into the forest.

Elise put her hand on Tomahoff's shoulder. "A nuclear weapon has just been used near Bonn."

He flinched. A hot flush of fear surged through his brain. "Which side burned it?"

"NATO. They're losing the war, just as we'd planned."

He was stunned speechless, staring blindly at the road ahead. *Just as we'd planned . . .* "What do they pay you for?" he whispered. "If you can't even plan a successful defense?"

"That's a good question. One the Soviets are certain to ask themselves."

He struggled to grasp her implications. "You're trying to convince them the seer's a fake?"

"Or at least that it doesn't work. Our kidnapping of Rajid will look like an attempt to salvage something from our failure."

"And this whole war," he whispered, his voice hoarse with emotion, "is a ruse."

"Oh no!" She sounded shocked. Then she seemed to reconsider. "Would we have engineered it? I don't know. Probably we could have found a more subtle way of proving our 'fallibility'. We didn't have too. This conflict was ordained a long time ago. The best we can hope to do is temper its intensity."

"If you die, will the seer still work?"

"Of course. That's why I'm here."

". . . and me?"

"I need your help, your strength. Sorry, Jim. I know you never wanted to see action like this, but you were in the right place at the wrong time. I had to draft you."

And how did I come to be in Schonhausen? he wondered. *Was that your doing too? Did you have me sent here because you knew I'd listen to your tales?*

The transit to the border was an exercise in evasion: dodging sky snipers and tank columns; lying in a ditch waiting for a convoy to pass; dropping scent capsules to confuse any patrolling dogs.

Finally, they jumped the third truck in a Soviet convoy carrying wounded soldiers and rode it the last kilometer into Czechoslovakia, clinging to the steel framework that supported the canvas canopy. At the checkpoint, the truck jerked to a stop. While he kept his face towards the canvas to hide his goggles, Tomahoff looked out from the corner of his eye. A shifting melange of noise surrounded them: rumbling engines; muttered Russian oaths; soldier bitching. A border guard came by. He glanced at them, stared for a few seconds as if he saw something not quite right . . . Then he shook his head and went on.

Tomahoff sighed, light headed with relief. Beside him, Elise shifted nervously. She was a shimmer, a phantasm cast in moonlight, an occasional shadow on the ground. No more substance than this, yet he followed her.

The truck lurched into gear. Two minutes past the border, they rounded a bend into a dense stand of forest. "Time!" Elise called.

Tomahoff counted to three, took a deep breath, then kicked away from the truck. He hit the ground rolling. Behind him, the convoy's headlights receded into the night.

Elise called a halt on a cratered slope above the road, where an allied bomber had dropped its load prematurely in an attempted strike against the highway. Tumbled into a gully at the foot of the hill were the still-warm carcasses of three burned-out Soviet tanks.

"Have you spotted the security facility where they're holding Rajid?" Elise asked, as she sat down beside Tomahoff. They'd switched their chill suits off to save power. "It's there, right across the road, dug into the hillside."

Tomahoff adjusted his goggles. The photomultipliers gathered in just enough light from moon and stars to show him a pair of reinforced steel doors set back against the far slope. "Yep, I've got it." He looked up. "So now what do we do?"

"Eat breakfast. After that, we get to work. We'll set up a string of cameras between here and the ambush point. They'll watch the road; let us know when Rajid is being moved."

"And me?" he asked, as he helped her unload the back pouch of her suit. "Are you ready to tell me what I'm here for?"

"Have you changed your mind?"

He arched his eyebrows. "Am I supposed to?"

"How could I know that?"

He shrugged.

"Jim," she sighed, "I wish you'd believe me. I *don't* know everything. I don't know what goes on in the heart of the Kremlin . . . or in the heart of a man."

Helicopters buzzed in the starry distance, a line of six Soviet gunships returning to the east. "And my assignment?" he asked. He didn't mean to be brusque, but he was uneasy. He sensed that something had changed in the hour since they'd dropped off the truck. The war had gone quiet; there was too little activity along the border. It was as if the armies were waiting . . . for what? The dawn? Or the holocaust?

Elise picked up a miniature camera lens from the collection of equipment that had come out of her pouch. "When we pop the gas canisters, Rajid will be out of it for a max of twenty minutes. You've got to move him during that time."

He groaned. "Oh man, grunt labor."

"Sorry, kid," she drawled in ancient Bogart-ese. "It's a lousy job, but someone's got to do it."

"Right." He watched her sort through her equipment: field rations, gas canisters, light explosives, a third chill suit for Rajid and an impressive collection of miniature photographic gear.

She set aside the explosives and the chill suit. "You carry these."

He looked at the little cylinders distastefully, then shrugged. "We're at war, aren't we?"

She didn't answer.

Dawn had begun to infiltrate the forest by the time they finished stringing the cameras. They'd come to a place two kilometers beyond the security facility, where the road jogged sharply south.

Elise dumped the last three cameras in a pile on the ground. "I have to make a trip into the woods," she said.

He nodded, and sat down to wait. When she'd been gone for a minute, he remembered the radio. Pushing back his hood, he felt around his neck for it and slipped it on. It was still tuned in to the local station. He turned it on, and a cultured German voice filled his ears.

"*. . . hostilities to cease at once, by order of NATO command. Troops are currently being withdrawn behind their respective international borders. Repeat: a ceasefire was declared at 0540. Civilians are to—*"

He jumped as leaves rustled behind him. With one hand he swept the radio from his head and switched off the transceiver. Then he turned to see Elise's calm face hovering eeriely above the brush.

Ceasefire! Did she know?

Of course she knew.

She'd been following the diplomatic exchange. She probably knew before the negotiators themselves reached a decision.

She switched off her suit and crouched beside him. "They'll call it the twenty-two hour war," she whispered. "It'll scare hell out of both sides. The truce will last a century."

"And Rajid?"

"Nothing's changed there. We still need to get him back."

But everything had changed! *Ceasefire.* "The border! The check point is going to close. We won't be able to get back across."

"There's still time. We can get him out and get back to the West before the border's reorganized."

Ceasefire.

"Can you call in air support? If we can get picked up right after we snatch him—" He stopped. She was shaking her head.

"No support. We have to get back on our own."

"But a chopper could—"

"No."

Tomahoff stared hard at Elise, accumulated doubts finally crystallizing in his mind. "Who issued my orders anyway?"

She looked away, her fingers tapping out indecision against her thigh.

"It was you, wasn't it?"

"Yes, Jim. It was."

"Then you're not sanctioned to be here."

He was thinking hard. He'd almost unraveled it: why Elise couldn't call for support; why Pieter had suddenly seemed so vulnerable. "The access codes!" he realized. "You said Pieter used access codes that could be deactivated. And that's just what happened last night, isn't it? He was badgering you with questions because he couldn't get any information on his own; he'd been cut off from the seer. And you couldn't call somebody up to say 'please turn the codes back on' because Pieter was supposed to be with the Soviets . . . Rajid, too! This rescue is a personal crusade . . . and if you let on what you're doing, your own codes will be neutralized. Maybe the whole seer!"

"No," she said quietly. "It would end with me. The West's defense structure would collapse without the seer."

He nodded, as understanding flooded his mind. "You said a Soviet seer would neutralize you. And that's exactly what NATO wants, isn't it? Because you're no longer under their control. Who does control you, Elise? Or are you the senior statesman of the next superpower?"

"It's not like that, Jim. Don't quit on me."

"But this is illegal! I have no orders to be here."

"Does it always take orders to make you get off your ass? What we're doing is *right*. The superpowers have made a mess of the world. It's time someone else tried to do a little better."

"And you've taken that burden upon yourself?"

"We had to, because we can see what will happen if we don't."

A motorcycle sped down the road. "I don't want to be your puppet," Tomahoff said.

"Whose puppet are you now?" She shook her head. "I don't want to control you, Jim. I *can't* control you. Any influence I have is on averages, not on individuals. Your free will remains intact. I'm only asking that you help me. I can't get Rajid out by myself."

I have no orders to be here!

"I could be imprisoned if I help you." She said nothing. "Elise, let it go! You predicted peace. Let it go at that."

Her lips came together in a hard line. "This isn't peace. It's a truce, that's all. Even a century is only temporary."

He searched her eyes, startled by the gravity of her voice. "And then? The final war?"

"That's right. It'll be the same old story. Fear. Mistrust. Accident. The End."

Tomahoff grunted. Pulling the radio phones from around his neck, he folded them neatly into a loop, then climbed to his feet. "The war's over," he said. "We should go back right now. Rajid's not worth risking life and career on." Her gaze held steady on his face. He looked away, twirling the radio on his finger, watching the smooth gray plastic blur with the speed of its rotation.

Rajid wasn't worth it, but Elise and her clan might be. Whoever they were, at least they were different; a third weight in the old balance of power, they held out the promise of something new. He flicked his fingers, letting the radio phones fly away. "Yeah, it'd be smart to go back . . . but I guess we'll go on instead."

A smile broke across her face. “Thanks, Jim.”

He grinned. Looking at her, he wondered what she saw on the edge of her long horizon.

She pulled her hood across her face until only her eyes were visible. “They’re bringing Rajid out now.” Leaves rustled. She touched his palm. “Shall we go?”

Holding her hand, he followed after her. He knew no orders would ever be written that would cover him on this one. He went anyway.

Career Decision was first published in Analog Science Fiction & Fact, in October 1988—when there still was a Soviet Union.

In The Tide

A curt summons brought me running to the primary control room. I arrived to find the Commonwealth Police at our doorstep. In their pockets huddled the System's grandest Makers, a plague of molecular machines poised to invade our rogue station should we refuse to cooperate with their commands. I gazed in dismay at a projection of their ship: malevolent black cruiser marked with the dancing Chinese characters I knew so well. Never had I expected to see that lethal signature so far beyond the borders of the Commonwealth. I looked to our leader, Dahlia Ivanov, anarchist, owner of our station and inventor-extraordinaire, seated like a queen on a dais at the control room's far end. One hundred sixty kilograms of billowing, low-gravity flesh should not be graceful. Dahlia defied that diction. With an elegant hand she fingered her single braid of thick orange hair as she awaited my assessment. "Whatever you have to do, don't let them aboard," I warned. "Don't even let them dock. We're contaminated with a thousand illegal molecules. If the police scent that they'll terminate this complex and—" *everyone of you.* I bowed my head. "Please forgive me. If I'd suspected they'd pursue me as far as Saturn system, I never would have imposed on you."

Dahlia snorted. "Oh, Aron dear, do stop moaning. And don't jump to conclusions. I've summoned you for advice, not as a sacrifice. The police don't even know we have a deserter aboard."

Deserter. A cruel word, yet undeniably true. I'd been drafted into the police at an early age, having been foolish enough to display a youthful talent in molecular engineering. Finding police discipline a bit restrictive, I'd parted company with the service—a bit earlier than the legal niceties allowed. I drew a deep breath of relief. "All right. Then just who is it they pursue?"

"Indigo."

On a station that housed over six hundred malcontents and refugees, I doubted I could name six people lacking a criminal record. Yet if I had to try, Indigo would head the list. A Blue Series derivative human, Indigo had abandoned the company of her birth to work a rogue station bound for Pluto. "Indigo? What—?"

"Indigo, nothing. *We* owe them a debt for her services this past year. Now, Aron, from your experience in the police, how much delay will be tolerated before the station is seized?"

"The station seized?" I asked blankly.

"Yes, dear. Debt is a criminal offense in the Commonwealth."

"I know that! But we're not in the Commonwealth."

"Some issues transcend legal boundaries. How much time do you estimate we'll have to prepare our escape?"

"Escape? We can't go anywhere. South Station is still under construction." The ship that had brought us to Saturn system we now called north station. We'd tethered it to an asteroid (hauled on a long cable all the way from Jupiter) and spun the whole affair to give us gravity while we constructed South Station from scratch—a second ship to house our expanding population. When South Station was complete, the tether would be cut and the two ships would launch separately for Neptune. But that was more than two months away. I reminded Dahlia of this. "Two months is no better than a year. The police won't wait two days if they think they've found their quarry. And even if we were ready to launch today, we couldn't outrun their guns."

"He's right, you know," a calm contralto voice observed.

And so I was. Though as I recognized her voice, I suddenly wished I'd been less right and more gallant. I turned, as the only derivative human aboard our rogue station entered the control room. Indigo: cool and clever, smooth and hard. Distant. And utterly beautiful. She shrugged, a full-body gesture that ran like a wave through the shimmering, shining platelets of gold and blue that were her skin. Her armor. Her sequined birthday suit designed to protect her from the cold and vacuum of Outside. "Aron is right," she said again, stroking her golden kisheer, the living respirator that lay like a cowl across her throat while she breathed the air of the station. "I won't put you all at risk. I'll go back with them, if it comes to that."

"You will not!" My shout surprised even me. "Uh, what I mean . . ." I stammered, "is—"

In the three-quarter gee pull of the station, she turned slowly towards me, and once again I felt nothing but admiration for her designers. Certainly, they'd been esthetes. Their care could be seen in every aspect of Indigo, from her tiny, decorous breasts, the erect nipples visible beneath a teasing layer of armored skin;

to her spidery hands, graced with fingers so long, they ought to have tangled but somehow never did;

to her feet: twice as long as nature intended, with opposable toes that could purchase a solid grip on any handhold. Yet never awkward. Their length gave her a long, rolling gate that only exaggerated her femininity.

As to her sexual abilities, I had only Dahlia's account that she remained human, though sterile. A subsidiary organ (scarcely visible because it too was finished in armored skin) protected her vulnerable parts from vacuum while modestly concealing the evidence of her private nature from my eyes. Nothing else was hidden. Indigo wore no clothes because she had no need of them. She was complete as she'd been made.

Suddenly conscious of my ill manners, my gaze fell. I was in love with our Indigo of course, but to what end? She'd shown me no favor, given no answer to my tentative advances. What could I read from that but a gentle "no"? To offer love where it's not wanted is an insult Indigo did not deserve. To pursue her further would mean a loss of face for both of us.

Sadly, the delicate manners of civilized places are not common on a rogue station. Other men had offered her sex in no uncertain terms. Many times on my construction shift, I'd heard the post-mortem dissection of some failed suit, and the ribald speculation on the reasons behind her choice of sexual isolation. To me the explanation seemed obvious: biology. Surely Indigo possessed a natural desire for her own kind. Why should she take a human companion?

Gathering up the scraps of my dignity, I tried to compose myself, saying, "I don't understand the problem, Indigo. Who's the claimant on this debt?"

She looked at me . . . looked *through* me really, her graceful face locked forever in an expression of saintly contemplation. Who could say what emotions passed behind that unchangeable mask? She said: "My former company claims the debt—SunBelt Enterprises." Her gaze shifted to the projection of the approaching ship. "Technically, I can work anywhere I choose. But my employer has to pay royalties to SunBelt . . . for the genetic work that went into my design."

"Oh." That made a cold kind of sense. "Well then. Why don't we just pay them, and—"

Indigo's lips parted and she laughed, a sound high and sweet, though no smile interrupted the perfect blue smoothness of her face. "You don't know what SunBelt charges for my services."

"Yes, they're very jealous of their Blue Series," Dahlia said. "Terribly afraid some pirate like us will clone them."

"How much?" I asked, not sure I wanted to know.

Dahlia pursed her lips and stared thoughtfully at the ceiling. "Less charges for towing back to Jupiter, and— Hmm, they might accept South Station as payment."

"South Station . . . ?" Seven months of labor had gone into the construction of South Station. "That's ridiculous." Nobody argued with me.

"You're acquainted with the defense structure of police cruisers, aren't you, Aron, dear?" Dahlia asked. "Perhaps you could manage to infect this ship with a flock of Makers, something that might play hard with their life support and weapons systems before self-destructing? Give them something to think about besides us?"

I stared at her in shock. "*Infect* their ship?" I had no doubt I could construct an appropriate molecular machine for any assault Dahlia might devise. I was less sure Dahlia understood how well the police were defended against such microscopic invaders by their own formidable Makers. "Absolutely not ever in the life of the Universe," I said. "It would be an act of suicide."

Dahlia frowned. Then she patted me on the shoulder. "That's all right, dear." Looking at Indigo, she shook her head sadly.

Indigo shrugged. "I'll go back with them. You can claim that you scooped me out of the Void, which is true enough, and that you were only waiting for SunBelt to come pick me up. That way you won't owe them a thing."

I must have looked hopelessly confused, because Dahlia turned to me in sympathy and explained: "Indigo was the victim of a construction accident in the Jovian system. A miscreant tug launched her towards the radiation belts. SunBelt executives saw no chance of rescuing her in time, so . . ." Dahlia shrugged.

I turned to Indigo. "They left you to die?" She looked through me in her usual disconcerting way, saying nothing. And of course I could read nothing from the set expression of her face. Even her eyes gave me no hint of her inner feelings. Deep-set, dark and with a gleam that was not-quite-human, they gazed at the world from behind smoked windows of organic 'glass.' Helplessly, I rounded on Dahlia. "*Do* something! There must be something else we can trade!"

"Perhaps there is," Indigo said softly. "If we want to risk it." I felt a chill stroll up my spine, a premonition tossed in my lap by some vexing twist in space/time. She said to Dahlia: "Aron has discovered a mining ship marooned in Saturn's B ring. Three ships, in fact, all abandoned by their former owner—" brittle humor crackled through her voice "—SunBelt Enterprises, Inc. If we could bring one out—"

I groaned. I'd mentioned the ships two days ago in a shallow attempt to amuse her. I'd been playing with the station's optical telescope when she'd chanced to pass by. "Take a look at this," I said, laying claim to her attention. Amidst a projection of Saturn's brightly colored rings wandered a tiny spot of shadow. "That's a robotic mining ship once owned by SunBelt Enterprises—your former company, so I've heard?" (I hadn't known her history then! How crass I must have sounded.) "Look close, and you can see the company name printed on the spine of the ship." At least, if I squinted just right I *thought* I could make it out: SunBelt.

Indigo shook her head. "You're imagining it. SunBelt doesn't mark their ships like that."

"I'm *not*," I protested. But I couldn't prove the point. "Anyway, this is one of three ships SunBelt designed to harvest volatiles in the belts. All three are still down there—abandoned—after a working life of . . . oh, five to ten minutes. They're derelicts now."

"What happened?"

I smiled, pleased that I'd caught her interest. "That's a mystery. Radio contact with the ships ended after the first few minutes. Satellite observation ultimately confirmed no activity. Repair pods were sent in, but those were never heard from again either. At the time there were protests about mining operations ruining the esthetic value of the rings. That was nineteen years ago."

"Environmentalists?" She spit the word with some distaste. That was her corporate background. Environmentalists traditionally played a hard and dirty game with the big industrial companies; sometimes company personnel found themselves employed in battle zones.

I nodded. "Apparently the activists poisoned the ring with a very talented strain of Makers—an *uncataloged* variety designed to infect and destroy the control centers of spacecraft." Possession of an uncataloged molecular machine is a capital crime in the Commonwealth . . . which is why our rogue station had sought the freedom of the outer worlds. "The Maker's molecular structure is still unknown, because no probe has ever returned a sample of ring dust for analysis."

Molecular structure is everything. Design the proper molecule and you'll have a microscopic servant capable of re-assembling, cell by cell, a badly damaged human body, or of weaving carbon atoms into diamond fiber, or, with more destructive intent, dis-assembling the walls of an orbiting city into their component elements, exposing the inhabitants to hard vacuum.

Speed and scale preclude direct human control of these microscopic processes, so the responsibility falls to a sub-class of constructed molecules: the Makers.

Makers are the molecular equivalent of programmable computers. Like viruses, they can cause millions of copies of themselves to be manufactured, and then proceed in invisible legions to carry out their programs. Unlike viruses, they can deliberately modify their instructions (and structures) when circumstances demand. The only defense against attack by a Maker is another Maker. Nineteen years ago, in a lightning-fast microscopic war, the Makers that polluted Saturn's rings had quashed the best defensive molecules SunBelt then possessed . . . but if Indigo had been impressed by that startling fact, she'd given no sign of it.

Now, with the Commonwealth Police bearing down upon us, I wondered what hope she saw in my tale of lost ships. I shook my head. "Indigo, you know we can't go down into the rings. The belts are poisoned with uncataloged Makers. Nobody comes out of there."

When Dahlia's eyes glinted orange, I knew I'd said exactly the wrong thing. "Our defensive Makers can neutralize any plague in the System," she insisted. "*Faster* than your police models." Her gaze shifted to Indigo. "If you want to do it, dear, I'm right behind you."

We told the police Indigo was on Tethys and would be returning on a heavily laden ice freighter in two days time. They politely agreed to await her arrival . . . though I suspected they experienced a mild disappointment over losing an opportunity to inspect our station. Meanwhile, we commandeered a tug that had come over from South Station to resupply.

Fading odors of stale coffee and dried fish greeted us as we boarded. Someone's half-finished lunch clung velcroed to the wall. Near the door, beneath a column of Chinese characters expressing hopes for good fortune, hung a tool belt, a cutting torch and a net bag containing three rolls of half-meter wide silver tape—a highly visible adhesive used to mark construction sites. I shoved these into an empty locker while Indigo disposed of the trash. A few minutes later, we left the station behind.

"Indigo?"

"Yes, Aron?"

My hands closed in rage as an image of my beloved falling alone towards certain death in the radiation belts of Jupiter played in my mind. "SunBelt doesn't deserve you. I would never abandon you."

"Why . . . thank you, Aron."

I looked up at the catch in her voice, but her eyes told me nothing.

We were alone on the tug. When, despite my emphatic objections, Dahlia and Indigo agreed to this scheme, I was left with nothing to do but volunteer my services. I'd expected Dahlia to accompany us, but apparently she'd thought better of it. I had to admire her for that.

"There it is," Indigo said. I looked out the viewport to see Saturn, his yellow face marred by a white spiral of storm winds. The southern hemisphere of the planet rose like a great, dull sun out of the plain of the rings. And there indeed, roaming towards sunset, was the mining ship we hoped to salvage.

Our approach would not be simple. Saturn's moons combined with their parent to create a complex gravitational field in the belt, generating braids and streams and waves of force that continuously churned the material in the rings. I left the problem in Indigo's capable hands, and turned once again to the diagnostic kit Dahlia had given me. Wafer-thin and no larger than my palm, the kit was a miniature laboratory capable of analyzing the structure of any active molecules we might encounter in the ring and of devising a Maker to neutralize them. Dahlia assured us it couldn't be defeated by a strain of Makers nearly twenty years obsolete.

Sometime later a dreadful *ping!* rang through the tug's hull. "Ice fragment," Indigo said shortly. "The ship will be singing before long."

So right, as usual. As we descended into the ring, we dodged the largest of the drifting icebergs: dangerous obstacles tens of meters across. But the myriad smaller chunks and particles of ice we simply pushed aside . . . or obliterated. A metaphor comes to mind: hailstorm. Soon, the ship rang so loudly under the barrage that conversation became impossible. Indigo shrugged the golden cowl of her kisheer up over her ears to seal them from the noise.

Seventeen minutes after the inal ping a final nudge of deceleration sent me leaning against my harness. The hailstorm had subsided as the tug closed on ring velocity; now it spoke in a faint susurration, like secrets whispered between decks. I stared out the viewport. Ahead of us, a following sun had turned the ring dust into a fine-grained fog. The miner was barely visible: it seemed more like a dark scar on my retina than a solid object actually embedded in that field of white.

I unstrapped and drifted from my chair. The time had come to collect a sample of ring dust. My suit hung in a locker. I removed it and shook it out. It was the best I could afford to buy during my hurried departure from the Commonwealth: light and slim, with a passive thermal system powered by body heat. As I pulled it on, molecular machines in the fabric shaped it to fit perfectly to my body. They also held it rigid against pressure. I could move only because microscopic sensors woven throughout the suit instructed the fabric to yield.

I retrieved the diagnostic kit, pulled on the helmet, then turned to key open the shield door. The interior panel slid aside to reveal the gelatinous lock.

Rumor reports that Dahlia designed the lock on a day when she was exasperated with all things mechanical. When I first encountered it, it nearly scared the–

But pardon me. I find my metaphors grow increasingly crude the farther I travel from Sol. Suffice to say I was not at all comfortable with the idea of a gel-like semipermeable membrane as the only barrier between me and hard vacuum. Time modifies prejudice. Now the slow cycling of standard locks seems a tedious process.

I turned to wave to Indigo, then plunged into the lock. Where the dense gel wouldn't yield to the uniform pressure of cabin air pushing outwards on its surface, it gave easily before the isolated force I exerted as I pulled hard against the hand-grips. For a moment I was a swimmer seeking the far side of a pool of gelatin. Then my helmeted head emerged Outside. I clipped my safety line to the nearest mooring and swung out of the way while the membrane self-sealed behind me.

Random static generated by the electrical currents in the ring crackled in my helmet. When I released my handhold, minute tidal forces began to draw me gradually, gradually away from the ship. I checked the kit. Green lights glowed reassuringly on its face. A sigh of relief escaped me. I'd had real doubts about our defensive Makers, but it looked like they'd keep the environmentalist's poison from savaging us. I hit the intake.

Microscopic particles of dust drift everywhere in the ring, so it was no surprise when the kit immediately recorded a hit. A blue light winked on, indicating the tiny chemical laboratory had undertaken an analysis. And then it winked out. The kit's entire face went black. No green lights. No red. Nothing.

I checked the on/off toggle. Jiggled it a few times. Nothing.

"Indigo." Some odd corner of my mind noted with pride that I managed to screen most of the panic from my voice. "Indigo, the poison's infected the kit." I waited a moment for her to answer. "Indigo?"

Silence filled my helmet, undisturbed even by the crackle of static. Realization swept like a thermal pulse across my brain. "*The radio's been disabled!*"

What had become of our defenses? Was nothing safe? For a horrible moment I imagined my suit collapsing around me as voracious Makers rearranged its molecular structure. With trembling hands I pulled on the tether, sure that it would disintegrate under pressure. It held, solid as ever, and I quickly hauled myself back to the silent tug.

What could I do? Our defensive Makers were worthless. If I pushed my way back through the lock, I would infect the ship instantly. If I stayed here . . .

My gaze strayed to the robotic miner, now only a few hundred meters away. The instruments aboard that ship had never been exposed to vacuum. Yet in minutes the ring poison had penetrated the ship's seals and killed it.

So it was only a matter of time until the infection found its way aboard the tug.

Another thought occurred to me then. While the air I breathed was recycled through a biological filter, that filter received nutrients through the actions of a delicate pump. If the pump failed, then nutrients could no longer reach the filter. The biological membrane would die within a few short hours . . . and I would rapidly follow.

I flung myself through the lock, grabbing blindly at the handholds. There might still be a chance to escape the rings. If we burned all our fuel now, we could pick up enough velocity to throw ourselves clear. We wouldn't need to control the tug after that. Dahlia could pluck us out of the Void. . . .

"Indigo!" I shouted, as I emerged on the other side. I unsealed my helmet and opened it a crack. "Indigo! We've got to get out of here before it's—"

Too late. The caterwauling of a half dozen alarms assaulted my ears. The console glowed cherry red with warnings. Orange emergency lights bathed the cabin in an eerie glow. "Total system failure," Indigo informed me, shouting to be heard over the din. "The damn defensive Makers *failed!*" Indigo never swore. We must be in deep, deep trouble.

I watched her helplessly as she rummaged through the equipment lockers. "Who's responsible for this tug?" she snapped. "Why isn't the equipment where it's supposed to be? Ah . . ."

She retrieved the small cutting torch I'd stashed in a locker and test fired it at a bulkhead. "Hey!" I shouted, as the beam burned a tiny hole through the wall.

There was a *pop!*, then a high-pitched whistle as precious air streamed into the Void. "Still works," Indigo said, grim satisfaction in her voice. Slapping the handgrip, she added, "It's low-tech. No artificial intelligence in its processor." The whistle rose in pitch, then cut off abruptly as repair molecules in the ship's skin quickly healed the wound.

Invented intelligence did seem to be the target of the uncataloged Makers. From the ship's electronic nervous system, to our ill-fated defensive molecules, everything capable of artificial thought had been neutralized. The simpler molecular machines such as those in the fabric of my suit and in the tug's wall which responded mechanically to appropriate stimuli, remained intact. So did the two nodes of natural intelligence aboard ship, for which I was truly grateful.

"We have to tether the tug to the miner," Indigo announced. "Then we can use our difference in velocity to swing around and launch ourselves out of the ring."

My eyes opened wide. I'd seen the miner. And our velocities weren't that different. "We're going too slow," I objected. "And even if it could work, *I don't have time!*" I told her about the pump that nourished my rebreather. "It *does* have computer components. It's going to fail . . . if it hasn't already."

Indigo had been in the act of fastening a tool kit around her waist. Now she froze. "A pump? The system's not organic?"

"Not completely. The maintenance is mechanical." Suddenly I sensed how false her former confidence had been.

"My blood nourishes the kisheer," she whispered. "I thought . . ." Her gaze fixed on an infinite point. "Aron, I just don't know what else we can do without help from above." One by one the tug's alarms were failing, as the poison penetrated deeper into ship's systems. The console had gone dark. "Damn, we need the radio!"

I shook my head. "Even that wouldn't help. We can't ask Dahlia to send another tug—"

She interrupted me with a curt gesture. "We can! If it doesn't come all the way into the rings . . ."

Hope leaped in my throat. "You have an idea?"

She sighed. "It's no good if we can't communicate it to Dahlia."

"Tell me! Tell me, and we'll find a way to talk to the station. I promise."

When compared to their breadth, the rings are the thinnest objects in the solar system. Clean space, unpolluted by ring poisons, where rescue vehicles could operate without difficulty, waited less than a kilometer away. As Indigo sketched her plan, I realized she could get us there.

Trailing the station in its orbit around Saturn lay the husk of the little asteroid whose innards had been converted into South Station. Following in the same orbit, neatly coiled and stored in a pod, came the hundred-klick cable that had served as a tow rope when the asteroid was yanked from the stockpile of a mining company doing business in Jovian orbit. "That cable can serve as a tether," Indigo explained. "A small engine can carry the free end down to us. We'll fix it to the miner, and—" Her hands made a blooming gesture, full of expectations—

—and hope flowered in my mind. "Ah! Of course! A tug or two on the other end and we escape along with the prize. Can it be done?"

"Why not? With working tugs as a counterweight, we can spin the whole system. Ninety degrees through the first rotation and we'll be well clear of the rings."

I grinned. Like an analog of the station on a huge scale, we could use Saturn's tidal forces to construct a temporary elevator out of the rings. As the giant contraption turned, we'd be lifted to life. Filled with the dizzying joy only a reprieve from certain death can bring, I grabbed up Indigo's hand in mine, and kissed it. Her skin felt warm against my lips. Glassy smooth and warm, despite the scales of her bejeweled hide. I looked up in mild surprise.

"We still have to find a way to get word to Dahlia," she cautioned, stroking my cheek with an enchanting tenderness that confused the words in my mouth and left me warm and flustered. With feather-light fingers she caressed my ear, brushed my neck, blessed my lips. And the sun filled me. A blinding thrust of heat that seared my brain and burned it clean. Without a thought, I slipped my arms about her waist, pressed my cheek against her belly. Slowly, dreamily, I let my lips wander across her glassy skin. In that moment, I cared not at all about the rings, the Makers, or our own dire circumstances. Fortunately, Indigo possessed more sense than I. "Aron." She stopped me with two fingers placed against my lips. "We'll have to get started soon."

I craned my head back to see her face, my arms still locked around her. She didn't seem to mind my advances—truly—or I wouldn't have continued. Gratefully, I pressed my cheek once more against her belly . . . and felt an answering pressure as her legs encircled mine. "Time to go," she whispered, and gently, she disentangled herself. Moving swiftly, she retrieved my helmet from the corner where it had drifted and helped me fit it once again to my suit, all the while sketching the details of her plan. I listened absently.

"Questions?" she asked, as she concluded.

"What? No. None." I longed to reach out and touch her face, taste her breasts. But our relationship remained unclear. Had I dishonored her with my affection? Had I dishonored myself? Or were we lovers now? I couldn't tell. And I had to know! Courtship should be a subtle thing, but suddenly there was no time. "Wait, there is one question. Indigo, could you love a fully human man?"

She froze. "You ask me that? Do you care?"

I blinked. "Of course I care! I love you!"

Though her face remained impassive, anger sparked her voice. "Do you? I never noticed a sign of *that*, though I looked. But then, who could read *you*? So formal and so reserved. You wear your civil manners like a mask!" And with that she slammed my helmet closed and sealed it, locking me in a cage of silence. I was far too astonished to object.

Turning half away from me, she jerked her kisheer up over her mouth and nose. The living organ immediately melded with the tissue of her respiratory system, providing her with oxygen while she returned to it the carbon dioxide it needed to survive. Settled in its active position, it looked like a respirator draped in a gold kerchief. Glaring at me once through her windowed eyes, she turned and dove through the lock.

I followed at a slower pace. Already the air in my suit tasted hot and thick with CO_2 as the efficiency of the biofilter began to decline. I swallowed hard. Another few hours without a nutrient bath to nourish the organics, and the air would be too fetid to breathe.

Following Indigo's instructions, I used the cutting torch to free a tow cable that had been locked down in its cradle at the stern of the tug. Indigo took the free end. Coiling herself against the side of the tug, she sprang backwards using every bit of force her long legs could muster. The cable paid out behind her. Hooking the torch to my belt, I watched her go.

Our path had crossed the miner's orbit since my first foray Outside. Now the derelict ship lay some two hundred meters out and to our stern. Indigo almost missed it.

Briefly, I saw her silhouetted against the huge, dark cave of the intake throat, a tiny doll cast adrift. Then she was past it, moving at an angle to the hull, still three meters inside the miner's orbit. The receding sunlight glinted off her blue-gold skin. I held my breath. And slowly, I saw the gap that separated her from our prize begin to close.

SunBelt Enterprises had invested heavily in this mining machine. It loomed like a menacing storm in the diffuse white light of the rings, three times the length of north station and twice as broad. Indigo swept past nearly the full length of the hull before she finally found a handhold. Slowly, she began to climb across the rust-colored metal, a lonely figure marooned on an island in a strange, dusty sea of powder and ice. As I watched her, I wondered: *could she love me?* That she might, had left me both flushed with joy and desperately afraid I might fail her. I checked the tow cable—still slack, as it would be for some time to come while the two vessels drifted gradually apart—then I returned alone to the tug's tiny cabin and set about trying to rewire the radio.

The cabin air grew slowly foul around me as I worked. Odd thoughts wandered through my brain, pessimistic threads that finally wound together into a single question: Were we being irresponsible in our attempt to escape the rings? Given the Makers' fierce appetite for machine intelligence, what might the consequences be if even a single molecule escaped sterilization . . . ? But my desire to live over-rode my conscience and I determined to keep silent on this point. I've never claimed to be a moral man.

In the end, my attempt to rebuild the radio proved futile. I couldn't coax even one tiny circuit back to life. My head ached from the effort, and finally, I gave it up, exhausted.

The time had come to go Outside and find Indigo. I sealed my helmet. And immediately, I realized I'd made a terrible mistake.

Without my breath to circulate air, the decay in the organic filter had accelerated. It felt as if I were breathing through a hot wad of insulation. Nothing to be done about it now. I crawled through the lock, to find that our orbit had brought us around to Saturn's night.

A few bright stars glinted through the ring dust. A roving moon cast a little light. In its thin beams I saw Indigo working her way back across the now taut tow rope. But it was another sight that drew my eye. During the past hours, the tug had swung around the miner, until now I could see a different side of the huge ship.

Smug! That's how I felt when I saw the proof that I was a better observer than Indigo. For emblazoned in mottled yellow roman letters across the miner's back was the word SUNBELT, just as I'd described it to her two days ago when I'd coaxed her to join me at the station's telescope. In smaller script following, I mentally translated the Chinese characters: *Saturn Division, SunBelt Enterprises, Inc.* This was our way out! If I could read those giant letters from the station's altitude, then Dahlia could too. And I knew exactly how to overwrite a brief message of my own, two simple characters that would explain our situation.

I whooped, wasting precious oxygen, then turned and dove back through the lock just as Indigo reached the tug. Yanking off my helmet, I breathed thankfully of foul air. When Indigo emerged behind me, I turned around and kissed her cheek. "The rolls of tape!" I shouted. "We can *write* a message to Dahlia."

She spit out her kisheer. "Aron, are you all right? The air in here . . ."

"I know, I know. Keep moving, or you'll be breathing your own exhalations." I yanked open a locker and grabbed the net bag that held the half-meter wide marking tape. After removing a tangled wad of multi-colored wires, several bits of broken plastic and a piece of torn packing foam, I held the bag up to Indigo in triumph. "We can *write* a message to Dahlia. We're going to make it!"

It was *not* lack of oxygen. I swear I saw her smile. After sealing up my suit, we hurried through the lock, and together began the long, hand-over-hand journey across the tow rope.

Black shadows had stolen across the periphery of my vision by the time we reached the miner. My senses blurred as my oxygen-starved brain stumbled over simple thoughts. Through the confusion, I felt Indigo take my arm. She pulled me with her as she worked her way around the miner, and finally, she pointed to a broad, flat surface.

I stared at the site, wondering what significance it had for her. Finally, she tugged at the net bag that I carried on my waist. *Ah . . . !*

Quickly I tethered myself to a handhold, then pulled out a roll of tape, searching in the faint light for the tab that should mark its beginning. A flush of fear drove through my veins when I couldn't find the tab. Then it was there, beneath my trembling fingers. One half of it had been torn away. I yanked at the remaining piece. It shattered like a fragile leaf of glass! I screamed in frustration. Then, pulling a screwdriver from my belt, I began to pry at the tape's end. A half-dozen silver chips broke off, like flecks of old paint chiseled from a wall. "*No!*" I whispered. "Please, no." I tried again, but I couldn't free the end. The tape had fused! Somehow the adhesive had leaked through its protective backing, sealing the roll, layer after layer, into a solid cylinder. Cold washed over me as I remembered the motley collection of debris I'd discarded from the bag—scrap wire, useless packing. It was all clear to me now. What I held was rubbish, trash, the contents of a garbage bag! I hurled the roll in a rage.

Startled, Indigo twisted to catch it, missed, then turned and snatched the bag away from me. Hurriedly she removed a second roll, examined it and embarked upon the same awful process of discovery I'd just endured. When she tossed the roll over her shoulder, I knew it was all up for us. Still, I waited with stubborn hope while she examined the last roll of tape. That too, she eventually cast away. It tumbled end-over-end, sparkling in the moonlight until it disappeared into the Void.

I felt a touch against my shoulder and turned to see Indigo. Gently she embraced me, her head against my shoulder, her legs wrapped around mine. The torch, still tethered to my belt, she brushed aside. I held her tight, while inside me, rage burned. *I couldn't let her die!*

But what could I do? My muzzy brain offered no solution.

Off beyond Indigo's shoulder a tiny moon was falling through its orbit. I watched it. How fast it seemed to move! When a blue flame burst from its end, I started in surprise. A spacecraft? Observing us? How close could it be? The fire disappeared, but not before it had ignited a vision in my brain. Could I offer up a flame in return? My hand sought out the torch. The instrument's invisible beam could not be used as a signal, but perhaps . . .

Indigo must have sensed that something had changed, because she pushed away from me. With my arms free, I wrested the torch from my belt and ignited it. I was laughing, I think. At least I remember strange bubbles of humor fizzing through my brain. Squeezing my eyes shut, I summoned a vision of the Chinese characters I had to draw. Then, in huge zig-zag lines of heat, I began to scribe a message in the miner's skin: 人 (human) joined on a long, long rope to 天 (heaven).

Indigo tells me a rocket came on a tongue of fire, and fused itself in an explosive weld to the miner's back, the tether trailing behind it for a hundred kilometers. I have no recollection of the event myself. I didn't live to see it.

"Oh yes, it was a close thing for you, Aron, dear," Dahlia confirmed, not for the first time. She looked across my hospital bed at Indigo, who sat on the other side. Then shaking her head, she rapped her soft fist against my skull. "There was *so* much damage in here. I do hope we put things right."

I'd spent the thirty-seven days since my death in coma, while molecular machines completed repairs on my damaged cells. In that time my voice had grown rusty from lack of use. "But did you sell the miner?" I croaked.

"Oh, yes, dear. We'll be safely off to Neptune by the time the police think to trouble us again."

I turned to Indigo, and wondered if it would do to offer my hand. She seemed to sense my uncertainty, for she settled the problem by trading me a kiss. Her mouth shocked me: hot and rough, lined with a thousand little tongues that trembled like beating cilia. I responded as any gentleman would—eagerly—while wondering what other secrets her body held. I fervently hoped I'd be given the opportunity to find out. Yet when our lips finally parted, a question lay between us. "Does SunBelt mean nothing to you, Indigo? Can you live, never seeing another of your kind?"

Behind me Dahlia clucked, while Indigo looked typically inscrutable. "Blue Series derivatives have been selected for body form," Dahlia said. "Very little work has been done on their psychology. Indigo—and every other Blue—is as attracted to original humans as any of their ancestors ever were. I'm afraid *you're* the one with the unusual sexual preference, Aron."

Can I be blamed for a rapid change of subject? Sheepishly, I asked, "How did you finally sterilize the miner?"

"We didn't," Indigo said.

"What?" I sat up in shock.

"Tut, tut, Aron," Dahlia said. "Don't look at us like that! There was no *need* to sterilize the miner. An environmentalist designed the ring Makers, remember? Checks were built into the system to forestall a plague. As soon as the little monsters are removed from the ring gravitational fields, they dissociate."

I frowned. "So you never did get to analyze them?"

An orange light ignited in Dahlia's eyes. "No. The clever little bastards. But don't you worry, dear! I'll learn. I will learn."

I didn't doubt it.

Dahlia left then, but Indigo stayed. "I suppose this hospital is a fine place," I said, turning to her. "But when am I to be released?"

"Tomorrow." She took my hand. "But we don't have to wait that long."

I smiled. Suddenly, we understood each other perfectly. "No," I agreed. "We don't."

She kissed me again, and in a soft voice told me what would please her. I did the best I could. Caught up in the tide of her affection, I was a happy man.

In The Tide was first published in Analog Science Fiction & Fact, in September 1989. This short story was actually a "study" in much the same way that a painter will do sketches before tackling the big oil painting. I used In The Tide to develop a feeling for the nanotech-drenched story world that later led to The Nanotech Succession books. I also used it to develop the type of evolved-human character that ultimately led to Nikko in The Bohr Maker. It's a scheme I heartily recommend! Get paid developing the ideas for your novels. Where's the downside of that?

Small Victories

(1)

Puma's hawk sighted the stranger on a cold morning when the wind off the Barrens had eased just enough to allow the blowing curtains of dust in the lower atmosphere to settle to the ground. "Hey, there's somebody out there," Puma called, his adolescent voice cracking in surprise.

A throat mike picked up his words and cast them to Jynis on the sage flats below. She switched off the torch she'd been using to weld a cracked seam on the sand-blasted cabin of the half-track and glanced up. Puma was crouched on a flat rock above the field station, studying the display on his pocket computer. An implant on the hawk's optic nerve transmitted what the bird saw to the computer, where it was translated into an image that had meaning to a human mind.

"Geology team?" Jynis called curiously. Paris Ridge was a remote field station, far to the north of the City of Necessity, and they had few visitors. Just the occasional geologist, or sometimes an army scout out to patrol the border.

"No way," Puma said. "On foot and in trouble. Face down in the sand. Look."

Jynis set down the torch and slipped her own pc from a hip-holster. She opened it. On-screen was the fractured landscape of Paris Ridge as seen from a great height. She made out the scattered white shapes of her oryx herd moving slowly down a ridge. The sight of the animals reminded her that she needed to get out there this morning, give the experimental antelope their weekly supplementary feeding—

There! Jynis finally found what had caught Puma's eye. Almost lost against a background of scattered stones and sparse native grasses—a tiny, prostrate figure in a camouflage suit of desert rust, an air-pack strapped to his back. The skin on the nape of her neck prickled under a sudden sense of peril. "Gotta be a truck, Puma."

"Don't see it."

Wind hissed past the corners of her respirator and tugged at her dirty white parka. Puma's voice arrived over her ear phones. "Better hurry."

"Sure." The native air was thin and mean. If the stranger's oxygen tanks were empty, he wouldn't last long.

Jynis walked from behind the 'track into the full force of the wind. "Storm blowin' up again," she observed.

The field station was situated high on Paris Ridge, on a long slope overlooking the rising swell of the Barrens. Wind-driven plumes of red sand drifted across the lifeless plain. A lowering sun burned dully through the dust-laden skies. They could shelter safe from any sand storm in the field station—the artificial cave had been dug back into the hillside so that only the outer door of the airlock was exposed—while in the half-track they'd be vulnerable. "How far you make it?"

"Seven miles," Puma said. "Maybe thirty minutes."

Jynis nodded. "Call Hobo Flats. See if they know something."

Then she switched off her throat mike. "Shani!" she called. "Shani, come to mama."

Shani had been playing with pebbles she'd found around the roots of the introduced sage. Now she toddled toward her mother, awkward in her padded suit, her exposed cheeks chapped red by the wind. Jynis reached down to pick her up. "We're going for a ride," she said.

Shani grinned and grabbed at the mask of Jynis' respirator. With an angry hiss, Jynis jerked her head back out of reach. "*Don't touch!*" she snapped.

Baby Shani didn't have a respirator. Neither did thirteen year old Puma or any of the other kids conceived in Necessity. They'd been deliberately designed to suit the native air, gifted with respiratory systems completely adapted to the miserly atmosphere of this cold desert world. Never for them the burden of an air-pack.

"No answer from Hobo Flats," Puma called.

"Try again later." Jynis wasn't concerned. Radio reception was a chancy thing. Ridges and gullies blocked the signal. Sand storms blew the antennas down. One satellite in synchronous orbit might have solved most of the problems, but manufacturing a satellite and the rocket to launch it was far beyond the reach of the divided and warring colonies. Too much had been abandoned at landing. Whole histories, whole technologies, deliberately destroyed by colony elders determined to leave the old sinful ways behind. Until necessity forced some of them to seek a compromise with their new world.

Puma tossed back the hood of his parka and came bounding down the slope. In the afternoon light his blond hair gleamed faintly pink. Even with his barrel chest, he looked as human as anyone born before the rift. *As human as me*, Jynis thought. Yet he owned something no one before his generation ever had: a third lung. An organ of reduced size, densely packed with alveoli that combed the air for sparse oxygen molecules with the efficiency of a dust miner filtering storm clouds for gold.

Jynis breathed in the bitter, plastic taste of her respirator. She would never have Puma's and Shani's advantages. She'd been conceived in Iyusha nearly eighteen years ago, before the rift, before the civil war, before a dissenting faction of colony elders had decided that their children must *evolve* if they were to have any real hope of long-term survival on a world so unkind.

Jynis pounded a touchplate on the side of the half-track and the airlock snapped opened. "You want to ride outside?" she called to Puma.

"Yeah."

Shani wriggled impatiently while the lock cycled, then they were inside the truck. Jynis helped Shani out of her gloves and parka, then strapped her into her seat. Gazing at the child's dark brown hair and wide eyes, she couldn't help thinking of Shani's father. But Greg had been dead two years, murdered on the border by Iyushans even before his daughter had been conceived.

Jynis gave Shani a quick kiss on the forehead, then settled into the driver's seat and started the engine.

The Paris Ridge oryx herd had reached the stranger first. The genetically modified antelope were nosing at the body when Jynis brought the truck to a stop. The rising wind that ruffled their thick white fur had already half-buried the stranger's legs in fine red sand.

Jynis wasted no time. Leaving Shani in the truck to finish her nap, she threw on her air-pack and respirator and headed for the lock. By the time she got outside, Puma had already pushed his way through the oryx herd and was crouching over the body. The hawk was perched on a nearby rock, its wings partly spread to balance it against the wind.

Jynis hurried forward, poking gently at the flanks of the milling oryxes to get them to move out of her way. Their long, straight horns flashed in the light as they nuzzled her for food. She'd hand-raised most of them at the field station, and they associated human scent with handouts. Usually she enjoyed their attention. But today their supplementary rations were due and they knew it. They mobbed her, blocking her path, their sharp hooves stomping on her booted feet.

"*Shaw!* Move!" she shouted, waving her hands to shoo them back. Their heads bobbed aggressively; they stood their ground. So she whipped out her pc, entered the oryxes' frequency, and tapped in a code that would stimulate the hormonal implant that each animal carried, calling for a mild case of the jitters.

The white antelope responded almost immediately. Their aggressive behavior stopped. A few snorted nervously, and then the entire herd began to move slowly away. Jynis bounded forward, then dropped to her knees at Puma's side.

The stranger lay face down, unmoving. A blue tinge discolored his cheeks; his lips were pale. He'd torn off his respirator. It was still in his hand, the straps tangled. "He alive?" Jynis asked.

Puma shrugged. "Sort of. Hypoxic. Air-pack's empty. Know him?" Puma swept back the man's long black hair so Jynis could see his features. She caught her breath. He was a young man, probably in his late teens, with rough, chiseled features and a fresh scar across his temple. Jynis felt her heart pounding in her ears. She was sure she'd never seen him before, and that could mean only one thing.

"Looks familiar," Puma announced.

"Oh yeah?" Jynis could feel her anger building. Reaching under the stranger's collar, she felt around for a moment, then pulled out a necklace. On the short, heavy chain hung a deep purple enameled replica of the Iyushan lily. "Since when are you familiar with Iyushans?"

Puma drew back like a cat that had encountered a fetid smell. He plucked at her arm, pulling her back. "Come on. Let's go."

She shook him off. "Uh-uh."

"Leave him!" Puma shouted, startling the hawk into flight. "We don't owe him anything."

"No," she growled. "But he owes us." She yanked on the chain, feeling her hatred like a heady wine. "Bet he was planning on making targets out of us, Puma. Sit up on that ridge over the station and pick us off as we come out the door. But he miscalculated. Ran out of oh-two. Too bad."

"Come on, Jynis," Puma pleaded.

She could hear the fear in his voice, but it meant nothing to her. "Look at him. He's old enough. Been a soldier a few years now. Think maybe he's the one that got Greg?" Her grip on the chain tightened. She twisted it around, wanting to choke the last air out of this son-of-a-bitch, wanting to do it for Greg, and for Shani, who would never know her father.

"Jynis!" Puma shrieked.

She gasped and dropped the chain. Puma was staring at her, terror in his eyes. She looked away. "Help me get him into the truck," she said gruffly. "They'll want to interrogate him at Necessity . . . before they hang him."

Visibility had dropped to twelve meters; the half-track's cabin was filled with the hiss of blowing sand. Jynis drove grimly, talking to Puma now and then to make sure he was all right. She'd brought the hawk in and chained it to its perch in the back of the truck. But Puma was harder to control. He'd insisted on riding outside despite the weather. She'd tried to persuade him to come in, but he refused to share air with an Iyushan. *Little prig*, she thought. *And where do you think you'll sleep tonight?*

They'd laid the stranger on a bunk in the half-track's pressurized cabin. Jynis had lashed his hands and feet to the bedframe, then strapped a respirator over his nose and mouth, locking down the demand button so the oxygen would flow free. She waited just long enough to see a flush of color rise in his cheeks before hurrying forward to start the journey home. Shani still slept in her seat, oblivious to the sound of the wind and the rough terrain.

"So someone really did find me in time." She jumped at the unexpected voice. "Or are you an angel bearing me up to Heaven?"

A glance over her shoulder showed her the Iyushan in his bunk, propped up on his elbows, his hands and feet still firmly secured. He'd worked the respirator down around his throat. His hard, chiseled face was pinched with exhaustion.

"The name is Jynis Ngutavai," she said, her gaze fixed on the rough terrain ahead. "Of Necessity."

"Cuvey Dubuisson. I've come a long way to find you, Jynis."

Dubuisson? Her knuckles went white on the steering wheel. She felt a prickly sweat break out on her cheeks. "Cuvey . . . Dubuisson?"

"I think you know my mother," he said sadly. "I don't."

She felt her mouth go dry. The words did not want to emerge, but she forced them. "Are you . . . ?"

"I'm your brother. Jynis, I was afraid you wouldn't even know my name."

She touched her throat mike with a trembling hand. "Gotta stop a minute, Puma. He's puking."

"Need help?"

"No. Take a minute."

She brought the truck to a halt, set the brake, unfastened her safety harness. Then she slowly turned around, taking another look at this stranger.

Mother had talked about Cuvey. He'd been two years old when the original colony broke apart. She'd left him and her husband in Iyusha, stealing away with the other radicals while Jynis was only a cluster of dividing cells in her womb.

Looks familiar, Puma had said. Sure, Jynis realized. Looked like herself in masculine issue.

"Why come here?" she asked, her voice sharp with suspicion.

"To see you, Jynis." In the back of the truck, the hooded hawk moved restlessly on its perch, its feathers rustling softly. Cuvey's head snapped around at the sound. He half-ducked, and a stifled cry escaped his lips.

Jynis caught her breath, then quickly looked away. An unpalatable combination of embarrassment and fear made her voice harsh. "You running from the war?"

"No!"

She could hear him breathing in deep, shaky gasps. But she wouldn't look at him. She kept her eyes carefully averted. This kind of fear was a private thing.

"I'm still in it," he growled. "I'm going back. I just wanted to see you, that's all."

"Why?"

"You my sister or not?"

She finally looked at him again. He nodded, his face a mask of tension. "I'm not here to hurt you," he said. "I'd never hurt you. You don't need these straps." He nodded at the bindings on his hands and feet.

She glanced at the straps, feeling a faint flush in her cheeks. "Why no truck?"

His gaze shifted. He seemed to be searching for an answer. Then: "I'm AWOL," he blurted. "Iyusha doesn't know I'm here." He looked up. His gaze locked onto hers with an intensity that made her shiver. "My buddy Royce, he heard your name on the radio. He and Fa'a . . . they said they'd cover for me if I wanted to come see how you were doing. But I couldn't get a truck. So I walked."

"That's impossible."

"It's not. Two packs and a thin mix. I walked all night."

"You didn't make it."

His breathing started to get raggedy again, but he fought hard to hide it. "I did make it. I'm here, aren't I? Now come untie me. There's a girl."

She'd risen from her seat without thinking. Now she moved toward him, her heart thundering in her chest. She crept to the foot of the bunk where she'd secured him, fascinated by his presence. She saw herself in his eyes. She tried to see her father. She'd never seen her father. *Dubuisson.*

"Free me, Jynis."

She touched one of the straps, but caution still held her back. "Why risk it?" she asked, surprised by the note of pain in her own voice.

"We're family. That's reason enough."

"It wasn't reason enough for mother and father to stay together."

He nodded sadly. "'S true. But we're not like them, Jynis. We're not like them. Come. You don't want to see your own brother hanged?" He gazed at her, his eyes dark and unreadable. There was much that he wasn't telling. She knew it. But she gave in anyway. She'd dreamed about him so many years.

Leaning forward, she cautiously unstrapped one of his hands. She half-expected him to go for her then. But he only reached slowly over to undo the other straps. She backed away a few steps, even so. This was treason. The elders at Necessity would unhinge if they knew. The thought secretly delighted her. Discipline in Necessity was always so hard.

"Hey, Jynis." Puma's voice came in over her ear phones. "Fixed him up? Need to move on. Wind's bad. Sand's thick."

Absently, Jynis touched her throat mike, her gaze fixed on Cuvey as he stood on stiff legs. "Done here, Puma. Ready to move." She switched off the throat mike and spoke to Cuvey. "He won't like it. You go home tomorrow and I'll make it okay."

"Sure. I've got to get back to my unit. Give me a ride part way to the border?"

She nodded, then turned to make her way back to the driver's seat. With her back to him, she felt fear run between her shoulder blades. But he made no aggressive move; only followed her forward docilely enough. She glanced at Baby Shani still sleeping in the shotgun seat. "I'll move her," she muttered.

Cuvey looked at the baby while Jynis unstrapped her. "Whose?" he asked in open surprise.

Jynis snorted. "Mine 'course. Think I run a babysitting service way out here?" She picked up Shani and cradled her against her shoulder while the little one moaned and smacked her lips. "Wanna let me get by?"

Cuvey stepped out of the way, the surprise on his face turning to suspicion. "How old is she?"

"Year and a half." Jynis set her in the backseat and strapped her in, then turned to look at Cuvey. "You got a problem?"

"You had her when you were fifteen."

"Uh huh."

"That her daddy outside?"

"Huh. Puma. He's a kid."

"Then where's her daddy?"

"You think she doesn't have a daddy, that it? You heard the rumors. You think maybe the elders just shot me up with some anonymous doctored seed?" He glared at her, but he didn't say anything. His face was dark with anger. "Well Shani does have a daddy. Down in the graveyard at Necessity. He was murdered on the border. Maybe by you."

Cuvey looked straight into her eyes. Memories seemed to march across his face like the shadows cast by blowing sand. Then: "Easy, Jynis," he said. "You're putting words in my mouth. I think you're too young, that's all."

She jerked her gaze away. "Sit down. We've got to get going."

He nodded and dropped into the shotgun seat. Jynis moved up to drive, suddenly sure she'd made a serious mistake. No.

The mistake was Cuvey's, for coming here at all. A boy's stupid, romantic lark. But the problem belonged to Jynis. Because Cuvey had been right—she couldn't let him hang.

She started up the truck, then touched her throat mike. "Secure, Puma?"

"Yeah. Let's go."

She released the brake and started edging the truck down an easy slope.

"That kid," Cuvey said. "Why does he stay outside?"

"Doesn't like the way Iyushans smell."

Cuvey smiled at that. He had a nice smile. Jynis felt her suspicions begin to fade. She turned her full attention to her driving.

The grade was beginning to steepen. She responded by turning the half-track slightly to ease the angle of descent. She could no longer see the ground. The wind had stirred up a mist of fine sand that streamed knee deep up the face of the slope, hiding rocks and rifts beneath its shimmering surface. She slowed the 'track to a crawl and switched on her throat mike. "Puma, hop down and check out this slope for me. I think I remember boulders—"

"On it."

A moment later he was in front of the 'track, wading through the streaming sand. A soft oath escaped Cuvey's lips. Startled, Jynis glanced at him. He was staring at Puma, his face drawn in disbelief. "That boy's out there without a respirator."

"Yeah," she agreed, letting the truck roll slowly after Puma.

"But . . . how? No one can get by on native air . . ."

Jynis' brows rose in surprise. "You don't know about our kids? Huh. Guess they're too young to be fightin' you at the border." She nodded at Puma. "But that's what the war's about, Cuvey."

"I-I knew your elders abandoned us because they were not content with their heritage. They wanted to breed a new race of humans—"

"No! Not breed. *Design.*"

"Uh huh. I didn't know you'd gone so far."

"Not me," Jynis said bitterly. "I haven't gone anywhere. Strictly ancestral type. Outdated."

Cuvey continued to stare at Puma, as if he still couldn't quite believe it. "He's an artificial man."

Quietly, Jynis said, "They don't tell you much in Iyusha, do they?"

Cuvey hesitated. She felt his gaze, though she kept her own fixed on the slope outside. Then, ". . . *maybe not*." The admission sounded pained. Jynis felt suddenly sorry for him—it was no easy thing to discover that your own fine body was seriously deficient when compared to a kid from across the border—and that your elders didn't trust you with that truth.

Jynis felt a need to drive the point home. "Puma's better than us," she said.

From the corner of her eye she could see Cuvey flinch. "Do you believe that?"

"Know it. See it each day. Me 'n you are cripples next to Puma 'n Shani, 'n all the other kids at Necessity. Would be nothing for Puma to walk to the border. That trek almost killed you."

Cuvey had nothing to say for nearly a minute. Jynis could feel him weighing the consequences of what he'd just learned. When he did speak, his voice was hoarse. "Does it hurt you?" he asked. "To be obsolete?"

Jynis bit her lip. For a moment she almost envied Cuvey. In his world he was as good as the next man. No better. No worse. Part of a whole. Things were different in Necessity, where the elders were struggling to build a world that would never include them.

Ahead, Puma signaled *Right. Right!* Jynis' attention snapped back to him. She was carefully guiding the half-track along the indicated path when the boy disappeared—he was there one moment and gone the next, swallowed up by the swirling sand.

"Puma!" she shouted, then switched on the throat mike and called his name again. There was no answer. Either his equipment was broken, or—

She slammed on the brakes. Loose sand shifted under the treads and the truck started to slide. She threw it into reverse and ground back up the slope to stable footing. Then she shut the engine down and scrambled for her air-pack.

"Puma," she called. "Puma, answer me now." He didn't respond. She found herself breathing hard. "Puma, I'm coming for you. Don't know if you can hear, but sit tight." She wrestled her pack on, then pulled the respirator over her face. Cuvey was right behind her. He found his own pack and disconnected the oh-two feedlines Jynis had rigged on it. Shani started to grumble in her sleep and a moment later she was awake and crying irritably "*Mama-ma-ma-ma . . .*"

Jynis stared at her in a sudden agony of indecision. She wanted to leave her in the truck. But the truck was parked on a steep slope. If it slipped, or rocked in the wind . . .

Cuvey seemed to share her thoughts. "You stay. I'll find Puma."

"No!"

He froze. "You still don't trust me? You want me to stay here?" He had the lock open. "But if you don't trust me, you can't leave me with the truck. And if Puma's hurt, maybe you're going to need my help."

Jynis hesitated while the seconds swept past. But she had no real choice. "All right. But first get the rescue pack. There, in the locker." She hustled Shani out of her seat and wrestled her into her parka, while muttering ineffective phrases of comfort to the unhappy child. Then she and Shani, Cuvey and the rescue pack, all squeezed into the lock.

The door closed, and Jynis found herself pressed up against Cuvey, supremely conscious of the hard reality of his body. *My brother*, she thought, and for a moment the little chamber sparked with a sense of unreality.

Then the outer door opened and she was moving cautiously down the slope, a step behind Cuvey, with Shani cradled in her arms.

At the point Puma had disappeared, they found a wind-smoothed gorge, an ancient fault line less than two meters across. Blowing sand obscured the bottom of the crevice. There was no sign of Puma.

They scouted along the rim until they found an outcropping of boulders. Then they took a rope from the rescue pack, tied a loop in the end of it and hooked it over a solid-looking rock. Jynis tossed the coil into the gully and watched it spin out. The wind caught it and swept it to one side.

"Now," Cuvey said, shouting to be heard over the wind. "Are you going to climb down with the baby in your arms, or will you let me go?"

Jynis squirmed. But again there was no choice. She bit her lip and nodded curtly. "You go. I'll hold the rope. Yank it when you've got him."

"Right." He hooked the rescue pack over his arm, looped the rope behind him and stepped backwards into the void. The wind tore at him as he descended. Almost immediately, he disappeared into the blowing sand.

Jynis watched him go. She squatted by the crevice, one hand around Shani, the other on the rope. What would Cuvey do when he found Puma? the *artificial* man? The bitter dispute between Necessity and Iyusha didn't stop at family lines. She knew that well enough.

"Puma," she whispered helplessly. And then she said it louder. "Puma!"

"Jynis?" The voice in her ear phones was weak; laced with

pain . . . almost lost behind the static generated by blowing sand. "You here?"

"Near, Puma. What happened?"

"Lip of the gorge . . . gave way. Leg's . . . broken—femur. Hey. Hi Jynis. Didn't know you knew how . . . to rappel."

"Don't, Puma. 'S not me."

He must have realized then who it was, and tried to move. Tears started in her eyes at his scream of pain. "Puma!" she called. "Puma, answer me, please." There was only the crackle of static. "Puma, wake up, wake up! Puma!"

She started back up the slope. When she reached the truck she hit the emergency override on the lock, blowing the cabin's seal, venting the interior. Shani was crying against her chest. Jynis held her tightly, while rummaging frantically through the lockers, looking for the pistol that she kept just in case one of the oryx injured itself too badly to be treated. She found it, then dug out the ammunition and loaded, while trying to balance wailing Shani. She started for the lock.

A figure filled the opening. Cuvey. She turned the pistol on him. "Where's Puma?" she demanded. "And don't tell me he's dead!"

"He's not." Cuvey looked carefully past the weapon. "Though he does have a compound fracture. I put an air splint on it, but I'll need a stretcher to get him out. Do you have one?"

"A stretcher?" She looked at the gun in sudden confusion. Then, with a grimace, she shoved it into her pocket. She started back toward the lockers, then hesitated. "Cuvey . . . why help us?"

His dark eyes were angry as he gazed at her over the rim of his respirator. "You're family, Jynis. Why is that so hard for you to understand?"

She shrugged, shamefaced. Then she went to the lockers, where she pulled out the bag that held the dis-assembled stretcher.

"I'll need another rope," Cuvey said.

She found one for him. Some twenty minutes later, they had Puma safe aboard the truck.

(2)

Cuvey resisted sleep for as long as he could, knowing what sleep would bring. He sat up late, talking to Jynis and listening to the sand storm hiss and howl outside the door of the underground field station. It was a big storm. Big enough to keep everyone pinned down in shelters, friend and enemy alike. Big enough to keep the radio out of commission. Or at least Jynis would believe that. He'd surreptitiously disconnected the antenna cable, just to be sure.

He jumped at the touch of Jynis' hand against his shoulder. "Lie down," she said. "It's late. You don't have to stay up to entertain me."

She'd doped up Puma. He was snoring on a pallet a few feet away in the low-ceilinged bedchamber. Once again, Cuvey found his restless gaze fixed on the boy. Puma's blond hair gleamed in the yellow light and his cheeks were rosy with fever. He lay half on his back, his chest exposed by the blanket that covered his injured leg. Cuvey stared at him, waiting for him to breathe, watching for the telltale rise and fall of his chest, unconsciously holding his own breath until his lungs burned for lack of oxygen. Puma slept on, drawing breaths in the oxygen-rich atmosphere of the cache that were so shallow the motion was undetectable.

Why had the elders said nothing about Puma . . . and all the other kids like him? Cuvey's gaze touched on Baby Shani, asleep in her mother's bed. It was inconceivable to him that the elders didn't know about this new generation. They must know. If Jynis made no secret of it, neither would Necessity. Yet the elders had never hinted at how rapidly the enemy was changing. Even his own dad, who'd sat on the governing council for as long as Cuvey could remember, had said nothing . . .

Puma was still a boy. But he'd be a man soon. How easy would it be for a man like Puma to cross the border on foot, moving at night, independent of an air supply? He could carry explosives instead of oxygen. He could reach Iyusha within two or three days.

No wonder the elders were pressing this war *now*.

Cuvey lay back on his pallet, trying to control his own harsh breathing. His eyes were dry and heavy with fatigue. It'd been well over a day since he'd had a wink and he knew he couldn't hold off sleep much longer. Still, he didn't want to sleep. He didn't like to sleep. If only he could skip tonight and go straight to tomorrow, even though tomorrow would only bring another phase of the war.

Jynis smiled at him. "Can barely keep your eyes open," she chided. "Why fight so hard to stay awake?" By her tone, he knew she didn't really expect an answer. He watched her as she turned down the wall light until it was a faint, gold ember.

His heart fluttered in the near darkness. He didn't want to sleep. "Do you look like our mother?" he asked impulsively.

"No." Her voice came out of the shadows. "Not at all." He could hear her lying down. He could feel his own eyes flutter shut, and then the weight of the darkness as it rolled in close around him, like a ghost that had been waiting long to take him. He gave in and let it have him, because he'd tried before and found that it was impossible to stay awake forever.

The darkness deepened. He could hear a distant wind blowing. It drew nearer, and nearer, until blowing sand stung his cheeks. Blood exploded in his rifle sights, redder than the red rocks of the Barrens. God stood beside him, an invisible presence that offered no guidance, only judgment. "*It's not fair!*" Cuvey screamed at Him. Flames ran through a tunnel, then burst outward into the night, like the sizzling tongue of a great dragon buried in the ground. Cuvey whooped in joy, half-drunk with easy triumph. He capered with Royce across the sand while the dragon tongue lit up the night, burning the empty field station at Hobo Flats. The mission was half done and they hadn't killed anybody. God was pleased. He knew it. God was pleased.

But the enemy couldn't leave it at that, couldn't let things be. *We didn't kill anyone!* Cuvey whispered fiercely.

The flames must have drawn the old man home. He'd come in from the desert, gimping and stumbling over the rocks, his respirator whistling with the force of his draught. Cuvey quiet now in the shadows. God conveniently absent.

Fa'a was up on the ridge with the truck and he took that moment to start the engine. The vehicle exploded in a geyser of flame, as if the dragon's back had been stabbed and fire had burst from the wound. Cuvey stared in disbelief at the fierce pyre that consumed his friend, his only way home. *We didn't kill anyone! Not this time.*

Then the old man chuckled, only a few feet away. "Gotcha, you bastards."

Cuvey stayed cool. This wasn't his first time. He moved in silence, a shadow within a shadow. A bad dream. The old man didn't laugh when the bullet took him through the heart. In the light of the dying fires, he appeared mildly surprised.

Cuvey stomped over to the corpse. He kicked at it, hating the elders, all of them, Iyushan and enemy alike. They were all one. They'd spent years together on the colony ship. They'd celebrated together the day they'd made landing on this God forsaken world and they'd torched the ship together, burned their last bridge joyfully together. They were all friends. They couldn't bear to kill each other. So they begat kids and sent them out to do the killing.

Near dawn Royce found the old woman. She was holed up in a truck less than a mile from the burned out field station. Royce was low on oh-two and he wanted that truck. Cuvey felt the same. No old woman was going to keep them from getting home.

Royce went in first. Cuvey hung back on the ridge, hunkered down with his rifle, keeping the old lady in his sights. He couldn't shoot through the windshield. The glass was tempered to withstand sand storms; a bullet wouldn't pierce it and he had no explosives. She could have just stayed in there until their oh-two ran out and she'd have been perfectly safe. But she knew her old man wasn't coming back to her and she wanted Royce in trade.

She saw Royce out in the rocks. She put on her air-pack, got her rifle, and opened the lock. Cuvey had her clear in his sights. He could have killed her then, but the look in her eyes stopped him cold. Such a look of hatred he'd never seen, and it froze him. She used the moment to blow a hole in Royce's heart. Cuvey fired then, but it was too late. He was alone.

Bone and blood coated the walls of the truck's lock. The old woman's body was slumped across the floor, her skull half gone and brains looking like spoiled jelly. Cuvey blew the seal, frantic to get past the mess. Inside, the engine compartment was wide open, with engine parts spread across the floor. Cuvey gazed at the scene, feeling the weight of God there beside him. And he started to laugh. He fell to his knees and laughed, until his respirator began to honk a warning of low oh-two. Then he pulled himself together and waded through the parts, kicking and cursing at the useless collection of metal. He knew he was looking at a minimum of a day's work to put it back together. No wonder the old folks hadn't made it back to the field station last night.

He stood in the middle of the mess, wondering what to do. He could try to reassemble the engine. But more than likely something needed to be replaced. Couldn't exactly call into Necessity for spare parts. And by the end of the day, when the old folks didn't check in, somebody might think of sending a patrol out this way.

He crouched on the floor, his head down between his knees. He was almost out of oh-two and his respirator howled the emergency with every breath.

They'd been so confident when they'd set out—he and Royce and Fa'a. It was to be a lightning mission. Hit the Hobo Flats field station. Torch it. Hit the Paris Ridge field station. Torch it. Run for home in time for breakfast in the mess hall. His dad had even come to see them off. "Your sister's at Paris Ridge," he'd said, as the boys checked their equipment. "Bring her home."

Cuvey's head snapped up. *Jynis*. If only he could make it to Paris Ridge, he would find Jynis. She'd been stolen away from home even before she was born, but Cuvey still felt as if he knew her. In his dreams he'd come for her a hundred times, to rescue her from the enemy. In his dreams, she was just like him.

He ransacked the truck, looking for extra air packs. But the old bitch had drained them. So he stripped the pack off her back. Then he set out for Paris Ridge. By the time he ran out of oh-two, the wind had scoured the blood from his hands.

The wind was still howling when he finally woke. He opened his eyes to near darkness. Baby Shani was standing next to his pallet, staring at him. He smiled at her. It was hard to think of this little girl as the enemy. She didn't look like a freak. He wondered if Dad would say kill her anyway. His smile faded, and Shani toddled off toward her mother's bed. Suppressing a groan, Cuvey raised his head and looked around.

Jynis and Puma were still asleep. In the windowless shelter he couldn't tell if it was night or day, but he had no desire to encounter more dreams. So he kicked off his thin blanket, shrugged on his shirt and headed for the kitchen to brew a pot of tea. Baby Shani joined him a minute later. He coaxed her onto his lap where she explored the stubble on his cheeks with a child's curious hand. He'd been so surprised to discover he had a niece. Children always surprised him with their own reality, with their instinctive refusal to fit within the confines of a strategic equation that would classify them as unripe ammunition for the war.

He tickled Shani, and she laughed. What to do with her? The war wasn't over. He still had to burn this shelter. And Dad hadn't said anything about bringing an altered grandchild back to Iyusha.

His gaze shifted from the child to the parka Jynis had worn yesterday. She'd left it draped on the back of a chair. As he looked at it, an icy feeling stole across his belly. He felt fairly sure that the gun Jynis had turned on him yesterday was still there in the pocket of the parka. He wanted to forget it was there. He hated this war. But God was watching.

Carrying Shani in the crook of his arm, he stood up and walked around the table. He patted the parka until he found the weapon, then he dropped it in a deep pocket of his pants. The tea was ready. He poured himself a cup.

(3)

Jynis slept late. Shani was already gone from the bed by the time she woke. "Shani?" she called, lifting her head. Puma was still asleep, but Cuvey's pallet was empty.

She was on her feet in an instant, stumbling out of the bed-chamber and into the kitchen. Cuvey looked up at her as she came in. He was stretched out on the cold floor, a steaming cup of tea at his elbow while he watched Shani play with the touch pad of Puma's sturdy pocket computer. The little pc's had lately become favorite toys.

"Good morning," Cuvey said, greeting Jynis with a gentle smile. "It is morning, isn't it?"

Jynis shoved her hair out of her face; her heart still pounded from the flash of adrenaline. "More or less," she growled, unaccountably angry. She listened to the wind. It didn't sound as fierce as it had last night. Maybe the storm was easing. Maybe Cuvey could go home today after all. She hoped so.

"Get you some tea?" Cuvey asked.

"In a minute. I need to check on Puma." She returned to the bedchamber, running her fingers self-consciously through her hair, trying to straighten it. She must look awful.

She crouched beside Puma. He was stirring in his sleep. She laid a gentle hand on his forehead. He'd been feverish when they'd brought him in yesterday, but after a night's sleep he'd cooled down some. She spoke his name softly. His eyes fluttered, then focused on her. He hardly seemed to breathe, so saturated was his system with oxygen in the rich atmosphere of the shelter. In these circumstances, his body accepted a high CO-2 level to keep him from becoming giddy. "Hey," he muttered. "We still alive?"

"Sure." She smiled, and stroked his cheek. "You scared me bad."

"That Iyushan scared *me*. Saw him in the dust; thought I was dead. How'd I get away?"

"Don't remember?" she asked curiously.

"No."

"He hauled you out."

Puma gave her a quizzical look. "Why?"

"'Cause he's my brother, Puma. Out of Iyusha."

Puma's jaw worked as he struggled with that. Finally: "He tell you that?"

She scowled. "*You* said he looks familiar. Who does he look like?"

Puma just gazed at her, his eyes sullen. "Where is he?"

"In the kitchen, playing with Shani."

"You left him alone with her!" He started to get up, but Jynis pushed him back down on the pallet. She tangled her fingers in his pretty blond hair and gave it a good, hard pull. "Not hearin' me, Puma!" she hissed at him. "Cuvey's my brother. Not here to hurt us. Not here at all, officially. 'N you're not gonna' breathe one word of this to Necessity." She yanked on his hair. "Got it?"

He yelped and slapped at her hand. She let him go. "You're crazy, Jynis," he said. "He's gonna kill you."

"Didn't kill *you*," she growled. "That tell you somethin'?"

She helped Puma to the toilet, then brought him breakfast. When she returned to the kitchen the pc was still on the floor, but Cuvey and Shani had disappeared. She found them in the air room, just inside the lock. The electrolysis plant was housed there, and the tanks of hydrogen and oxygen. Cuvey held Shani in the crook of his arm. Together, they admired the hawk on its perch near the door. "Don't let her close," Jynis warned. "Hawk's mean." Cuvey stepped back a pace, while the bird preened restlessly.

Jynis glanced at the windspeed meter. It showed barely fifty miles an hour. She pulled on a thick, gauntleted glove, then freed the hawk from its perch. "Weather's calming down," she said to Cuvey. "We need to go."

"I'll check out the respirators."

"Good." She set the hawk down on the floor of the lock, then stepped back and closed the door. Pumps began draining the excess air. "Come on, Shani," she called. "Time to dress." Cuvey passed the baby to her, though he seemed reluctant to give her up.

"She breathes shallow and slow," he said.

"Yeah."

"But she doesn't seem . . . *wrong*."

Jynis gave him a scathing glance and started to turn away. She was surprised by his hand, hard on her shoulder.

"It's not my word, Jynis. It's what they say in Iyusha. Shani's a beautiful child." The tension in his eyes startled her. "How deep is the change?" he asked.

"Huh?"

"Is it heritable?"

She gazed at him for a long moment, trying to decipher his intentions. "Why, Cuvey? You're thinking what?"

He blinked, and suddenly his expression grew hard. "Just curious." He reached for the respirators, and started to strip and clean them. "How soon can you get ready? I have to get back before my officer finds I'm AWOL."

"Twenty minutes?"

"Good."

She stopped by the radio to check in with Necessity. But the unit only pulled in static. The antenna must be down. She cursed softly. If Necessity didn't make contact with her today, they'd steer a border patrol this way. She and Cuvey would have to hurry.

She moved quickly, changing Shani, giving her a bite to eat, getting herself dressed. Puma watched her sullenly. "He's gotta be a criminal," Puma said. "How can you just let him go?"

She pulled on a fresh shirt and stomped into her boots. "He's my brother. How can I let him hang?"

"Everybody's got family on the other side."

"Cuvey's not on the other side," she pointed out. "He's here."

But Puma persisted. "You were ready to kill him yesterday."

"Didn't know who he was."

"Still don't. Maybe he *did* kill Greg. Ask him?"

"Shove off."

"At least leave Shani here."

She gazed at him thoughtfully, then nodded. Cuvey's interest in the child unsettled her. Better to leave her here with Puma. "Okay."

"*Jynis!*" Cuvey shouted from the other side of the shelter. "You ready?"

"Three minutes!" she called. She went to the kitchen; picked up Puma's pocket computer from the floor and set it on the table. Then she retrieved her equipment belt and strapped it on. Her own pc was still in the holster. It pressed against her thigh. She tapped absently at its housing. Puma's doubt was working on her nerves. She went over again in her mind what she was doing, but the conclusion came out the same. She just couldn't let Cuvey hang.

"Jynis," Puma called softly. She went back to the bedchamber and looked in. Shani was playing on the floor with her blocks. Puma was frowning thoughtfully. "Did you ever contact Hobo Flats?"

"No. Radio's down."

"Try the hawk?"

"Later, Puma. Gotta go."

"Then get me my pc and I'll do it!"

She scowled at him in irritation. She didn't want Puma making trouble. "No," she said. "You rest. I'll take care of it." She slipped her own computer out of its holster and opened it, then leaned in the doorway and tapped in a string of commands. The hawk had flown north. She called it around to the east, guiding it toward Hobo Flats. Suddenly Cuvey was at her shoulder. She jumped, startled by his silent approach. Soldier quiet. He already had his air-pack on. His respirator dangled around his neck.

"What are you doing?" he asked.

"Lookin' around. Couldn't raise Hobo Flats yesterday. Maybe some trouble there."

"Looking around?" Cuvey gazed over her shoulder at the computer display, then frowned darkly. "That picture's not real time."

"Sure is," Jynis told him. "It's out of the hawk. Iyusha doesn't do this?"

Outside, the air was still thick with dust suspended by the storm. Visibility wasn't good. But through the haze she thought she saw a truck stalled in the Barrens. *Stop hawk!* she thought, and tapped in the command. *Turn about and circle that.*

The hawk's vision was very good. As it flew lower, she could see the truck's open lock. She could see the swollen body sprawled across the floor there, chest up, mouth open. But the head was half gone. She felt Cuvey move away from her side, and her gaze turned to follow him. Their eyes met, and she saw the truth in his cold stare. "*You bastard!*" she hissed.

Suddenly her pistol appeared in his hand. He stepped back into the kitchen, grabbed her parka from the back of a chair and held it out to her. "Put this on," he said. "We're leaving."

She stared at the gun as if it were a willful thing. She told herself he would never hurt her. Told herself that over and over again. "No," she answered, closing the pc and slipping it back into the holster. "Go alone. Murderer."

"Put it on!" Cuvey shouted. "You don't belong with these freaks. You're coming home with me."

"No."

He snarled at her. But to her surprise, he lowered the gun. "Fine then, little sister. Stay."

He dropped the parka on the table, then turned and strode toward the front of the shelter. Jynis glanced at Puma. He was huddled in a corner of the bedchamber, Shani sheltered behind him. "Get dressed," she growled at him. Then she turned, grabbed a knife from the kitchen, and ran cautiously after Cuvey.

She found him in the air room. He didn't seem surprised to see her. He turned the gun on her again. "Stay back," he said. But she had no desire to approach. "This world belongs to Iyusha, not to the traitors at Necessity."

"You came here to kill us."

"Not you. There's not enough of us left. Dad wants you home."

"I am home."

Cuvey scowled darkly. His gaze left her, to scan the pressure gages on the air room wall. "Your hydrogen tanks are full. Ah, oxygen too." Reaching out, he turned the couplings, one for each tank. The hiss-roar of escaping gases filled the room.

"What are you doing?" Jynis yelped. She leaped for the panel. "That's hydrogen. One spark and—"

Cuvey knocked the knife from her hand in one practiced blow. "BOOM," he whispered, as she scrambled back out of reach. "Now get in the lock."

"But Shani! 'N Puma . . ."

"Get your little baby if you like. But get in the lock."

She darted back to the bedchamber and went to her knees beside Puma. He'd dressed Shani in her thermal suit, and was struggling into his own parka. "Hurry up! Hurry up!" she screamed at him. "He's going to blow the shelter!" She helped him with the parka, then hauled him to his feet. He grunted with pain; his face went pale. She looped his arm around her shoulders. "Try to walk." Shani was clinging to her leg, howling to be picked up. Jynis reached a hand down to her.

Suddenly Cuvey was there. He snatched up the child and strode wordlessly forward. "Come on, Puma," Jynis pleaded. As she went through the kitchen, she grabbed her own parka. Puma's face was beaded with sweat. "Come on," she told him. "We can make it."

They reached the air room. The pressurized tanks were still dumping their mix into the atmosphere of the shelter. Cuvey was waiting in the lock, wearing his respirator. He held Shani with one arm, the pistol with the other. The welding torch stuck out of the pocket of his parka and Jynis' air-pack was at his feet. He shoved the pistol in Puma's face as Jynis crowded him into the lock. She slapped the button to cycle the lock, and the door closed. "This is why you came here, isn't it?" Jynis shouted at him over the sound of the pumps. She wanted to grab her air-pack, but she'd have to drop Puma to do it.

Cuvey leaned forward, pressing the muzzle of the gun against Puma's cheek. "We had a team on every field station between here and Necessity. I could have been on any one of them. But I came to Paris Ridge for you. I'm gonna' bring you home."

The outer door opened. Jynis' ears popped at the pressure change. She drew in a lungful of thin native air and held onto Puma.

Cuvey put Shani down, then took out the welding torch. "Out," he said quietly.

Jynis grabbed Shani's hand, then nudged Puma. "Let's go."

He leaned on her lightly, trying to take most of his own weight. After ten steps she was breathing like a runner at the end of a race. She stopped and looked back. Cuvey had the torch lit. He leaned down and placed it carefully on the floor of the lock next to her air-pack, then he stood back as the door began to close.

"*My pack!*" Jynis whispered.

"Never mind!" Puma cried. "Gotta' get out of here!"

They had twenty seconds before the lock's inner door opened and the torch ignited the cloud of hydrogen gas. Counting the time, Jynis staggered across the sage flats, hauling Shani with one hand, supporting Puma with the other. At twelve seconds Cuvey caught them. He grabbed Shani. Jynis blacked out.

She opened her eyes to see the hawk circling far overhead—dark wings against a rusty sky. Puma lay beside her, eyes closed, breath drawn in ragged gasps. He sweated pain. She sat up slowly, listening to the low roar of flash fire, sensing it in the ground. Even that effort required oxygen; she started breathing fast and deep—impoverished air bearing the scent of sage. She started when she saw Cuvey.

He stood not five meters away, cradling Shani in his arms and watching as the door of the shelter melted in the searing heat.

Shani was crying. Jynis struggled to open her eyes, to bring her mind up to the level on which Shani existed. It seemed a long time before she could manage it. But at last the dusky shadows that obscured her vision began to part. Shapes appeared: the tall columns that supported the bunks in the back of the truck; the rattling bank of lockers. Jynis turned over—it was all she could manage—and found Shani in the bunk beside her, her little face sticky with snot, and red from crying. The world began to spin. She grasped that she was about to black out again, so she concentrated on her breathing, drawing in huge lungfuls of air in quest of sparse oxygen molecules. Shani's face stabilized.

Cautiously, Jynis moved a hand and started to stroke the baby's cheek. Shani seemed oblivious to her efforts. The bunk bounced and rattled, the engine gunned sporadically, and with a sudden, profound inspiration, Jynis realized the truck was in motion.

She smiled. Puma was taking her home to Necessity. Good. She hadn't seen her mother in so long.

Too bad he'd forgotten to pressurize the truck. Natural mistake, of course. Low oh-two was right for him. Right for her. Helped her sleep. She just wanted to sleep. But Shani kept on crying, a grating, wailing sound that cut through the lulling noises of the truck in motion to scour at the fibers of her body.

"Shani," she whispered. "Shani, don't cry."

Puma had broken his leg. The thought popped into her head as Shani paused in her lament to gulp at a lungful of air. Puma had broken his leg.

Something about that . . .

She groped for the elusive thought. Impossible, impossible. What? To drive the truck? With a broken leg.

Her eyes snapped wide open, and she lifted her head a spare inch. She could just make out the back of the driver's head. His hair was black, not blond, and it was bisected by the strap of a respirator. Cuvey.

Then where was Puma? She couldn't remember; couldn't think at all. At least Shani was winding down. Something had caught the baby's attention. She sat up, swaying and bobbing with the motion of the truck. Then she reached out toward Jynis' hip. Jynis followed the pudgy hand with her eyes, and smiled. Shani wanted the pc in her hip holster. The little computer had lately become one of her favorite toys. "Go ahead," Jynis murmured, her eyes half-closed. "You can play with it."

Shani tugged, wrestling with it until it popped out of the holster. Jynis helped her open it on the narrow space of the bunk. It was still tuned to the hawk's optic nerve. On the little screen she could see the rough, red rock country of the northern Barrens. A truck moved rapidly up the wind-smoothed floor of a shallow gully, trailing a high plume of dust behind it as it headed for the border. The oryx herd grazed in a little rill to the east.

Jynis felt her heart quicken as she gazed at the antelope. They were overdue for their supplementary feeding. She should have cared for them yesterday, but the storm had forced her inside. She could call them now. They'd come running to the sound of the truck. They'd mob the vehicle. Cuvey would have to slow his headlong rush back to Iyusha.

She thought for a moment, then carefully entered a code that would stimulate a craving among the onyxes for the minerals in their supplementary feed.

(4)

Cuvey drove the truck as fast as he dared. He felt the press of time like a poison in his blood. The coordinated attack on the line of field stations was over a day old. If not for the storm, this part of the desert would already be crawling with enemy patrols. Now that the storm was past, he had at most a few hours to get away. He skidded the truck around a bend, then gunned the engine, racing down the wind-smoothed floor of the shallow gully, heading for the border.

Suddenly a fleet white beast leaped in front of the truck, followed instantly by another, and another, and another. He screamed in surprise, and hauled hard on the steering stick. There was a sickening thump, and then the truck caromed across the gully floor, climbing the narrow embankment for a few meters before slamming into the vertical wall. He jerked and pulled on the steering stick, but the truck was already toppling. It slammed over onto the ground and skidded on its side before coming to a stop.

Cuvey found himself hanging from his safety harness. Blood and bits of white hide smeared the outside of the window. Farther down the gully a herd of white, shaggy, horned antelope milled beside the steep walls.

He felt a fire ignite in his belly, a growing pressure that threatened to choke him and suddenly he was screaming in pure rage. He snapped out of his safety straps and kicked at the console, cursing the truck and the antelope and this barren world that had never offered anything that, in the end, had not proved to be a poison to his soul.

Even Shani. As an Iyushan, he was supposed to hate her. He'd tried to hate her. He knew she was *wrong*. But she was part of him. A beautiful child. And he knew, deep inside, with a fatalistic certainty, that he would never live long enough to see another child born in his family.

The baby's cries sliced into his rage, dividing and draining it. "Shani?" he called, suddenly frantic. "Jynis?" He climbed out of his seat and clambered through the overturned truck.

He found Shani in the space between two bunks. She had a red, swelling bump on her forehead, but she cried lustily and stood up to reach out to him. Shani. He grabbed her and held her tight, astonished by the warmth of her cheek against his neck. He kissed her hair, knowing he should have left her with Puma, back at the burned out station. But he couldn't bear to leave her. Oh God, he was so tired of this war.

"*Mama-ma-ma-ma,*" Shani was crying.

"Where's your mama?" Cuvey whispered. He looked past Shani. His gaze found Jynis. Her body was draped over one of the bunk's support columns. She wasn't moving. Cuvey went to her. He set Shani carefully down against the overturned bunk, then bent over Jynis. Her breathing was as shallow as a whisper. Her lips were turning blue.

He ducked his head and yanked the respirator off his face, then slapped it over her nose and mouth and pressed the demand button, forcing air at her. "*Breathe!*" he hissed in her ear. "*Breathe, Jynis.*"

He'd kept Jynis on native air too long. The truck's tanks were empty. He didn't have another air pack. He'd thought it would be all right, but he'd let it go on too long. Everything came back to poison his soul. "*Breathe!*"

Her chest rose slightly. Her eyes fluttered. Then she drew a deeper breath. "Shani?" she whispered.

"She's all right," Cuvey said, around an intense pain deep in his throat. He took the respirator back and drew a couple of breaths, then returned it to Jynis. She finally opened her eyes and looked at him. He couldn't read her expression. "The truck's wrecked," he told her. "We're going to have to walk. It'll only take a few hours."

She passed the mask back to him. "You torched my air-pack."

He didn't want to talk about that. He'd thought things might go easier if he could keep Jynis dependent on him. "Don't worry," he said. "We can buddy breathe, and get there on one pack. It won't be easy, but we can get close enough to the border for a patrol to come over and pick us up."

"Uh-uh. I'm not going with you."

"You have to. This is the only air-pack."

"No thanks. I'll pressurize the truck, and wait for my people to come."

"The truck's tanks are empty."

She glared at him like he was a foul, deformed creature from the fields of Hell. "You're a liar."

"No. See for yourself. The tanks bled dry after you blew the lock." He helped her move forward and she found that it was true. There was no air left on the truck except what was in Cuvey's pack.

"Let's go," Cuvey said. "Every breath we take here is wasted." He passed the respirator back to her, but she'd already turned away. She was making her way back towards the bunks, breathing hard. She stumbled, and almost went down. "Jynis!"

He caught up with her and slapped the respirator over her face. She breathed deeply, gratefully, leaning against his arm. "Have to . . . find the pc," she gasped.

They found it against the bottom of a bunk. It still worked. Cuvey studied the picture a moment, then decided the hawk had gone east. On screen, he could make out a plume of dust near Hobo Flats. Fear prickled across his skin, leaving a thin film of sweat.

"They're coming," Jynis said.

Cuvey shook his head. "They might not get here for three or four hours! You won't last that long on native air."

Shani had crawled into her mother's lap. Jynis stroked the baby's hair. She said nothing, but tears started in her eyes.

"Jynis!" he screamed at her.

"You started it!" she snapped back. "It's not my fault. It's 'cause *we're* wrong. You 'n me 'n all the elders. We're wrong for this world. Don't belong here. We're too fragile. But Shani will still be here when they come. And Puma. And Puma . . ." She looked up at him, her eyes wide with fear. "*What did you do with Puma?* Did you murder him too?"

Cuvey denied it with a shake of his head. "No. I just left him. *He'll* be all right. Not like you and me."

He sat back, leaving the respirator with Jynis. He felt taken by a great wave of weakness that seemed to roll down out of the sky. It coiled like a noose around his neck, choking him. He saw himself swinging from the gallows at Necessity. A cry burbled up from his throat, but he bit it off before it could emerge. He reached for the respirator and breathed deeply, then passed it back to Jynis. He could strangle in this atmosphere just the same as in a noose. It was all the same. Because Jynis was right. They weren't made for this world.

He chuckled softly, self-deprecatingly. "All my life I've dreamed of you, Jynis. I wanted to be your hero, the one who brought you home."

She'd been engrossed with the pc, tapping in commands to the hawk, but now she looked up at him, her eyes narrowed combatively. "I won't go with you."

He nodded, remembering the terrible blue color of her lips. A few minutes more without supplementary oxygen, and she might have died. Her image shifted in his mind. Her blue countenance became a metaphor for Iyusha: an oxygen-starved body politic slowly suffocating on a hostile world. "Resuscitation unlikely," he muttered. A cold sweat broke out across his cheeks. A few minutes ago he'd been determined to bring Jynis back to Iyusha. Now he had to wonder: why? To watch her die with the failing colony?

He shook his head. "It's all gone wrong," he said, half to himself. "Iyusha's finished. We're going to lose this war. The land and the air are our enemies, and we are bound to lose." He looked up. "Jynis—I was wrong to try to take you. I know it's too late, but . . . *I'm sorry.*"

She looked away, one hand swiping quickly at her eyes. “Let it go,” she said. “We understand each other now.”

He nodded, conceding that.

When she looked back at him, there was an odd gleam in her eyes. “Know if the truck’s radio still works?”

He shrugged. “Why?”

She tipped the pc’s screen toward him. “Look. Iyushan patrol less than twenty miles to the north. Call them. Tell them to come get you.”

(5)

Jynis didn’t understand why she was doing this. Cuvey was a murderer. He’d killed the staff at Hobo Flats, she had no doubt of that. Their deaths were his fault, his responsibility. He was an enemy soldier, and if he weren’t her brother, he would have killed her too. “Call them,” she repeated.

He responded with a resentful gaze. “I won’t do it. They’ll get here before your people. They’ll take you and Shani back to Iyusha. I can’t let that happen now.”

“Don’t tell them we’re here. Walk out a couple miles. Meet them.”

“And leave you on native air.”

“Done it before. Lasted over an hour.” She touched his cheek. “Be picked up in time. Don’t worry. Now call them. Please. *Don’t* want to see you hang.”

He looked at her doubtfully. She nodded encouragement. And finally, he reached for the radio with a trembling hand.

He stayed as long as he could. But as both patrols drew near, they knew it was time for him to go. “This war’s over for me,” he told her. “I’m tired of serving the elders. I won’t do their killing for them again.”

She nodded and hugged him. Peace was a distant thought, a dream that had soaked into the sand, to disappear with the blood of sundered families. She took one last pull from the respirator, then let him go, feeling oddly triumphant, as if she'd won something precious this day. She grinned at him and waved goodbye.

But as she watched him jog up the gully, she knew she was making too much of it. The war wasn't over. Cuvey was alive now, but he could be dead tomorrow by a sniper's bullet. And she was so exhausted, she knew there was a real possibility she wouldn't survive until her rescue. Yet . . . she had gained *something*. A moment outside the war. A chance to act on her own conscience, from her own heart. Duty and history be damned. It was a giddy feeling. A giddy feeling . . .

She sighed as her thoughts began to dissolve in the dearth of oxygen. She cradled Shani on her chest, dreaming of life, of change. She would let herself sleep now. But as her eyes fluttered shut . . . she swore to this world that she *would* wake up . . . again.

Small Victories is a novelette originally published in Analog Science Fiction & Fact, in September 1993.

Liberator

Alone in her darkened bedroom, Hanan took a few furtive minutes to compose a ghost copy of herself. The task was automated. She had only to initiate it, and an electronic copy of her persona would be drawn from her brain by the billion threads of the atrium that grew through her neural tissue.

Now you'll be free, her mother's voice seemed to whisper from out of the distant past.

But the freedom belonged to the ghost, not to Hanan.

Still, this simulation of her consciousness was both accurate and self aware. She thought of it as a second self. It could travel where she could not, and when it returned its memories would become her own.

She rocked slowly in the recliner while the ghost took shape, listening cautiously for the sound of Seyyed's footsteps on the carpet outside her open door.

A high-pitched chirping distracted her. It arose from behind the dresser and was immediately followed by a dry rustle. Hanan tensed. The little secret one must be very hungry to make such noise. She issued a quick electronic signal through the atrium and immediately the tiny bat sprang from its lair behind the dresser and shot across the room, tumbling into her lap. She picked it up carefully, its claws sharp against her skin as it sought a hold of its own.

I've hurt no one, Hanan thought, stroking the enhanced bat's soft black fur. She'd had the creature smuggled into the country years ago inside a food shipment bound for the impoverished children in the Ovens District. Its body was small enough to fit easily against her palm. She cradled it in her hands, fascinated by the unrelieved homeliness of the creature. With tiny eyes half-hidden under a heavy brow, its features seemed compressed into a perpetually sad expression. Its ears looked rumpled, its snout too heavy, its nostrils oddly like a dog's.

Her atrium alerted her: the ghost was complete. So she signaled the bat to make ready to receive it, then she downloaded the substitute persona from her atrium into its. Now she existed both inside and outside the bat as two separate and independent entities, two diverging minds.

But as always, she found it difficult to let the other go, to fully trust the ghost to do as she would do (though it was herself). So she hesitated, stroking the bat, running her fingers along a thin bone near the base of one wing until she felt the nodule, the suicide device implanted by the off-world corporation that had assembled this creature. If the bat were ever discovered, the atrium would signal the nodule to burst, spilling a self-motile poison into the bat's bloodstream. Within a second and a half, the poison would migrate to the brain, destroying the tissue there and erasing all evidence of the atrium and the ghost.

Reassured by this hard lump beneath her fingertip, Hanan stood, the tiny creature still in her hands, and walked to the doorway that opened onto the veranda. Lifting aside the gauzy curtain, she released the bat. It leapt from her hold, and disappeared into the dark.

"Hanan?"

She turned swiftly, to see Seyyed in the other doorway. "Oh! You startled me. I was . . . thinking."

He smiled tenderly and came to her. "About what? Not Uncle, I hope."

She shivered. "Not Uncle, no. I've had enough of Uncle for one day."

He touched her cheek. "But you're worried."

She smiled teasingly, knowing from long practice how to distract him. "So make me unworried."

He grinned, and accepted the challenge.

Later though, sleep wouldn't come. Seyyed's ministrations had failed to banish her brittle mood and she lay in the dark, listening to his soft breathing and remembering the day just past, as if she could draw some benefit from its casually demeaning events if only she saw things in the right light . . .

She'd been in her study, carefully explaining her instructions to the manservant: "There's a tiny hotel next to the fireworks factory in the Ovens district. An orphaned girl lives in a lean-to in the back—ten or twelve years old, she works in the hotel as a maid and has five younger siblings in her care. Gather them all up and escort them to Sister Maria's school. The nuns have made a place for them."

"Yes, ma'am."

"As always, you mustn't identify me."

"I understand, ma'am."

It was then that she noticed her daughter Sari standing forlornly in the doorway. She dismissed the manservant and called Sari in. "Darling, what's the matter?"

Sari ran to her, snuggling into her open arms. "Mama, why is Uncle here?" she asked plaintively. "He scares me."

"Hush, darling," Hanan whispered. "He's here to see Daddy, that's all. They have business. And you shouldn't be afraid of Uncle. He loves you."

"Then why are *you* afraid of him, Mama?"

Hanan glanced through the study's open doorway. She could see straight through the sitting room to the veranda beyond, where Seyyed chatted with Uncle beneath the mist roof that sheltered the mansion's enclosed courtyard. Seyyed could be companionable with anyone, even a beast like Uncle. "Uncle loves you," Hanan insisted. "And me too. You must remember that family is more important to him than anything."

"But I can never please him! When I served him juice, he only told me to walk more softly, and set the glass down more carefully and to stop trying to fix my hair myself—he said it's ugly, and I should let you do it." Her wide dark eyes finally spilled tears across her brown cheeks.

Hanan's heart began to burn. Why did Uncle come here if he could only find fault with her family? Why had he always been such a hateful man? But she wiped Sari's tears away, saying: "Uncle just wants you to be the very best young woman you can be, so that you'll reflect well upon your family. Now go. Find your brother. He must come say hello or Uncle will be so insulted, he may never come to visit us again!"

The jest drew a crooked little smile from Sari. "*If only it were that easy!*" she whispered. Then she ran off to the playroom to look for Hamal.

Hanan straightened. Turning, she looked once more to the veranda, only to find Uncle's stern gaze fixed upon her. For a moment she panicked. Had he heard Sari? But no. He smiled and beckoned to her. Obediently, she left the study, her bare feet silent on the plush, patterned carpets, her narrow silk skirt sliding softly against her legs.

"Ah, Hanan," Uncle said, with a smile like a shark. "Come join us. Seyyed tells me you've found places for three more families amongst the charitable schools."

"Yes," Hanan said, accepting a proffered seat. "And one more just today. But there's so little room available, and so many deserving."

"Probably not so many as you think," Uncle said, leaning back in his chair, his fingers laced over a satisfied belly. "If the slum dwellers had the intellect to appreciate a better life, the President would build schools in the Ovens and educate everyone. Of course, that *was* tried before, wasn't it?"

Hanan lowered her gaze, responding in the docile way that kept her safe before this man. "Yes, Uncle." But in the polished silver sides of the coffee service she thought she caught a glimpse of her mother's face, the wide dark eyes fixed on her in unflinching accusation. Hanan shivered. Anna Soukotta had been dead for thirteen years.

Uncle turned to Seyyed. "Can you imagine trying to build a school in the Ovens?" he said. "We'd have to provide a nursery for the twelve year olds to drop off their children." He chuckled at the image, while Seyyed said something innocuous, his cool dark eyes vaguely uncomfortable.

Hanan stole another glimpse at the reflecting silver, but this time she saw only an image of herself. Hanan-the-Perfect, she thought mockingly, a woman with unusually fair skin, full lips, and balanced features, her conduct always gracious and dignified, her philanthropy well known, a doting mother of two, the loving wife of a successful business man, niece of the chief of secret police, loyal servant of the state. That was how the world saw her. In her own mind it was a different picture: Hanan-the-Imposter, the Fraud who lived every day in dreadful fear that she would be exposed.

Nervously, she searched the image. *You can't see it*, she thought. There was no outward sign of the atrium and no one had ever guessed at its existence, not even Seyyed. Yet it was there, just the same. A bio-electronic portal inside her brain that could put her in touch with the world net if only she dared to use it for that. An extra sense organ that would let her host guests in electronic copy, except that she would never risk having anyone there. The atrium had been designed by foreigners and implanted in her by her mother when she was a child. *Now you'll be free*, Anna Soukotta had always insisted. But the atrium was illegal, and Hanan knew it for a lethal defect that would kill her someday as surely as an aneurysm brooding in the brain of an old woman.

Anna Soukotta had dismissed such concerns. She'd brazenly pursued her political agenda, campaigning in the slums for universal education, decrying government censorship, and collecting enemies like other women collected perfume. Uncle had ordered his younger brother to divorce her. He'd refused.

But Uncle wasn't a man to be disobeyed. Even after twenty four years Hanan could still remember the scent and the sound of panic at Anna Soukotta's last political rally as government troops began firing into the crowd. And the officer, faceless behind his riot shield, who'd dragged her screaming away from the security of her father's arms moments before a fusillade of bullets tore through him.

To Uncle, nothing was more important than family . . . except the family's reputation. Given a reason, he'd sacrifice Hanan just as easily as he'd sacrificed her father.

Seyyed touched her hand and she jumped. "Hanan, Uncle is speaking to you."

"Where is your son?" Uncle repeated, his voice sharp with nascent suspicion. "Seyyed tells me he made a perfect score on his latest math test and I wanted to congratulate him."

Hanan flushed. "My apologies, Uncle. When Hamal studies, the rest of the world is nothing to him. Sari has gone to fetch him."

Uncle's lips turned in a cold smile. "Ah yes. Hamal's a smart boy. He'll be on the President's staff some day."

"Yes, Uncle."

Yes, Uncle. Yes, Uncle. Yes, Uncle: her angry thoughts mocked the meaningless chant. She'd die before she'd allow Uncle to turn sweet Hamal into one of his protégés.

Her gaze wandered beyond the veranda railing and up, to the courtyard's translucent "ceiling"—a cloud of mist sprayed by nozzles placed around the rectangular roof line. As the mist evaporated, it cooled the air so that the courtyard remained comfortable even while the city outside baked under cloudless skies.

Footsteps hammered on the courtyard's tiled path. "Hello, Uncle!" Hamal shouted as he ran amongst the ferns and carefully tended flowers.

"Hello there, young man!" Uncle turned to Hanan, his teeth bared in satisfaction. "Why do you always look so worried?" he demanded. "The boy pleases me. You've been a good mother."

"A good mother?" Seyyed echoed. "Other women are simply good mothers. Hanan is an angel. Her children are her life." And he gave her a quick wink, to let her know the pride he felt in her.

The ghost of Hanan rode the little bat to Hell. The journey was short—just over a kilometer—but then Hell had established many franchises upon the Earth during the long history of humankind. Along the way the bat followed an erratic flight path as it hunted mosquitoes and moths, its sonar picking their tiny shapes out of the night sky. Hanan's disembodied ghost let it feed, though she cut off the line of raw sensory data that brought her the sonar images. She preferred the darting, dancing infrared picture of the city captured through the bat's artificial eyes. Once the bat had eaten a good meal, she took control of its volition through its behavioral modification net.

The bat had been equipped with a very fine system of scent discrimination. Hanan's ghost used this now to locate the girl who'd lived behind the hotel, calling up the child's individual scent pattern from her atrium's library. She guided the creature along the edge of the slums. Even here, beyond the zone of official poverty, the streets were clogged with temporary shelters, tents and tarps and cardboard boxes that the government permitted to exist only between ten at night and five in the morning, when they must be removed to make way for the day's business traffic.

So many people! Their numbers still overwhelmed Hanan. How could so many survive such terrible conditions for so long? There was never enough food or water. Disease was rampant, and parents rarely lived long enough to instruct their children, so that each generation was forced to create a culture anew . . . a faint and diminishing echo of the once increscent and intricate past.

The bat caught a whiff of the programmed scent. It stalled and dived, pursuing the trail. Hanan was startled to see that she was already over Sister Maria's school. She pulled the bat off the scent. It wasn't necessary for her to see the child again; it was enough to know that she was under Sister Maria's care. There were others to think of now.

Hanan turned the bat towards the heart of the Ovens and hunted them out, one by one: the children she'd come to think of as her wards. She'd call them out of the slums only when she could secure a place for them in one of the schools or missions that took in homeless children. Until then she would only watch. Anna Soukotta had proved the futility of trying to improve conditions on the inside. Her benign social movement had boiled into riot. Her political campaigns had become rites of murder. She herself had finally been assassinated in exile.

Dawn was near by the time Hanan's ghost left the last of her children. The bat was exhausted. The time had come to go home. She fed her own scent profile to the bat, then turned it towards the affluent heart of the city. But it struggled against her lead. It turned back towards the Ovens. She felt a stab of concern—the bat had never disobeyed her before. Then real fear brushed her as she realized that the bat *was* obedient. It had already found her scent trail. In the Ovens. At night.

This was impossible. She must be asleep in her bedroom, in the distant heart of the city. And yet, in the riot of molecular data that filled the night, one trail burned clear. It was the scent of herself.

She gave the bat its head. It fluttered swiftly through the slum, unnoticed by the weary squatters who were already rolling up their shacks in anticipation of the dawn. The scent trail grew stronger. She could no longer doubt that her true self had come to this ghastly place. But why? Only her charity reached here. Never herself or anyone in her family.

The eastern sky had begun to lighten when she saw a large building looming just ahead. The structure seemed out of place in this ramshackle neighborhood, too new and too well tended. The bat wheeled over the building's high wall and dove into a shadowed courtyard. Sonar filled the dark spaces with smudges of vegetation and the lightning gold streaks of startled insects. The bat alighted on a reed shade that covered a dark window. The shade rattled briefly. No light glinted through its slats; the room beyond was dark. Yet she could hear voices. Female voices speaking soft good mornings. The Hanan scent trail was very strong.

The ghost suffered a mental shudder. What circumstance had brought her true self here? Had she been the victim of some crime? A kidnapping?

Where were the children?

Panic spun like a wind devil through her mind. She sampled the air. But she could scent no trace of the children and that absence brought a sense of relief.

Dawn light reached into the courtyard as the bat clambered around the edge of the shade to the interior of the open window. With infrared eyes, the bat distinguished four figures in the room, all female, still lying upon their sleeping pads, but awake. One of the four seemed old and frail, her shoulders hunched as she sat up on her mat. Two were younger, although mature. The fourth was small and lithe, a girl halfway to woman-hood. This child stood up, laughing at some joke that she'd been told. Then she turned to the window and pulled at the cords on the side, rolling up the shade. The startled bat burst into flight, squeaking slightly as it wheeled about the room above the frightened, upturned faces of the women. They cried out in wonder, even as they ducked to avoid the leathery wings. Then the bat dashed out of the open window, Hanan frantically urging it towards home.

It wasn't me, Hanan thought. She sat alone on the veranda, still stunned at the news brought home by her ghost.

The children were with their tutors. Seyyed had gone out on business. The servants had cleared the breakfast dishes. But Hanan continued to sit, remembering the upturned face her ghost had seen in the dawn light. A girl's face, a child of thirteen or fourteen, just past the age of menarche. Hanan remembered that face. It had belonged to her once, when she was thirteen, or fourteen.

It wasn't me.

Yet it was. The scent trail was exactly the same as her own, made so by the changes of puberty. No two people had the same scent signatures, she knew this. Except identical twins. And the girl in the slum could not be her twin. Hanan was thirty eight years old. "*Mother, did you hate me this much?*" she whispered.

Anna Soukotta had despised custom and tradition. She'd never respected the laws that protected the morality and sanctity of human life. She'd believed in the usefulness of atriums and of genetic engineering and population control. She'd believed that all human beings lived lives of equal consequence. She'd been an outsider amongst her own people, a rabble rouser bent on challenging the status quo. Her politics had infuriated Uncle. To punish her, he'd taken Hanan away after his brother was killed. And mother had never tried to reclaim her . . .

"I wasn't the daughter you wanted." Intuitively, Hanan understood. She visualized her mother as she must have been then, angry, without a husband, exiled from her family and her class, her own daughter a traitor to her political movement . . . yet still undefeated, uncowed. Stubbornly demanding her agenda from life. "To try again—only you would have thought of it, Mother." Tears squeezed from Hanan's eyes; tears of anger, and rejection. To take a failed daughter back to the womb. Remake her. Set her on a new path. Change the formula of child-rearing so that the end product would be more . . . *worthy*.

Hanan's heart swelled with anger, until it was crushed by the heaving confines of her chest. *I am not that bad! I didn't deserve to be replaced.*

"Ma'am, are you all right?"

Her chin jerked up, eyes wide in fear. The manservant stood hesitantly beside the breakfast table. Hanan fought her agitation, forcing a stiff calm onto her face. "Yes, I'm fine. Please leave me alone now."

The manservant nodded uncertainly, and left. In a state of forced detachment, Hanan considered her situation. She had a double living in the Ovens, almost certainly an illegal clone, much younger than herself. Uncle must not discover it. He would kill it if he did.

Fervently, she wished that it had never lived, and yet . . . she didn't want to see it die. An intense curiosity burned in her mind. What was the other like? What was *she* like, in other circumstances?

She stood up abruptly and hurried to her room, quickly changing from her morning gown into a loose-fitting pantsuit and jeweled sandals. A scarf went over her head.

"Find the manservant," she told the house. "I'm going out."

Hanan rode in the back seat of the Mercedes while the manservant drove. The roads were rough and traffic was slow, the trucks and cars tangling with brightly painted trishaws pedaled by sweating men with huge thighs. Hanan stared out the window, unseeing, until the car drew up in front of a little shop advertising herbal remedies. She emerged into the sun's searing rays. "Stay here," she told the manservant as he hurried to help her with the door. "I'll only be a moment." He frowned unhappily. It was his duty to keep her in sight at all times. But her stern scowl convinced him that this time there would be an exception. She entered the shop and the door closed between them.

A young woman emerged from a backroom to greet her. Hanan turned over a credit card. "I'd like to purchase information," she said. "A new, two-story building. Walled courtyard. Between Chu Fong's store and the canal. What is it?"

The woman fingered Hanan's credit card, her eyes vacant for a moment as she thought. "Ah. You mean the mission."

"A Christian mission?" Hanan was surprised. Mother had never thought much of Christians, or Muslims, or anyone else of faith.

"No. They call it The Tenacious Flower Mission. Secular." She glanced down at the credit card, then back up at Hanan. "Expensive."

"I'll pay."

"It's a political refuge. For the followers of Anna Soukotta. They say her daughter lives there."

Hanan felt her hands begin to tremble. She pressed them firmly against her sides. "Thank you," she said, and nodded. The young woman scanned her credit card and deducted an amount that Hanan didn't bother to check.

That night Hanan sent her ghost back to the Tenacious Flower Mission. The bat was hungry, and difficult to control. The ghost let it hunt insects for a few minutes in the courtyard before forcing it down under the eaves of the building. She searched for her own scent and came across it almost immediately. It led through an open window. She hesitated a moment. She'd never taken the bat deep inside a strange building. What if someone saw her?

The air was thick with the scent trails of many individuals. What if someone attacked her with a broom? The bat could be killed. But curiosity forced her on. She crawled to the edge of the window and peered in at a small bedroom, vacant now, the sleeping pads and blankets neatly laid out on the floor. A single, battery-powered light was mounted near the doorway. Hanan launched herself into the dim yellow glow and crossed the room, alighting on the door frame. She peered past that to see a long, dark hallway, lit only by the dull glow of lights from adjoining rooms.

The scent trail led to the right. She followed it, flying close to the ceiling, darting through the shadows almost faster than a human eye could follow. She flitted past a doorway. The scent of herself almost overwhelmed her. She squeaked and wheeled, her feet clawing for a grip on the door jamb.

Voices came to her from the room beyond. She peered past the doorway. The radiant light of a lantern hanging from the ceiling almost blinded her in the second before the bat's enhanced eyes could adjust. Then she saw herself. A pretty young girl in a button-front gauze shirt and blue sarong, her black hair bound in a neat bun against the back of her neck. In a gentle voice she coached seven grown men in the art of reading. Each man held an electronic book. By turns they read passages from it. Hanan's ghost recognized the text. Hadn't mother read her the draft when she was only ten years old? She hadn't understood the meaning then, but the words had stuck. *Empowerment: the Common Person's Guide to Freedom*, by Anna Soukotta, had been banned in the republic for over twenty years.

The clone's name was Ari. A simple, common name. She worked as a teacher at the Tenacious Flower Mission. And, it was claimed, she was the daughter of Anna Soukotta. These were the only facts Hanan had obtained after an hour's observation. She needed to know more, to ask questions. Time, then, to visit Ari in person.

The manservant accompanied her into the Ovens. He frowned disapprovingly when she told him their destination, but he said nothing. When they arrived at the mission, he armed the Mercedes, then followed Hanan through the open gates.

Pathways paved with flakes of recycled concrete criss-crossed through the mission's courtyard. Newly planted fruit trees and thriving vegetables filled the gardens. Vines grew on the walls. A few white-haired women tended the plants. They paused in their work to watch Hanan. One of them spoke a soft greeting, which Hanan politely returned. "Wait for me here," she told the manservant. Then she mounted the steps and entered the mission building.

It was cool inside only by contrast to the blazing heat in the courtyard. Hanan missed the gentle purr of the mist nozzles that cooled her own garden. As she began to look about, a woman very near her own age appeared from a hallway. She was dressed in neat though worn clothing. "Madam?" she asked, with a friendly smile.

"Good day," Hanan said. "Forgive me for not having an appointment, but I've come to see Ari. I've heard much about her that I approve, and I'd like to meet her myself, perhaps make a contribution to her cause."

The woman's open expression immediately tightened with suspicion. "We have an Ari here," she said. "But she's just a novice teacher. Perhaps you meant—"

"No," Hanan interrupted, determined to come swiftly to her point. "I meant Ari, the daughter of Anna Soukotta."

The woman stiffened. Her face took on the cool, unyielding character of an ivory carving. "There's no such person here," she said shortly. "And we have no political affiliation. We're simply a school for the poor. You cannot be a friend if you repeat that name under our roof."

Hanan's voice didn't change in tone. "Please tell Ari that the *first* daughter of Anna Soukotta is here to see her."

The woman squinted in hard suspicion. But as she examined Hanan's face, fear trembled across her lips. "You are . . . ?"

"Yes. You recognize me, don't you?"

"Yes. I-I—"

"Just bring Ari. I wish to meet her."

The woman nodded uncertainly. "Please to . . . follow me." She beckoned, and Hanan trailed her through a hallway lit only by diffuse daylight drifting in from adjacent rooms. She smelled flowers and frying vegetables. So much less intense than the same odors encountered through the bat's sensorium.

They came to a doorway. The woman peered past the edge of the curtain that covered it. Hanan could hear Ari's voice coming soft from the room beyond. "She's teaching a class," the woman said.

"Summon her now. It would be dangerous for all of us if I'm here too long."

"Yes ma'am." With a delicate hand, she lifted the curtain. "*Ari!*" she called in a whispered hiss. "*Ari!*"

Ari looked up in mild surprise. Hanan stared at her greedily. So young, so pretty.

"Ari, come," the woman called nervously, as the men in the classroom turned to stare. "It's important."

Ari excused herself, and came in soft steps to the door. Her gaze swept past the woman, to fix on Hanan. There was recognition in her eyes. "So you've come already."

They sat on cushions on the floor of a room whose sliding shoji doors had been thrown open to the heat of the courtyard. Ari served her fruit juice without ice. "How did you find me?" she asked.

"I can't say that. Be satisfied that no one else knows you're here."

"You understand what I am?"

Hanan squinted. "Do *you* know?"

Ari nodded warily. "Mother believed in honesty in all things. Nothing has been kept from me. I know that I am you, set upon a different path."

Hanan felt a shudder of despair rush through her. She sipped her juice, focusing for a moment on the sweet, fruity flavors to distract her mind. "*Why?*" she asked at last.

"That question's been an agony to you, hasn't it?" Ari said. She sighed. "Anna Soukotta had lost her first daughter. She'd lost *you*, Hanan, my sister self. You must understand. She was alone. Her beloved husband was long dead, her daughter gone, her political career in shambles. She'd spent three years in the tidal prison. She wanted a *legacy*—"

"*I was not dead*," Hanan said, between clenched teeth.

Ari nodded sadly. "She knew that she'd wronged you. She wanted to atone for that. To do better . . ." Ari's voice trailed into silence. "I'm sorry. This must be so painful."

Hanan wrestled her passions into a still, warm mass. "She must have died shortly after you were born."

"Yes. I never knew her."

"But how did you survive?"

"The Followers cared for me."

Hanan's puzzlement must have shown, because Ari smiled in apology. "The Followers: three women devoted to Mother. They never married. They dedicated their lives to my upbringing and education. Through their memories, I've come to know our Mother. I owe them everything."

Hanan wondered how much the tool must owe its maker. "Then you continue our Mother's work."

"Yes, but more quietly than she. I'm neither her equal, nor her replacement. But I do what I can. As do you."

Hanan flinched. "What I do is insignificant."

"Not to those you help."

Hanan refused to argue her own competence. She'd long ago accepted what she was. She said: "You're teaching from illegal books."

"Yes."

Hanan stared at her hands. Her long fingers were laced together, working against each other. "This is very dangerous. If you're discovered, you could be executed. Your existence is illegal. If they learn what you really are . . ."

"Yes, the Followers have told me this. And I don't want to die. But the work is very important."

"You risk too much!"

"Please don't take offense. It's not likely anyone will discover that we're the same."

Anger flared in Hanan's chest. "You think that's it? You think I'm here because I'm worried about your connection to me?"

Ari looked suddenly uncertain. "You have children. It's natural to worry about . . . these things. Perhaps you shouldn't have come here."

"Perhaps you should be more secretive about your parentage."

But Ari shook her head. "I won't hide it. The name of Anna Soukotta gives me a voice here. And if I'm arrested, I'll be executed for my atrium, long before it's discovered—how did you put it?—*what I am*."

Hanan felt her heart stumble. "You have an atrium?" The words were thieves slipping past her teeth.

Ari nodded. "Mother gave it to me. She has said that atriums were made illegal only because they empower the people."

A soft moan of fear issued from Hanan's throat. Did Ari suspect her atrium was a duplicate too? "You shouldn't have told me that," she hissed, seeking to end this vein of conversation.

But Ari gazed at her with calm eyes and said: "I know mother gave you an atrium as well."

Hanan bit down on her cry of protest. Her lips pressed together in a thin, trembling line. She closed her eyes and envisioned oceans of ice; vast, sterile expanses of utter cold. Her heart slowed. Her breathing calmed. "Never say that again," she whispered. She opened her eyes, to see Ari gazing at her in concern.

"I'm sorry," Ari said. "Perhaps I shouldn't have— It might be better if you go now."

"Yes," Hanan agreed. "But I . . . I wish you'd give me your atrial address."

Ari smiled, as if she'd been waiting for such a request all along.

At home, Hanan sought out copies of Anna Soukotta's writings. There were none in Seyyed's library, of course. She inquired by e-mail at several political bulletin boards, but none of the operators knew her; no one would admit to possessing the illegal manuscripts. Finally, she ordered them from overseas.

All the while she watched herself from a distance, with disbelieving eyes. *Why am I doing this?* The question gnawed at her, though the answer was simple. She needed to understand her mother. She needed to know what had driven Anna Soukotta to seek a dangerous life when she might have lived to a very old age in comfort and joy.

Even more, Hanan needed to know why she herself had made a different choice.

The computer beeped the arrival of the texts. Hanan downloaded them into her electronic book, then took it with her when she curled up under the covers. The children were asleep. Seyyed was working on his accounts. Outside, the mist nozzles softly cooled the night. The bat was off watching over Ari.

Hanan switched on the book.

Uncle called early next morning to say that he would join them for breakfast. Hanan sat across the table from him, feeling like a rat caught in the cobra's gaze. Uncle seemed quite pleased with himself. He laughed and joked with Seyyed and Hamal. He even complimented Sari on the flower arrangement she'd prepared for the table. All the while Hanan could feel the cobra's measuring eye as he prepared to strike. She forced herself to eat a bowl of fruit and a dish of rice. Let the cobra have a fat rat; she refused to allow him to feed upon her guilt.

"There is a minor matter we need to discuss, Seyyed," Uncle said, after the breakfast dishes had been cleared away and the children sent off to their studies. "Perhaps your office would be more appropriate?"

"Of course, Uncle."

"Oh." He looked at Hanan slyly. "Would you join us too?"

She nodded. Her breakfast was a painful weight in her stomach. *Let him eat a sick rat*, she thought.

She sat upon a couch in Seyyed's office. Uncle took the recliner. Seyyed called for tea, then seated himself at her side. Uncle smiled at them. "You've always made me proud, Hanan."

She blinked, taken aback.

Uncle pretended not to notice. "I will say upfront that there is nothing more important than family. You know this is so, Hanan, because I took you in when my brother died and raised you as the child I never had. I didn't do this because of any love I held for you. As we both must acknowledge, I barely knew you at the time. To be cruelly blunt, I suspected I was making a grave error in bringing you into my house, perhaps even risking my political career. Yet I adopted you anyway, because you were my brother's daughter."

"Yes, Uncle. And I am always grateful."

He feigned surprise. "Are you? But your mother was a seductive woman, Hanan. She led my brother away from decent society, and corrupted him with her venal ways."

Hanan felt her cheeks heat up. In shame or anger? She couldn't tell. She bowed her head; studied her long fingers interlocked in a temple built of tension. Seyyed's own dark hand eclipsed hers. He squeezed slightly, to let her know his love. "Surely Hanan has proven herself worthy of your generosity, Uncle," he said. Hanan could hear a faint thread of anger in his voice, just enough to let Uncle know he wouldn't tolerate further insults to his wife. Hanan bowed her head still farther; her shoulders hunched as she silently chastised herself. Did she think she was risking only herself by pursuing Ari? Had she forgotten that Seyyed too could be hurt?

"Hanan has been a perfect daughter for me," Uncle said gently. "A blessing to a man who never enjoyed children of his own."

Hanan looked up in surprise . . . to meet the cobra's certain gaze.

"But Anna Soukotta was a seductive woman. *And* she was your mother. It's only natural for you to feel curiosity about her life. Frankly, I'm surprised you waited this long."

"Uncle, I'm sorry—!" Hanan cried. Seyyed grunted a startled question. Uncle sliced the air with his hand in a gesture that demanded silence.

"You have two perfect children, Hanan. And an esteemed husband who loves you. Remember them, late at night, when restless yearnings take hold of you. Think of them. Go to your husband's bed. You'll be yourself again by morning."

Hanan squeezed Seyyed's hand and nodded. "Thank you, Uncle," she whispered, shivering with relief. "Thank you."

"What did you think you were doing?" Seyyed shouted. "Did you think no one would notice? Does our security mean so little to you? Why, Hanan? Just tell me why! You hated your mother; that's what you've always said."

Hanan huddled on the couch and sobbed. Each angry word from Seyyed was a blow to her flesh. Other husbands screamed at their wives, beat their wives. But not Seyyed. Each day of their life together was a day of love. Now she'd hurt him. "I'm sorry, Seyyed. I don't know why I did it. I don't know what came over me. I just—" She groped for an explanation, something to say that might soothe him. "I heard that in the Ovens people are talking about Anna Soukotta again. I . . . I never really knew her. I wanted to know why so many people loved her . . . when I did not. I wondered what it was about Anna Soukotta that could inspire people after all these years. I might have wondered if I had any of that in myself . . . if anyone would continue to attend to me after such a span of time."

"I'm here, aren't I?" His voice was pained. He was down on his knees beside her. He put his arms around her neck. "You have inspired me, Hanan. I have loved you, and thanked Allah for you, every day of our marriage. I couldn't bear to lose you. Please don't risk Uncle's anger. You and I, we live in a perfect world. Don't break it."

"I don't want to, Seyyed! You and the children are my life. I would die without you."

"Then you will never do this again."

She felt the cool touch of his cheek against her own. Smelled the male scent of him. Pulled him closer until his breath was warm on her ear. "What if Uncle had not adopted me?" she whispered her nightmare. "Where would I be now?"

"It doesn't matter."

"Seyyed!" She pleaded for understanding. "Haven't you ever wondered how you might have turned out under different circumstances? Look at *my* life. What if Father hadn't been killed? What if Mother had really loved me? Who would I be today?"

"You would be no one, because you would be dead. Hanan! Remember it's me who loves you."

The argument petered out, but his anxiety remained. He seemed almost afraid to leave her alone that day. They made love on the couch. He served her tea. She sang a love song for him while they worked together in the garden, gathering flowers for his office while Sari and Hamal played a noisy game of tag. And she knew that he was right. They lived in a perfect world. Why then couldn't she forget about Ari?

Night came, and she and Seyyed made love again. He fell asleep in her bed, something he hadn't done for many years. But Hanan remained awake. She sat, watching his breathing, the peaceful lines of his face as he slept. She knew the flaws in him: his shortness of temper when interrupted in his work; his impatience when the children made errors; his insistence on her impeccable appearance, at home or in public. He was not an easy man to live with. But sleep banished all the nettles. Times like this, he seemed an almost perfect being. And that only enhanced her anguish.

She kissed him softly on the forehead—an ambivalent apology for her imminent betrayal. He was her sun. But Ari was a terrible moon shadow gliding darkly across his face. Rising from the bed, she called the bat.

It had been out hunting insects near the house. When she plucked it from the curtain its fur was slightly damp from the mist nozzles. She studied its face in the dim illumination of a night light mounted low on the wall. A homely creature, dark and secretive, without influence in the world. This was her true face. The beauty that Seyyed treasured was only a mask. If he could see inside her, this is what she'd look like. Nothing at all like Ari.

No, Ari was a being entirely different. Ari was her diametric opposite. Boldly using the name of Anna Soukotta. Teaching openly from illicit texts. Shaping the world. Ari couldn't be her double. "*I must protect her*." This had become a mandate in Hanan's mind, for reasons maternal. She'd come to see Ari in the same way she saw her children—derived from herself, but utterly different.

Inside her atrium Hanan assembled a ghost, then downloaded it into the bat. "Watch over her," she whispered, as she set the creature free in the night.

Explosives! The bat had carried Hanan's ghost deep into the Ovens before she detected the molecular trace. It excited a priority code in the bat's data bank and the creature wheeled about automatically to pick up the track again. The scent was a blazing gold arrow, pointing down an alley towards the Tenacious Flower Mission. Hanan urged the bat to top speed.

She found the first mine placed on the mission wall not an arm's length from the gate. It was hidden behind a squatter's tent in which four young children slept with their mother. Hanan hesitated for almost twenty seconds while the bat searched out more mines. Finally she consulted her atrial library for Ari's address. Never before had she phoned anyone from an atrium. It was too dangerous. Such conversations were too easily overheard. But tonight she had no choice.

"Get out!" she cried, as soon as Ari acknowledged her. "Get out! The building's mined, inside and out. My Uncle has found you already. There are explosives planted on the walls. There's one by your bedroom. Run, run, run!"

Ari's voice came to her, weighted with stress. "How do you know? Hanan, where are you? What have you heard?"

"Run, Ari. There's no time to explain."

"What kind of explosives are they? Maybe they can be disarmed."

"No, it's too late. There are too many. Run now. I don't know when they're set to go off." She circled the courtyard, her sonar pinging against walls and windows. To her relief, she heard Ari shout an echo of her warning. People awakened. Her sonar caught them as they ran sleepily through the courtyard and out to the street. Ari was with them. Hanan followed her. Watched her run in her nightshirt through the alleys ringing the mission, shouting and banging on tents to awaken the squatters. "Get clear of the walls!" she yelled. "Get clear of the walls! We're under attack!"

"Ari!" Hanan called. "You must save yourself. Get away—"

The explosives went off. Each one had been expertly placed, and most of their force was directed into the building. Still, the explosion knocked the bat into the air and deafened its sonar receptors. Hanan could barely control it as it tried to flee in panic. "Ari! Ari!" she cried. "Answer me, child. Are you all right?" As she brought the bat around, she could see the mission: a jumbled pile of dust and mortar, some of the debris on fire. Bodies lay in the streets around it. Moans of anguish filled the air. She sought Ari's molecular trail, but the explosion had blown all scent tracks out of the air. "*ARI!*"

"I'm here, Hanan." Her voice sounded strained, as if she spoke through gritted teeth.

"You're hurt."

"Just a little. Oh, Hanan, why did they do this to us?"

Hanan found her kneeling in the street, cradling in her lap the bloodied body of one of the Followers—the old woman with the hunched shoulders.

"I'll have money sent to you," Hanan said. "I'll find you a new place to live."

Ari lifted her face to the night. Tears ran down her cheeks. "I don't know where you are, Hanan, but I thank you. You saved many lives tonight. I only wish you could have saved just one more."

Back at home, the true Hanan still lay awake in her bedroom. When the sound of a distant explosion reached the house, she sat up, her ears straining the dark for more information. After awhile, she heard sirens. Seyyed stirred sleepily, asked her what was the matter. "There was an explosion in the Ovens." He went back to sleep. She got out of bed. It was past midnight. Worry fluttered against her breast like moths against a window. She put on fresh clothes then went to the study to use the telephone. She started to punch in Ari's atrial address, then remembered: the phone kept a record of all outgoing calls. She put the receiver down and stared into space.

The telephone beeped softly.

She started, then picked up the receiver, only to hear a dial tone. The soft beeping went on, and suddenly she realized it wasn't the phone at all, but the atrium inside her head. She hadn't heard that sound since Mama had tried to get her to use her atrium so many years ago. She shivered. Mama had been the only one to ever call her. No one else knew her atrial address.

The beeping went on.

What to do? She remembered. Tentatively she requested a caller I.D.

Information flooded her mind like a lost thought suddenly recalled. The caller was herself. The ghost of herself riding the bat. She hesitated. She'd never conferred with her ghost before, afraid of what that might say about her soul (divided? or existing outside her, so that she was . . . not?) And it had seemed a vanity too, a greater crime than simply absorbing the memories of the ghost and reflecting upon them as she would upon experiences encountered in a dream . . .

"Ah . . . Hello?" she said tentatively, unsure if she must speak aloud.

"Get out!" her own voice seemed to shout in her ear. "I had to telephone Ari. Now they know about us. Get out of the house before they come for you."

Hanan's eyes flew wide. "But the children—!"

"Leave them. Seyyed will care for them. Uncle can't touch Seyyed."

"I-I can't—"

"Uncle knows about the atrium. Get out now, before it's too late."

"But where can I go?" she cried, looking around in panic, as if the answer lay somewhere in the walls of a home that could no longer shelter her. "There's nowhere to go. I can't get out of the country."

"Go to Ari. It's our only chance."

"To the mission? That's no shelter."

"To the streets! The mission has been bombed into rubble. Hide in the streets, but go *now*!"

Hanan hurried toward the stairs, her slippers soundless on the polished wooden floor. Uncle was coming. She was leaving her children. She must go in their rooms and look at them one last time. But there was no time. They would hate her when she was gone. Seyyed would hate her. Once out the door, she could never come back. And no time to say goodbye.

"*Mama*?"

Sari's frightened whisper reached her as she started down the stairs. "Sari! You must go back to bed."

"Mama, where are you going? What's wrong?"

Hanan gazed back at her, agonized. She looked so frightened! Hanan wanted to hold her, hug her, tell her that everything would be all right. Her mouth opened, but the lie that she'd intended didn't fill it. Instead the truth raced out. "Sari, I have to go away! I've done something— something—" Tears blurred her vision. "Uncle will be coming for me. I have to be gone before he comes. Sari, I love you—"

Sari surged forward and flung her arms around Hanan. "Take me with you! Don't leave me here with Uncle."

Hanan stumbled back in shock. "I can't take you, Sari. It's too awful. You must stay here. Daddy will protect you."

Her arms tightened around Hanan and she began to sob. "No! Uncle tells Daddy what to do. And Uncle will hate me when you're gone. Take me with you, mama. You can't leave me here."

Hanan shook her head. She could never take Sari into the streets, into that Hell. Sari would die there. "Let me go, let me go!" She fought to break the sobbing child's grip.

"Hanan!"

She looked up to see Seyyed, his hair tousled, fear in his eyes. Her gaze shifted back to Ari. "Go to your father," she ordered in a cold, commanding voice. "He'll protect you." Then she shoved the child away and hurried down the stairs.

Seyyed bounded after her. "Hanan!"

She spun about, her hand out to ward him off. "Don't question me!" she cried. "And don't try to protect me. You are innocent. The less you know—"

The door behind her burst open. Seyyed looked past her, and she could read her fate in his expression, and in the single word shaped by his silent lips. *Uncle*.

Slowly, she turned.

Uncle stood just inside the doorway, his hard gaze fixed on her, his lips parted to show his teeth. Four powerful looking young men in military uniforms stepped around him and took up positions on either side. "Traitor!" he shouted at her. "Deceiver! *Soukotta!*" In his mouth, the name was an oath. "Your ghost was out there tonight. Did you really think you could keep an atrium hidden from me?"

Pent-up anger slammed like a pressure wave through Hanan's brain. "I *did* hide it from you. For years and years. Didn't you ever suspect? Didn't you ever sense what mother had done to me?"

"Soukotta?" he screamed. His face darkened in rage, and she realized he'd been struck yet again by an old enemy. "Soukotta did this? Why didn't you tell me?"

"You killed my father for less! I didn't want to die."

"Leave her alone!" Seyyed shouted. "She's *my* wife." He tried to step in front of her, but Uncle flicked a finger at the soldiers and two of them hustled him aside.

Uncle produced a kem-wand. Hanan had seen the device in police movies. It was armed with a microscopic medical robot intelligent enough to recognize and destroy any artificial organs in her body. She stumbled backwards, but one of the soldiers caught her arms. Seyyed was screaming.

"Take Sari out of the room!" Hanan cried. Too late. The wand touched her cheek. She felt a sharp sting, then a tiny worm went speeding through her flesh to her brain. It attacked her mind, entangling itself in the threads of her vision until her sight contorted into a firestorm of hellish lights. She lost her body. Lost all sense of the world. A river roared in her ears. She knew it to be the sound of time rushing by. The days of her past pummeled her, then sped on in no good order. She tried to grasp at them, but they swept past her fingers like a river's current, immaterial energy impossible to seize.

The water closed over her face. She drifted, rolling slowly against the bottom while dreams picked at her whitened flesh. Odd, chaotic, fragmented dreams that gradually faded into darkness.

When she finally awoke, she found herself abed, in the room in which she'd grown up in Uncle's house. By the light and the heat and long experience, she knew it must be afternoon.

She was not dead. She studied this fact for a moment, astounded. She didn't even seem to be disabled . . . except for the atrium. That didn't respond and she had to assume it was really gone. Had her mind been damaged by the loss? She searched her memories, but they seemed complete. She didn't bother to ask herself how she would recognize a loss.

The door opened and Uncle came in. His rage was gone. By the expression on his face, he seemed almost sorry. "Hanan."

He pulled a wing chair up to the bed and sat down. "You must forgive me my anger. I thought you'd deliberately withheld the secret of this atrium from me. But of course, it wasn't your fault. Soukotta did this to you."

She listened, amazed at the prospect that he might forgive her. She wanted to know more, but another question was more pressing. "Uncle—Sari and Seyyed, and Hamal—are they all right?"

Uncle shrugged. "You can imagine. It's been traumatic."

She nodded. She could imagine all too well. "I was afraid to tell you, Uncle," she whispered. "I didn't know what you'd think."

He gestured helplessly. "At least your mind wasn't damaged. The neurologist tells me you'll be fine." He tapped his fingers against his thigh. "Hanan, I can understand you keeping the atrium a secret. It must have been horrible for you. I'm not quite so certain why you used it in the cause of a rebellion."

Hanan felt a cold sweat break out across her cheeks. Her body ached with a desire for her children.

"Sari isn't well," Uncle said, watching her closely. "She wouldn't be comforted last night, and finally had to be sedated. When Hamal awoke this morning and learned what had happened, he argued with his father and tried to strike him. Seyyed is considering a divorce." Uncle leaned closer. "Who was the girl at the mission, Hanan? This one you called 'Ari?'"

Hanan went very still. There could be only one reason Uncle had asked her this question. Ari must still be free. She looked sideways at Uncle. "I don't know who she is. I met her by chance. She seemed like an upstanding person. I wanted to make a donation to the mission. I didn't know she taught Mother's philosophies—"

"Don't lie to me, Hanan. I already have cause enough to be annoyed with you. Who is this Ari?"

Hanan realized that Uncle would have had hundreds of people from around the mission interrogated. He would have heard that

Ari claimed Anna Soukotta for her mother. “Ari may be my sister,” Hanan allowed. “We look very much alike. Did you know that?” She felt a hysterical giggle deep in her chest; swallowed hard to contain it.

“Ah, yes,” Uncle said. “So you’ve heard this rumor that she’s your sister. I hoped that was your motive. I can understand it. It’s virtuous to be interested in your family.” He nodded in satisfaction. “Family is the most important thing.”

“I believe that, Uncle,” Hanan said carefully. “But do *you* believe she’s family? If Ari really is my Father’s child, she’ll be illegal—conceived after his death.”

He shrugged his disinterest. “The perpetrator of that has already been punished.”

Her lips formed a small round o. So the rules could bend for Uncle’s family. Hope fluttered in her chest. Now that her atrium was gone, and Ari’s origins forgiven, couldn’t her life be repaired? “Uncle, might we bring Ari home? If she’s really my sister, she belongs with me.”

A brittle smile moved Uncle’s lips. “That was my thought. But we have to find her first. The longer it takes to find her, the more frustrated my men will become. Anger may drive them to make a blunder that we’ll all regret . . .”

Hanan didn’t mistake his meaning. “I understand, Uncle. And if I knew how to help you, I would.”

He left. Hanan waited a moment, then tried the door, but it was locked. There was no phone in the room. She paced the length of the patterned carpet, thoughts of her family and of Ari mixing incoherently with thoughts of herself, of soldiers hunting, of the choices she’d made in her life. The afternoon faded and night came on. A servant brought her a meal. She ate it by the glass window that overlooked the courtyard. The air in Uncle’s house was cold and sterile with air-conditioning. The servant returned to claim her tray. She sat by the window, thinking, waiting for news of Ari. She started when a soft scratching sounded against the glass.

At first she saw only a dead brown leaf clinging to the outside sill. Then she realized it was the bat. How could it have found her? Then she leaned forward in horror, staring into its tiny, artificial eyes as they sought her through the window. Her ghost must still exist behind those eyes. A part of her that she could now never reclaim. And then a second realization: her ghost must know where Ari was hidden. If only it could tell her. Then she might guide Uncle to Ari before the ruthless soldiers did her harm.

She stood up and shoved her chair out of the way. There were louvers beneath the large window. Judging by the gray scum in their seams, they probably hadn't been opened in years. She pushed on one. It resisted at first, then slowly turned. The bat fluttered down to the opening and clambered into the room. Belatedly, Hanan wondered if an alarm would sound.

She picked up the bat, cradling its soft furry body against her cheek. She knew that she should summon Uncle, show the creature to him, explain everything. He would measure her honesty by that. He would also destroy the bat, and Ari would be lost.

She held the bat in front of her face. If she spoke, her ghost would hear her, and understand. "Find Ari," she said. "Tell her to call Uncle. She must give herself up. If she does, Uncle will forgive her. He understands that she's *family*. And she can survive the loss of the atrium. Tell her to come home." She shoved the bat back out past the louvers just as Uncle opened the door.

"*Ari!*" Hanan's ghost shouted desperation at the fugitive's address.

"Hanan?" The answering voice was sleepy, uncertain.

"Yes, of course!" Hanan cried. She was trapped. Trapped! A ghost condemned to remain forever outside her own body. Never would she feel its pleasures again. Never to make love to Seyyed, to cuddle Sari, to kiss Hamal. Never to walk or run or eat or cry. But she was not powerless. She sensed that Sari and Hamal might have a mother again if Ari were delivered to Uncle. From the fear-focused viewpoint of her new existence, nothing else seemed to matter.

"I'm coming back, Ari," she called over the telephone network, as she drove on tired wings through the humming city. "I have a message from your sister: they're hunting you, but we have a chance to survive . . . if you call Uncle."

"*What?*"

Quickly, the ghost explained: "You have no choice. You can't hide forever. They *will* find you. But Uncle knows that you're family, that you're the sister of Hanan. He'll forgive you. He'll take you in because you're his brother's child, just as he did for Hanan. Your sister has given up her atrium. You must do the same. But she says you can survive that. You must come home."

"Give up the atrium?"

"Yes. In trade for a peaceful life, a perfect life." She'd finally caught Ari's scent. It was a discontinuous trace at first, but then the track widened into a clear path through the streets. The ghost flew low, to drink it in, skimming the startled, upturned faces of the street people.

"Give up my mother too?"

Now the ghost saw, just ahead, the crumbling apothecary shop where Ari had taken refuge. She flitted under the eaves and quickly located the hole in the termite-eaten boards she'd discovered earlier that night. She crawled through, until she could poke her tiny snout into the room. Light came from a flash light set into a niche on the wall. Ari sat on a worn brown cushion that might have been stripped from an old sofa. A salve glinted on her arms and bare shoulders, where it had been applied to her burns. Three other people huddled near her, two of them with small revolvers resting in their laps. "Our mother betrayed the family and destroyed our father," the ghost said.

Ari's lips twisted in irritation. "Your *Uncle* destroyed our father."

The ghost knew this to be true. So she didn't argue. She used it against Ari. "Uncle will destroy you too. You must come home."

"No." Simple as that. Not even questioning the offer. A bald 'no' and the ghost felt her world begin to fray. Ari said: "You never understood who mother was, did you, Hanan? I always envied you because you knew her. But perhaps I was wrong. You may have been too close to her to see. But through death and distance, *my* mother has taught me things that are more important than simple family. I'm here to give voice to the many who have no voice. I am my mother's tool. I am her servant. I am *home*. Tell Uncle he must hunt me down."

"No, Ari! You must reconsider," the ghost cried. "If you don't come home, I'll never have my children back. Ari, they'll be without a mother. Come home, come home. They are your children too—"

Ari cut the connection. The ghost stared at her, aghast. She tried to call her again, but Ari refused to answer. The child sat in the cool, dim interior of the apothecary shop, staring across the room at nothing. Tears welled up in her eyes and eased down across her cheeks. Still, she refused to answer.

So Hanan entered a new address, and identified herself: "Uncle. It's Hanan."

Uncle's gruff voice came to her a moment later as he spoke into his telephone. "Who is this?"

"Hanan," she repeated, feeling a whisper-hiss of anger break through her habitual submission. This was Uncle and he was a murderer and she'd always known it. But there had always been too much to lose to risk turning against him. Even now.

"You're not Hanan," he said. "I know where Hanan is."

The anger grew, like a tiny fire burning in a dark closet, heating the fuel around it before bursting into a violent blaze. "I'm Hanan's *ghost*," she said, in crisp, clear syllables. "You trapped me outside of my body, Uncle, when you destroyed my atrium. How will I ever go home now?"

"You must erase yourself," Uncle said. Did she hear a note of fear in his voice? "You are an illegal simulation."

"I am with Ari."

There was a moment of silence, a great warring silence in which Uncle debated the possibilities entailed in this phone call. Finally he said: "Where is she?"

"Will you let your Hanan go home?"

"This is no time to bargain."

"It's the only time I'll have something to bargain *with*."

Uncle took a moment to consider this. Then: "All right. If we find Ari, I'll send my Hanan home. And then you'll return to my house, and fly to my hand, where I will kill you."

Hanan quailed. There could be no afterlife for a simple electronic ghost. Her end would be an empty end, an arrested signal, darkness.

"Hanan?" Uncle probed for a response.

"Will you swear to only capture Ari then?" she whispered. "And not kill her? I know this is best for her. But you must promise she won't be killed."

"If she's my brother's daughter, I'll do what I can."

And that was the most she'd get out of Uncle, she knew. So she gave him directions to the apothecary shop.

Sometime in the hours between midnight and dawn, as the true Hanan paced the width of her prison bedroom or sat stiff-backed in the chair beside the window, a realization came to her, one absurdly obvious in retrospect. She'd always been a prisoner under Uncle's care. Before, the cage had been large enough to contain Seyyed and the children and she'd let that soothe her, blind her. But it had been a cage, nonetheless. Now that the boundaries of her life had shrunk, she felt them more.

She paced across the room, stared at the closed louvers, then paced again. What was happening out there? She'd heard nothing since she'd released the bat. Uncle had refused to give her any information, though she'd explained to him about the bat and why she'd used it once again. Through it all his face had been a wooden mask. She had no way to tell if he believed her.

She stared at the louvers. If she could remove them one by one, she could slip out the window, perhaps climb down to the ground floor. There might be a way out of the courtyard, a chance to contact Seyyed. Together they could spirit the children out of the country . . .

But Uncle would see to it that they were caught. Seyyed would be shot, and the orphaned children raised under Uncle's supervision. Her heart seemed to stretch in a painful wail. There was too much to lose, too much to lose. She must wait. Dawn was at hand. Be patient. Ari would come home and everything would be all right.

The door burst open, and she jumped as if she'd been shot. Uncle. He had an object in his hands. He held it up for her to see. The bat. He held it by the wing tips. Half its head had been blown away. Her heartbeat quickened. Tension threatened to burst from her breast in a violent scream. Uncle said: "I wanted you to know that your soul is no longer divided."

She nodded slowly. "And . . . Ari?" Her throat was so dry, she could barely speak.

"Ah yes. Ari." He released the bat's wings, and casually tossed it into a corner trash can. "I've been thinking a lot about Ari tonight, and I've grown curious. How did you know she was your sister?"

Hanan shook her head slowly, dismayed at the direction Uncle was taking. "A guess Uncle," she lied softly. "Her looks; her situation. A few questions to the mission sisters."

"But you never had her tested."

She shook her head, unable to force from her tongue even a single word reply.

"Well I have. And she's not your sister, is she?"

Hanan felt a great whirl of gray storm flood her mind. If Uncle knew that, then Ari must have surrendered. Or been captured. Or killed. She grabbed the back of the chair for support. "You said you'd protect her!"

Uncle seemed unconcerned. "You told me you never spoke with anyone through the atrium," he said. "Or accessed any library."

She nodded shakily. "That's true, Uncle. Until I-I warned Ari."

"Then how did you learn to clone yourself?"

Her lips parted in astonishment. "I didn't do that, Uncle. It was my mother."

"Anna Soukotta never had time for children."

Hanan nodded eagerly. "She must have come to regret that. So in her last years she conceived of Ari. What other choice did she have? My father was already dead. He couldn't sire a new child."

"I understand the guilt a child may suffer. You were always an unworthy daughter in your mother's eyes. Did you think you might turn out better the second time around?"

"I didn't do it, Uncle," she insisted. He must believe her! How could he not believe her?

He said: "Anna Soukotta resided in a state prison for the two years before her death. She died without ever leaving her cell. It would have been impossible for her to create this abomination."

"No. She was in exile!" Hanan wailed. "It was on the news. I saw it. An assassin killed her in exile."

"A politically convenient story. One that you counted on, I see." He turned to go.

Hanan surged after him. She grabbed his arm. "Uncle! You must believe me—"

His fist struck her in the eye. Her head snapped back. The floor slammed against her shoulder. Colored jets of pain erupted in her field of vision as she struggled to her feet. "Uncle! Wait. Don't go!" The door closed behind him. She threw herself against it, screaming. "I didn't do it, Uncle! I didn't do it. It was my mother. My mother! I am innocent. Innocent. Innocent. Please, give me back my life . . ." She pounded on the door until her fists were numb, and then she sank down to the floor, her spine pressed against the wall. Tears rolled down her face.

Nothing's more important than family. That's why Uncle had carried on a murder spree against his own. First father, then mother, then Ari . . . all to protect the family's propriety. Hanan would be the next victim. She would die for something she hadn't done. And how long could Seyyed survive her? Uncle must suspect Seyyed now, or at least mistrust him. She remembered the bat, stretched between Uncle's fingers. When Seyyed was gone, Uncle would have Sari and Hamal. Another generation of the family to instruct. And when instruction failed, to murder.

She stood slowly, and walked to the trash can. Stared down at the carcass of the bat. Its head had been destroyed by the bullet that killed it, but the rest of the body was intact. She knelt and picked it up, then ran her finger slowly along a tiny bone in the right wing until she felt the nodule. There. It hadn't been broken. She smiled. The atrium must have been destroyed before it could issue its suicide signal. She hunched over, trying to hide what she did from the surveillance cameras. Then she pulled the wing close to her face and bit hard into the bone. Squeezing the nodule out of the torn wing, she caught it in her hand.

Uncle returned at mid-morning to offer her his own kind of clemency. "Nothing is more important than family," he explained, his face a cold study in anger. "That's why I've never put a member of my family on trial. A trial would be humiliating and degrading, and would expose us to ridicule. I believe that justice should be served within the privacy of the family unit."

Hanan rose from the table where she'd been sitting, and stepped across the room towards him. "Is that why you had my father murdered?" she asked quietly. "Instead of trying him for treason?"

Uncle's scowl deepened, but he ignored her question. He said: "A suicide, committed out of remorse, would staunch this scandal."

"I see." She stepped closer still. "And did you assist my mother in suicide as well?"

He bared his teeth in what might have been a grin. This was a subject that pleased him. "Oh yes. I had her shot."

Hanan nodded slowly, rolling the nodule she'd recovered from the bat between thumb and forefinger. The poison it contained was effective only inside a bloodstream. "And Ari, you shot her as well. Even after you *promised* to protect her."

Uncle grunted noncommittally.

"Well, I do agree with you," Hanan whispered, so that he had to lean forward to hear her. "A suicide committed out of remorse would save us all much anxiety." And she crushed the nodule between her finger tips, coating her nails with the clear jelly inside. She had only seconds before exposure to oxygen denatured the poison. She stepped forward. Raised her hand as if about to beg for clemency. Then she raked her nails down the length of his throat, drawing broad lines of blood.

He reared back. "*Bitch!*" But a moment later his hands were grasping at his throat. His eyes widened, then rolled back in his head. His body began to twitch. Tiny spasms at first, escalating rapidly until he looked like a stick doll shaken on the end of a string. He collapsed to the floor, still shivering, his feet thumping loudly against the carpet while his bowel and bladder gave way.

Hanan turned away in horror. She fled to the bathroom and frantically scrubbed at the jelly still clinging to her fingers. A moment later she was on her knees, heaving on the floor. When the spasm passed, she sat up. Perspiration soaked her face. She stood up on shaking legs and washed her face, careful not to look into the room. She straightened her hair, then set to cleaning the mess on the bathroom floor. When that was done, she returned to the room. Uncle lay on his back, his eyes wide, his tongue protruding from his mouth. Hanan shivered. Now she knew what murder felt like.

She cast about over the floor until she found the broken nodule. She picked it up with shaking fingers and rubbed it on Uncle's nails. Then she raked them against the wounds on his throat until tiny bits of flesh and blood had lodged beneath the nails. This poor deceit wouldn't fool a proper investigation. But she doubted there would ever be one. Uncle had too many secrets that could too easily be revealed.

She returned to the bathroom and scrubbed her hands again, then left the room. She walked silently down the empty hallway. Family business was private business. There were no soldiers set to guard her. In Uncle's room she found a scarf to cover her head, and dark glasses to go over her eyes. In his office she found numerous debit cards that didn't require an I.D.

She left by the servants' door. The old woman who'd cooked for Uncle for thirty years stood motionless in a corner of the kitchen as Hanan passed. "*Soukotta,*" she whispered at Hanan's back. It had the sound of a benediction.

Outside, the light and the heat destroyed Hanan's calm. She looked about, panic rising in her chest. Her heart thundered against her ribs as she hesitated, uncertain of which way to go. She had no plan of escape, other than a vague notion of disappearing into the Ovens. Certainly she could not go home. She was a traitor, and the president's men would come after her if they thought she was still alive. So she must disappear. Convince the world that Uncle had achieved justice in his own silent, secret way.

She hurried along the sidewalk, head down, ears and eyes tuned to the activity around her. Few people were about. The police kept the vendors and homeless off the streets of Uncle's neighborhood. Hanan would have preferred the clatter of the Ovens. She was too obvious here. She felt as if the security system in every house she passed tracked her progress.

She'd only gone a few hundred meters when she heard a car approaching from behind. It was going too fast. She began to move towards the inside of the walk.

In this neighborhood, every house was a compound. Tall stucco walls lined the street and there was nowhere to duck out of sight. She fixed her gaze on a cross street twenty meters ahead. When she felt the car swerve towards her, she began to run.

"Wait!" someone shouted. "We're friends!"

She ran harder. The hot air over the sidewalk swept past her face like the breath of a kiln. The car coasted up beside her, skidded half on the sidewalk. A door opened, and a man she didn't recognize leaped out. She dodged and tried to run the other way, but he was faster. He caught her, one arm around her chest, squeezing so that she could hardly breathe. His other hand went over her mouth, the salty taste of his sweat burning her lips. He dragged her back to the car and fell onto the seat, on top of her. The door slammed shut and the car zoomed off. Seconds later, the sunlight disappeared. The car was driving down a steep slope, tires squealing. It came to a sudden stop in a dimly lit garage. The doors opened, and her assailant hauled her out, his hand still over her mouth.

"*Through here!*" a woman hissed, and they hauled Hanan downstairs. A door snicked shut behind them, and they were left in utter darkness. The man took his hand away from Hanan's mouth, but he didn't let her go. "You're with friends," he whispered.

She could sense the presence of several people now, the shuffling of feet, the moisture of their breath thick in the air. A flashlight came on. Its narrow beam flashed across her eyes, then came to rest against the floor. In its reflected light, one face stood out amongst the small crowd in the tunnel. "*Ari?*" she whispered.

The second daughter of Anna Soukotta had a smile on her face. Hanan looked at her with amazement. "Forgive me, forgive me," she muttered. "When Uncle came to me this morning . . ." She shook her head in confusion. "I was sure you must be dead."

"It was close," Ari admitted. "The soldiers learned we were at the apothecary shop. But our lookouts saw them coming. We were out the back door. They hit me with a poison pellet—see here?" She showed Hanan a small wound on her upper arm. "It went right through the muscle. The drug knocked me out. But my friends were able to carry me to safety."

"I'm so glad," Hanan whispered.

"The soldiers spent an hour looking for that pellet. I suppose they wanted a tissue sample."

"Did they find it?"

Ari sobered. "I'm sorry, Hanan. I didn't realize until later what your Uncle could learn from that."

Hanan hid her face behind her hands. "You shame me! Don't apologize to me. My ghost was probably the one who turned you in. I really believed Uncle when he said he'd let you live."

Ari gazed down at the dusty floor. "I heard later that the soldiers had shot a tiny bat they'd rousted from the shop's rotten walls. I wondered if that was you."

Hanan nodded miserably. She felt herself at the bottom of a very deep pit. "I always had more than I could bear to lose."

"You love your family. There's no shame in that. Risk is easy when you have no one and nothing to lose."

Hanan shook her head in wonder. "Are you really only fourteen?"

Ari shrugged thoughtfully. "My ghosts have gathered over a hundred years of experience. But I still feel that I'm just a tool, constructed by expert crafters."

"I want to help you."

"Now that *you're* on your own?"

Hanan nodded. "Uncle is gone now. But Sari and Hamal and Seyyed still live in the cage he built for them." That had been tolerable, when she too lived inside. Now the view was different.

"It'll be a long war," Ari warned. "And we have no way to take you out of the country."

"I wouldn't leave. There's too much work to be done here. Our mother's work."

Hanan didn't mention what Uncle had said about Anna Soukotta dying in a prison cell. She sensed that Ari needed the myth of her mother's love to sustain her inner strength. Ari *was* a tool, but of the Followers, not of Anna Soukotta. Let her serve her purpose well.

Liberator is a novelette that was first published in The Magazine of Fantasy & Science Fiction, in June 1993.

Old Mother

Long strings of firecrackers sparked and exploded in the moment of the New Year, roaring across the seaside pavilion like an assault of armies. The violent odor of gunpowder invaded the clouds of salt spray thrown up by the huge combers that boomed against the beach: a baseline rhythm for the drums and gongs that drove the lion to dance. The lion was a fantastic animal, fifteen feet from nose to tail, neurocell plastic glittering white and red and gold, great green eyes winking under heavy lashes, huge maw snapping open and shut as it charged about the crowd pursuing invisible demons. Asha ducked and stumbled backwards, laughing, as the lion raced past her. Clay caught her; stood her back up on her feet again with a grin. The drums pounded a blood rhythm into her head, a pulse that hammered at her doubt. She crowed with a hundred other voices when the lion reared up on its hind legs to roar at the stars winking overhead.

The stars, the stars. They teased her in the night, faint and shimmering in mystery. Never confuse the stars with the planets. The planets were bright and close and too well understood. But the stars . . . no one had ever tried for the stars before. That would soon change. This time tomorrow she'd be off on the first leg of her journey to *Dragon*—almost-living biometal ship that had been growing in orbit for five years. All was ready now.

"Time to make the offering!" Clay shouted over the thunder of surf and drums. *A farmer would remember that*, Asha thought. Even in the new century, it didn't hurt a farmer to pay attention to luck and omens and gods.

Nodding, she reached into her skirt pocket. Little rectangles of gold foil were already shimmering in the torch light, held over the heads of the crowd by eager hands. Asha added her own to the glitter. Clay's strong hand encircled hers, left over right. For luck, for prosperity. She smiled and leaned against him, feeling the strength of the land in his body, his lean muscles like the binding roots of the orchard he tended on his grandmother's farm. For a moment, fear glittered in her sight like starlight on broken glass. But she turned away from it. That was for tomorrow. Tonight they would dance together to the rhythm of the drums.

The lion was working the other side of the crowd now. She could see its handler, seated behind the musicians, studying a video display of the pavilion, directing the lion's dance with the aid of a collision avoidance program. And his partner beside him—Clay's grandmother, Electra—a dark and heavy old artist in a flowing blue dress who used smart paint and guile to make lifeless things suddenly seem alive. Around Electra, reality became slippery. Any inanimate object could suddenly awaken to a new and animate identity. Nothing was fixed. Nothing was quantifiable. She'd raised Clay in a world in which dreamtime could hardly be distinguished from the waking state.

Asha's gaze fixed on Electra's wide, brown face, on her dark eyes that managed to scowl despite the joyful bent of her mouth. Clay had been nothing more than a bit of embryonic tissue when his grandmother had taken him in. She'd raised him in her womb, nursed him at her breast, filled him with her own primal vision of the land as a mother deity and they'd been happy—until Asha came along.

From across the pavilion Electra seemed to sense Asha's gaze. Her head turned; triumph sparked in her eyes. Then a drunk tourist whirled across Asha's line of sight, blond hair flying as she spun her own dance to the New Year. Asha tipped her head back to look over her shoulder at Clay. He mis-read her mood and kissed her, his scraggly black moustache rough against her lips.

"You two ought to be married!"

Asha looked around, startled to see the blond tourist swaying in front of her. The woman lifted a lei of knotted *hala* leaves from around her own shoulders and held it up with a brilliant smile. Then she reached out and quickly tied it around Clay and Asha's outstretched hands, binding them tightly together. "Make your offering to the lion," she advised. "And leave the bondage on until it falls off naturally. Then you'll be married well and long. I guarantee it! And I am a licensed witch!"

She whirled away to spread her benedictions elsewhere, while their friends laughed around them. "You have to marry him now, Asha!" "Go for it, Clay!" "Do it for real! Log it on the P.A. net." *Do it, do it, do it*, the chant started at once on all sides. Then the lion charged. People screamed and fell back. The great beast wove up and down against the straining crowd, its mouth snapping shut over gold foil after gold foil. "Feed the lion," Clay intoned in her ear.

Together they extended their offering. Asha stared at their bound hands for a moment, touched by a sense of wonder. Clay's hand was trembling as it closed over hers.

Suddenly, multi-colored jets of flame ignited overhead. Paper lanterns began to burn with the ferocity of rocket fuel. The lion snorted in fear and bounded backwards while Asha ducked instinctively, pulling Clay down with her. Within seconds the fire cut through the rope that suspended the lanterns above the pavilion. The rope fell to the concrete floor in neat, arm-length sections that began to writhe, gleaming and hissing and rearing up, forked tongues tasting the sudden scent of fear. Asha recognized the arrow-head and spiny tail of death adders, serpents that had long ago cut a niche for themselves in the island's deranged ecology. The crowd gasped and fell back before the snakes' collective gaze. For a moment silence engulfed the pavilion while the angry snakes flattened their coils against the ground and debated attack. But they waited too long. The lion had recovered. It charged toward the line of death adders on great, padded feet. They seemed to sense it and turned as if to flee, but too late. The lion caught them and crushed them. One by one they exploded in purple fire under its trampling feet, each ignition accompanied by hysterical screams of approval from the crowd. Asha's throat was raw with her own passion as she cheered the destruction of what must be Electra's artful demons.

"*The lion!*" Clay cried, reminding her why they were there. And suddenly it was upon them.

Clay yanked their bound hands up with the offering and the lion's maw flew open like double doors slammed wide. It's red tongue lolled. It pounced upon the foil, its jaws slamming shut bare millimeters from their finger tips. The offering slipped out of their hands. The lion batted its brilliant green eyes and moved on.

Asha sagged against Clay, a grin on her face and a sense of elation in her heart. Across the pavilion Electra wore an expression that made her death adders seem almost kind.

"You have to do it," Stuart said seriously. "I've heard of that witch. She has a lot of celebrity clients. They say she gives good advice." Like Asha, Stuart was Cured. But he'd been on Maui only six months.

"Do it," Kemmy agreed. Another Cured, on her last month before eviction back to the Celestial Cities. "Make the marriage official. You know you want to."

"But it won't work," Asha said softly. She glanced at Clay from under lowered eyes . . . an unCured farmer rooted to his land. He'd said nothing since they'd made their offering to the lion. He sat on the picnic bench, staring at their bound hands clasped together on the table. Of the mixed emotions on his face, worry was the one she recognized most clearly.

The euphoria of the dance had faded for her too, leaving behind only a great hollow fear of the morning's reality. She bit her lip. "How can we do it? Tomorrow—no, it's already today—today will be our last day togeth—"

Clay flinched. But Atlanta laughed. "What's tomorrow? Tomorrow may never come."

"For you," Asha whispered, knowing no one would hear her over the surf. Atlanta was unCured. Time was more uncertain for her. She'd lived near the beach at Makena since she was seven and she'd go on living there until she'd used up all her tomorrows and died of old age.

The Cured had made a different deal. They'd bought youth. Didn't cost much. Just their land, their homes. Whatever bound them to Mother Earth. Cost calculated on a sliding scale according to net worth. *We turn no one down.*

Youth, and a luxury apartment in the Celestial Cities. Fair enough, Asha thought. Old Mother had no room for ageless geezers determined to live forever. Asha reckoned they were lucky to get one year in ten in the cradle. But her year was up. New Year's Day. Vacation over. Time to move on—without Clay. She'd chosen *Dragon*, and if she ever came home again, it would not be in Clay's lifetime.

She sighed deeply. To love a man who refused to take the Cure, who was as tightly rooted to the Earth as the trees he tended on his grandmother's farm: it was absurd, and yet it *was*. Until it all ended tomorrow.

The chant started up around them again: *Do it, do it, do it.*

So-called friends feeding like psychological vampires on their dilemma. *Do it, do it, do it.* For they wanted a fine, romantic story to tell in the years to come.

Still, Clay said nothing.

Asha felt hands at her elbows. "Come on! There's a public access booth on the corner." Sheer force of numbers moved them. Clay didn't resist. Asha didn't want to. By the time they reached the booth, someone had already called up the wedding contract and filled in the blanks from their public access bios.

"All it takes is your signature!" Stuart shoved a screen pen into Asha's hand.

She held it, open-mouthed, while her eyes scanned the contract. They couldn't do this. She knew it was wrong. Marriage was not meant to last only a day.

Then Clay took the pen out of her hand and signed. He studied his signature for a moment, his face uncertain, bemused. Then he looked at her, the expectation in his eyes bordering on fear. Asha knew they were making a mistake. But she could not disappoint those eyes. She took the proffered pen and signed. The computer downloaded the contract with their signatures into the public access net. The screen cleared. A new message appeared: *Congratulations to the new Mr. & Mrs.!*

Morning found them in Clay's room at his grandmother's farm house. Asha had awakened here many times over the long summer and fall, so that the scene held for her a pleasant familiarity. Outside, she knew, the air would be crisp and cold this far up the flank of the old volcano. But Clay's room was warm and pleasant.

Clay was still asleep. But he must have been awake earlier, because someone had told the curtains to open, admitting the blindingly bright rays of the morning sun as it climbed over the mountain's shoulder. Asha stretched, blinking in the sunshine.

A few meters beyond the window was the upper persimmon orchard. It covered the rising slopes of the old farm for nearly half a mile. The trees' knobby gray limbs draped their supporting scaffoldings, stark and leafless in winter.

Asha lifted her head. Her long black hair was matted with dried perspiration and smelled of smoke. It fell about her brown shoulders in a tangled mane. She smiled at Clay as he lay on his back, his left hand twisted around on the pillow where it was joined to her right. It had been interesting making love with that bondage. Using the toilet had been a bit embarrassing. But she imagined they could make up for that in the shower. She giggled and nuzzled his chest to wake him. "Clay."

His eyes opened briefly, then squeezed shut again. He threw his arm over his face. Then he sat up suddenly, grinning. He checked their bondage and looked at her. "It was real."

She nodded slowly, unwilling to look further ahead than this moment. He leaned over and kissed her. The sun seemed to press them together with a heat that threatened to melt and mingle their bodies. But after a few minutes, Clay pulled away. He leaned back against the pillow with a sigh, his dark eyes half-closed in the light. "How I love the sun," he mused. He raised his bound hand and hers, studying the knotted *hala* cord in the sunshine. Abruptly, his idle smile winked out. "The house doesn't know your voice. How'd you open the curtains?"

"I didn't. I thought you did."

His eyes widened in sudden fear. Startled, Asha followed his gaze to the *hala* cord. It seemed to shimmer for a moment. Then the green color flowed out of it, as if sucked out by the sunlight. It turned a tired gray with darker stripes. It developed scales. Angry eyes glittered in a tiny, arrow-head. A baby death adder, wrapped twice around their wrists, its slit of a mouth biting its own bony tail with needle-sharp teeth.

Asha gasped and yanked her hand away from the hated thing.

The snake disintegrated. It fell across the bed in a thousand tattered shreds of *hala* leaf.

The bond was broken.

Asha found herself crouched like a cat on the foot of the bed, her breath tearing in and out of her lungs. Clay was on the floor, his left hand still extended towards her. He looked at her in shock that quickly hardened into anger. Leaping to his feet, he threw his head back and bellowed "*Grandmother!*"

"Clay—"

He turned to her, teeth bared. "It was grandmother."

Asha nodded slowly. The old lady had shown off her talents last night. "It was the sunlight. She must have sprayed the substrate on while we were sleeping, and the program was activated by sunlight." As if by explaining the vision, she could make it less real.

"You two had no right to make this marriage."

Asha flinched at the unexpected voice. Clay's grandmother was standing in the door. Asha slipped off the bed, pulling a blanket around her body. Electra was a tall, imposing woman—unCured—and unbent by age or disappointment. Her thick gray hair, swept up on her head and bound with a string of cowry shells, emphasized her regal carriage. A lifetime spent in this farmhouse, watching friends and family give in to fear or doubt and move away, take the Cure, had left a tang of bitterness in her personality, like the aftertaste of medicinal tea. But she'd hung on, thriving on a profound sense of place, on a certainty that she was no entity unto herself but that her consciousness flowed into the land and the consciousness of the land into her in a relationship that would not tolerate physical separation, and that couldn't be bettered by the simple longevity promised by the Cure. Her gaze skewered Asha. "You're a thief," she said, in a voice filled with quiet menace. "You came here, and accepted my hospitality, all the while contriving to steal my legacy."

Then she turned her wrath on Clay. "And you. What do you mean by this marriage? Do you mean to go away from here? Do you mean to seek the Cure and leave me and this farm? You are the last one, Clay. The last one. All my children have betrayed me and left this land that nurtured them. Are you going to leave too?"

Clay crumpled before her like hollow aluminum under a fist. "It's not like that, grandmother. You know I'd never leave." He glanced nervously at Asha. "She's my wife now. She can stay with me until I die. Won't you, Asha?"

Asha felt her mouth open. Tears started in her eyes.

Electra took one look at her face and hissed in disgust. "She won't stay with you. Look at her. She'll be gone before the sun sets and she'll never set foot on this land again." She stomped her hefty heel and turned to go. "You belong to this land, Clay," she called over her shoulder. "Your life is here."

Asha listened to the soft thump of footsteps as Electra walked barefoot down the hallway of the sprawling house. When silence had descended once again, she turned to Clay. "We have to talk—"

Her words seemed to break him from a trance. "I don't want to talk!" he screamed at her. He grabbed his pants from the back of the chair and stepped into them, the armor weave hugging his thighs like a second skin.

"Clay—!"

He yanked a stained and tattered sweater over his head. "Get dressed," he growled. "And get out. Go away now because I don't want to see you again." He slammed open the back door of the bedroom and stomped into the boots that were waiting outside on the porch.

"Clay, wait!" she pleaded with him. But she might have spoken to the wind. He leaped off the porch and took off running through the orchard, flushing a bevy of doves from the frost-burned kikuyu grass under the leafless trees.

Asha found him nearly an hour later at the top of the orchard, seated on the ground with his back against one of the trees, pruning shears idle in his hands while he stared out at a view that encompassed the house and the lower orchard, and below that, in a vista that seemed to fall away forever, the isthmus of Maui thirty five hundred feet below, and onward, the western mountains and the long blue march of the sea. A grand, pastoral spectacle that never failed to stir in Asha a sense of awe. *Yet I'm leaving.* In this moment, her intention seemed nonsensical. There could be no finer home in all the Universe than right here with Clay. Yet she remained determined to go. In the light of paradise her innate restless nature was revealed: a kind of insanity.

Clay refused to look up as she approached. She ducked under the scaffolding that supported the gnarled tree limbs and crouched down beside him. Thick clouds had come up since the blazing sunrise. They clung to the upper slope of the old volcano, white and gray and deepest black, so close overhead that the farm, less than halfway up the mountain's flank, seemed perched under a roof at the top of the world.

Asha loved this mountain. She'd been born in a house less than five miles from here, had spent much of her childhood on the slopes of this volcano. But when she was eleven, her parents had sought the Cure, taking her with them to live in the Celestial Cities. A year ago she'd acquired a special pass, and come back, to spend her last days on Earth while *Dragon* was readied. With all the world to choose from, she'd returned to this mountain. It was home, she realized. It always would be. More so now than ever.

As she looked at Clay, she could feel her heart begin to race even above the accelerated pace it had taken for the climb. "Your grandmother's right," she said. "I am a thief. I do want you. It's not too late to change your mind. There's room on *Dragon* for you. You know I've made it so."

He stared glumly downslope, making no answer. Her fists clenched in frustration. Didn't he realize she had to leave by sunset? How could the unCured be so profligate with time? She reached down, brushed aside a layer of dead leaves with her hand and plunged her fingers into the soft soil, pulling out a fistful of dirt. "Look at this, Clay." She grabbed his hand and poured the cold soil into his palm. "This is what you're suffering for. Dirt. Earth. Soil. You were even named for it! *Clay*."

His fist closed over the rich, dark earth. He finally turned to look at her. "I'm just a simple farmer, Asha. I belong here with the land. Why can't you understand that?"

She looked up at the heavy clouds. She could feel their cold, moist breath blowing down on her—an ineffective draught against the heat of her rising anger. She knocked the dirt out of his hand. "I wish this mountain could conjure up one last lava flow—aimed right across this farm! Maybe that would free you from this place."

He rubbed his palm against his pants to wipe the remaining dirt away. Then he took her hand in his. "You came to *me*, Asha. I didn't seek you out. You came here to my island, my home and you made me love you. Now you want to change everything I am, everything I stand for. But why should I change for you? You've taken the Cure. You have forever to live. Would it hurt you so much to stay here a single lifetime, and keep me company while I die?"

His hand felt warm and rough against her own. She imagined this hand growing older, more calloused, as the years rolled by and old age slowly claimed him. What would it be like to live a lifetime with him? To watch him grow old and weak and weary while her own youth remained as constant as the stars. She shivered, knowing she could never endure it, knowing that she would nag him every day to seek the Cure until the love between them finally soured into hate. *Dragon* would be long gone without her, and she still would not have Clay.

“Walk with me,” Clay said.

She nodded. They sidled out from under the tree, then walked hand in hand past the upper boundary of the orchard. She paused by a rock outcropping on the edge of the forest. The successive bands of two ancient lava flows and one ash fall could easily be counted in the exposed rock. Clay had chiseled off the weathered gray surface of both bands, carving the black rock underneath into intricate scenes of farm life: planting, spring growth, the constant battle with birds and insects, the harvest, the bare branches of winter and children playing amongst the trees. That last bit was purely imaginary. Clay had been the last child to grow up on this farm. She touched the scene wistfully. His skill still astounded her. Yet his stubbornness made her want to cry in frustration. For Clay would never carve a free stone. He used his art only on the substrate, on the structure of the mountain itself so that his work could never be moved from the land.

Perhaps she was foolish to try to shake him loose; perhaps that’s what she loved in him. Certainly there was a seduction in his permanence, a dream-like quality to the smooth, predictable pattern that had been laid down for his life.

He tugged at her hand impatiently. He hadn’t brought her here to see his art. They walked on through the forest of black wattle, their boots crunching against a thin carpet of tiny fallen leaves and seed pods. Daylight dimmed under the closely spaced trees. The trunks overhead creaked against each other as the wind stirred their tops.

“If I took the Cure I’d have to leave this land,” Clay said. “I’d have to ask permission to return, obtain a special permit just to visit this farm once every ten years. And it wouldn’t even be mine anymore. Can you see me living in an apartment in one of the Celestial Cities?”

She tried to imagine it, but the image wouldn’t gel. “No,” she admitted. "But we won't be living in the CC. We're bound for another world, Clay, one that no one has ever seen before—"

"As beautiful as this one?" Clay asked. "My family has lived on this land for five generations—"

Asha yanked her hand out of his in a sudden surge of anger. "They've all left!" she said. "All but you and your grandmother. Even your parents ran out on you. Before you were born. They paid for their freedom with you, Clay. They gave you to your grandmother as *solace* when they abandoned her for the Cure. Have you ever seen your mother? Do you ever hear from her? And where are you going to get a wife? Except for a few nostalgic tourists like me, this island is almost abandoned! What's the point of staying on? To grow old without children. To be the last beat of a generational rhythm that will end with your death."

Clay's eyes flashed. "There *are* families left; women who believe in the old ways. Atlanta for one—"

"Then what are you doing here with me?"

His anger faded. A bemused smile crossed his lips and he shrugged helplessly. "What's a simple man supposed to do, when his heart is stolen by the cruel hand of a heavenly goddess?"

"*You* are cruel," she answered resentfully. "I've never taken anything from you that you didn't offer willingly."

He shrugged, as if that didn't count. "Come. I want to show you something."

They came to the edge of a steep ravine, one of many that ran like wrinkles of age down the face of the mountain. He followed a faint track down, a deer trail she guessed, that skirted sheer cliffs and crumbling slopes. If there were any snakes around, surely they'd flee at the noise.

She saw no more of his carvings, though there was abundant exposed rock. At the bottom, dragonflies hovered and dipped over a few stagnant pools left by the last rain.

Clay began to climb the other side. She looked after him in dismay. "Clay, you're not serious." The whole far side of the ravine was covered with a thicket of blackberries. Asha had no desire to challenge those brambles . . . or the slithery creatures she felt sure must abide there.

"It's not far," Clay said, looking back over his shoulder. "And I've cut a path. Come on."

The "path" was little more than a rabbit run. She had to crawl on all fours, and the brambles still grabbed at her sweater and caught her hair. She cursed as a thorn pierced her palm, but she struggled on, until she found Clay crouched in front of a dark hole on the precarious slope. As she came up, he turned around without a word and wriggled through the hole, his shoulders scraping the edges as he squeezed through. "Clay!" she cried, as he disappeared inside.

She hesitated. She did not like small dark places. And for the first time in their relationship she was afraid of what he might intend. She listened to the mournful sound of the wind in the trees; the angry buzzing of a solitary yellow jacket. Then she cursed again, and followed him into the cave.

The entrance was a narrow crevice, taller than it was wide. She could fit through on her belly, but barely. Clay must have wriggled through on his side. She crawled for at least ten feet, until she ran into a wall. It was absolutely dark this far in. She felt with her hands until she found a small opening below her and to the right. Her hands were shaking and her breath came in harsh little gasps. She could hear no sound from Clay. There was no way she could turn around. How long would it take her to wriggle out backwards? She twisted her body around to the side and crawled into the little invisible hole.

This passage was even tighter than the first. Icy water dripped onto the back of her neck. Spidery tree roots grabbed at her hair. Tears of despair started in her eyes as she worked her way down the steeply sloping crevice. Then suddenly the darkness expanded. She could lift her head; taste a draught of cold, moist, stale air. She felt carefully around, but could find no walls except the one behind her. "Clay?" she whispered.

"Over here." His voice came to her through the dark, strong, amused. A light flicked on and she could see him across the cavern, flashlight in hand, sitting in a niche halfway up the cave wall like an icon set in the wall of a church.

The cave wasn't as large as it had felt. Perhaps a hundred people could fit inside. She began to pick her way towards him across jumbled rocks. "Why are we here?"

He smiled at her, that beatific smile that had caught her eye last spring when she'd first seen him fishing on the beach at Makena. "This is where I'll come when my life is at an end."

"Clay, stop it." She halted halfway across the cave floor.

Clay said: "I think ninety-nine years is enough for any man. I should be able to make it to ninety-nine, don't you think? Baring any major accident."

"You could easily make it to a hundred and fifteen before old age takes you."

"Could be. But ninety-nine is enough." His eyes gleamed with a fey light. "I like it here, don't you?"

She looked around. The cave was an old lava tube that looked as if it had suffered in an earthquake. The walls were broken and crumbling. White calcite crystals showed here and there in snowy patches on the roof, otherwise the rock was unspectacular. She saw no carvings. Neither were there bones or other obvious sign of prehistoric burials. She shrugged and crossed her arms over her chest. "I've heard there are interesting insects to be found in caves like this."

He laughed, as bright and cheerful now as if he'd taken the sun inside him. "And they'll have me in the end."

"When you are ninety-nine." She could feel a nascent purpose building in the air, and resolved to wait quietly for its appearance.

"Yes," Clay said. "It'll only be a few years from your point of view. I hear the clocks will run very slowly aboard ship when *Dragon* makes her run between the stars. I want you to think of me."

"I will do that."

"You'll probably be the last one alive to remember me."

"I feel the obligation. I'll remember you well."

His eyes were glittering in the flashlight's illumination. "I'll squeeze out all the time I can. I'll wait until the last day of my ninety-ninth year, the day before I'm one hundred. Then I'll come to this cave, and I'll sit right here in the dark until I die. Think of me: a naked old man on a shelf."

"You'll be too fat to fit through the entrance."

He gave her a nasty look. "You don't get it, do you, Asha? This cavern is a special place. No one ever saw it before me. You're only the second human being to come here. Doesn't that interest you? Isn't it important? Why are you leaving on *Dragon* except to see things no one has ever seen before? Well here. I've fulfilled your wish and you didn't even have to leave Earth. What do you think?"

She squatted down slowly on the cave floor, cold seeping into her body through the soles of her boots. Her gaze swept the black walls once again. "It's just a cave, Clay."

To her surprise, he nodded, satisfaction rolling like a wave across his face. "That's right. And even if it were halfway across the Universe, it would still be just a cave. It has no soul. No one's ever lived here. No one's ever died here. Nothing's ever happened here at all. Who cares?"

"What are you trying to tell me?"

"That you have to *live* in a place to imbue it with soul. Someday my grandmother will die. But she won't be gone from my life. I'll know her in the trees that she planted as a young woman, in the paintings that hang in our house, in the songs that I sing that I first heard from her lips." His eyes grew distant. "Everything on our farm has been touched or shaped by someone who loves me. By someone in my family. Even if they never knew me. Even if they died a hundred years before I was born, their love still fills my home. They knew I'd live here someday."

His gaze shifted back to Asha. "You'll never know the satisfaction my grandmother enjoys. You'll spend yourself searching for mysteries, but you won't find them. In the end, everything out there will be mundane, as secular and uninteresting as this cave. The only real mysteries are those of the human heart."

Was that true? Was it? She couldn't deny it outright. She'd seen the grandeur of nature and of human things. Palaces in the sky and mountains upon the Earth. Vast oceans, and solar sails. And she'd known wonder and awe and joy at her surrounds—but never in absolute quantity. Always, under the surface, doubt whispered and made her uneasy. The beauty of the grandest vista, the perfection of the tiniest insect—what did it mean? In the end, she'd turn away, dissatisfied. The only experience she'd ever had that left her fully easy and content was her sexual relations with Clay.

The notion of being driven by biology didn't offend her. But could Clay be right? Was the human mind so constructed that it could not be satisfied except by something as simple and commonplace as love? "There's more," she said. "I know it. I want to see other places, Clay. It's the way I am." She gazed up at him. He still sat in his niche, one knee drawn up to his chin, the other leg dangling. He watched her—critically—as a director might watch a play. She took a step towards him. Then another. "And I will not stay here to watch you grow old!"

He pulled his leg up and looked at her sharply. A new excitement glinted in his eyes. "Let's gamble our love," he said.

"What do you mean?"

"Let's make a bet on it. I want to stay. You want to go. We can't settle this rationally, so let's give it to chance. Do you think you could find your way out of here in the dark?"

She scowled. "Sure. It's just a simple chamber, and—" She looked around. Where was the entrance hole? She couldn't see it. Suddenly, she was unsure of the exact direction.

But Clay overlooked her distress. "Good," he said. "Then we're on." He hefted the flashlight and threw it across the chamber. It shattered against the wall and the light went out. His voice came out of the darkness, proud, challenging. "You lead us out of here, and I'll leave with you."

Her mouth was suddenly dry. "You'll take the Cure? You'll leave this place?"

"I'll do that." His voice had gone hoarse. "For you. For you."

He'd given up! Given in. Her heart pounded in an adrenaline rush of joy as she turned back the way she'd come. But . . . *which* way? False colors danced before her eyes as her brain drew hallucinations to populate the darkness. Which way had she come? "What if we can't find the way out?" she asked.

A bitter laugh greeted her question. "Then obviously: you stay here on the shelf with me."

"That's not funny, Clay."

"It isn't meant to be."

So perhaps he hadn't given in quite yet. "You think you'll keep me in here just long enough to miss my passage, right? That's the game you're playing."

"Is it a bet?"

She chuckled. She wasn't afraid of the dark. And she wasn't afraid of losing either. "You're on." She heard him climbing down from his niche. She imagined his body, lean and strong in the dark. Imagined his hands, from out of nowhere, clasping her. She giggled. This could be fun.

Suddenly there was a clatter of rockfall. Clay grunted and cursed. "*Ow!* What the—?"

"What happened? Are you all right?"

"Something bit me." He sounded as if he were speaking through gritted teeth. "On my shoulder. *Uh—!* Dammit!" She heard him slapping at the wall. "Sucker got me twice."

"Clay, what is it?"

"I don't know! Something . . . Shit. Adder . . . " His voice lurched towards her. Suddenly he fell against her, and they both went down. A rock dug into her side, and she winced in pain. "Aw man," Clay moaned. "My shoulder's going numb already—"

"Clay, if this is a joke—!"

Then she felt his shoulder and the line of his neck. They were already swollen.

The paramedic completed her examination of Clay while her equipment was still being ported into the cave. She rocked back on her heels, to meet Asha's gaze. "There's nothing we can do," she said. "I'm sorry. If we'd been on the scene when it happened . . ." She shrugged helplessly. "But he's gone."

Asha nodded. The snake's neurotoxins had stopped Clay's heart long before she'd found her way out of the cave. It had taken her nearly three hours to discover that the cave entrance lay under a shelf that appeared to be part of the cave floor. Nearly three hours. In other circumstances, that wouldn't have been so long. In retrospect, the task Clay set her had been easy. *Lead us out of here, and I'll leave with you.*

"You'll still do that," she promised, kissing gently his cold lips. Then she looked up at the paramedic. "I want to take him out of here now."

It required another hour to bring the body out the narrow cave entrance and up the side of the gully. Clay's grandmother stood on the edge of the slope, watching the progress of the gurney, her wringing hands the only sign of the distress she must be enduring. Where would her love go now? Asha stood behind her, listening to the soft beat of an approaching helicopter. A police officer had tagged a landing zone between the orchard and the wood. She watched him as he waved the ship in. "I'm Clay's wife now," she said to Electra's back. "Officially, that makes me next-of-kin."

Electra didn't respond, but Asha could sense the bitterness of her thoughts. *Thief!*

"I'm taking Clay for the Cure," Asha said.

For a moment Electra continued unmoved. Then a shudder ran through her body, as if Asha had reached out and physically shaken her. "They told me he was dead," she whispered. She looked over her shoulder. For the first time in that terrible afternoon she met Asha's gaze. "They told me he was *dead*."

Asha had never shared Clay's fondness for this domineering old woman. How could she, when circumstance had pitted them against each other from the start? Yet they'd both loved Clay. She was acutely conscious of that as the gurney bearing Clay's white-wrapped body was lifted over the lip of the ravine. "Yes," she explained softly. "By the standards of the unCured, Clay is dead." She stepped aside to let the body pass. "But his pattern remains. The structure of the cells within his brain is still apparent. It'll be no great challenge for the technicians of the Celestial Cities to restore him." She tore her gaze away from the body as it was being loaded on the helicopter. Her gaze fixed on Electra. "But when he's restored he'll also be Cured. His life here is over."

Yes, she was stealing him away, *like a thief* . . .

A medic leaned out of the helicopter to look at her. "You the wife?" he shouted over the beat of the rotors. "You want to ride along while we put him in cold storage? Then come on!"

She started forward. But guilt stung at her conscience, slowing her. She was leaving Electra with nothing, not a grave to visit, or a presence to be half-sensed from the corner of the eye. She looked back. "Clay was ready to go!" she blurted. "He just couldn't bring himself to make the decision."

Electra's chin rose. "That's what you've never understood: the decision wasn't his to make." Her tired face seemed suddenly flush with pride. "He belonged to the land. The land looked into his heart . . . and *let him* go."

Asha's lips parted in astonishment. A half-sensed truth rang inside her like a bell note on the edge of hearing. "*The land?*"

The medic leaned out of the helicopter again. "Come on, ma'am. Let's go!"

His shout jarred her from her reverie, shattering a vision that suddenly seemed lost to all recollection. "Coming!" she called, and ran hard for the helicopter. Electra shouted something after her. She caught the words as she scrambled into the cabin:

"*A tree may be cut down for wood to make a ship, but it will always bear the grain of its youth!*"

"Wouldn't have it any other way," Asha cried. She waved fiercely as the helicopter began to lift. In the beat of the rotors she could hear the sound of drums, in the purr of the engine, the throaty roar of a lion.

Old Mother was first published in The Magazine of Fantasy & Science Fiction, in April 1995.

The Bird Catcher's Children

Harysen crouched amongst the thick mosses and fine-leafed vegetation of the forest floor. The rain dripped around him, drizzling off his graying hair and the mildewed lens of his camera. He'd lived in this forest for nearly a month now and in that time the rain had never stopped. It cloaked the forest in a misty curtain, like some jealous spirit unwilling to share even a glimpse of its dominion with the world beyond.

And worse, several days ago Harysen had felt obliged to abandon his raincoat. The constant drips and drops had rattled so obtrusively against the plastic coat that he'd stopped wearing it after he'd spotted the wild children. Now he was always wet. He hunkered close to the ground, soaked to the skin and freezing as he awkwardly tried to make his long, husky frame invisible amongst the rain-bejeweled vegetation.

Across a fog-shrouded clearing he could see the two children. He'd observed them often enough to overhear their names: Menoot and Ukra. They were perched high in a giant of a tree that had just reached full flower. They waited, motionless and almost invisible amongst the bright orange blossoms, camouflaged by the cloaks they wore, fine cloaks woven of tens of thousands of feathers all dark green, gray and brown.

The children were hunting birds . . . or the things that passed for birds here. Nasty little four-legged, feathered reptiles. Miniature dinosaurs with bad dispositions. Avesaurs is what the park wardens called them. A few of them were capable of gliding, but none could really fly. The feathers were for warmth, or perhaps for courtship. Harysen wasn't sure. To him, the children were far more interesting.

A sharp squawk recalled his attention. A flock of bright orange birds no bigger than his fist had appeared in the lush green foliage of a neighboring tree. As Harysen watched, the flock of ten or twelve individuals scrambled through the dripping canopy and into the blossoming tree.

Instantly, an avesaurian cacophony descended upon the forest. The children had painted the tree's branches with a sticky resin. The little orange avesaurs were trapped in the goo. They squawked and screamed and flapped, their calls resounding off the canopy, the forest floor.

The little girl, Ukra, half-stood on her perch amongst the branches. She was probably about eight years old, no more. An ululation arose from her throat, and she skittered through the bobbing tree limbs, chasing the last few holdouts back to the area of sticky branches. One orange avesaur took off in a long glide to a neighboring tree. The others stuck.

The boy, Menoot, chirped in a kind of mocking imitation of his frantic prey. The tree branches dipped and swayed as he scuttled to the nearest orange bird. Menoot looked about ten, his long, coppery hair secured in a hundred skinny braids. His feather cloak made no rustle at all as he moved; it shifted on his back, utterly silent. He tossed one side of it over his shoulder. Underneath he wore brown leather breeches. His feet and chest were bare.

He dipped two fingers in a pouch that he wore at his waist, then he reached for one of the squawking, panicked birds. Grabbing its beak, he tucked it under its wing. Then he massaged its feet, rubbing a salve on the avesaur's clawed toes that dissolved the sticky resin and freed the frantic creature. Then Menoot picked it up and thoroughly cleaned its feet. He cradled it for a moment against his chest while his hand flicked rapidly across its back, almost too fast to follow, and then the bird was free, running off across the branches to disappear amongst the foliage. In the boy's fingers Harysen could just make out a small collection of orange feathers. These went into another pouch at Menoot's belt and then he moved on to another bird.

Only then did Harysen remember to take pictures. The camera lens wandered between the boy and his sister. The camera disk whirled. Then abruptly the image of Ukra and Menoot vanished from the viewfinder, to be replaced by an out-of-focus, dark brown field. Startled, Harysen looked up.

Standing in front of him was a short, wiry man, heavily bearded, with blue eyes and a dark complexion. Like the bird-catching boy, this man wore only leather breeches and a long feather cape. But his cape was of striking colors: crescents of electric blue rocking across a brilliant yellow field. And like the boy, his hair was fixed in tiny braids, though his were enlivened with strings of feathers to match the cloak. Harysen had never seen this man before, but he knew he must be Menoot's and Ukra's father.

His gaze raked across Harysen—his inferior height and bulk seemed to trouble him not at all—and suddenly Harysen felt like a guilty adolescent rather than the self-assured artist who'd commanded the attention of society for over two decades. The bird catcher spoke: "Why have you come here?" he demanded. "And why are you harassing my children?"

Harysen felt a rush of surprise. The bird catcher's perfect English seemed at odds with the man's exotic appearance. But why?

This man was no more native to Weyken than Harysen himself. He was a renegade, a runaway from the cities, a squatter living here in defiance of Congressional edicts that declared the very presence of human beings on natural worlds to be an illegal pollution.

Harysen rested a strong hand on his camera, resisting the instinctive urge to a combative response. "You've got it wrong, friend," he said in a low, rugged voice. "I'm no threat to your family. And I'd never let on to the park wardens you're here. I've come to work, that's all. I do sculpture—carvings in wood and bone."

"And you're on Weyken with permission, huh? A special man."

Harysen chuckled, determined to be agreeable. "The government let me come. I wanted to study nature--"

"And with a whole planet full of nature, why did you make yourself *our* neighbor?"

Harysen scowled to cover a sudden surge of guilt. The bird catcher was right, of course. He'd built his house in this part of the forest because he'd *wanted* neighbors. He'd wanted to be close to the squatters, to watch them, to learn how they lived. Because the only part of nature that had ever really interested him was human nature. But such reasons would seem frivolous to this man. He stiffened, as he glimpsed a flicker of his own mortality in the bird catcher's eyes.

Suddenly, a startled shout sounded from the tree tops. The bird catcher spun around, his gaze fixed on his children. "Red dragons!" the little girl cried. In a blur of motion the bird catcher disappeared up the nearest tree, climbing the rough-barked trunk with fingers and toes.

Harysen twisted around, his gaze scanning the tree tops. Three scarlet avesaurs were approaching through the canopy. From their nose to their hind legs they were as long as Menoot. Their short feathered limbs scrabbled through the branches, their black eyes flashed as they raced towards the captured flock of orange avesaurs. With their blocky snouts and decorative plumes they looked like miniature Chinese dragons armed with a heron's stabbing beak.

Harysen found himself running awkwardly across the forest floor, stumbling over roots and fallen branches. The children were in the dragons' path. And they weren't moving. "Get out! Get away!" Harysen shouted in a booming voice. But his warning was eclipsed by a tremendous roar from the tree tops, a predator's howl of rage.

The dragons stopped abruptly. The roar sounded again, and suddenly the red avesaurs switched directions and fled, disappearing within seconds into the dense foliage of the canopy. Harysen turned around, searching the branches for this new danger. But he saw only the bird catcher moving carefully towards his children.

Harysen leaned against a tree, his head down as he tried to catch his breath. When he looked up again, Menoot, Ukra and their father were calmly freeing the captured flock of little orange avesaurs, carefully cleaning each member, while exacting as tribute a small wad of orange feathers. Together the family required only a few minutes to finish. Then they cleaned the tree branches and vanished into the canopy.

Harysen sat in his living room, in the odd house he'd ordered built on the brink of a precipitous gully, cradling in his hand a glass of bourbon and water, no ice. He lived without refrigeration or air-conditioning. The entire planet of Weyken was an official wilderness, so the park wardens had decreed that the house must have no central power. The only machinery Harysen had been allowed were a few small shop tools, an electronic notebook and of course, the transit booth.

But Harysen counted the limited accommodations as one of Weyken's attractions. He'd grown tired of an environment programmed to address his every need; of an audience that adored everything he made, be it quality or crap. Something in him had longed to escape the absurd safety of society, to reach for the primitive: to be on his own, to warm his ration packs in a real fire, to breath air generated by a living forest, to be close to the land and his own instincts—this was an experience he'd sought all his life.

He'd even let himself hope that Weyken would prove a cure for the strength-sucking sense of futility that had haunted him these past few years. Now he laughed at the thought. Weyken hadn't changed anything. He was play-acting here, and he knew it.

He gazed past the open glass doors to the patio, watching a small brown bird hop across the heavy vine that had climbed up the posts of his house. The vine twined about the covered patio, its heart-shaped leaves a lovely shade of spring green, its flowers like small beads of purple glass. The bird had woven a nest among the branches, and just this morning Harysen had counted three white eggs.

He thought about doing some work. His publicist had convinced a Congressional committee that this forest would inspire him—with its incredible diversity of life, with its magnificent selection of hardwoods. Special legislation had been passed allowing him to come here. Back in the world, expectations were high.

"I am the eyes of my age," he announced to the little bird that hopped about the twining vine, poking its head in and out amongst the leaves as it searched for insects. "My hands have made the art that will define this time in history."

The little brown bird remained wisely unimpressed, as was Harysen himself. He was a sculptor, that was all. And the work he'd done in the past mostly pleased him. But it was *past*, leaving always the question *what next?*

For almost a year, the answer had been *nothing*. His ex-wife had adopted the habit of chastising him daily. His agent had grown surly. The hoity-toity art crowd had begun to bid up the prices on his work in a slow-boiling round of speculation.

And then he'd read about Weyken. A few weeks later, to his profound surprise, he'd found himself with permission to go on an 'artist's retreat' on the uninhabited world—to become the only alien creature in a biological preserve that encompassed the entire planet.

Only later did he discover the squatters. His research turned up at least six groups in widely scattered locations throughout the southern cloud forest. The wardens seemed unaware of their presence. Harysen did nothing to enlighten them. But he did change the location of his house, because suddenly he was far more fascinated by the biological potential of his own species than by that of the entire ecosphere of a nearly unknown world.

Looking past the patio doors, Harysen toasted the antics of the small bird, then tossed back the last of the watered bourbon. It glissaded down his throat, leaving a trail of warmth that never quite seemed to reach his blood anymore. Shoving his chair back with a loud scrape, he stood, intending to put a few more pellets on the fire.

His eye caught a flash of color in the forest. He looked again, and saw the bird catcher stepping out from the vegetation beyond the patio, his bright blue and yellow cape glistening in the misty light.

"Well, well," Harysen muttered to himself, his surprise quickly evolving into caution as the bird catcher crossed the patio and entered the house.

The man was a head shorter than Harysen, but his sinewy shoulders left open the question of who held the advantage in strength. He fixed Harysen with a severe gaze. "Why have you been spying on my children?"

Harysen scowled. He really wasn't good at diplomacy. Still, he was determined to try. "The same reason they've been watching me, I expect. Simple curiosity. You know, they sometimes leave gifts of green wood for me on the forest floor where I'm sure to find them."

And in return Harysen had carved the kids a few toys—tiny avesaurs and spoons and abstract ornaments. He left the trinkets in the forest because the children refused to approach him.

"You've taken pictures of my children," the bird catcher accused. He started moving about the rustic living room.

Harysen watched him suspiciously. "The pictures are harmless," he said. "They're for my personal use; I won't publish them. And the wardens will never see them."

The bird catcher had found Harysen's electronic notebook. He picked it up, examined it for a moment, then strode with it from the living room into the hallway.

"Hey, wait a minute!" Harysen started after him. Oval windows looked out into the forest on either side of the passage. Then the hall opened up into the studio. On the workbench was a large battery-powered saw, lying amidst all the hand tools Harysen used in his work. The bird catcher's glance skipped over the saw before fixing on the dark, depthless door of the transit booth.

Then he was up the stairs, two at a time.

Harysen abandoned the diplomatic approach. "That's my bedroom!" he roared, bounding after the man. "And this is my house. What are you after, anyway?" Harysen reached the top of the stairs and turned into the bedroom. A window-wall looked out over the gully and the gently falling rain.

The bird catcher stood silhouetted against the wall, his cape tossed back over his bare shoulders. "Where are the pictures?" he demanded.

Harysen nodded grimly. "All right. I'll concede the picture taking was out of line. An invasion of your privacy." He walked to the cabinet and opened the door. The camera was on the shelf. He pulled the disk out of it, and turned that over to the bird catcher. "Destroy it if you like."

The bird catcher took the disk, slipped it into a pouch at his waist, then held out his hand. "And the rest of them?"

"What?"

"I'll take the rest of your disks—and the camera as well—just to be on the safe side."

Harysen bridled. "I won't give you my camera. I need it for my work." He crossed his muscular arms over his chest.

With reptilian speed, the bird catcher stepped past Harysen, seized the camera from the cabinet shelf, then turned and flung it straight at the panel of rain-streaked glass. It struck the pane and shattered, while the glass resounded with a metallic wail. "The rest of the disks," the man said again. "I'll take them now."

Harysen studied the ruined camera. Then he looked back at the squatter and nodded slowly. He'd come here to learn, not to fight. "I'll get them for you."

The disks had fluttered like silver fish as they tumbled down, down the deep ravine, finally disappearing into a fog bank far below. The electric saw and notebook had followed, and then the small kit of power tools.

"Why did you come here?" the bird catcher asked again.

Harysen scowled, feeling himself a hypocrite in the other man's eyes.

"Weyken is a living world. Listen to its rhythm, and you'll know your tech doesn't belong here."

"Nothing of us belongs here," Harysen growled. "We're all trespassers."

The bird catcher looked at him as if he were a rather unappetizing morsel. "Who decided that?" Then the man turned swiftly about and started down the path. "I will move my family," he called back over his shoulder. "And you will have an artist's perfect isolation."

Harysen sat up late into the night, bourbon in hand, staring out the open living room door to the vine-wrapped patio while the rain tapped and slid through the twining leaves. Now and then he heard a roar far off in the forest. Occasionally he heard a rustling in the brush nearby, and then he would stiffen, alert for danger. But no ravenous feathered dinosaur materialized, and he went back to his gloomy thoughts.

He must have nodded off eventually, because when he awoke, gray dawn was seeping through the clouds. He heard the crack of a stick, a soft giggle, the tapping of the rain. He sat up abruptly, the sounds echoing strangely in his memory and he was suddenly unsure if he'd heard them at all, or if it had been the last remnant of a dream. He listened, his ears straining past the patter of the rain, his eyes searching the leafy face of the forest beyond his patio.

The giggle had belonged to the boy. He was almost sure of it. He stood slowly and walked to the open doorway. "Menoot?" he called gruffly. "Ukra? Are you there?" The children were like the birds they hunted—up at dawn and nowhere to be seen after sunset. He took a step farther. "There's no need to be afraid, Menoot. I'm your friend."

But there was no answer from the forest, and after fifteen minutes of patient waiting and calling he gave up, still uncertain if anyone had been near at all.

He was walking back across the stone-laid patio when his gaze was caught by three small white eggs on the ground. He bent and scooped them up, recognizing them as the eggs of the little brown bird nesting in the vine.

The shells were empty. Each one had been neatly pierced and sucked dry. He hissed in sudden anger. Had the children done this? Or some other creature? He started to fling them into the forest. But at the last moment he noticed the nest wasn't empty. There were still three eggs in it. But they were different—slightly smaller and light pink instead of white. The little brown avesaur was perched on the roof, staring at him anxiously. He tossed the white shells away and walked back into the house. By the time he had the fire up and breakfast heating, the foolish brown bird had settled contentedly on the adopted clutch of eggs.

It had been so long since he'd done any real work. And for most of a year that hadn't bothered him. But this morning he felt restless, and intensely bored. He went to his studio. The yawning door of the transit booth seemed vaguely threatening, so he turned his back to it, studying instead the shelf that held stumps and chunks of fallen trees that he'd gathered in the forest.

It was so damp here, it was hard to find a piece of wood that was fallen but not rotted. But he'd gotten a few chunks, the largest no bigger than his head. And the children had brought a few more. Someday soon he'd cut some green wood and haul it back to the studio to dry. Someday soon.

He ran his finger over the scavenged wood. The pieces ranged in color from blond to coppery red. He chose a honey-colored piece and took it to the workbench, then set himself on a stool and studied it for awhile, letting it speak to him of its own nature. He smiled to himself as shapes began to move in a slow swirl through his mind. The wood was playing with him, giving him only glimpses of its soul. He couldn't see the final product yet, but he could see how to get there, so he took up a little hand saw and began to cut. A few grains of sawdust speckled the bench.

Something creaked behind him. A soft foot step on the floor. He jumped. The saw snapped out of his hand and clattered to the ground.

He whirled around to see a synthetic warden emerging from the depthless gray door of the transit booth. He glimpsed it for only a moment: a faceless, man-shaped figure of white ivory less than a meter high, still wet from the reproductive gel. Then its surface camouflage kicked in. Its skin mimicked the gray of the transit booth, the white of the walls, the green of the forest beyond the windows . . . an undefined blur of motion as it strode from the studio into the hallway.

Harysen suddenly remembered himself. "Stop right there!" he shouted after the retreating synth. "Where are you going? What business do you have here? I've requested no assistance. Come back here!" But the synthetic warden ignored him. It probably housed only a partial persona, just enough intelligence to execute its task.

Harysen abandoned his work to run after it, driven by a sudden, nasty fear. "Hey you!" he roared, following the synth out of the house. "Stop right now or I'll break you in two." But even as his words echoed across the ravine, the camouflaged synth vanished into the greenery of the forest.

Goddamn, if it's come for them . . . Goddamn if it's found them . . . I won't let it . . . I can't let it . . .

Harysen's breath wheezed in and out past his throat in great, painful gasps as he trailed the nearly invisible synth through the forest. He wasn't used to moving at this pace. He kept tripping over rotten stumps or slipping on patches of mud and with every step he fell farther and farther behind. Finally, he stopped.

All he could hear was the ragged heaving of his own lungs. So he held his breath a moment. His heart boomed in his ears. Distant birds called. Rain pattered on leaves.

It occurred to him he had no idea where he was.

Slowly he surveyed the ground around him, but footprints disappeared almost instantly in the spongy humus. He raised a trembling hand to wipe at the sweat and rain on his forehead. He told himself there could be many reasons why the synthetic warden had come. He told himself it was not his fault. He told himself lies.

If only he could warn the bird catcher's family. Surely with a few minutes warning they could disappear into the forest? The synth was stupid. It carried only a partial persona. The bird catcher could outwit it easily if only he had a few minutes warning . . .

Harysen let his head fall back and he yelled. He screamed. He howled until his throat was raw. "*Menoot! Ukra! Run away! A warden is here! Save yourselves! Run, run, run!*"

Finally, he gave up. The rain was falling harder now. He was soaked to the skin and starting to shake, not necessarily from the cold. He tried to collect himself. Down slope, he thought, recalling the topo map he'd explored with such pleasure when he'd been planning his stay on Weyken. *The bird catchers live down the slope from me.*

He carefully examined the forest around him and after a few seconds decided that there *was* a discernable slope. He started trotting slowly down hill, casting about for some kind of sign and after awhile he found what might have been a footpath, though whether it had been made by human feet or by the scaled toes of some ground-dwelling avesaur he couldn't tell. He followed it anyway and eventually it brought him to a neatly constructed tree house mounted in the lower limbs of two forest giants. The house was made of thatch, and there was an abstract feather ornament of red and blue hung near the door.

He thought he smelled wood smoke on the air, but the scent was coy in the rain.

"Hello?" he called tentatively. There was no answer. He climbed a ladder and looked inside the door. Embers glowed in the ash bed of a stone hearth. A slumped figure lay on the floor. Harysen hurried over to it, and crouched down.

It was the remains of a woman. The synth had used a bio-accelerator spray on her. Her body was crumbling into a sweet-smelling waxy brown heap that would be indistinguishable from soil in another few hours.

Harysen stood slowly and glanced through the rest of the house. There was little to see. Some sleeping pallets. Baskets of nuts hung near the fire where the heat would help keep mildew away. Fruit hung from the rafters. A half-completed green feather cloak stretched on a rack. A bright blue and yellow cloak thrown casually on the floor . . . the same cloak the bird catcher had worn. He stooped to pick it up, and discovered beneath it another rapidly decaying form.

He sank to the ground. His face pressed against the soft feathers of the cloak while his body shook in bouts of rage and grief.

It might have been near noon when thunder rumbled in the skies and the rain pushed itself to a new level of intensity. Harysen left then, taking the cloak with him. He climbed slowly down the ladder, keeping his gaze carefully raised so he wouldn't glimpse the bodies of Menoot and Ukra. Let the forest take them. They belonged to the forest.

He wandered aimlessly for awhile, having no idea how to get home. He started imagining his own body as a decaying heap on the forest floor and he was honest enough to see the justice in that but nevertheless the idea didn't appeal to him. So he kept going.

Around midafternoon he was pushing tiredly through a head-high stand of some purple-flowering shrub when he almost stumbled into the deep abyss of the gully. He backpedaled in panic, staring at the misty depths of the cleft while his heart thudded in surprise. But after a moment, he realized he was no longer lost. If he followed the gulch upslope, he'd eventually come to his house. And so he did, late in the wet afternoon.

He'd left the patio doors open. As he entered the house he thought he saw a shadow pass swiftly up the hallway, but he heard nothing and when he checked through the house it was empty. He threw the blue and yellow cloak across his bed and thought sourly about the possibility of an avesaur lurking in a closet or behind a curtain. He went downstairs to close the patio doors.

But as he touched the handle he heard an odd hissing and a tiny moaning sound—a soft, high note of madness. He felt the hair on the back of his neck rise. His first impulse was to slam the doors tight and lock them. But it was such a tiny sound . . .

He stepped out onto the patio, into the gray light of late afternoon. The air was dank and the rain was drip-drip-dripping down on his already saturated clothes. The hiss and moan sounded again, and with a wash of relief he realized what it was. He approached the nest of the unassuming avesaur that had been cuckolded by another bird, and peered in.

The adopted eggs had hatched. There were three chicks in the nest and their beauty took his breath away. They were tiny, perfectly formed creatures much like earthly cats but with long, sinuous necks, their bodies covered with iridescent feathers of green and blue. They hissed and moaned, while he smiled in delight.

Carefully, he picked one up, cradling it in his hands. It struggled to escape. He tried to calm it. He whispered to it as if it were a human baby. It swung its long neck around and sank its sharp beak deep into the thick flesh below his thumb. He yelped and dropped it quickly back into the nest while the rain washed a large droplet of blood from his hand. Silently, he berated himself. It was an avesaur. A savage, foul-natured bird. Not a source of comfort. Not a human thing.

He walked back into the house, stripped off all his clothes and left them in a heap by the patio doors, which he closed firmly. Then he found his packet of bourbon, went upstairs, crawled into bed and wept until the drink ferried him slowly into sleep.

When he awoke it was deep dark. The rain was pounding on the window of his bedroom, rattling menacingly against the glass. And over the sound of the rain he heard other noises downstairs. Voices? Just on the edge of hearing.

He strained to catch the words, but the harder he listened, the fainter the sound grew.

He shivered, knowing he should never have come here. If he'd stayed away, the park wardens never would have noticed the squatters.

But he'd come, intent on observing the squatters' lives . . . as if those lives were a performance that he could admire or revile. Now the players had vanished, their existence shattered by the simple fact of his presence. His simple presence.

It seemed very cold this night.

He reached out to pull a blanket around his bare skin. But his hand encountered feathers. He yanked his hand back in shock, expecting a sharp beak to snap at his fingers. The voices had faded. Only the sound of the rain was left. He reached out again, tentatively this time, and laid his hand on the feathered cloak. He pulled it slowly up to his chin. It slid across the bed without making a sound.

But as he closed his eyes, a resounding blow hit the roof of the house. *Boom!* Right over his head. He ducked instinctively, his heart drumming and his fingers cold as the whole structure of the house shook with the impact. He waited for a second blow, but a minute passed and there was nothing but the fluid grumble of a rogue wind in the gully.

Outside the window, the darkness was easing. He could make out shapes and silhouettes, the familiar outlines of the landscape beyond the glass.

With a mental effort he put away his fears—didn't dispose of them!—just put them away for the moment. He dressed, then wrapped himself in the feather cloak, feeling oddly grand and foolish. Then he went outside to investigate the damage to his roof.

A tree branch had fallen on the house. He laughed when he saw it, chiding himself for his night terrors. It wasn't even a large branch, though it was heavy. The broken end shone white in the gray morning light with the brilliance of fresh bone. Where had it come from? He tipped his head back, noting the forest giant that had dropped it. He could see the break—a white tear in the trunk of a slender tree that towered nearly a hundred feet over his head.

A gift, he thought. This is a gift from the forest. And he felt stricken, as an old, almost forgotten sensation slid into his arms, his fingers. A restless, murmuring wind in his blood demanding that he work.

Loathing himself, he bent down to examine the wood, wondering if he dare carve it while it was still green. His soul felt as dark as a rain-filled night. A family had died because of him. But his art was reborn.

The wood was the hardest, most beautiful, whitest wood he'd ever seen. Like ivory, like bone. His blades touched it, scraped it, shaping and sawing across a grain so fine it was almost invisible. And gradually, as the day passed, a composition emerged from the wood.

At dusk he sat back to examine it. He was ravenously hungry, his eyes were aching and his bladder was painfully full. But he stared at the object, surprised at what he saw.

It was a fluid, abstract image of a couple embracing, sharing a passionate kiss that implied a solid union, that promised children. And they were dressed in feathered capes, feathers twined in their hair. It was beautiful. It pleased him as nothing he'd made before ever had. He studied it in wonder, thinking he would send it back through the transit booth, show his agent, his ex-wife, let them know his career wasn't finished yet—

Feathers shook behind him. Coarse, rattly feathers. Claws scraped on the studio floor.

Harysen spun around to see a red dragon crouched in the doorway. It looked huge in that enclosed space, glaring at him with wicked black eyes. It reared up on its hind legs, the long talons of its fore paws rattling against each other with a sound like rain on glass. Then it dove at him.

Using its beak as a spear, it jabbed at his face. It raked at him with its talons. He screamed and fell back against the wood rack. The dragon bounded after him, its beak stabbing at his eyes. He slapped it away.

It came at him again. Its beak struck the back of his hand. Blood spurted from the wound. He howled in rage and kicked at the dragon. It fluttered back a few steps. He looked up, just as a second dragon launched itself at him from the studio window.

He raised his hands to shield his face. The avesaur's body struck him. Its beak stabbed at his throat. He cried out, and whirled away.

From the corner of his eye he saw the first bird, stabbing fiercely at his sculpture. Meanwhile, a third individual and a fourth had appeared at the window. Coarse scarlet feathers rustled, rattled. They launched their attack.

He ducked to the floor, beating back the flock of dragons with his hands. Blood was running freely from his scalp when he caught sight of the feather cloak. It hung from the stool where he'd tossed it when he'd started carving that morning.

Now he grabbed it; yanked it down on the floor beside him. The unexpected motion startled the dragons. They backed off for a second. Long enough for him to find his feet. Then he was running. Flashing past the oval windows of the hallway, through the living room, exploding past the patio doors, the cape waving along behind him.

At the edge of the forest he paused a moment to glance back over his shoulder. There were at least a dozen more of the red dragons moving in the trees overhead, descending on his house.

He spent the night in the forest, surrounded by the utter darkness, by the voices of the night creatures. He huddled under a fern frond, not far from the house, wrapped in the feather cloak. The rain fell against the feathers and rolled away without touching him. The night moved slowly forward. The forest voices changed. But Harysen continued to sit.

His injuries were superficial, but they still hurt. He was thankful for the cloak. It was a skin that kept him dry and warm through the lightless night. That kept him alive, he thought. He wondered at the art that had gone into making it. How had squatters from the cities learned to make an object at once so beautiful and functional? Where eons of evolution would have been required to shape a similar adaptation in any other creature, these squatters had done it in less than one generation. And he'd destroyed them.

Are we a form of pollution? he wondered.

The bird catchers had never ravished the forest.

Given: a new world and a few humans to occupy it. What would the result be after a thousand generations?

The park wardens insisted any human interference would spoil a world and leave it an environmental hell. But Harysen wasn't so sure. Might it be possible to slip into a new world as quietly as a graft that only made a tree stronger? Was it fair to the squatters to prejudge the outcome? Was it fair to the forest not to?

Harysen dozed and woke and dozed some more until dawn light finally started to filter through the forest canopy. When there was enough light to see by, he crawled out from under the fern and stood. His legs and back were horribly stiff and he felt light-headed from lack of food. Yet he knew too little about the forest to forage for a meal. If he wanted something to eat, he'd have to reclaim his house.

He stretched and caught a few drops of rain on his tongue and then he set off in the direction of home. It wasn't far. He'd made sure last night that he wouldn't get lost. So after a minute or two he was standing behind the last screen of vegetation, studying the house.

The patio doors hung open. The morning sun probed the interior, illuminating rent sofas and torn rugs. Ashes had been kicked out of the fireplace and lumps of bird crap sullied the floor or dripped in obscene smears on the walls. The destruction appalled him. It had the aspect of a conscious attack against his person, his life. He told himself that was ridiculous. But he had to swallow hard against an ugly knot of superstitious fear.

He waited and watched for some twenty minutes but saw no sign of activity, so finally he moved cautiously towards the house. His bare feet squished in the mud, then he stepped out onto the patio. He peered into the house. Broken glass shimmered in the hallway where some of the oval windows had been shattered. A few red feathers were scattered across the floor. But the house seemed silent, empty.

A sudden chittering overhead made him jump. He looked up to see the little brown avesaur that lived in the vine. Its head poked down through the leaves as it challenged him, seemingly ready to launch itself at his face. He stepped back in pained surprise. What was going on? The little creature had never minded his presence before.

He glanced at the nest. Then he turned around to take a closer look. The nest was gone! Not just empty, but gone. The beautiful baby avesaurs—he imagined them being eaten by the red dragons and the thought sickened him. The brown bird raced down the vine, snapping and cursing at him. He retreated into the house.

He heard the voices again as he went up the hallway. There could be no doubt this time. He stepped carefully past the broken glass, his heart hammering in his ears. Then he looked in the studio.

It was in worse shape than the living room. Everything had been knocked over and destroyed, the windows broken. He saw the sculpture he'd made yesterday. It was lying upside down in a corner, severely pecked, looking like a disfigured honeycomb. No trace of the original design remained. Fury ran through his brain, but stopped short when he caught sight of the children.

They were crouched in front of the depthless gray door of the transit booth. Both were shirtless, dressed only in brown leather breeches. Their camouflage capes were cast back over their shoulders. The girl, Ukra, had her coppery hair bound up in a huge fluffy pony tail on the top of her head. Menoot still wore his countless tiny braids. They had the little brown avesaur's nest on the floor between them. One of the three adopted chicks was missing.

Ukra glanced over her shoulder at Harysen. "What is this?" she asked, indicating the transit booth. "We saw that little hiding man disappear here. Did Mom and Dad go with it?"

Harysen felt his throat knot up. She must have seen the crumbling mounds of organic matter in her home. But why should she recognize those as her mother and father?

Menoot was staring intently at the transit booth's blank door. He put his hand in; watched it disappear. Withdrew it and watched it reappear. Then he picked up one of the two remaining hatchlings and inserted it into the door.

"Here! Don't do that!" Harysen cried. Too late. The boy withdrew his hand, and the chick was gone.

"Where did it go?" he muttered. He reached in and groped around, but his hand emerged empty. He coiled it into a fist and glared at Harysen. "Where's our Mom and Dad?"

Harysen glanced at the transit booth's control panel. It was set for the capitol city, probably the warden's headquarters. He leaned forward, his hand twitching nervously. The children were squatting right in front of the door. With one step he could grab them and fling them through. In a few days they'd be reconstituted in the city, where the authorities would see to it they were properly cared for. Yes. That was the thing to do. It would be best for them. What hope did they have here?

The little girl watched him with wide eyes, the feathers in her hair moving minutely in a stray current of air. Who could predict the outcome? Harysen wondered.

He yielded his advantage and squatted on the floor, face-to-face with the kids. They didn't belong in the city anymore than the avesaurs.

"Your parents are gone," he said softly. "They can't come back."

"They're dead, aren't they?" Menoot asked. "My Dad told me this might happen."

Harysen nodded gravely. Ukra began to cry. He offered her his arms and she came to him, her decorative feathers tickling his chin, her tears warm against his chest. Her hair smelled of the forest. He breathed in the scent. It filled him; warmed him; left him briefly terrified. His arms tightened around her.

"We have to go away," he said hoarsely, astonished at how easily the decision had been made. "Maybe we can find some of the other people who've settled in this forest."

The boy gazed at him with steely eyes. "Will the hiding man come for you too?"

Harysen considered this. "I'm here with permission. But the wardens will look in on me. If I disappear they might even look for me . . . unless they believe I'm . . ."

He was thinking about the white wood, and how smooth and hard it felt, so much like bone. "If they found human bones they'd have to assume I was dead. They might not even bother to confirm whether the bones were real or not." The boy looked at him with puzzled eyes.

"Will you help me learn the forest?" Harysen asked. Menoot nodded slowly. "And I'll help you to learn—" But what could he offer, really? Guidance? History? Seasoned wisdom? The opinions of other worlds? That all seemed of small value here. Maybe it was enough to offer the simple evidence that children grew up into adults.

He set the girl on her feet and kissed her on the cheek, then he retrieved the remains of his sculpture. He showed it to the kids. "Do you know where I can get more of this white wood?"

Ukra flushed red and ducked her face. Menoot looked stricken. "You want to call the red dragons back?" he asked.

"What?"

"The red dragons always come to the white wood," Ukra said, looking up. "Mom says when the wood's cut, it has a smell. The smell's the same whether beetles damage the wood, or people cut it."

"And the red dragons come to eat the beetles," Harysen concluded for her. "Then this wood was a gift from you?"

To Harysen's surprise, he saw tears start in Menoot's eyes. "We wanted you out of the house," he said, his voice high and uneven. "We wanted to see if Mom and Dad, if— We're sorry."

"It's all right," Harysen said.

"You carved the wood," the girl said. "The smell of it was

everywhere. The birds went a little crazy. We didn't mean to wreck your whole house."

"It's all right," Harysen repeated. "I don't expect I'll be living here much longer. Can you get me the white wood?"

Menoot nodded miserably.

Weeks later, when the wardens finally sent a synth to look in on Harysen, all that was found of him were a few broken pieces of skull and mandible, both thoroughly pecked.

The wardens were secretly pleased to be rid of this alien infestation, and they moved quickly to ensure that another would not occur. Before any higher authority could interfere, they ruled the death as accidental, sprayed the house with a bio-accelerator and destroyed the transit booth. Once again, Weyken was a closed world.

Back in the cities the art community decided that Harysen's work was worth at least ten times any previous estimates. While in the forest, the rhythms of life began to change.

The Bird Catcher's Children is a novelette that was first published in The Magazine of Fantasy & Science Fiction, in January 1997. The "synthetic warden" in this story bears a strong resemblance to the warden used in my novel Deception Well. I'd forgotten about that.

Hooks, Nets, and Time

The ocean ran through his dreams. The panting breath of the wavelets as they rose and fell against the pylons became his own breath, a slow, deep rhythm in his lungs that forced him to run. His footfalls reverberated against the black plastic photovoltaic field that doubled as a deck: a square track five kilometers long, encompassing the perimeter of the shark pen. Starlight glinted off the water; glistened in the film of sweat that coated his pumping arms. The rubber soles of his running shoes beat out an ancient cursorial rhythm, a telling vibration transmitted through the deck to the perforated steel walls of the shark pen and then to the coral foundations of the station some twelve fathoms below. Crippled Tiburon would be lurking there near the bottom, listening, measuring the vibrations in his ancient, clever mind, waiting for the hour when his fins had fully regrown and his strength was at once new . . . and old.

A thin wail twisted through the humid night. Tiburon heard it in the depths and thrashed his powerful tail. The wail grew into a distant howl of terror.

A faint splash.

Zayder sat up abruptly. The dream peeled away like burned film, leaving him in another version of the night. He'd fallen asleep on a lounge chair again, in the open air, on the deck of the Ocean Hazards Collection Station that he managed alone. The blocky silhouette of the shed rose behind him. The structure seemed to be an ugly afterthought to the automated design of the UN mandated OHC Station. Still, it served him for housing, and storage for the shark farm: luxury quarters compared to the fishing boats he'd grown up on.

Out on the water, the distant lights of a freighter interrupted the blanket of starlight. In the pen, the swish and splash of a shark fin accented the peaceful wash of the ocean.

Zayder leaned forward, ignoring the dry moss of a hangover that clung to his tongue and the roof of his mouth. He listened, unsure if the howl had been part of his dream. His pulse still hammered in his ears. He'd heard howls like that before: once as a kid, when a man fell off the shark boats in the Sulu Sea. And again, one night when Mr. Ryan came to the station. Zayder had only feigned drinking the cordial that should have sent him into a drugged sleep. That night he'd watched surreptitiously as a bound man went screaming to the sharks.

He listened. He thought he could detect a distant, angry voice from the direction of the freighter, but that was all. And what if he heard more? What was he supposed to do if he discovered mayhem and murder on the high seas? Call Mr. Ryan and complain about the neighbors?

He chose to believe that it had been a dream.

Dawn came. Zayder woke, washed his face, put on his running shoes. Another day. He would spend the morning doing maintenance on the robotic garbage trawlers that had come into the station overnight from their long forays into the South China Sea. In the afternoon he would mutilate sharks, harvesting the regrown fins of the captive beasts for sale on the Chinese market—the prized ingredient in shark fin soup. So much to look forward to.

But first he would run.

He set off at an easy pace on the only route the station offered: a 5K lap around the photovoltaic decking built atop the steel mesh wall of the shark pen. At high tide the deck was a meter above the water, with the open sea on one side and the enclosed waters of the pen on the other.

Zayder had run this makeshift track twice every morning for almost a year. Boredom had been left behind long ago. Now, his mind automatically faded into a passive altered state before he finished the first hundred meters. Conversations rose from his past to fill his consciousness, insignificant exchanges: a joke offered to college acquaintances in a bar; polite questioning of a professor; a cautious response to the inquiries of a government personnel officer hiring biologists for the wildlife refuge at Moro Bay; and yet another personnel officer, hiring for the marine sanctuary in the Gulf of California, and another and another, until they all seemed to be different versions of the same bad news: *I'm sorry. You have an excellent record and your thesis is impressive, but I'm afraid you're not quite right for us.*

He studied every word, searching for some point where—if only he'd phrased things differently—events would have taken a more positive path. An absurd exercise. He already knew the point when his career in marine biology had been lost. It had happened even before he knew what a career was, when he'd been arrested at seventeen for poaching.

It had meant nothing to him at the time. He'd been working for his Dad, hunting pelagic sharks for a dealer, who preserved the bodies and sold them as dramatic ornaments for coastal mansions. Zayder's family had been deep water fishermen for generations. But as natural resources dwindled, what had been an honest occupation gradually became a crime, and an arrest for poaching just another risk of the business.

But the wealthy patrons who supported refuges and sanctuaries around the world didn't see it in that practical light. No refuge manager would want his patron's newsletter to ring with the headline: *Former poacher hired as field biologist.*

It had never mattered how well he did in school.

But he'd come too far in life to go back to the boats, so he'd taken a job with Mr. Ryan instead. Ryan did not believe in nonprofit enterprises. When a U.N. mandate required every corporate entity that generated potential ocean garbage to construct and maintain an Ocean Hazards Collection Station, Ryan had expanded on the design by adding the shark pen.

Shark fins were much in demand and now nearly unobtainable since the wild populations had been hunted almost to extinction. Tiburon's fins alone would fetch twice Zayder's yearly wages each time they could be regrown and harvested. Ryan's select market held the great white shark in high esteem: no other great white had been reported in nearly five years. Speculation held the captive animal to be the last of its species.

But beyond the income from fins, the station was useful to Ryan in other ways. So Zayder finally found himself employed again, master of a remote world built on a reef in the South China Sea.

The deep blue sky lightened as he ran. The pink fair-weather clouds that hugged the horizon gradually brightened until they were bathed in brilliant white. A moment later the rim of the sun appeared above the water. Zayder ducked his head, his thoughts blown back to the present by the sudden blast of daylight.

A hundred meters out on the sun-burnished water a black torpedo armed with a spine of pentagonal fins scudded towards the station: one of the robotic garbage trawlers being driven home by a combination of the light breeze against its adjustable fins, and a solar-powered engine. Its collecting tentacles trailed a hundred meters behind it: some on the surface, some searching out the depths below. Most of them were laden with a motley collection of old plastics, netting, glass, metal and organic debris bound for the station's recycling bins.

Zayder slowed to watch the trawler come in. At the same moment a white-noise explosion of water erupted from the pen, scarcely a body length away. Startled instinct slammed him backward as the geyser of white water lunged toward him. A solid shape appeared as the pearly water fell away. He recognized the massive, lead-gray profile of a great white shark, its fins fully grown and its maw open, its upper jaw thrust forward to expose rows of triangular teeth. *Tiburon!*

Spray washed over Zayder as he threw himself back, a split second before the five-meter shark slammed onto the deck. The whole structure shuddered. Fracture lines bloomed in the photovoltaic panels beneath Tiburon's belly. The shark fixed him with its manic black eyes. It thrashed on the deck, jaws snapping in an effort to get at him. He felt the rush of air as the teeth closed within centimeters of his ankle.

"*You bastard!*" he screamed. He jumped back again. The shark thrust forward. Its torso was draped on the deck, but its great tail was still in the water, fanning the surface into a violent foam. "Back in, you fucker!" Zayder screamed.

The shark snapped twice more, then grew still. Its eyes still fixed on him, it slid silently back into the water.

Zayder stood on the deck, his shoulders heaving, a torrent of curses spilling from his mouth. Tiburon was the oldest, biggest monster in the pen. Zayder had harvested his fins five times, each time salving the wounds with a regenerative balm that forced the valuable fins to regrow. Five times he'd nursed Tiburon in the recovery channels, where pumps forced a steady torrent of water over the helpless shark as it writhed on the bottom of a narrow steel chute.

"I'll take your fins again this afternoon," Zayder growled. Cautiously, he stepped forward, to peer over the edge of the deck. Tiburon was a skulking shadow a fathom down.

Suddenly the shark turned, cruising slowly out about fifty meters toward the center of the pen until Zayder lost sight of it. A moment later Tiburon reappeared, still a fathom below the surface, his great tail flailing as he charged the wall of the shark pen. Zayder got ready to dodge a second lunge. But Tiburon had his own designs. He rammed the wall of the pen with his snout. The blow shook the structure. Zayder stumbled, swaying to keep his balance. He almost went down.

What the hell was going on? Was the damn fish trying to knock him off the deck?

Tiburon took off again for the center of the pen. Zayder turned, ready to run for the shed and his tranquilizing harpoon, when a low moan reached his ears. "*Help, man. Help me*," a tired voice croaked.

It came from the ocean side of the deck. Zayder glanced over his shoulder. Tiburon had turned. Quickly, Zayder dropped to his knees and leaned over the decking to spy a young man—probably no more than twenty—adrift in the light swell, a few meters outside the steel mesh. The sun shone full in his pale face as his bare feet tread the water in quick, frantic strokes. His dark hair floated like an ink cloud around his shoulders, blending imperceptibly with his black shirt. He sputtered, his eyes pleading with Zayder for help.

Looking at him, Zayder grinned in sudden relief. No wonder the shark had been pumped into a manic state. Tiburon had smelled game in the water. And just where had this stray fish come from? He could guess. The garbage trawlers had brought bodies in before—though never live ones. The trawler tentacles were designed to detect and avoid living organic structures. But Zayder knew that clothing could confuse them.

Just then, the shark rammed the wall of the pen again. The deck shuddered. "Not this time, you man-eating bastard," Zayder muttered.

He dropped to his belly and reached out a hand to the foundering stranger. The water was a meter and a half below. "Here," he barked. "See if you can reach me. I'll pull you up."

The kid shook his head, his mouth twisting in pain. "Can't," he panted. "Hands are bound."

Zayder scowled. And who had bound his hands and dropped him into the sea? Maybe it was better not to know. Zayder didn't want to get sucked into the personal affairs of men like Ryan.

The stranger seemed to read his thoughts. He closed his eyes, leaned back farther in the water and stopped kicking, as if waiting for Zayder to decide whether he would live or die. Zayder cursed softly.

Men like Ryan might have a choice. But he wanted never to be a man like Ryan. Quickly stripping off his shoes, he slipped over the side of the deck and into the water.

The ocean's cool and pleasant hand enfolded him, quenching his doubts. He stroked to the stranger, hooked an arm across his chest and dragged him along the pen wall, nearly sixty meters to a maintenance ladder. He tried not to see the huge shadow that cruised back and forth, back and forth, just a few meters away on the other side of the steel mesh. But he could feel the kid watching.

Zayder didn't blame him. The mesh wasn't designed to inspire confidence. It had a gauge wide enough to allow Zayder to wriggle through if he had to. The shark seemed appallingly near.

To distract the kid, he asked: "How'd you get the garbage trawler to let you go?"

The kid's eyes squinched shut. Then in hoarse English, dignified with a slight British accent, he explained: "I was floating motionless in the water when the trawler took me. It grabbed me around the chest, and dragged me. It was moving so fast, I couldn't fight it. I thought I was going to drown. Then it stopped here. I twisted and kicked until it let me go . . . *why?* Motion . . . characteristic of living organisms. The trawler's . . . not supposed to be hazard to sea life . . . so I suspect motion . . . stimulated my release."

Zayder began to regret asking the question. Who the hell was this kid?

He reached the ladder, then hooked an arm around the lowest rung, heaved the kid over his shoulder and climbed out. "I think I can walk," the kid gasped. Zayder didn't believe him. He laid him carefully on the deck, then checked for Tiburon. The fish was cruising out toward the center of the pen again, so Zayder took a moment to check the bindings that held the kid's arms pinioned behind his back.

He discovered two ropes: one at the elbows, one at the wrists. The kid's palms were pale and wrinkled from exposure to water. A lacy network of blood seeped across them from his finger tips. His finger tips? Zayder felt a chill across the back of his neck. This kid had no finger tips. His fingers were torn, bloody stubs, taken off at the first joint. "Holy mother," he whispered. "Who did this to you?"

The kid blinked, an odd look of wonder on his face as he lay on the deck. "The shark," he whispered in his cultured accent. "I was holding onto the mesh. My fingers were inside. I didn't see it coming." He turned his head, to look out across the pen. Zayder followed his gaze. Tiburon had turned. He was driving hard for the mesh again. "I never saw a shark before." He smiled in a dizzy, distracted way. "I can't believe how lucky I am to see one."

Zayder scooped him up and ran for the shed as Tiburon hit the mesh one more time.

The kid had passed out by the time Zayder got him inside. Blood oozed from his fingers onto the bedding, but the severed arteries had closed down and the flow was minuscule. Zayder bandaged each finger. In the air-conditioned shed the kid's skin felt cold, so Zayder stripped off his wet clothes and bundled him in a stale-smelling blanket. Then he sat down on the floor beside the pile of clothing, pausing only to note the pricey designer names before going through the pockets.

He found a credit card and an I.D., both in the name of Commarin Wong. And he found an electronic device, a black cylinder some seven centimeters long and one in diameter. It had an on/off button and a working light. The corporate name embossed on the housing was *Guidestar*, a company that dealt in geographical positioning equipment. Zayder guessed that the device was a transponder, presently inactive. But who was it intended to signal?

He slipped the instrument into his own pocket as his earlier worries returned. Just who had tossed this kid overboard? And wouldn't they come looking for him if they learned he was alive? He gathered up the wet clothes. He should get rid of them, in case anyone came looking.

He'd started to stand, when he caught sight of the bloodstained sheets. Damn. He'd have to get rid of the sheets too. And then there was the matter of the kid himself: Commarin Wong. The name tickled some partial memory. *Commarin Wong*. As if he should have recognized it.

The kid groaned in his sleep. A moment later his eyelids fluttered. He stared at the ceiling for a moment, then he turned his head. His gaze took in Zayder's face, before fixing on the company graphic on the breast of Zayder's t-shirt: *Ryanco*. What little color there was in Commarin's pale face drained away.

Zayder felt fear run in harsh prickles across his own skin. He didn't want to cross Ryan. He should call in; report the incident.

He cursed his shark-hunting youth, and the arrest that had ultimately forced him to work for human sharks. He cursed himself, because he wasn't one of them. "Why does Mr. Ryan want you dead?" he asked, his voice deliberately hard edged.

A faint, self-deprecating smile flickered across Commarin's pale lips. "He doesn't want me dead," he said, his voice barely more than a whisper, hoarse from a night of strangling on salt water. "He wants me back."

Zayder resented what he believed to be a lie. "That was you screaming last night, wasn't it? They bound your hands and threw you off that freighter, right? Well, you might have noticed, *Commarin Wong*, they didn't send a boat after you."

Again, that self-effacing flash of a smile. "That's what happened," he agreed. "But you have the advantage of me."

"The name's Zayder Silveira. Mr. Ryan's my boss, and I need this job."

"Zayder Silveira?" Commarin shoved himself up on an elbow. "I've heard of you. I read your doctoral thesis, *An Observational History of a Juvenile Great White Shark*. It was a stunning exercise in open ocean research. I'm honored to meet you."

Zayder blinked, astonished at this outburst, and the unexpected reminder of better days. The juvenile stage of the white shark's life cycle had been virtually unknown before he'd netted his subject in the Indian Ocean. He'd tagged the little shark, then followed its beacon for three months. But his research ended prematurely when it trailed the scent of death to carcasses entangled in an abandoned drift net. Before long the white shark became entangled too.

That study had turned out to be the last published account of a living great white. Zayder had hooked Tiburon three years later, but by then he'd been working for Ryan.

"Are you continuing your shark studies here?" Commarin asked. He seemed suddenly invigorated: his dark eyes sparkled with curiosity, his pale cheeks bore a faint flush of excitement. He seemed to have forgotten his injuries, his precarious existence of a few minutes before as he pressed Zayder for more information. "Is Ryan supporting your research?"

Watching him, Zayder felt a flash of anger. He hadn't pulled a man from the ocean. He'd only salvaged a spoiled corporate brat who didn't know enough about the real world to appreciate his own jeopardy.

"Yeah," Zayder said, his voice ugly with sarcasm. "I came here to study the sharks. That's right. Mr. Ryan's real interested in natural history."

Commarin's expression dimmed. He looked away. "You're right, of course. Ryan's not interested in natural history. I know that. It's all money to him." He knotted the blanket in his fist. "That's why I had to leave."

His voice had descended to a barely audible whisper, but there was something compelling in it, leading Zayder to wonder if his judgment had been too harsh. He stood up thoughtfully, and fetched Commarin some water. "Why did you leave?" he asked, as Commarin drank thirstily.

Commarin lowered the cup. For the first time, he seemed angry. "Ryan's my patron, you know. He considers me his prodigy. He's supported me since I was five, the best schools, all of that. I took my degree in genetics. It's what he wanted; not what I wanted. I wanted to study natural history, like you."

Commarin Wong. Zayder grimaced as he suddenly recognized the name. Commarin Wong was the new star of Ryan's genetic labs. Far more than a corporate brat, he was a hand-fed prince raised to augment Ryan's empire.

"That's the expression most colleagues get when they realize who I am," Commarin said resentfully.

Zayder felt himself backing away emotionally. "I'm no colleague of yours," he growled. "I don't know anything about constructing genetically-specific drugs—and I don't want to. I'm just a grunt Ryan hired to oversee his favorite hobby."

"No, you're not," Commarin shot back. "You're the poacher who took a degree in natural history. A poacher. With a black mark like that, it's no wonder you couldn't get a real job. So now you work for Ryan."

"You know, you're a real wise-ass."

"I work for Ryan too."

"Sounds like you owe him."

"I'm not his slave. I'm not going back."

Zayder nodded slowly. Hell, if he had any choice, he'd run too. "So what happened on that ship?"

The fire went out of Commarin. He lay back against the pillow. "I stowed away on one of Ryan's ships. It seemed like the perfect opportunity. But I didn't do my research first. It seems the captain has had an ongoing problem with stowaways trying to reach the Americas. He didn't appreciate my presence."

"Neither do I. But why didn't you just tell him you were a corporate brat on Ryan's A list?"

"Don't you think I tried? He didn't believe me."

By the time Zayder got Commarin fed and asleep, the morning was almost gone. He dismissed any thought of doing the scheduled maintenance on the garbage trawlers, and instead got his harpoon. It was time to go after Tiburon.

The harpoon's darts were armed with a neurotoxin that would stimulate the shark to bask at the surface in a state of slowly-moving somnolence in which it could be roped and winched to the recovery channels for surgery.

Zayder walked up and down the deck, squinting against the glare on the water as he tried to identify Tiburon amongst the many shadows that swam slowly through the midlevels of the pen. He hoped to take Tiburon without entering the water. He let his feet pound a rhythm on the deck for half an hour, but the great white never surfaced. Giving up, he went to the shed and pulled out his diving gear.

He didn't go into the water often, but sometimes it was necessary. It wasn't so dangerous. There were only two or three really aggressive sharks, and he could hold them off with the harpoon.

He was coupling the respirator to the tank when Commarin emerged from the cabin, dressed in a set of Zayder's company shorts and t-shirt, the clothing oversized on his smaller frame. He looked drained, but sound.

He watched Zayder for a moment, but his restless gaze didn't linger. It scanned the sky, the ocean, the surface waters of the pen. "You haven't said what you're going to do about me."

Zayder grunted. He hadn't decided.

"You found the transponder?" Commarin asked.

Zayder scowled. "Was that your sissy stick? To call Mr. Ryan when you'd had enough salt water and decided to be a good boy?"

Commarin smiled tightly. "I'm not alone," he said. "I have friends in Brazil. They're waiting for my signal to pick me up."

Zayder punched a flow button on the respirator. He noted in satisfaction that the harsh rush of air made Commarin jump. "You're a lucky man to have a job waiting for you. What'll you be doing? Making lethal genetic weapons for the other side?"

"No. I'll be working on the genetics of endangered species in the Brazilian preserves."

Zayder froze. He'd tried to get work at a preserve in Brazil, one that supported a riparian environment that ran all the way to the sea. Sharks were known to feed in the murky waters of a river's mouth, where the occasional animal carcass would wash out from the forest. *Such a lucky man.*

A gray fin cut the water in the pen, just a few meters away.

Zayder tended over a hundred sharks in this pen. They rarely attacked each other, as he kept them satiated on the organic garbage the trawlers brought in.

He watched the fin glide by. He'd learned to recognize each shark as an individual. This one he could identify by the fin alone. "*Tiburon*," he whispered.

Silently, he laid the tank on the deck and picked up the harpoon.

Commarin must have noted the change in his gaze, because he turned. His eyes widened as the shark doubled back. It glided even closer to the deck this time. As it slid by, its head rose half out of the water and its ancient eyes fixed on Commarin.

Zayder had seen this sort of behavior before. "That's Tiburon," he said. "The one that took off your finger tips. Sharks pick their victim. Guess he figures you belong to him now."

"Are they so intelligent?" Commarin asked. He hurried to the edge of the deck, where he dropped to his knees and leaned out over the water.

Zayder's eyes went wide. Tiburon was only a few meters off the deck. The great fish turned suddenly, his tail churning the water as he raced back toward Commarin.

Zayder got there first. He grabbed Commarin by his shirt, yanked him to his feet and threw him back towards the shed. The shark turned abruptly and descended back into the water without striking.

"You gotta death wish?" Zayder shouted.

Commarin didn't answer. His face reflected fear as he looked out across the ocean, where the low rumble of a distant helicopter had suddenly become audible. Zayder darted to the ocean edge of the deck. He saw the machine, a speck on the horizon, skimming the waves as it bore straight for the station. He turned to Commarin. "Looks like Ryan's found your trail."

Commarin nodded grimly.

"I could try to hide you. But it's useless. If they suspect you're here, they'll search the station."

"It's all right," Commarin said, his expression suddenly as empty as the shark's. "I won't make trouble for you."

Zayder could remember the desire. It was not so long ago when he'd still allowed himself to dream of the great marine preserves off Australia, off Africa. All he'd ever wanted was to know the ocean, to untangle its secrets. He would have done anything to be permitted to study in those preserves.

Commarin shared that hunger. He'd gambled his life for it, on a wire-thin chance to evade Ryan. And he was about to lose.

Zayder's gaze fixed on the diving equipment on the deck. "Underwater," he muttered. Then he looked up at Commarin. "They might not look for you underwater."

He sent Commarin to a network of caves in the reef, just outside the steel mesh wall of the shark pen. He had him take the bloody bedding and clothing with him, because there wasn't time for it to be fully consumed in the recyclers. "You can stay down for fifty minutes, no more."

From inside the pen, Tiburon watched Commarin drop into the water; the shark disappeared into the depths in parallel with the young man.

Zayder returned to the shed to find the helicopter already down, the rotor slowing to visibility as the craft bobbed on pontoons a few meters off the station. The helicopter's doors had been removed. Mr. Ryan liked it that way.

A bodyguard leaned out from the passenger side to catch the rope Zayder tossed. Another half-rose from his position in the back seat, his automatic weapon cradled across his chest. Ryan held the pilot's seat.

After the rope was secured, Zayder pulled the helicopter close to the deck so the party could climb up. Then he let it drift a few meters out on the swell.

The two bodyguards ignored him. Weapons in hand, they set off through the station. Ryan turned to Zayder. He was a big man, thick necked and well muscled like the bodyguards. He stepped into the building's shade and removed his sunglasses. From his Chinese mother, he had dark hair and pale skin. From his Caucasian father, he had blue eyes and the bearing of a shark. "A valuable man was lost at sea last night," he told Zayder. "The incident occurred near here."

Zayder nodded. "A garbage trawler brought him in."

Ryan smiled coldly. "I missed your report," he said. "Where is he?"

Zayder glanced nervously at the waters of the pen. The smile on Ryan's face disappeared, to be replaced by a stony frown. "I didn't get to him in time," Zayder said. "At dawn I saw the great white feeding on the body. The trawler must have classified it as organic garbage and dumped it into the pen."

The pale color of Ryan's face deepened to the coppery blush of sunset. "You didn't try to recover the remains?"

Zayder stared at him impassively. Ryan, still bristling, returned his stare for a long moment. Then suddenly he seemed to relax. The color in his cheeks eased and a sly look came over his face. "Bring me the shark," he said. "I want its fins."

Zayder started. But Ryan had already turned away from him. He barked a brief order, and the two bodyguards reappeared from the shed. "We're going shark hunting," Ryan told them. He turned to Zayder. "Perhaps we can still recover some evidence of our young man from the belly of the shark."

Zayder felt a cold flush of horror. "*No!* The great white may be the last of its species. If you slit its belly, you'll kill it. You'll kill the species."

Ryan's eyes narrowed. "That would be a terrible thing," he

agreed. "And I would be very upset if I did such a thing, only to find its belly empty." He pressed his finger against Zayder's chest, then drew a hard line down to his belly. "I might feel the need to similarly gut the man who had misled me."

The bodyguards leveled their weapons at Zayder's chest. Zayder stiffened, but his gaze remained fixed on Ryan's face. "I'll need the harpoon," he said. It was still lying on the deck, where he'd left it after his aborted hunt for Tiburon.

Ryan took a step back, then stooped to pick it up. "I'll handle the weapon," he said. "You find the shark."

Sharks were unpredictable. Zayder had never developed a reliable way of calling them, except to chum the water with blood. Ryan knew that. But Ryan wanted Tiburon *now*. Zayder squinted as his gaze swept across the surface waters of the pen. It had been ten minutes since Commarin slipped into the ocean. Tiburon had followed him down. Zayder remembered the fury of the shark that morning, when the pen walls had kept it from its selected prey. "All right," he said. "I think I know where I can find him."

Zayder led them along the deck, some three hundred meters, until they neared the point above the underwater caves in which Commarin was hiding. He imagined Tiburon below, listening to the vibrations of their footsteps, the shark's blood fury roused by the scent of inaccessible Commarin. He searched the clear blue water inside the pen. Smaller sharks swept past, their movements quick, agitated. Cautiously, Zayder crouched at the edge of the deck. He could feel Ryan's presence close behind him. "Well?" Ryan demanded.

Zayder thought he saw a huge gray shadow in sinuous motion far below. *Come on, Tiburon. You vicious old bastard.*

The shadow turned, circled, then began driving towards the surface. Zayder looked up to see Ryan staring at the charging shark. "He's the last of his species," Zayder said. "And he tends to hold a grudge."

Ryan raised the harpoon; took aim. The bodyguards moved up beside him, edging close to the deck, even leaning over, so they could see the action. The shadow of the shark seemed to grow enormously large as it approached. Sweat appeared on Ryan's cheeks. "*It's not slowing down!*" he hissed.

Zayder readied himself. As Tiburon burst from the water, Zayder dove diagonally across the deck—and collided with Ryan! Ryan blocked his way—and he'd failed to fire the harpoon. Instead, he'd thrown himself back, rolling to safety across the deck as the shark crashed onto the black surface of the photovoltaic cells. Zayder scrambled to escape Tiburon's snapping jaws. But the shark was faster. He felt the huge triangular teeth rake furrows in his leg. He screamed and clawed at the deck, slithering away. Twisting around, he looked back in time to see the thrashing shark snap at one of the bodyguards. It took the stunned man in its massive jaws and bit down. The man never even screamed as his spine was snapped. Then the shark shook its massive head. Blood flew as it dropped its victim. It turned to the second bodyguard and lunged, snapping once, twice as the screaming man scrabbled across a deck that was suddenly slick with blood. Tiburon's maw closed on the man's leg, taking it off just above the knee.

Then, as if he'd collected his due, the shark slipped quietly back into the water.

Zayder found himself on hands and knees in the center of the blood-washed deck. The wounded man was screaming. The bleeding corpse shuddered on the deck. His own leg felt as if fiery brands were burning into his flesh. He choked on the pain.

Suddenly, the bolt of the harpoon was thrust in his face. He stared at the double image of the steel point as it hovered, out of focus, scant centimeters from his eyes. He looked past the point to see Ryan standing over him, face flushed with fury.

"Where is Commarin?" Ryan shouted. "Where is he?"

"Tiburon," Zayder gasped. "I told you—"

"No more lies! That shark has not fed. Where is he? Where is Commarin? Tell me now, or you'll die. Tell me, because I'm going to find him anyway."

The screams of the wounded man were growing feebler. He was bleeding to death while his boss continued to pursue the quarry.

In the pen, the waters were no longer calm. Sharks were gathering, drawn by the huge quantities of blood draining into the water. Zayder glanced at the frothing, whirling maelstrom of fins, knowing his own death would lie there if he gave into Ryan.

Tiburon had never given in. Not even after his fins had been cut off five times, five times regrown in the coursing waters of the recovery channels. He'd just gotten bigger and meaner; faster, stronger. Maybe soon, he'd be able to jump over the deck to freedom.

All this passed through his mind in the space of a trembling breath. And then he made his decision. "Fuck you, Ryan," he muttered.

Ducking quickly, he rolled off the deck. He heard Ryan scream at him, but the sound was cut off by the water as he plunged into the pen, just on the edge of the frenzy.

Zayder opened his eyes to the brine. He saw dark shadows dart toward him. The water was murky with blood. He stretched out his body and reached for the mesh of the shark pen's wall. He kicked. Harsh skin scraped his ribs as a shark brushed against him. He kicked harder. His fingers found the mesh. A gray shape loomed out of the froth and murk. Maw open, teeth bared, it bore down on him. He jammed his head through the mesh; wriggled to get his shoulders through. The shark turned and darted away, its dentate skin scraping his thigh as he pulled himself all the way through.

He surfaced under the deck, gasping for air. His eyes were closed in a grimace of pain as he fought the urge to scream. Ryan was on the deck, just above. But there was so much blood in the water! Ryan would have to believe he was dead. He would have to.

"*Zayder!*" a voice hissed, not an arm's length from his ear.

He jumped in shock. His eyes flew open to see Commarin adrift in the water beside him, still wearing the diving gear, his bandaged hands awkward as he paddled to stay afloat.

A wave of dizziness swept over him. He could sense blood from the wound in his leg pumping into the ocean. He could still feel the frantic thrashings of the frenzy in the currents driven through the mesh. His trembling hands stroked the water. "Ryan knows you're here," he whispered to Commarin. "His goons are dead. But he's the worst of them."

He reached into his pocket to remove the transponder. Sinking deeper into the water, he thrust it at Commarin. "Take this," he hissed. "Make your way around the pen until you find a garbage trawler in port. Check the ready lights on the berth. Find one that's nearly charged. Use your knife to remove the tentacles, then tie yourself to it. It'll take you a hundred klicks out by morning if it senses no weight on its limbs. Your friends will be able to retrieve you safely."

"You're coming too," Commarin said anxiously.

Zayder's lip curled in anger. "Don't think so, Commarin. Tiburon nicked my leg. Blood's still flowing. I've got to get out of the water."

"But Ryan's there."

"I've dealt with sharks before. Now go. Go! Get out of here. I want to see Ryan lose for a change."

But Commarin shook his head. "Not a chance. I got you into this mess. I'm not going to abandon you now. Look, if we can get to that helicopter, we can both get out of here."

"I don't know how to fly a helicopter."

"I do."

Staying under the deck, they moved around the perimeter of the shark pen toward the shed and the moored helicopter. A long gray shadow dogged them on the other side of the mesh: Tiburon. Coursing back and forth, back and forth, the shark's ceaseless motion focused on their slow progress.

They reached the shed without incident. The helicopter bobbed on the light swell only a few meters away. There was no sign of Ryan.

"He was uninjured," Zayder hissed. "He'll have called for reinforcements by now."

The light tread of a foot overhead alerted them. The shark swam past, turned, swam past again.

"Commarin!" Ryan's voice boomed over the hiss/roar of the swell rising and falling against the mesh. "I know where you are, Commarin. Your toothy escort is less shy about showing himself than you are. Come out, Commarin. There's little to fear. You know I'm a practical man."

To Zayder the words seemed amplified, reverberating under the deck. The voice might have been that of the shark, a dual entity, inescapable in its reach. He leaned back in the water, conscious of a soft roar in his ears that was the helpless static of oxygen-starved nerves. Some part of him knew he was bleeding to death. Salt water splashed into his mouth. He started to choke. He reached for the mesh to keep from sinking, but suddenly Commarin was there, buoying him up with bandaged hands, hissing something about Tiburon. And then: "We have to try to swim underwater to the other side of the helicopter."

Zayder shook his head, fumbling to find the words to express his fears. "No good!" he whispered. "Ryan's armed. Even if you managed to take off, Ryan could still bring you down. Have to get rid of Ryan first."

But how? His mind seemed to be bobbing about on the surface of a swell. He had trouble focusing on a single train of thought.

He felt as if the trailing tentacles of a garbage trawler had become tangled in his brain, each tentacle pulling the neural tissue in a different direction.

One tentacle, one direction. Garbage in, garbage out. He twisted around in Commarin's arms. "A garbage trawler brought you in."

Commarin nodded slowly.

"Find one that's charged and ready."

"No. I told you I won't leave without you."

Ryan's voice boomed again from overhead. "Commarin, Commarin, why so stubborn? When are you going to realize that hiding under the deck is no solution?"

"Not you," Zayder whispered. His gaze wandered to the deck overhead. "I was thinking this time we could go trawling for sharks."

Commarin frowned, but he helped Zayder swim to the nearest trawler's berth. Zayder glanced at the maintenance panel. It indicated the unit was charged and ready to go, awaiting only its turn in the schedule. Tiburon slipped past inside the pen. Zayder was peripherally aware of the wake of the great fish as he lifted his hand to touch the panel. "You want to send it early," he told Commarin, his voice barely audible, even in his own ears. "You press this. But first we take off the tentacles, all but one."

It was an easy operation. The snap-in modules popped out, until only one was left. "Unwind it a bit," Zayder said, clinging to the trawler's housing. "It won't stick to your skin; only to your clothes." Ducking underwater, he struggled out of his company t-shirt, then resurfaced. He took the end of the tentacle in his bare hands. It felt smooth and soft and only mildly sticky. "When I hit the deck," he said, "you launch the trawler."

"Zayder—"

Zayder grabbed the maintenance ladder and started climbing, his steps deliberately loud against the peaceful mutter of the ocean. His head crested the deck, and he saw Ryan.

Ryan looked surprised to see him. He brought up the muzzle of his weapon. "I thought you'd be shark food by now."

"Commarin's hurt," Zayder croaked. "Help haul him up. Can't do it myself. Injured . . ."

Ryan crept forward cautiously. A meter and a half away, he leaned over the edge of the deck, as if to check whether Commarin really was clinging to the ladder. Zayder judged it his best moment.

He launched himself onto the deck, hitting it belly first and sliding toward the startled Ryan with the tentacle held in his outstretched hands. It wouldn't cling to living flesh. But it would happily wrap around Ryan's clothed leg.

Zayder threw it against him as he slid past. Ryan dropped the gun. He bent down, his bare fingers tearing at the tentacle. "*Now, Commarin!*" Zayder screamed.

But Commarin had already launched the garbage trawler. Zayder saw the finned torpedo from the corner of his eye, speeding out to sea. Ryan saw it too; saw the connection that bound him to it. He gave one hard yank on the tentacle as a snarl escaped his lips, and then the craft yanked him into the water. Zayder watched him go: dark, fishy figure in a white, foaming wake.

The garbage trawler would stay out until it had accumulated its weight capacity or until thirty days had passed, whichever came first. Given that it had only one tentacle to gather trash from the water, Zayder knew that it would not return in Ryan's lifetime. He closed his eyes, and laid back against the deck.

It was the roar of the helicopter that roused him. He awoke to find himself strapped into the passenger seat as the craft slowly lifted into the air. Looking down through the open doorway, he could see the shed, the recovery chutes, the black photovoltaic panels that defined the pen, the sinuous bodies of the collection of captive sharks. He thought he could pick out Tiburon among them. He'd taken the great white's fins five times, and every time, he'd forced them to regrow.

He turned quickly to Commarin. "Go back," he croaked. "Go back a moment."

"There's no time! Ryan's people will be here—"

"There," Zayder said, pointing to the shattered section of deck where Tiburon had lunged at him only that morning. The bodies of Ryan's men weren't far away. "Please, Commarin."

Reluctantly, Commarin set the craft down in the water just outside the pen. "What are you going to—"

Zayder unlatched his shoulder belt and stepped out into the water.

"Zayder, wait!"

With Commarin yelling at his back, he stroked to the nearest trawler's berth. It was the machine that had brought Commarin in; nearly half charged now. Half would be enough. Zayder seized one of the tentacles, pulled it out of the module, and dragged it to the mesh. Tiburon cruised into sight. Zayder laughed bitterly. "Looking for another taste of me, you old bastard?" He waited for the shark to pass, then wrapped the tentacle around the mesh and watched it take hold. Then he went back to the trawler and activated it.

It hummed softly for a moment, then sped out of its housing, the tentacle paying out behind it. Zayder ducked under the tentacle and stroked back to the idling helicopter as quickly as he could. Commarin helped him climb aboard. "What the hell are you doing?" he demanded, as Zayder collapsed into the seat.

"Just get us out of here, quick," Zayder muttered.

The tentacle had already payed out to its maximum reach. Zayder could see the mesh bowing outward under the strain. "Hit it, Tiburon," he muttered. "Hit it hard."

The shark seemed to hear him. Or perhaps its carefully cultured fury alone led it to attack the mesh. But as the helicopter lifted, Zayder saw the long gray shadow charge the wall of the pen.

The impact caused the deck to visibly shudder. The cracked photovoltaic panel split fully in two. The trawler lurched forward, submerged for a moment, then bobbed to the surface again as the tentacle snapped.

Zayder screamed in fury! The pen had held, and the sharks were still trapped in the artificial confines of a tiny, protected ocean. The helicopter lifted higher into the afternoon. The dark shapes of the great fish swam in their ancient, enduring journey, round and round the closed walls of their sanctuary. All but one.

Zayder saw it as Commarin banked the helicopter. The afternoon sun blazed on the blue water, but beneath the brilliant play of light, an anomalous patch of night sped into the open ocean. He saw it for a second, maybe two, and then the fish sought deeper waters, its sinister shape disappearing into the blue.

"It's a man eater," Commarin said. "It killed two men."

"It's part of this world."

Commarin shook his head. "It's part of the past. It'll be hunted down."

"I know." And when Tiburon was finally taken by hook or net, the species would be extinct. No sanctuary or reserve could change that.

Had the notion of sanctuary always been illusory?

His leg throbbed where the shark's teeth had raked him. "I'm going back to the fishing boats," he said.

Commarin looked startled. "No. You're a trained scientist. Come with me. There'll be a place for you—"

But Zayder wasn't listening. In his mind he followed Tiburon through the deep, as a fisherman would, a hunter: the original students of the natural world.

He followed the great shark all the way back to his own fading origins. There were no sanctuaries in the open ocean—not for pelagic sharks or for deep-water fishermen. There never could be. But he would go back. He would fish, until that life was finally, fully played out on the open sea.

Hooks, Nets, and Time is a novelette originally published in The Magazine of Fantasy & Science Fiction, in August 1997.

The Flood

Mike lay awake in the night on a bed of damp leaves in the towering shelter of a eucalyptus grove, listening to the pounding surf. His young wife Holly slept on the ground beside him, clutching their thin blanket to her chin, her legs half-tangled with his. He rested his hand lightly on her rib cage, feeling her breathe.

Nights were the worst. At night he couldn't see the waters coming. So he listened to the surf, trying to measure the volume of the ocean by the sound. He'd seen the ocean rise as much as thirty meters in a night. Rising. Never receding.

Fear slipped like oil across his skin—cold, encompassing fear. Through his mind's eye he watched Holly drowning, her face pale and exhausted as she finally slipped beneath the relentless waters. Still, that sort of death was ancient and familiar.

God, God, God.

Sudden sweat coated his body despite the chill of the night. His stomach seemed to fold into a fist. This, he thought, would be a good time to recall some profound and comforting passage from the Bible. But he didn't know any. Religion had never been his thing.

Still, God was ever in his thoughts these days, as he watched the world drown.

How could He let this happen?

Mike did not believe in the beneficence of God. He was not even sure he believed in the deity Himself. And alone amongst the survivors, he refused to accept that the end of the world might be a good thing.

Sometime before dawn the rising waters must have claimed a gentler shoreline, because the noise of the surf subsided. Mike slept then, waking only when the sun was well up. He cuddled against Holly on their bed of leaves, gazing downslope at the ocean. He could see it just beyond the grove of trees. Its surface was glassy in the crisp, still air of morning, the waters pale green over a pasture that had flooded in the night. Gentle swells rolled in from the deep to sweep upslope through the eucalyptus grove in flat hissing crescents.

Mike watched them in a half-conscious state, pleasantly distanced from both his worrisome dreams and untenable reality, until a slight breeze rustled through the tree tops, reminding him that he still needed to devise a sail for his newly finished boat.

Holly stirred sleepily. He bent over her, gently brushing aside her long dark hair to kiss her cheek, feeling yet again the sour clench of fear. He would not let her be taken. He could not. It would be better to drown. But better still to steal her away on his boat. Soon. Maybe even today.

She blinked and stretched, then smiled at him, a serene joy glowing in her dark eyes. "Mike. Do you feel it, Mike? It's very close now."

"We don't have any food left," he told her.

She shrugged, sitting up, her long tanned legs goose-bumped in the morning chill. "We don't need any food. Today will be the last day. I can feel it."

As if to emphasize her words another wave slid up through the grove to swish against her feet, laying down a crescent of sand before subsiding. Mike found himself staring at the dread signature. In the weeks since the flood began, he'd watched the sand and waves take over roads, houses, forests, pastures, farms, as the ocean steadily rose, drowning the island that had always been their home. They'd retreated upslope as the waters advanced, but the highest point on the island had been only five hundred meters above sea level—

Mike squinted down at the new shoreline. Now, he guessed the highest point might clear thirty meters. He frowned, trying to recall the exact geography of the island before the flood. Hadn't the meadow where he'd built his boat been *more* than thirty meters below the summit?

"The ark!" he yelped, leaping to his feet. "Holly . . . " He grabbed her hand and yanked her up. The roar of the night's surf resounded in his mind. His boat had been well above the waterline at nightfall, but now—

He ran through the grove, dragging Holly with him. He was afraid to leave her alone, afraid she would disappear like so many others.

"Mike," she panted, bounding along in his rough wake. "It's all right, Mike. You don't need the boat. Everything will be all right."

But he couldn't believe her. He'd never been able to believe.

They splashed through a retreating wave, through rotten leaves half-buried in sand. Their feet sank deep into the unstable mix. Tiny air bubbles erupted on the forming beach. Then they reached the edge of the grove and burst into the open.

Sunlight sparkled on green water. Children frolicked in the swell, riding the shore break at the edge of the insatiable ocean.

Finally letting go of Holly's hand, Mike scrambled up a scrub-covered ridge of ancient lava. By the time he reached the top, the cool air was tearing in and out of his lungs. He stood on the crest and looked down at his project.

Yesterday evening, the boat had rested solidly on its platform, fifteen meters above the waterline and nearly completed, a tiny ark made of green eucalyptus wood. But the surf had seized it in the night, throwing it against the jagged lava of the ridge. The shattered pieces bobbed and tumbled with the incoming waves.

Holly joined him, her breast heaving with exertion beneath the scanty coverage of her tank top. She glanced at the wreckage, hardly seeing it. "Come and swim, Mike," she pleaded. Her eyes were wide and soft. "The water's warm. The waves aren't big. It's a perfect day. A gift from God."

On the summit of the island a huge white wooden cross glowed in the morning light, a memory of earlier days.

Most of the people who'd lived on the island before the flood had already been taken away. There were only forty or fifty left, waiting patiently for their turn on the ropes.

Mike tore his gaze away from the shattered boat, and rounded on Holly. "Wake up!" he shouted. "Wake up. You've been walking around in a daze for weeks. You and everyone else while an act of genocide has been going on around you. We're dying, Holly. Family by family, your god is killing us."

Holly's gaze seemed suddenly weighted in concern. She raised her hand to brush Mike's wild hair away from his face, off his ears, as if by that simple measure she hoped to change a basic deficiency in his vision, in his hearing.

Mike knocked her hand away. "I'm not deaf and I'm not blind!" he shouted. "I can see what's going on—"

"But you can't feel it," she said softly.

"No. No you're right. I can't feel it. I can't." His hands clenched into fists. He closed his eyes as anguish flooded his mind. "Why me, Holly? Why am I the only one who can't *believe*—"

A far-away rumble cut off his lament. The sound resembled the thunder of a distant jet, summoning a memory of childhood when he'd lain awake at night listening to the passage of an anomalous craft far overhead, imagining that what he heard was no commercial airliner on an unusual route; that instead the nightfarer was a B-52, armed with nuclear missiles bound for a hardened target in Siberia. The overflight that presaged the end of the world.

His childhood fears had faded with the cold war, had dulled with maturity. Now they were back, haunting him, as the end of the world loomed in unexpected reality.

He looked out across the ocean, where he counted three twisting wires of brilliant golden light. They were thin, like cracks in the sky letting in the light of heaven. But vast, appearing to extend far beyond the brilliant blue bowl of the sky, disappearing into some nebulous distance that seemed somehow utterly different from the sky Mike had known all his life. Light bleeding from some other place. Some other world. Hungry light, that preyed on hope and faith.

The distant jet-roar faded to silence as the wires of light approached across the water. They swayed as they moved, not behaving at all like ordinary light, but instead bending and floating like extremely low-density matter. Once again, Mike felt himself astounded at their thinness. The first one swept across the shallows toward the children playing in the waves. At this distance it was easy to see that it was no thicker than the mooring lines once used to tie cruise ships to the docks.

The children had spotted the rope. Their joyous cries could be heard from the ridge as they scrambled and dove toward the light. Mike wanted to scream at them to stop, to run away. But they *believed* . . . .

A young girl just short of puberty reached the rope first. She grabbed it with her right hand and was immediately yanked off her feet. She rose skyward. At the same time she seemed to shrink so that she was drawn *into* the column of light. Mike watched as she became a tiny silhouette within the golden glow, a dark figure receding at fabulous speed across a vast dimension that did not exist in this world. He watched until she became a black point on the visual horizon. And then he watched her disappear.

Other children followed her, six, then seven of them before the rope left the now-empty water and swept ashore, zig-zagging across the newly-laid beach as it offered itself to the eager, waiting parents.

Mike fell to his knees, sickened. He bent over, holding his stomach. He wanted to puke. Holly crouched beside him. "It's all right, Mike," she soothed. "It's all right. God has come for us. You don't have to be afraid."

Her words made his hackles rise. Was a rope finally out to lure the two of them? After weeks of watching everyone they'd ever known disappear up the ropes, was this their time? His fingers clawed at the ground. Why couldn't he feel the grace the others felt? Why couldn't he *believe*?

A deep electric hum assaulted his ears. He felt his hair lift slightly, as if a field of static electricity had suddenly swept around him. Looking up, he saw a second golden rope racing in from the ocean towards the ridge. "*No!*" he shouted.

He dove at Holly, knocking her to the ground. He held her there with his weight, pinning her arms against her sides. "I won't let you go to it!" he screamed at her. "I won't let you go."

The rope was dancing, swaying up the jagged slope of the ridge. Holly's eyes filled with tears. A trace of blood netted her lip. Her jaw trembled. "Please Mike. Let me go. It's my time. It's our time. I don't know why you can't feel it. But I do know you love me. You have to trust me. You have to let me believe for you—"

He kissed her to stop the flow of words. His lips pressed against hers, his tongue probed her mouth, he tasted the sweet salt of her blood. It crossed the membranes of his mouth like a drug. Her love flowed into him, her trust, her faith. He felt a warm, golden glow fill him. He let go of her arms, to cradle her beautiful face in his hands. And then they were sitting up, spooning, her arms tight around the small of his back. And somehow after that he found himself on his feet. She stood facing him, holding both his hands. A column of gold rose behind her. Her warm dark eyes were locked on his. She nodded encouragement. Moving backward, she led him first one step, then another. Letting his left hand go, she half-turned to seize the rope. "*Faith,*" she whispered.

Her body arched in sudden ecstasy as she was yanked up the rope. The gasp that escaped her lips was a knife that cut through Mike's consciousness. He stiffened, as a dirty old awareness flooded his mind. "Holly, no!" he roared.

She was receding up the rope, her right side shrinking, darkening into a silhouette as she was swept into the narrow chasm of golden light, her left side yet in the flooded world. "*Holly!*"

He found that he still held her left hand. Now he seized it with both his hands and pulled. Her body continued to shrink, to recede into impossible distance. Her arm stretched in a long black ribbon. Then her hand turned palm up in his grip, and vanished. He found himself grasping at empty air.

A scream of utter rage ripped from his throat. Tears flooded his face.

The golden light hummed and shifted, awaiting him.

"*Not me,*" he choked. "I won't go with you. Murderer! Murderer!" He turned and fled into the forest.

The island was empty, all the people finally gone.

Mike climbed the hill and sat at the base of the cross. Cool air washed over his face, while scudding clouds played with the sun's light. The remaining land mass was no more than a quarter mile across now. Uninterrupted ocean surrounded him on all sides, the water appearing to rise up like a shallow bowl, with himself trapped in the bottom. How high would the waters rise? High enough to drown even continental mountains?

There is not that much water in the world!

Movement caught his eye. A sparkle of white against the cloud-shadowed sea. A bird, he realized. And as it drew nearer he recognized the wandering albatross, gliding on its white wings just above the crest of the swell. A solitary creature.

He watched it in gratitude, and not a little wonder, realizing only then how much he'd missed the non-human life of the island. For the cats and dogs, birds, and cattle had disappeared with their masters. Even the fish had vanished from the ocean. He wondered if this bird could be as hungry as he.

It stayed with him, flying a restless circuit around the shrinking island as the flood waters continued to rise. By noon, when hunger and thirst and utter isolation began to play upon his mind, it became the focus of his delirium. He found himself flying on long wings around and around the white wooden cross as if he flew on the end of a chain. He wanted to turn tail to it. He wanted to glide across the open ocean into the blue promise of homogenous vistas: *just a little farther now, and you will find land, life*.

But the bird refused to leave.

The afternoon passed. Mike felt his skin burn in the intermittent sun. Thirst seemed to swell his tongue into a dry, dusty sponge. Hunger knotted his belly. He watched the waves roll in, from all sides now, higher and higher until by late afternoon they met at the bottom of the cross.

He climbed the monument to escape the churning tumult of water that consumed the last bit of land. He hauled himself up on the crossbar, then hugged the post while the waters roiled below him, slowly yet inevitability rising. Soon he would drown. Were there fish left in the water to eat him? Were there still microbes that might break down his flesh? Perhaps he would sink to the bottom and become covered with sediment and be converted to a fossil, the only evidence left of the original animal life of this world. For he sensed that the world was being cleansed, prepared for an entirely separate history to follow.

Tears filled his eyes as he looked out across the watery wasteland. He couldn't imagine worshipping any deity capable of creating this murderous scene.

All Gone.

The vast and empty ocean seemed to resound with that statement of finality.

All Gone.

When the last creatures were flushed out by the flood, the world would be clean, ready to be remade, renewed.

Mike held on. By evening the ocean was nearly calm. The golden colors of sunset played across the uninterrupted horizon. He gazed at the sight, feeling the burnished colors enter his soul and warm him. Last day.

He started, as the albatross swept past. It had been drawing nearer all day, perhaps emboldened by the retreat of the land. Now it floated by, scarcely an arm's length away, the wind abuzz in its feathers, a slight noise that seemed to grow in volume as the bird receded until the buzz became the ominous rumble of distant thunder, distant jets.

Mike looked up, to see a golden rope dancing on the horizon. A single rope. It was the first time he'd ever seen just one. His heart began to hammer as the old fury returned. He clung to the cross and screamed at the usurper, his voice rolling across the calm waters. "*Liar! Murderer!*"

A cold swell rose up to touch his dangling feet, bringing with it a sudden darkness. Fury flowed away, leaving behind the painful vacuum of despair. He bowed his head against the post and cried until the thunder faded and the hum of the rope filled his ears, until the deceiver's golden glow burned through his closed eyes.

He still didn't believe in the beneficence of God. He knew the flood was an act of genocide and the rope was a con game. Knew it by the anguish in his soul. But it didn't matter anymore. He was human, and he must follow his people, be it to hell or oblivion. He opened his eyes. The rope danced before him, an inexplicable gold cable let down at the end of the world. The albatross floated on a breeze, seemingly watching, waiting for his lead.

He grasped the rope in both hands, and was gone.

The Flood was first published in More Amazing Stories, edited by Kim Mohan and published by Tor Books in Feb. 1998.

Goddesses

(i)

In the birthing room of a tiny clinic, in a town in Southern India, holding the hand of another man's wife, Michael Fielding felt chaos rise quietly through the world. Like the gentle flood of an untamed river, it seeped into his life, dissolving the past, laying down the mud that would grow the future.

Jaya's hand tightened on his. Her lips parted, ruby-red jewels set against her cream-coffee skin, their color that of a tailored strain of bacteria cohabiting in her cells.

"Another's starting," she whispered. Exhaustion feathered her words. "Michael . . . all the old women lied . . . when they promised it would be easier . . . the second time."

"You're almost there," he assured her. "You're doing terrific."

Sheo's voice backed him up, speaking from the beige picture-frame of the open portal, sitting on the rickety metal table at the head of the bed. It was a voice-only connection, so the portal's screen displayed a generic sequence of abstract art. "Michael's right, my love. You are wonderful."

"Sheo?" Jaya's dark eyes opened. She turned toward Michael, but she wasn't looking at him. Instead, her gaze fixed on the lens of his net visor that concealed his eyes like gray sunglasses. She seemed to search the shades for some trace of her husband. Her expression was captured by tiny cameras on the shades' frame. Processors translated her image to digital code, then shunted it to Sheo's mobile address, across town or across the continent—Michael had lost track of how far Sheo had progressed in his frantic journey to meet his wife.

Jaya should have been home in Bangalore, enjoying the services of the finest hospital in the country. She did not belong in this primitive clinic, where the obstetrician was a face on a monitor, checking on her through a stereoscopic camera that pointed between her legs.

Of course it was Michael's fault. He'd been in-country two weeks, the new district director for Global Shear. It was an assignment he'd coveted, but with only five days notice before his transfer from the Hong Kong office, he had not been ready for it.

Jaya took pity on him. Claiming her maternity leave might otherwise end in terminal boredom, she took a train to Four Villages, to help Michael find his way through barriers of language and local custom.

He and Jaya had both interned at Global Shear, members of a five person training team so cohesive that, ten years after the course work ended, four of them still met almost daily on a virtual terrace to exchange the news of their private lives and their careers. When Jaya stepped off the train to embrace Michael on the dusty platform, it was the first time they had ever met in real space . . . and it hadn't mattered. If they had grown up in the same house, Michael could not have felt any closer to her.

Now the baby was coming three weeks early.

Everything happened so much faster these days.

Sheo's voice crooned through the portal speaker, calm as a holy man preaching peace and brotherhood. "You're strong and you're beautiful, Jaya. And you've done this before. Our beautiful Gita—"

Fury heated Jaya's black eyes. "That was six years ago! Now I am old! And you're not here."

"I've got a zip," he explained quickly. "I'm leaving the airport now. I'll be there in just a few more minutes."

"He'll be here," Michael whispered, fervently hoping it was true. With a white cotton cloth, he daubed at the sweat gleaming on Jaya's forehead and cheeks. The clinic's air-conditioning had been shut off at midnight. It would not be restored until after dawn, when the sun rose high enough to activate the rooftop solar tiles. Windows had been thrown open to the night. In the distance, a train murmured, base whispers interrupted by rhythmic thumps, that went on and on and on until Michael felt the train must surely run all the way to Bangalore.

Jaya's eyes closed. The muscles in her face emerged in severe outline as the contraction climaxed. Michael dipped the cloth in a bowl of water and wiped at her forehead, until she growled at him to leave her alone.

Down between her legs, the midwife, who spoke excellent English, sighed happily. "Ah, he's almost here. Gently now, lady. Push gently, so he doesn't tear you."

"Where are you, Sheo?" Jaya cried. "It's happening *now*."

"I'm here!" The calmness in Sheo's voice had cracked. "I'm outside."

A scree of dirty brakes and the growl of wet pavement under tires testified to the arrival of his zip. "Get your ass in here, Sheo," Michael growled.

Jaya gasped. From the foot of the bed, the midwife cried, "Here is the head! He's here . . . just a little more, a little more . . . there!"

And Jaya's breath blew out in a long, crying exhalation. "There my lady, now only his body to come, easy, easy."

Sheo stumbled past the curtain, struggling to pull an old set of surgical scrubs over his beige business shirt. A nurse followed after him, her face stern as she fought to grab the gown's dangling ties.

Sheo still wore his own shades, and as he cried out Jaya's name a whistle of feedback snapped out of the portal on the bedside table. Michael leaned over and slapped the thing off.

Then the baby was there. The midwife had the child in her hands, but as she gazed at it, her happy expression drained away. Her mouth shrank to a pucker. Her eyes seemed to recede within a mantle of soft, aging flesh. The stern nurse saw the change. She leaned past the midwife's shoulder to look at the child, and her eyes went wide with an ugly surprise.

For a dreadful moment Michael was sure the baby was dead. Then he heard the tiny red thing whimper. He saw its arm move, its little fingers clench in a fierce fist. Was it deformed then? Impossible. Jaya had employed the best obstetric care. If there had been a problem, she would have known.

Sheo crouched at Jaya's side. He whispered to her, he kissed her face. Neither of them had noticed the midwife and her distress, and for that Michael felt thankful. But he had to see the baby.

At his approach, the midwife looked up warily. She pulled the baby close to her breast as if to hide whatever damning evidence she had seen.

"No," Michael said. "Let me see."

She seemed ready to resist, but then she sighed, and held the child out.

The little girl was a mess. White goop filled a sea of wrinkles. There were downy patches of dark hair on her shoulders, and her face was flushed red. Michael grinned. A typical newborn. He turned to Jaya. "She's beautiful. A beautiful little girl."

The doctor on the monitor agreed, and still Michael felt as if a shadow had swum sinuous through this night, drawing all of them a little deeper into the haunted past.

Michael had been warned about the strangeness of this place.

It was not quite three weeks since the wall screen in his Hong Kong office had opened on an image of Karen Hampton, smiling slyly from behind her desk, with the Singapore skyline visible through the window at her back.

She'd asked if he still had a taste for challenges, and he'd risen like a shark on blood scent.

Karen Hampton was in her sixties, and Michael could only think of her as *classy*. Her skin was fair, her features petite, her manner of dress stiff-Gotham-upper-crust, but when she laughed, Karen Hampton sounded like a trucker bellied up to a bar. She was laughing now. "That's my Michael! Still hungry." Then her face grew stern. No longer the sympathetic mentor shepherding his career, she transformed into the unflappable director of Global Shear Asia. "I want you to be the next site director at Four Villages."

He could not believe what he was hearing. "Karen! Hell yes. You know I've wanted this from the concept stage."

Her gaze didn't soften. "I know, but nevertheless, I'm advising you to think hard about it, Michael. This is not so much a favor, as a chance to ruin your career."

Four Villages was a quiet experiment that could change the path of development in impoverished regions throughout the world. Global Shear had won a ten year contract as civil administrator in the district—and not as a glorified cooperative extension service. They had been hired to overhaul a failed bureaucracy, and to that end, many traditional government functions, from real property inventories to taxation, had been placed in the corporation's hands.

"You aren't going to show a positive balance sheet for at least five years," Karen warned him. "Maybe longer. We have been hired to grow an economy. Within ten years, we must develop four essential aspects of a sustainable trade system: infrastructure, information, financing, and trust. I put trust last, not because it is the least important, but because it is the most important. Only when trust is firmly established, and our presence here welcomed by a majority of residents, will we begin to see a profit."

Global Shear's contract would be financed partly through the World Bank, but primarily through a carefully defined flat tax, so that the corporation's income would rise with economic activity. In a region of sixteen million people, the profit potential was enormous. So were the challenges, of course, but if the job was easy, it would have already been done.

"We will be wrecking traditional relationships between farmers, landlords, and business people," Karen warned. "We will be stumbling through issues of religion, caste, and gender. We will be accused of corrupting traditional culture and it will be true. To many, we will be the enemy. But at the same time, if we deal honestly and enthusiastically with everyone, self-interest will convince the majority that we are performing a right and proper job. The poor are the majority here, Michael. Your goal is to change that fact. Your biggest challenge will be your own preconceptions.

"You've worked in Sarajevo, Kurdistan, Rangoon, Hong Kong, but nothing you've experienced will leave you feeling as displaced as you will feel after a few weeks in Four Villages. This project is not about New Delhi. It's definitely not about Bangalore. It's not about the educated, westernized Indians you have worked with in our offices around the world. It's different. Remember that, and you might make it through your first month. It's also utterly human. Remember that as well, and you might outlast your predecessor, who succumbed to culture shock in less than a year."

Karen had warned him, and after two weeks in-country, Michael knew she hadn't exaggerated. If not for Jaya he might have been lost, but even Jaya was a foreigner here. How many evenings had they spent in despairing laughter, trying to decode the bizarre demands of a merchant or a farmer or a local police officer? Or the medical staff in a rural hospital?

In the clinic's dimly-lit hallway, Michael met the stern-faced nurse, pulling fresh sheets from a closet. He approached her, driven by a need to understand. "Why did you look that way, when you saw Jaya's baby? As if something about her frightened you?"

The nurse's face was hard, like well-aged wax. "I don't know what you mean, Mr. Fielding. It's as you said, a beautiful baby girl."

"Please." Michael moved half a step closer. At six foot one, he towered over the nurse. On some level he knew he was using his height to bully her, but he had never had it in him to look away from a bad situation. "You saw something. Please tell me what it was."

The moan of another woman's labor seeped from behind drawn curtains. Anger flashed in the nurse's eyes. "I saw that she is a girl."

"Of course she's a girl, but what's wrong with her?"

"That is enough." The nurse slipped past him with her burden of sheets.

"Wait," Michael pleaded. "I don't understand."

She looked back at him. Had her expression softened? "It is nothing, sir. Just a surprise. Mostly, these women have boys. When they have girls, it is usually a mistake."

"A mistake?"

"I am glad it's not a mistake this time."

Later, Michael walked the dim corridor with Sheo, while the nurses tended to Jaya and changed her gown. "They were shocked you had a daughter."

Sheo's lips pursed in a long sigh, while outside, rain pattered in peaceful rhythm. "The old ways are dying out, but change doesn't happen everywhere at once. This is my second daughter, and I would not wish it any different. But for a family living a traditional life, a daughter is not an asset. For the very poor, she can be a financial disaster. Illiterate, subservient, she is of little use. It will cost her family to raise her, train her, and then they will have to pay another family to take her in."

"The midwife said most ladies here have boys."

"Did she? Well. There is always talk."

"Infanticide?" The word softened, set against the rain.

"It starts much earlier, I think." Sheo shook his head. "But don't talk of these things now, Michael. Not on my daughter's birthday. She's beautiful, isn't she? As beautiful as her mother."

(ii)

One more battle nearly won.

Cody Graham leaned back in the shotgun seat of the two person ATV, tired but psyched following an afternoon spent roving the thriving grasslands of Project Site 270. "It feels so *good* to get out of the office!"

She glanced at Ben Whitman, hunched under his Green Stomp cap as he worked the ATV up the slope. The kid was smiling. Enough of a smile that Cody caught a flash of teeth. She congratulated herself. It was the most expressive response she'd managed to wring out of nineteen year old Ben. Not that he was unfriendly, or even shy. Just a bit reserved. Nervous maybe, in the presence of the big-shot boss.

"You've done a great job here," she added, as the ATV ploughed a path through waist-high grasses.

"You keep saying that."

"Oh, and you do a great self-check. Nice, clean toxin smears."

"Oh thanks. Clean pee. My specialty."

Cody laughed. For six months Ben had been Green Stomp's only full time employee at 270. Clean-up at the hazardous waste site was nearing completion. Staff activity had been reduced to a daily round of detailed soil assays, with the occasional application of a spray or injection of nutrient-fortified bacteria to areas where microbial activity had declined. The bacteria worked to break down toxic molecules into safe and simple carbon groups—food for less exotic microbes serving as natural decomposers within the soil. An inspection tour of 270 by the federal oversight officer was scheduled in three weeks, so Cody had set up a tour of her own in advance of that, to look for any outstanding problems. She hadn't found any. Green Stomp would close out 270 as a showcase project.

Ben's hands tightened on the wheel as the ATV bounced upslope to the project office: a green-gold, wind-engineered tent anchored to an elevated platform. The graceful tent was a huge step above the ugly mobile trailers Cody had used eleven years ago when she and her partners tackled their first bioremediation project. Using both natural and genetically-tailored soil bacteria, along with select plants, they had set out to clean a hazardous waste site contaminated with perchloroethylene.

PCE was a common—and carcinogenic—industrial chemical. For many years it was believed that no microbe could break it down to harmless components. Then in 1997, researchers unveiled a new bacterium, found in the sludge of an abandoned sewage plant, that could do just that. Genetic tailoring modified the strain to work in dryland environments, and since then, thousands of polluted sites had been restored.

"You know," Ben said, his voice strained and his knuckles showing white as he gripped the wheel, "when 270 closes down, I'm going to be out of a job."

Cody's smile broadened. "That's the second reason I came down here. I wanted to talk to you about that."

While Ben prepped his soil samples for mailing to Green Stomp's central lab, Cody laid claim to the administrator's office. With a cup of fresh coffee in hand, she leaned back in the chair, kicking her feet up on the empty desk top. The office looked out on the lush grassland of the project site. She could see the trail taken by the ATV, and—hazed by distance—she could just glimpse the glittering surface of the Missouri River through gaps in the broken levee.

Three years ago Project Site 270 had been farm country—prime farm country, at least when spring flooding was minimal and the levees held. In the spring of '09 the levees gave way. Floodwaters destroyed the freshly-planted crop, at the same time spreading sewage, spilled petroleum products and the hazardous waste from illegal dumping across the fertile land. It had happened many times before, but in '09 a new ingredient was added. Under the pressure of rust and water, several abandoned storage tanks cracked, leaking a grim cocktail of restricted pesticides into the muddy aftermath of the flood. The disaster went undiscovered for weeks, until wildlife started turning up dead.

Cody scowled as a doe emerged from a windbreak of poplars to the north. Animals were reservoirs of fat-soluble pesticides; the stuff concentrated in their tissues as they ate contaminated plants. Fences had been built to keep deer off the project site. Traps had been laid to contain smaller species that could not be fenced out. But no containment system was perfect. "Yo, Ben!" she called. "Looks like you've got a breach in the fence."

He appeared from the direction of the lunch room, a steaming cup of coffee in hand. "That doe again?"

"It's a doe."

He looked out the window. "I think she's getting in at the foot of the bluff by the river. I swear she hangs out there and waits until the motion sensors are switched off."

"Can you remove her today?"

"Sure. Before I go home."

Until the land was certified clean, Green Stomp's contract called for all large wildlife to be expelled.

Cody nodded at a chair on the other side of the desk. "Have a seat, Ben. We need to talk about your future."

"Then I've got one?"

He looked so anxious Cody had to smile. It was scary to be out of a job. Unemployment benefits didn't last long. No one starved, of course. You could crunch government crackers until the next millennium and never run short of nutrients thanks to the new mondo-wheats. But it wasn't fun. "Sit down," Cody urged again, and this time Ben sat, cradling his coffee cup in his hands, staring at the steam that curled up from its black surface.

"Your supervisor speaks highly of you," Cody said. "Six months working alone, and you haven't missed a day or screwed up a sample."

Ben looked up. He pushed his cap back on his head. "She said to talk to you about continuing with the company."

"Good advice. Are you willing to move?"

He frowned over that. Cody suspected he'd spent his whole life here, along the river. "Sure. I guess. Like to where?"

Cody looked up at the ceiling. She pursed her lips. "Say . . . to Belize? Or Sierra Leone. Maybe even Siberia?"

A look of despair came over Ben's face. Cody slipped her feet off the desk, immediately sorry. "I'm joking! We're just a little company, strictly North American. The biggest adventure you could expect is the wilds of Pennsylvania."

"I'll take it," Ben said, with painful solemnity. "I'm not the smartest guy around, but I know how to work. I don't get bored. I don't slack."

"I don't hire grunt labor," Cody told him, "for anything more than short term. You'd have to be willing to go back to school. If things work out, Green Stomp could eventually sponsor you for an online degree."

Again he stared at the steaming cup clenched in his white-knuckled hand. "I never did too good in school."

"Want to try again?"

He raised his eyes to look at her. She saw fear there, and hunger. A fierce hunger.

Say yes, she urged him silently.

Ben was a smart kid. That was easy to tell after working with him only one afternoon, but it was equally obvious someone had been carping in his ear all his life that he was basically a dumb shit who would never amount to anything. It was hard to counter that early life influence.

"How much school?" he asked.

Cody grinned wickedly. She had spent her own formative years in a private boarding school, as a charity case on a corporate scholarship, seeing her mother only on rare weekends. Those had been the hardest years of her life, but receiving the scholarship to attend Prescott Academy had also been her biggest break. She bore no sympathy for anyone out to shirk an education. "Oh, ten or fifteen years of college should do it for you, Ben."

His lips twitched in a ghost of a smile. "At entry-level wages?"

"Pay commensurate with experience. Say yes, Ben."

He nodded slowly. "Okay then. Yes."

Cody had made Green Stomp's reputation by tackling the toughest, dirtiest jobs she could find. The harder the challenge, the more she liked it. Kicking apart toxic "non-biodegradable" molecules was a physical thrill. In her mind, it was the same as kicking down the mental walls that fenced people in. Like the one that said kids from bad neighborhoods couldn't make it in life. *Kick*. Or the one that said technology must eventually lead to apocalypse, whether through war, engineered disease, over-population or pollution. *Kick*. Cody had seen a lot of tough problems, but she hadn't seen the end of the world yet. Look hard enough, and problems could provide their own solutions. Green Stomp already held several patents on specialized strains of bacteria recovered from heavily polluted sites.

Now she tapped her data glove, waking up the portal standing open on the desk. The collapsible monitor had a display the size of an eight by twelve inch piece of paper. It was a quarter inch thick, and when not in use, it could be folded into thirds and slipped into a brief case. Now it stood open, leaning back on a T-shaped foot. "Hark, link to Jobsite."

The portal opened a cellular connection to Cody's server. Seconds later the screen came to life with an image of Jobsite's bioremediation lobby.

Cody turned the portal around so Ben could see. "Green Stomp gets about a third of our projects through Global Shear. You've heard of them? No? A multinational. We sold them a twenty percent share of Green Stomp in exchange for expansion capital, so they like to drop business in our direction. Plus I interned there, and several execs know and love me." She grinned.

Ben's smile was fleeting as he puzzled over the lobby architecture.

"Anyway," Cody went on, "another third of our projects represent repeat business from satisfied clients. We're grateful for that of course, but let me tell you a secret. The most interesting jobs come off the public link. Go ahead. Scroll through the list. Check it out."

The portal was keyed to Cody's voice. It didn't know Ben, so instead of speaking to it, he leaned forward, tentatively pressing the manual keys on the frame. "Do you ever get scared?" he asked, as his gaze flicked over the listings. "Do you ever worry you'll poison yourself?"

Cody leaned back in her chair, feeling her chest pull tight. "It's something you always have to keep in mind."

In fact, she'd already poisoned herself. Somehow, early in her career, she'd screwed up and a toxin had gotten into her blood, into her flesh, into the growing embryo in her womb. She'd been so careful at home: no alcohol, no coffee, no soda, no drugs. It hadn't mattered. When the pregnancy was terminated, Cody felt a chip of her soul flushed out along with her daughter. "These things happen," the doctor had assured her, but Cody needed to know *why*. She went looking for a causative event—and she found it when a bioassay of her own liver tissue revealed PCP contamination—the prime pollutant on every job site she'd worked the previous two years.

"Didn't you say you grew up on the west coast?" Ben asked, his pale cheeks aglow in the portal's light. "A place called Victoria Glen?"

"Yes."

"Well, guess what? It's on the job list."

Cody turned the portal back around, and frowned.

(iii)

When Michael left the clinic, night still drowned the street, thick and warm, like the spirit of some tropical ocean, ghosting in the rain. Inside, Jaya was teaching her newborn to nurse, while Sheo arranged their journey home.

Michael paused on the clinic's veranda, listening to cocks crowing the unseen dawn, and the musical patter of rain.

A headlight cruised the street. It hesitated just before the clinic, then it slid into the pull-out. Diffuse light from the clinic windows glinted on the narrow, beetle-shell chassis of a zip, painted pink and looking hardly large enough to hold a man. Powered by hydrogen fuel cells, its engine ran silent, so that its arrival was marked only by tire noise. Rain dashed through the beam of its dim headlight. The aerodynamic canopy rose a few inches. A boy of perhaps twelve or thirteen years peeked out, fixing Michael with a hopeful look.

Michael shook his head slightly. He hated to disappoint such an intrepid entrepreneur, up so early to find the fares that would pay off the loan on his zip, but his feelings were running high and he couldn't think of squeezing himself into the zip's stuffy little shell.

The boy shrugged, closed the canopy, and pulled away.

A cow lowed, and a rat scurried across the street. Michael hesitated, reminded that he was a stranger in this place. Still, he was not alone. His right index finger curled, to tap a point on the palm of his data glove. A green ready light came on in the corner of his shades. "Send voice mail to the Terrace," he whispered. A mike on his earpiece picked up the command. "Start: Jaya and Sheo are the proud parents of a beautiful and impatient little girl . . ."

He found himself smiling as he described the birth for their circle of friends. Then he touched his gloved palm again, sending the message to the Terrace.

Warm rain enfolded him as he stepped off the veranda, soaking his hair and transforming his silk shirt into a transparent film. The silk was artificial, spun in a local factory financed by Global Shear. Other grants had gone out to farmers and small business owners all over the district, but could it ever be enough?

Jaya's daughter had been born into a world of nearly eight billion people. A billion of them lived in India alone. Michael tried to imagine the scale of it, but he could not. *We are a river, flooding the world.* Inevitably remaking it.

A glyph blinked on in the corner of his shades, surrounded by a pink query circle. Michael recognized the symbol of the Terrace and smiled. "Link."

"Michael!" Etsuko's soft, clipped English laughed in his ear. "I guess you are a surrogate father now!"

"That's right, old man," Ryan chipped in, his Australian voice loud and bold. "You do have some images for us? Flash them."

"Archived," Michael said. "Sorry. Sort it out later, okay?"

"First timer," Ryan chided.

Etsuko asked, "Where are you now?"

"Walking home."

"Walking?" she echoed. "Isn't that dangerous?"

"Ah," Ryan scoffed. "He's a company big wig now, with his own eye in the sky following after him."

Michael groaned. "I keep forgetting about that." Global Shear had assigned him a permanent guard in the form of a mini-drone aircraft with a wingspan the length of his arm. Powered by solar cells and a lightweight battery system that could get it through the night, it tracked his movements, ever-poised to raise an alarm should anything go wrong.

"We're bored in our little cubbies," Ryan said. "Give us the scene."

Bored? If Ryan got bored, it was only on weekends, before the Asian markets opened. During the rest of the week he traded currencies under contract for a large Australian firm.

Etsuko worked in the calmer environment of a California-based multinational specializing in online education. She staffed the East Asian shift, so her workday often began in the warm, hazy afternoons of Santa Barbara.

Michael's day ran well behind theirs—a fact Ryan tended to forget. He tapped his glove, activating the cameras on his shades. *Pan left to right*: one and two story stucco and plastic dwellings loomed out of the darkness, squeezing against the rain-splattered street. A bicycle trundled past, its rider hidden beneath an umbrella, two squawking chickens strapped to the handlebars. From a few blocks away, the screech of wet brakes.

The video feed uploaded over cellular links. On the Terrace, Ryan would seem to be sitting at a patio table in the shade of a pepper tree, sipping java in mild morning sunlight, fenced in by the dense foliage of a mature garden, or perhaps gazing out over a seascape with a hint of salt tang in the air. Whatever environment was running, half of it had now vanished, replaced by Michael's input.

"God!" Ryan said, and Michael could hear his feet hit the floor. "It's still night there—and it's pouring."

"It's grand, isn't it?" Michael asked. He slicked his hair back, tasting the water on his lips. Precious water, falling like a blessing timed by forgotten gods. Rain had been absent for the two weeks he'd been in-country. As his census teams inventoried the tiny farms surrounding Four Villages, they faced farmers more and more anxious over the success of this season's crop of rice or peanuts, and increasingly unwilling to speak to the officials responsible for confirming their landholdings and setting their taxes. "The rain will help," Michael said firmly. Rain would ease everyone's mood, and in the long run even the most recalcitrant farmers would see that their interests were the same as Global Shear's.

Right?

A stray breeze puffed from an alley, carrying the dilute but distinct scent of an open sewer. Global Shear was responsible for developing infrastructure, overseeing environmental restoration, encouraging private credit, and enhancing agricultural extension services—all popular activities. But they were also the tax collector, and fairness demanded a thorough inventory of the district's landholdings, along with a clarification of boundaries and ownership—all the while smoothing the ruffled feathers of displaced local officials.

(*Diplomacy*, Karen Hampton would say, *is a grim necessity*.)

So were creative solutions. More than one company official had lobbied for a policy that would encourage family farms to merge into larger agricultural concerns so they could practice economies of scale, but such schemes didn't take into consideration the dense population.

Michael talked it over with Ryan and Etsuko as he made his way through the waking neighborhoods. "Hand labor still makes sense, for now. Replace the thousands of laborers with machines, and where will the laborers find work?"

At first glance, the sheer numbers of people seemed an intractable problem, but the truth lay deeper. When warfare and ethnic strife were kept at bay, birth rates plummeted. Four Villages was no exception. The town itself was an accident of geography, grown up fast and ugly from the melding of what had once been four separate hamlets. Most of the women here were having only two or three children . . .

Or was it two or three boys? Michael promised himself he would examine the statistics when he went into the office later in the day.

Lights were coming on in the houses, and the smell of cooking gruel drifted out into the street. "It's more than birth control," Etsuko was saying. "It's education, economic independence, a sense of confidence in the future . . ."

"Sure," Ryan agreed. "That and coveting your neighbor's success."

Michael burst out laughing. There *was* plenty of inspiration for the ambitious in Four Villages. On every street, affluent homes huddled next to shacks. Electric lights spilled from some windows, while others held the soft gleam of candles. A mixed neighborhood like this was a robust place—in sharp contrast to the cankerous hearts of the original villages, where ancient buildings housed fundamentalist Hindus, or fundamentalist Moslems, who still went about life as they had for centuries, in grinding poverty, practicing and defending their faith in settings that barely tolerated the presence of a Global Shear census taker.

The warm rain slackened as Michael turned onto a muddy lane scarred by zip tires. His residence was third on the right—a large house owned by Global Shear, its white-washed face abutting the street. The house was built around an enclosed courtyard, where a neglected garden faced a long, lingering death.

As Michael approached, the old house detected his presence and a welcoming light switched on. It illuminated the alcove—and a large, bundled object huddled against the heavy double doors.

"Hello," Ryan said. "What's this?"

Etsuko hissed sharply. "Michael, be careful."

He stopped in the middle of the lane, his instincts made wary by anti-terrorism training. He tried to see the anonymous object as some cloth-wrapped package stashed by a passing street merchant, perhaps to protect it from the rain. He tried to see it as trash.

Then the bundle stirred, faded cloth sliding aside as a head lifted, turned, and the face of a little girl blinked at him, dark eyes wide with confusion and fear.

"It's a kid," Ryan said. "Christ, look at her face. Somebody's punched her around."

Instead, Michael looked away from the bruises on her cheeks, wanting to believe they were only shadows. Gray mud streaked her black hair. A nose ring glinted silver. Her sari looked as if it had been purple once. Now it was a lifeless gray. Michael guessed her to be no more than thirteen years old.

The girl's right arm slid into view. No rings and no bracelets adorned that arm. It was a fleshless bone covered in light brown skin, so very thin there did not seem to be enough muscle mass even to raise that fragile hand. Nevertheless, she pressed it against the wall. She tried to stand, but her limbs would not be controlled, her balance was absent. Michael had once seen a dog taken by an epileptic seizure. The will to move existed, but it only reached the muscles in fits and starts. It was the same with this girl. After several seconds, she sank back to the alcove's tiled floor. She bowed her head. She pulled her sari up to cover her face while Michael stood in the street, gaping, trying to find some precedent in his world for her sudden appearance, clueless what to do.

He told himself it was a dream. How was he supposed to get in his house?

Etsuko's voice was tense: "Michael, I am searching for a local emergency number."

Ryan: "Haven't you got one on file, mate?"

"Corporate security," Michael said stiffly. "That's all. Etsuko?"

"I am contacting the police."

"Don't," Ryan said. "This isn't the silicon coast. If the cops could help, she would have gone to them."

Michael stared at the girl. For Christ's sake, he was a businessman, not a charity worker, and it had already been a long, sleepless night. Let this be a dream.

The girl tried again to get to her feet. Again, she slid back to the ground.

"Jesus, Michael," Ryan said. "Are you just going to stand there? Mate, you've got to do something."

Michael's conscience screamed the same thing, yet still he didn't move. "What can I do?"

Some dark voice whispered that he could walk away, get breakfast in town, go straight to the office, give the girl a chance to disappear.

"Call corporate security," Etsuko said crisply. "They will help. They will get you inside."

"Bloody hell," Ryan said. "Boosting her to the next street over won't help *her*."

"He's not Mother Theresa."

"You could try calling a neighbor, mate."

Michael shook his head. "No, I don't think so." Tragedy was too common here. Sympathy wore thin. Just yesterday he had seen motherly Mrs. Shastri brandishing a heavy stick as she chased a beggar out of the lane.

Michael sighed. She was only a little girl. Still, in her presence, he sensed again the ghostly inundation of chaos. "Witnesses," he muttered. "Ryan, Etsuko—record everything, because you're my witnesses. Got it?" He fervently hoped the spy plane was active overhead.

The girl cringed as he approached. It was a tiny gesture, but startling. "Hey," Michael said. "I won't hurt you." He knelt beside her. Gently, he lifted her sari away from her face.

"The dirty bastards," Ryan muttered.

The girl's cheeks were dark with bruises. Her sari was soaked and she was shivering. Next door, Mrs. Shastri shouted at the servant who cooked for the family. Michael tensed. He didn't want the old gossip to see this girl. "Come inside," he said softly.

"That's it, mate," Ryan encouraged him. "It's the right thing to do."

The confused look in the girl's eyes told him she did not understand.

The Shastri dog took that moment to run into the street, a tiny, white-furred terror bouncing on short legs, yapping a fierce challenge. "Watch out, mate!" Ryan cried. "Attack from the rear."

The girl gasped. The rat-dog took encouragement from that. It charged at Michael, its jaws snapping as it darted about, working up the nerve to bite.

Michael didn't think that would take long. Operating in survival mode now, he yelled at the house to open up. The triple bolts slipped in a simultaneous click, then the doors swung back. He launched a kick at the rat dog. Then he lifted the girl—

she weighed so little!—and stumbled with her into the house. As the doors closed, he heard Mrs. Shastri calling sweetly to her little terror.

Ryan was laughing. "Very smooth, mate. You're a hero."

"Shut up."

Soft lights had come on in the house, falling across new carpet, designer furnishings, and walls paneled in rich faux-teak. The air was dry and cool, almost sterile. "Welcome home, Mr. Fielding," the house said in its motherly voice. "You have five messages."

Michael stood just inside the doors, his shoulders heaving, more with panic than exertion. Looking down at the girl, he found she had fainted, gone limp in his arms. Oh, this looked just great, didn't it? Avaricious foreign businessman kidnaps helpless girl. The local tabloids could churn a million hits out of a headline like that. Christ.

"Now you're committed," Etsuko said. "You must take care of her."

"Yeah." Michael carried the girl into the living room, where he laid her down on the western-style couch . . . hoping she didn't have lice.

She looked so fragile. Tiny and breakable, as if her bones were thin glass copies of real bones, melting away in the heat of an inner fire. Her skin felt hot and her sari was covered in mud. The drawstring of a heavy cloth pouch was looped around her wrist. Michael slipped the pouch off and teased it open, feeling like a lout for abusing her privacy, feeling stupid for feeling like a lout. After all, he'd brought her into his house at no little risk to himself and she was helpless and he needed to know who she was, where she came from, and *who to call*. There had to be someone he could call.

He scowled at the contents of the pouch.

"What is it?" Etsuko asked.

"Dirt."

Well, not dirt exactly. More like a dark, loose humus smelling of garden shops and greenhouses.

"If that's her idea of a valuable," Ryan muttered. "She really is in a bad way."

Michael closed the pouch, leaving it by the French doors that opened onto the neglected courtyard.

"Michael, I've got to take off for awhile," Ryan said. "I've got an appointment that can't wait."

"Sure. Etsuko? I know you have work to do too. The house can record."

"You are sure?" she asked. "I can stay awhile."

"No, it's all right."

The link to the Terrace closed.

Michael looked at the girl. Her sari had fallen away, exposing her shoulders, her arms, her bruised face. Her skin was prickling, purpling in the air-conditioning. Of course her clothes were soaked. He was wet too. The chill air bit at his skin. He headed for the bedroom.

Stripping off his silk shirt, he pitched it into a laundry basket. Then he opened a linen chest at the foot of the bed and pulled out a clean blanket. He used it to cover the girl, who was muttering now, though she didn't wake.

Next, Michael started some tea in the kitchen. The power meter was low, but the sun would be up soon. Even with the rain, the roof top tiles would quickly recharge the house batteries, so there was no need to conserve. He pulled some leftover *samosas* out of the refrigerator. He heated some soup.

Sitting on a stool, he watched the soup spin in the microwave. He was thirty two years old, one of the youngest managers in charge of a major district contract.

So start thinking, doofus.

"Hey," he said softly. "I could call the clinic."

With curled fingers, Michael tapped a trigger point on his data glove. He was tempted to ask for Jaya, but he was *not* going to bother her, not now. So he asked for the midwife, who had seemed so relieved when Jaya had not rejected her baby girl.

After a few minutes a woman's voice came on the line. "Hello?" Suspicion and fear huddled in that one brief word. Her tone didn't change when Michael told her about the girl.

"This is a charity case, sir. You need to call a charity." She gave him the number of an organization.

Michael called the charity. Another woman answered. She listened to his story and blessed him, while Michael begged her to come pick the girl up. He would cover the cost of her care. Just return her to her family. Please?

"Mr. Fielding, given the circumstances in which this girl was found, it's likely she has no family."

"But she must have come from somewhere."

"Surely. But please understand. A girl like this has most likely been cast out of her home for . . . infidelity? Or sterility. These things happen, even in better neighborhoods."

Michael did not think this girl came from a better neighborhood. "Can you care for her then?"

"Sadly, no. We have no beds left. We would have to tend her on the street. Please understand, her circumstance is not unusual."

The microwave finished. Michael stared at it, fervently wishing the sun would rise, wanting to see light seep through the peach-colored blinds. "What's to become of her?"

"That is in the hands of God."

The woman promised to call around to other agencies. In the meantime, she would send someone over to check on the girl. Michael reminded her he would be more than willing to pay for the girl's care. She thanked him and linked off.

He slipped off his shades and peeled off the data glove. He sat on the stool, trying to visualize where this might go. He could not. He could not see even ten minutes ahead.

At least the soup was warm. He placed the bowl on a tray, along with a spoon, and then he zapped the *samosas* for a few seconds to warm them. They came out soggy, instead of the crisp, fried pastry they had once been, but he put them alongside the soup anyway. Then he carried the whole to the living room, where the girl was sitting up, looking around with a dazed expression. Her eyes went wide when she saw him.

Michael was suddenly conscious of his bare chest, bronzy skin over health club muscles. He suffered a devastating suspicion that he was communicating inaccurate innuendoes. Christ. He set the tray down on the low table fronting the couch, spilling a little of the soup. The girl pulled the blanket up to her chin. "For you," Michael said, his cheeks heating with a despairing flush. Then he hurried to the bedroom and got out a shirt.

When he looked again, the girl was sitting on the floor, holding the soup bowl in her delicate hands, drinking from the rim, her eyes closed, as if she were privileged to taste some nectar of the gods. Michael felt a rush of relief, thinking maybe, maybe he'd gotten it right. Then his gaze fell on the sofa, and he shuddered at what Mrs. Nandy, the cleaning lady, would say about those streaks of gray mud ground into the upholstery.

The house spoke English, but after some exploration of its options menu, Michael discovered it also had personalities schooled in Hindi and Tamil. He activated the Hindi personality, and then set about introducing it to the girl. That wasn't easy. She had said nothing so far, and the house needed a voice print as well as a visual image to accurately recognize her.

With two hands, Michael beckoned her away from where she huddled on the floor by the couch. She looked very frightened, but she followed him. When she stood in full view of the tiny cameras mounted in the corners of the room, he held up his palm, asking her to stop, to wait. "Hark," he said. "In Hindi-version, ask her to say hello."

Lilting words spilled forth in the soft voice of the house. The girl hunched, trembling. Her gaze searched the walls.

The house repeated its request. This time she looked at Michael. He nodded encouragement. Hesitantly, she placed her palms together. "Namaste," she whispered.

Michael smiled. "Ask her name."

The house spoke again, and her eyes grew wide with wonder. In a barely discernable voice she said, "*Rajban.*"

"Rajban?" Michael asked.

She nodded. Michael grinned and tapped his chest. "Michael," he told her. Then he bowed. When he looked up, her cheeks were flushed. Her lips toyed with a smile. She started to reach for her sari, to pull it across her face, but when she saw the mud on it she scowled and let it go.

Michael asked if she wanted more food. She declined. He told her someone was coming to help her. That brought a look of fear so that he wondered if the house had translated correctly. "Why don't you sit down?" he offered, indicating the couch. Rajban nodded, though she remained standing until he left the room.

Returning to his bedroom, he took a quick shower, waiting all the while for the house to announce the arrival of the charity worker. No announcement came.

"Link to the office," he instructed the house as he shaved. "Check Rajban's name and image against census records." It wasn't exactly legal to access the records for personal use, but this wasn't exactly personal.

The house started to reply in Hindi. He corrected it impatiently. "English for me," he said. "Hindi for Rajban. Now, continue."

"No identity or residence can be established from available census data," the house informed him.

Michael swore softly. So Rajban was a non-entity, her existence unrecorded by his intrepid census teams. Which meant she was either new in town, or a resident of one of the reticent fundamentalist neighborhoods.

"What does my schedule look like?"

"Daily exercise in the corporate gym from seven to eight," the feminine voice recited. "Then a breakfast meeting with Ms. Muthaye Lal of the Southern Banking Alliance from eight thirty until ten. A staff meeting from ten fifteen—"

"Can the SBA thing be postponed until tomorrow?"

"Inquiring. Please stand by."

Michael finished shaving. He cleaned the razor, then reached for a toothbrush.

"Ms. Lal is unable to schedule a meeting for tomorrow."

"Damn." He tapped the toothbrush on the counter. "This afternoon, then?"

"Inquiring. Please stand by." The response came quickly this time. "Ms. Lal is unable to schedule a meeting for this afternoon."

Michael sighed. No surprise. Everybody's schedule was full. Well, Ms. Muthaye Lal worked with poor women, through the SBA's community banking program. Perhaps she would have some advice for Rajban.

After Michael dressed, he looked into the living room. Rajban had fallen asleep on the floor beside the couch. He told himself it would be all right if he left for a few hours. The house would take care of her. And if she decided to leave. . .

His jaw clenched. That would be the easiest solution for him, wouldn't it? If she just disappeared.

"Call the charity again," he told the house. Again, the woman on the other end of the line promised to send someone by.

He waited an hour. No one came. Rajban still slept. Michael wished he was sleeping too. His eyes felt gritty, his body stiff.

His brain was functioning with all the racing speed of a third generation computer. He wondered if Jaya was awake.

In the bathroom medicine cabinet there was a box of Synthetic Sleep. Michael didn't often take metabolic drugs, but he'd been up all night, and if he wanted to get through this morning's meeting in coherent condition, he had to do something to convince his body that he'd had at least a few hours of rest. He peeled open the casing on one pill and swallowed it with a glass of water.

"Take care of Rajban," he told the house. "Teach her how you work. And *call me*, if you have any questions, any problems. Okay?"

(iv)

Rajban woke with a gritty throat. Her muscles ached. Her joints ached. Her heart was beating too fast. "Namaste?" she whispered.

The house informed her the man had gone out.

He had not hurt her. Not yet.

She looked around the room, unsure how she had come to be here, knowing only that it was shameful. Mother-in-law would never let her come home now.

It was Mother-in-law who had sent her away.

She padded through the house, not daring to touch anything. She even worried about the carpet under her feet.

Turning a corner, she found the great, double-doors that had sheltered her last night. Her heart beat even faster. Were the doors locked? She half-hoped they were. Out there, the horrible street waited for her. Nothing else. Yet she could not stay here. Hesitantly, her hand touched the latch, just to *see* if it was locked. She pressed on it—only a little!—and the latch leaped out of her grip, swinging down on its own with a multiple *click*. The doors started to open. A razor of light streamed in. Frantically, Rajban threw herself against the doors. She held them, so they stood open only a crack. The day's heat curled over her fingers, while outside, women talked in cultured, confident voices.

Listening to them, Rajban trembled. She did not dare show herself in such company. Leaning forward, she forced the doors to shut again.

Back in the living room, she stood beside another set of doors. These opened onto the courtyard. She stared through their glass panes at a half-dead garden surrounded by high walls. Potted banana trees stood on one side like dry old men. Bare skeletons of dead shrubs jutted between the weeds. Yellow leaves floated on the surface of rain puddles.

There was no one outside, so again Rajban tried the latch. These doors opened as easily as the others. Steamy air flowed over her, laden with the smell of wet soil and unhappy plants. Cautiously, she stepped outside.

A paved path wound between the weeds. She followed it, discovering a servant's door in the back wall, but it was locked and would not open.

The path brought her back to the house. She crouched in the open doorway, lost, not knowing what to do. Why was she here?

Clean, frigid air from the house mixed with dense, hot, scented air from the sweltering courtyard, like dream mixing with reality. Rajban struggled to separate the two, but they would not untwine. Hugging her knees to her chest, she rocked on her bare feet, seeing again the blinding flash of the morning sun reflected on the metal circles sewn into the hem of her sister-in-law's green sari. She squinted against the glare, and hurried on. *Hurry*. Her skin felt so hot. Her heart scrabbled like a wild mouse in a glass jar. Her veil kept slipping from her face, but she didn't dare stop to fix it. Sister-in-law's bare brown heels flashed beneath the swinging hem of her sari. Rajban struggled to keep up, fearful in the presence of so many strangers. In the two years since her marriage she had not left the house of her husband's family. The borders of her life had been fixed by the courtyard garden and the crumbling kitchen where she helped Mother-in-law prepare the meals.

Last year her husband went away.

In the months since, Rajban had often been sick, with fevers and chills that no one else in the family shared. Her work suffered. Now Mother-in-law was sending her away. "We have found a family in need of skilled hands to keep the house. They are a respectable family. You will serve them well. Gather your things. It is time to go."

There wasn't much to take. An extra sari. A necklace her mother had given her.

Before she left, Rajban slipped into the garden with a cloth bag from the kitchen. Fruit trees and vegetables thrived in boxes and tin cans and glass jars with drainage holes drilled carefully in the bottom. It had not always been so. When she first arrived in the household, the garden had been yellow and unhappy. But Rajban tended the soil as her mother had taught her, on their tiny farm in the country. She dug up patches of the courtyard with a heavy stick, mixing the dirt with chicken droppings and sometimes with night soil, but only when no one could see her, for her husband would never take her to bed again if he knew. When it rained, she caught the water that dripped from the rooftop, ladling it out over the dry days that would follow, praying softly as she worked. She turned the soil until it became soft, rich black, and sweet-smelling. One day as she turned it, she found a worm. Life from lifelessness. That day, she knew magic had flowed into the soil.

A sickly mandarin tree grew in the cracked half of an old water barrel. Rajban teased away several handfuls of surface dirt, then gently she mixed the black soil in. Within days the tree rejoiced in a flush of new green leaves.

Magic.

Rajban mixed the old dirt into her pile. She dug more dirt from the hard floor of the courtyard. She stirred the pile every day, and every few days she repotted another plant. The garden thrived, but it was not enough to keep Mother-in-law happy, so Rajban was being sent away. Quietly, she filled her cloth bag with handfuls of the magic soil. Then she smoothed the pile so no one would know.

A few minutes after following Sister-in-law out the door, Rajban could no longer guess the proper way home. Fearfully she watched the step-step of Sister-in-law's heels, the swing of her sari, the fierce flash of the sun in the decorative metal circles. And then somehow the green sari slipped out of sight.

Rajban wandered alone through the afternoon, not daring to think too hard. Night fell, and fear crawled in with the darkness. Respectable women were not found alone on the street at night.

Her fever saved her from rape. *She's dirty*, the boy who stole her mother's necklace growled to his companions. *A dirty, infected, dying whore*.

Now Rajban crouched in the courtyard doorway, shivering on the border between warm and cold, light and shadow, past and future, the dying garden on one side, the rich house on the other. An unexpected fury stirred in her breast and flushed across the palms of her hands.

Am I dying?

The possibility enraged her. She did not want to die. Emphatically not. Not now.

I want a baby, she thought. I want my mother. I want my own garden and a respectable life.

These things she would never have if she let herself die now.

Rajban is fifteen.

(v)

Michael arrived by zip at the address recorded on his schedule—a European-style restaurant, on the ground floor of a well-maintained home. A woman greeted him, speaking lightly-accented English. "Welcome, Mr. Fielding. Ms. Lal has just arrived. Won't you come in?"

Air-conditioning enfolded him. He followed the hostess past widely-spaced tables occupied by well-dressed patrons. At a corner table a woman in a traditional sari rose as he approached. His shades caught her ID and whispered it in his ear. *"Muthaye Lal, age twenty seven, employed by Southern Banking Association four years—"*

He tapped his glove, ending the recitation.

"Mr. Fielding, so glad you could come."

Coffee was poured, and a waiter brought a first course of papaya, pineapple and mango. Muthaye tasted it, and smiled. She was not a pretty woman, but her dark eyes were confident as they took Michael's measure. Her enunciation was crisply British. "I will admit to some disappointment, Mr. Fielding, when I learned Global Shear had appointed another foreigner to head this district's office, but your background speaks well for you. Are you familiar with the Southern Banking Association's microeconomics program?"

Michael sipped his coffee, admiring the way criticisms and compliments twined together in her speech, like the strands of a rope. Muthaye could have learned her negotiating tactics from Karen Hampton. Michael certainly had.

Rise to all challenges, especially if they've been promptly withdrawn.

He set the coffee down and smiled, choosing to answer the non-question first. "It's Global Shear policy to expand the international experience of our executives. Please don't take it personally. You probably know that seventy percent of our upper-level staff here at Four Villages is Indian."

Amusement danced in Muthaye's eyes. "And that Global Shear employs Indian executives in offices on three continents. Yes, I know, Mr. Fielding. Global Shear is a true multinational, with, I trust, community interests?"

"Of course. Cultural and economic vitality go hand in hand. That's our belief. And the SBA is well-known to us for its community endeavors. While I'm not familiar with the particulars of your microeconomics program, I have studied several others around the world."

Microeconomics had begun in Bangladesh, where a few hundred dollars loaned to a circle of impoverished women could seed a microenterprise that might eventually grow into a thriving business.

"Our program is well-established," Muthaye told him. "We have over 4000 women participating in Four Villages alone. Each one of them has developed an independence, a self-reliance their mothers never knew."

Michael nodded. To educate and empower women in underdeveloped areas had long been a key to economic progress. The women's lives were tied up in their children. Selflessness came easier to them than to their men. "Global Shear invests many millions of dollars every year in this cause, throughout the world—and the returns have been impressive."

"Ah. That would be in the form of taxes you collect?"

"A measure of economic vitality."

"And your source of income."

"Doing well by doing good—"

"Benefits everyone. Yes, Mr. Fielding, I do agree. I asked for this meeting to discuss with you yet another opportunity for Global Shear to do well by doing good. I would like you to sponsor a line of debit cards to be used by members of the Southern Banking Association. Most of our deposits are tiny, you understand. A few rupees at a time. The money comes in as coinage, and generally it goes out the same way. If the coinage can be exchanged for debit cards, loss from theft would plummet."

"Is theft such a problem for your women?"

A frown marred her brow. "It's often the husbands, you understand?"

Michael flashed on the image of an irate man confiscating his wife's meager earnings, to spend it on . . . ? Drink, perhaps. Or other women. The microeconomic banks had long been convinced that women were the financially responsible members of most marriages, and so most loans were made to women.

Muthaye signaled a waitress for more coffee. "There would, of course, be upfront costs should we institute debit cards. This is the reason we need a sponsor for the program. Our depositors simply do not possess the capital to acquire a debit card through normal routes. The economic scale we deal with is meaningless to anyone in the middle class, whether they live in India or the United States."

Michael nodded. "We're talking about account activity equivalent to a few dollars a week?"

"Exactly. Of course with debit cards, tax collection for Global Shear would be simplified. Taxes could be paid directly out of the electronic accounts, so that no time would be lost collecting and counting the rupees owed."

Michael reflected that most of Muthaye's clients would fall far below the threshold income for tax collection. "Do your depositors have the math skills to understand this kind of abstract system?"

"Education is a requirement for permanent membership in the SBA, Mr. Fielding. Also, the math we teach will be supplemented by bar graphs on the debit cards."

"Oh." Graphic cards would cost far more than those with a simple magnetic strip. "Well. I'll be happy to assign a staffer to this project. We'll assess costs, and give you an indication of the possibilities in a few days."

As they continued to discuss details, Michael's thoughts returned to Rajban. He wanted to call the house, to see if she was still there. He felt guilty about leaving her alone.

As the minutes wore on, he felt certain Rajban would take advantage of his absence, and leave. He realized now that he didn't want that. For where could she possibly go? Back home, he supposed. It would be better if she went home. Wouldn't it?

"Mr. Fielding?" Sharpness touched Muthaye's voice. "You seem distracted. Did you have another appointment?"

"Ah, no. Just a situation at home. My apologies—"

He felt the vibration of a call coming in, followed by a barely audible, trilling ring. Vibration/trilling, the combination repeating like a European siren. Michael tapped his data glove.

Take a message.

The shades would not accept the command. "*Urgent, urgent, urgent!*" the stealthy voice whispered back.

Muthaye was looking at him now with an amused expression. Michael apologized again as he took the call. The voice of Mrs. Nandy, his housekeeper, exploded in his ears. "There is a vagrant in the house, Mr. Fielding! It is a woman of shameful kind. I have her in a corner. She is filthy! Vermin-covered! Mr. Fielding, I will call the police!"

"No, no, no!" His voice boomed through the restaurant, causing heads to turn. "Leave her alone. She is a guest. A guest, you understand? I have asked her in—"

"Mr. Fielding! Vermin-covered! Dirty! This is a dirty woman! You cannot mean to have her keep your house—"

"No! Nothing like that. *You* are my housekeeper. Why don't you take the day off, Mrs. Nandy?" he added, trying hard for a soothing tonc. "Visit your grandchildren—"

"They are in school."

"Don't frighten her, Mrs. Nandy."

"She is vermin-covered!"

"Please?"

He looked at Muthaye, at her sharp, dark eyes. "Just leave the house, Mrs. Nandy. Take a holiday."

She finally agreed to go, though Michael didn't know if he could believe her. When the call ended, he looked at Muthaye. "My apologies again, but the situation at home—I really need to go." He started to stand. Then he changed his mind. He sat back down. Muthaye worked regularly with poor women just like Rajban.

Briefly, he told her about the girl he had found on his step. Muthaye's expression hardened as he described Rajban. Her lips set in a tight line and anger gleamed in her eyes. "The charity worker will not come," she said, when he had finished.

"What?" Michael spread his hands helplessly. "Twice she told me someone would be over as soon as possible."

"And no doubt that is true, but the possible comes with many restrictions. You are already caring for Rajban. There will always be cases more pressing than hers. Mr. Fielding, you have been very kind to help this girl. Hers is an old story, in a world that often despises its women. My mother suffered a similar fate. She was abandoned by her family, but she became educated. She learned economic independence. She insisted that I be educated too. She devoted her life to it."

Michael stared at Muthaye, trying to visualize her as a street waif. He could not. "Your mother did a fine job."

"Indeed. Are you going home straightaway?"

The twists and turns in her conversation put Michael on edge. "Yes. I need to check—"

"Good. May I accompany you, Mr. Fielding?"

"Well, yes, of course." He felt relieved at her offer, yet strangely resentful too. Muthaye would take over Rajban's care.

As if to prove it, she announced, "I will call a health aide from the women's league to meet us." She folded her portal and slipped it into her purse. "Ready?"

They found Rajban in the courtyard. She looked up as the French doors clicked open. Her bruised cheeks were flushed, her face shining with sweat. Fear huddled in her dark eyes. To Michael, she looked like an abused little girl. Muthaye crouched by her side. They talked a minute, then Rajban followed her into the house.

The house announced the arrival of a visitor.

"That will be the health aide," Muthaye told Michael. "Please escort her in."

Michael nodded, wondering when he had lost control of his own house.

The aide was a diminutive woman, yet intense as pepper sauce. With rapid gestures she spread a cloth on the living room floor, then arranged her equipment on it. Muthaye introduced her to Rajban. The three women ignored Michael, so he retreated to his home office. The workload did not stop accumulating just because he was absent.

He linked into the corporate office, downloaded a log of telephone messages, postponed the staff meeting, gave some cursory instructions about the SBA debit card plans. When he returned to the living room, the health aide was just slipping out the front door. Michael looked after her anxiously. "Where is she going? Is she done?"

"Yes, Mr. Fielding." Muthaye leaned forward and patted Rajban's hand. Then, with an unbecoming groan, she clambered to her feet. She seemed older than she had at breakfast, her confidence burned away. "You have been very kind to Rajban. She is deeply grateful."

"I, ah . . ."

Muthaye's smile was sad. "What else could you do? I understand, Mr. Fielding—"

"Call me Michael, please."

Muthaye nodded. "I know you didn't look for this burden, Michael, and I know the situation is awkward for you. I would ask though—and *I* am asking, not Rajban—that she be allowed to stay the night."

"Isn't there—"

"No. All formal shelters will be full. But by tomorrow, I may be able to find a home for her."

"She's sick, isn't she?"

Muthaye nodded. "She won't name her family. She doesn't want to shame them, especially her mother, who was very proud of the marriage she arranged for Rajban. Her parents are destitute, you understand, but women are becoming rare enough, that even daughters with no dowry may find husbands. Rajban's husband is the third son—"

"She's *married*?" Michael interrupted. "But she's just a little girl."

"She's fifteen," Muthaye said. "Child marriage has become fashionable again among certain fundamentalist groups. Rajban has been married two years. She and her husband lived in his mother's house, but her husband was sick. He went away last year and didn't come home. Rajban has never been pregnant, so she believes she is infertile, and so of no value. She has also been frequently sick this past year, and a burden on the family."

Michael felt the sweat of an old terror break out across his brow. "My God. She has AIDS, doesn't she?"

"That would be my guess. No doubt she caught it from her husband. Her family must have suspected the same, so they abandoned her."

"But she can be treated," Michael objected.

No one had to die of AIDS anymore, not if they took control of their lives, and lived the medical regimen.

"Given money, given time, yes, the disease can be put into remission," Muthaye agreed. Still, Michael heard resignation in her voice.

"Rajban has no money," he said.

Muthaye nodded. "Rajban has nothing."

(vi)

For Cody Graham, home was a luxury condo in the foothills above Denver. She caught a train from DIA, arriving home in late evening, at the same time as the dinner for two she had ordered along the way. The food went onto the table while her account was automatically billed. She took a quick shower. When she emerged, she found Wade had arrived. He was pouring Venezuelan spring water into lead-free wine glasses. "Hey," she said, toweling her hair dry. "You remembered."

"Of course I remembered." Wade arched an eyebrow in comic offense as he set the bottle on a tray.

Wade Collin was president and chief stockholder of a small but thriving biotech firm. His company was his life, and he regularly devoted seventy to eighty hours a week ensuring its success. It was an obsession that had brought his marriage to an end. "A good end for both of us," he claimed. "Marriage demands more time than I'll ever be willing to give it."

In his mid-fifties, with two grown children, Wade was still a handsome and vigorous man. He and Cody had been friends for years, and lovers for much of that time, brought together by need and by convenience. It was all either of them had time for. It was all they would admit to needing.

He studied her face, and gradually, the humor in his hazel eyes changed to concern. "Cody? Are you getting nervous?"

"No." She sighed, tossing the towel onto the back of the sofa. "It's just been a strange day. I found out that the neighborhood I grew up in has been designated a hazardous site. It's scheduled for remediation."

Wade scowled as he uncovered the dinner plates. "Inauspicious. Will you take it?"

"I don't know. I picked up the download packet, but I haven't looked through it yet." She dropped into one of the chairs. Fear was a fine mesh wound around her heart. "Truth is, I'm not at all sure I want to go back there."

Going back would mean facing again the stuff of vanquished nightmares: summer heat and summer anger and the urine-stink of crank houses, transformed into blazing infernos when their clandestine labs caught fire. And other, more personal things.

"You are getting nervous," Wade accused.

Cody shook out a napkin and grinned, hoping it didn't look too false. "Maybe just a little," she admitted. It had been six years since her horrible first pregnancy. She'd waited all that time, living a medical regimen while the toxin levels in her tissues declined. "I still want my daughter."

"Howling, screaming, smelly brats," Wade warned, sitting down beside her.

"Won't work," Cody assured him.

"Could be a boy."

Nope. Cody wouldn't say so out loud, but she knew it wouldn't be a boy.

She sipped at the Venezuelan water, imagining she could feel the babyjack in her womb. A slight pinching sensation—that's the identity she gave it. She hadn't told Wade it was in there.

Uterine implants were a form of selective birth control developed for couples with inherited genetic disorders. After conception, they screened the embryo's DNA for a suspected defect. If it was found, the implant would release a drug to block the natural production of progesterone and the pregnancy would fail.

Though it appeared nowhere in the company prospectus, the

most common "defect" the implants screened for was the sex of the embryo. Cody's babyjack would kick in if it detected a male embryo, causing a spontaneous abortion within several days of conception. That early in her term she might experience a slightly late, slightly heavy menstrual period. Nothing more.

Wade had waived parental rights to any child she might conceive. She had signed documents freeing him of obligation. They had submitted DNA samples to an anonymous testing service, where their chromosomes were sorted across a large series of DNA chips. No major incompatibilities had been found.

"Genetic maps," Cody mused, "health tests, trust funds, legal documents . . . am I neurotic? My mother conceived me in an alley behind a rave club when she was fifteen. He didn't want to use a condom because it was too constricting. They screwed for a week, then she never saw him again."

"So you both learned from her mistake."

"And we've both been over-compensating ever since."

He sighed, his sun-browned hand closing over hers. "You're a good person, Cody. You deserve more than this. You should have had the fairy tale."

She smiled. *I did.*

She'd had the marriage, the handsome husband, the baby on the way, and it had all blown up in her face. On some level, she'd always known it would. She'd already made it out of the brutal slum of Victoria Glen, and surely that was enough to ask of life? The castle on the hill could wait for the next generation.

(vii)

Muthaye left the house, promising to return as soon as possible. Michael did not like the sound of that. It reminded him too much of the woman from the charity, but what could he do? He had his own schedule to keep. This afternoon he was due at a publicity event on a local farm, the first to bring in a harvest of genetically engineered rice developed by a Japanese company and distributed by Global Shear.

He took another shower, and another tab of Synthetic Sleep. The pill's chemical cocktail was designed to mimic the metabolic effects of a few hours of rest. His body could not be fooled forever, but he should be okay until the evening.

In the living room, Rajban was crouching on the floor, staring out at the garden. Michael hesitated on his way to the front door. Something in her posture touched a memory in him: for a moment he was immersed again in the half-dark of a city night, and the awful silence that had followed her cold declaration, *There's nothing left, Michael. I'm leaving*. He felt as if his chest was made of glass, and the glass had shattered.

He shook his head. That was all long ago.

The house spoke in its soothing, feminine voice. "Your car is here." Then it repeated the news in Hindi. Rajban turned, her face an open question. Michael wished he could stay and talk to her. Instead, he put on his shades and he left.

The company car bounced and lurched along a dirt road in dire need of scraping. The driver was forced to dodge bicyclists and zips, an assortment of rusty old cars converted to ethylene, and hundreds of pedestrians. Fifteen miles an hour was a top speed rarely achieved, and Michael was twenty minutes late by the time he arrived at the demonstration farm.

No one noticed.

A huge canvas canopy with walls of transparent plastic had been set up in the farmyard. An air-conditioner powered by a portable generator blew an arctic chill into its interior, while outside, misters delivered fine sprays of water over the arriving guests. Michael soon found himself in conversation with an Ikeda tech and a reporter from CNN. "It's an ideal grain," the tech was saying. "Requiring less water and fertilizer than any other rice strain, while producing a polishable kernel with a high protein content."

"But," the reporter countered, "your opponents claim it's just this engineered hardiness, this ability to out-compete even the weeds that makes it a threat to the biosystem."

Michael dove into the debate with practiced ease. "Out-competing the weeds is something of an exaggeration. Ikeda rice is still a domesticated plant, requiring careful farming practices to thrive . . ."

Most of the afternoon was like that. The event was a press-op, and Michael's job was to sooth the usual fear of genetically-engineered food plants. Most wealthier countries forbid the importation or sale of engineered crops, fearing ecological disaster, or the discovery of some previously unknown toxic quality in the new food. At least, those were the reasons most often cited. Michael suspected it was really a fear of shouldering any more responsibility. Already the land, the climate, and even the ecology of the oceans had been transformed by human activity. If the formula of life itself was now to be rewritten, what would be left outside the range of human influence? Not much. Every disaster outside of seismic instability would then fall squarely at the feet of technology.

For now it didn't matter that Ikeda rice couldn't be sold across international borders. Small farmers could peddle their excess crops to the villagers. Large farms could ship to the cities. Someday though, international markets would need to open.

It was late afternoon when Michael slipped free of the press parade. He took a folding chair and set it up beneath the spreading branches of a banyan tree. He had hardly sat down when a party of young men emerged from the farmhouse. They laughed and teased one another, startling a long legged bird that had been hunting on the edge of a rice paddy. As the bird took flight, Michael found himself surrounded by six smiling youths, each neatly attired in dress shirts and cotton slacks, sandals on their feet. One of them introduced himself as Kanwal. He offered Michael a banana-mango smoothie obviously rescued from the tent.

"This is my father's farm," he informed Michael proudly. Then he explained that his friends were all from nearby farms.

Michael was halfway through the tall glass when he realized it had been spiked. With vodka? That would neatly counter the Synthetic Sleep.

Kanwal proudly tapped his chest. "I am seventeen this year. I have finished my public schooling. My father wants to buy a truck. He will start a business delivering fruit to the cities." Kanwal rolled his eyes. "He says he is getting too old for farm work. He wants to drive a truck while his sons do the tough work!"

The other boys erupted in laughter. Michael grinned too. "Your old man must think a lot of you."

"Oh, I don't know," Kanwal said. "I think he just wants to hit the road to look for a new wife."

The boys giggled and moaned. "He's old," someone muttered. "But not too old!"

"He wants us to believe it, anyway," Kanwal said. "But I'm seventeen! He should be looking for a wife for me."

"Isn't that your mother's business?" Michael asked.

Kanwal shrugged. "My mother is dead three years. My youngest brother does all the cooking now."

"No sisters?"

Kanwal made a face. "No. Of course not. My old man wanted to get ahead, not raise a servant for another man's family. We are very modern here. We don't believe in dowry. If I had a sister, my father would have to pay her dowry. Still, it makes it hard to find a wife. My father was married when he was fifteen. Look at us.

We are sixteen, seventeen, eighteen years old. No one has a wife. Hey." He turned to his friends. "Know who's making the most money these days? The marriage broker!"

The boys guffawed again, but Michael frowned. Kanwal noticed, and responded by rubbing Michael's shoulder in a friendly way. "You have a wife?"

Michael shook his head, declining to explain to Kanwal that though he'd been married at twenty four, it had not lasted two years. *There's nothing left, Michael.*

Kanwal might have read his mind. "Divorced?" he asked.

Michael scowled. "You watch too much TV."

Kanwal giggled, along with his friends. "American women like to have many husbands and only one son."

"We could use some American women here," one of the boys chimed in from the back of the group.

Michael felt the vodka inside him, dissolving his diplomacy. "Women are not toys. They're people, with their own dreams, their own ambitions."

"Oh yes," Kanwal agreed with a hearty nod. "They are goddesses." The boys all offered confirmation of this.

Kanwal went on, "This farm would be a happier place if we had a woman in the kitchen again. Hey, but no one wants to be a farmer anymore, not even my old man."

Michael sat up a little straighter. *This* sentiment had not been reported by his census teams. "Why do you say that? This farm has had a profitable year, despite poor weather."

"Oh, we're doing all right," Kanwal agreed. "But do you think it's easy? Laboring all day in the hot sun, and we don't even have a tractor. The water buffalo are still our tractor. It's shameful! I want to move to Bangalore, learn computers, work in an office."

"Ah Kanwal," one of his friends interrupted. "Everybody wants to work in an office, but it's the farm for us, you know it."

Kanwal gave his friend a dark look. "Not all of us. Every evening I walk all the way to town, just so I can spend half an hour at the home of a link-wallah, exploring the net. Half an hour! That's all he allows, because he has many clients, but half an hour is not enough time to get any real training—maybe if I could print out lessons, but I can't, because I don't have the paper. But I have a plan.

"I can read well. We all can. I've read every book in the two library booths at South Market. Do you know what we're doing? My friends and I? We're putting our money together to buy our own terminal. I have a friend in town who can get an uplink." Kanwal nodded, his dark eyes happy at his inner vision. "There is formal schooling online, from all over the world, and some of it at no cost. You hear how well I speak English? I learn fast. Hey." He looked at his friends again. "Maybe we're better off with no wives yet. No children to care for, right? Make our careers first. It's what the Bangalore families tell their young men." He turned back to Michael. "You have children, mister?"

"No," Michael said, feeling a sudden tightness in his gut. *There's nothing left, Michael. I'm leaving.*

Kanwal's brows rose in surprise. "No children? Not even from the wife who divorced you?"

"No," Michael repeated firmly, his cheeks heating with more than the torrid afternoon. She had not wanted to try again. *I'm leaving.*

From the back of the crowd the anonymous heckler spoke. "Hey Kanwal, waiting a few years for a wife doesn't sound too bad, but I don't think I want to wait *that* long."

The boys again erupted in laughter, while Michael's cheeks grew even hotter. He was only thirty two, but to be thirty two and without children . . . did that make him a failure in their eyes? It was a stunning thought, and one he didn't want to examine too closely.

Quickly he drained his vodka smoothie while Kanwal went

right on massaging his shoulder, his dark eyes shining with confidence, and ambition. "That's right, mister. You watch us. In two years, we will all be middle class like you."

(viii)

Two in the morning, and sleep wouldn't come. Cody listened to Wade's soft snoring. She could just make out his silhouette in the faint amber glow spilling from the bathroom nightlight. Maybe new life had begun in her womb tonight, maybe not. It would be a few days before she would know.

She got out of bed, feeling a lingering stickiness between her legs. She groped for a nightshirt and pulled it on, then padded into the living room, where the curtains stood open on a sweeping view of Denver's city lights.

She always took on the toughest jobs.

So why was she so damned scared of the project at Victoria Glen? She'd looked over the specs after dinner. They'd been nasty, but Cody had dealt with worse. *Kick. Kick!* No sweat.

Except she *was* sweating. Her palms were slick, and the soles of her feet.

So? She'd been scared before. The only thing to do was face it down.

She took a long swallow from the bottle of Venezuelan water, then she got her VR helmet from a closet. Sitting on the sofa, she pulled the helmet on, encasing herself in a safe black vault. Nice, simple environment. She almost felt she could go to sleep.

Almost.

She instructed the wireless system to link with her server, where she'd stored the download of the Victoria Glen site, prepared by a redevelopment company called New Land.

She gazed at a menu, then, "Document three-seven-zero," she whispered. "*Go*."

The menu faded as a world emerged, creeping in like sunrise over a tired city. New Land had recorded a full sensory walk-through. Cody's helmet translated the digital record, synthesizing sight, sound, temperature, and encoded odors. Her lungs filled with sun-warmed air, brewed over old wood and oil-stained asphalt.

She found herself afloat, a few feet above an empty street. It ran straight, like a canalized river cutting through a landscape of vacant lots and boarded-up houses. A few sparrows popped up and down in brush that sprouted around a chain-link fence. Warning signs glared from the abandoned buildings:

KEEP OUT.

HAZARDOUS MATERIALS SITE.

DANGER - NO TRESPASSING.

It took her a minute to realize this was Victoria Street, and that first house, with its sagging porch cuddled under a steeply sloping roof, that was Randi's house. It had been the upper limit of Cody's permitted territory, and a safe place to run if ever she needed shelter. The house next to it had been a rental, with a fleet of showy cars perpetually drifting in and out of the front yard. Only a rusted hulk was left now, crumbling in the shade of a large tree leaning over a gap-toothed fence from the yard next door.

Looking at the tree, Cody felt hollow inside. *Jacaranda*, she realized. As a kid she'd never known its name, just enjoyed gathering the purple blossoms that showered from it in the spring. She and Tanya would have pretend weddings and toss the fallen flowers in the air. Where had they learned that? Cody couldn't guess. Neither one of them had ever seen a wedding.

The tree looked so much bigger than she remembered.

Pushing the trackball forward, she went gliding down the street, a ghost returned to haunt the old neighborhood.

She drifted past the fence. She hardly dared to look, but there it was: A tiny block of a house, built close to the ground, like a bunker. The roof had gaps in it. Head wounds. The windows were boarded up. It didn't matter. It was all there. All of it, still lurking inside her mind. She closed her eyes, and reality thickened, like flesh on the bones of the past. Little Tanya from down the block was knocking on the door, jump rope in hand. It was a hot summer evening. Cody got her own rope, and they practiced together on the sidewalk, singing *seashells, taco bells, easy, ivy, over*. No way they were supposed to be outside that late, but mama was still at school and Tanya's big sister was sleeping.

They sang very softly, *seashells, taco bells*, so Passion wouldn't come charging at them out of his girlfriend's house across the street, screaming dumb-bitches-shut-up. His motorcycle was there, but his fuck-this-fuck-that music wasn't pounding the neighborhood, so she guessed he was asleep.

They were practicing cross-arms when a tanker truck came rumbling into sight from the direction of Randi's house. They stopped jumping, to watch it go by. It was a big truck. The tank had been painted gray. It didn't have the name of any gas station on it.

"Look," Tanya said. She pointed at the truck's undercarriage and giggled. "It's peeing."

A stream of liquid ran from beneath the truck, splashing black against the street. Tanya waved at the anonymous bulk of the driver. Across the street, Passion was screaming *What the fuck is that noise?*

Cody snatched the helmet off. Her heart felt like it had melted into her arteries, a pounding starfish in her chest. *Oh no, oh no*. She stared at the looming shapes of furniture in the dimly-lit room. She hadn't remembered the truck in years and years. Maybe it had felt too dangerous to remember. *Oh God, oh Jesus*. Her palms were sweating.

Just a few seconds after the truck had passed her eyes had started burning. She ran into the house and threw up. Passion was screaming outside, shooting his gun. Cody lay on the broken tiles of the bathroom floor and cried, she felt so sick, until mama came home and moved her into bed. She didn't say anything about the truck and its stinky pee, because she should never have been out on the sidewalk.

Carefully, Cody lay the helmet on the cushion beside her. Wade was snoring softly in the bedroom. The antique clock on the mantle was ticking, ticking.

What had gone into the street that night? And on other nights, what had spilled from the kitchen drug labs? From the ubiquitous activity of auto repair? From the city's fights against rats and roaches? What had trickled through the soil, into the ground water, returning through the faucet of the kitchen sink?

Splash of clear water into a plastic cup held in a little girl's hands; the dry tang of chlorine in her throat.

There had been toxins in her body that killed her daughter. Cody had always assumed it was *her* fault, that she'd been incautious on a job, that somehow she had poisoned herself, but what if it wasn't so?

Her lips pressed together in a hard line. Any hazardous substance report generated by the clean-up of Victoria Glen would be kept confidential by the redevelopment company. She'd be able to gain access only if she could offer compelling evidence of on-site injury, and that was doubtful. She'd only lived there until she was ten, until Mama got her the scholarship to Prescott Academy. Cody had left for boarding school and never had come back.

So there was only one way to learn what ten years on Victoria Street had done to her. She would have to take on the job herself.

(ix)

Rajban was up early. Michael found her in the kitchen when he woke, peeking into cabinets with all the stealth and caution of a kid looking for treasure but expecting to find a tiger. "Good morning," Michael said. She jumped, and the cabinet door banged shut. Her hands were already soiled with the gray dirt of the courtyard. Michael sighed. She certainly had an affinity for gardening.

Ignoring her fright, he beckoned to her to come to the sink, where he showed her how to slide her hands under the soap dispenser. The sensor popped a spray of soap onto her palm. She lathered it, carefully imitating Michael's every gesture. Water came from the tap in a tepid spray, like a stolen column of soft rain. Michael dried his hands, Rajban dried hers, and then together they made a breakfast of papayas, bread, and yogurt.

After they ate, Rajban disappeared into the garden, while Michael readied himself for work. Last of all, he picked up his shades. The Terrace glyph waited for him, surrounded by a pink query circle. He linked through. "Anybody there?"

No one answered. He left the link open, confident someone would check back before long. Next he put a call through to Muthaye, but she didn't pick up either. A moment later, the house announced a visitor at the door.

"Ooh, company," Ryan said, as the line to the Terrace went green.

Etsuko sounded puzzled. "Who is that?"

"No I.D.," Ryan muttered. "Pupils dilated, skin temperature slightly elevated. He's nervous."

"Or angry," Etsuko said. "Be careful, Michael."

"Hey," Michael said as the house repeated its announcement, this time in Hindi. "Good morning and all that. Back again, huh?"

"Been waiting all morning for your shades to activate," Ryan agreed. "You have to understand—your life is so much more interesting than ours. Now hurry up. Go find out what he wants before my next appointment."

Michael summoned an image of the visitor into his shades. "So I guess it's not Muthaye at the door?"

"No, mate. No such luck. A local gentleman, I should think. Looks a little stiff, if you ask me."

Etsuko snorted. "By your standards, Ryan, anyone could look stiff."

Rajban slipped in through the French doors. Michael sighed to see that her hands were dirty again. Some of the dirt had gotten on her face. Still, she looked at Michael with eyes that were brighter, fuller than they had been only yesterday. Then she looked at the door . . . hoping it was Muthaye too? Come back to visit her as promised.

"Say," Ryan said. "Maybe she knows the guy."

"Right." After all, someone had to be looking for Rajban, regardless of what Muthaye said. A brother, perhaps? Someone who cared. Michael slipped the shades off and handed them to Rajban, motioning that she should put them on. Tentatively, she obeyed. For several seconds she stared at the scene, while her mouth twisted in a small hard knot. Then she yanked the shades off, shoved them into Michael's hands, and ran for the courtyard.

Ryan said, "Women react that way to me too, from time to time."

No one laughed.

Michael stared after Rajban, dread gnawing like a rat at his chest. Despite Muthaye's words, he had envisioned only a happy reunion for her. What would his role become, if her family demanded her back, and she refused to go?

Stop guessing.

He slipped the shades back on and went to the front door. "Hark. Open it."

The stranger in the alcove was tall and lean, like a slice taken off a fuller man, then smoked until it hardened. His black hair was neatly cut and combed. His dark eyes were stern. They remained fixed on Michael through a slow, formal bow. "Namaste."

"Namaste," Michael murmured, feeling the hair on the back of his neck rise. There was something about this man that set him on edge. The intense stare, perhaps. The unsmiling face. The stiffness of his carriage. Smoked and hardened.

"I am Mr. Gharia," the stranger said, in lilting but well-pronounced English. "And you, I have been told, are Mr. Fielding. I have come to inquire about the woman."

Michael felt stubbornness descend into his spine, a quiet, steely resistance learned from the heroes of a hundred old cowboy movies. "Have you?"

Vaguely, he was aware of Etsuko muttering, "Gharia? Which Gharia? There are dozens in the census, approximate height and age . . ."

Mr. Gharia apparently had a stubbornness of his own. He raised his chin, and though his head came barely to Michael's shoulder, he seemed tall. "It is improper for this woman to be residing within your house."

Michael had never taken well to instructions on propriety. Remembering the look of fear and distaste on Rajban's face as she fled to the courtyard, he ventured a guess, and dressed it up as certainty, "This is not your woman."

Mr. Gharia looked taken aback at this discourteous response; perhaps a little confused, but by his reply Michael knew that his guess had been correct. "I am a friend of the family, sir."

When Michael didn't respond to this, Gharia's tone rose. "Sir, a widow deserves respect. This woman must be returned immediately to her family."

A widow. So her husband was dead. Muthaye had said he'd left home a full year ago. Michael had assumed he'd gone for treatment, yet now he was dead. Did Rajban know? Had anyone bothered to tell her? Thinking about it, Michael felt an anger as cool, as austere, as shadows under desert rock. "This woman has no family."

"Sir, you are mistaken."

"The family that she had cast her out like useless rubbish."

"I have come to inquire about her, to be sure she is the woman being sought."

"She is not that woman," Michael said. "She is a different woman altogether."

"Sir—"

"You would not have me put her on display, would you? Now sir, good day." He stepped back, allowing the door to close.

Gharia saw what he was about. "It doesn't matter who she is!" he said quickly. "*Any* Hindu woman must be ashamed to be kept as a whore. It is intolerable! It—" The door sealed, cutting off Gharia's tirade with the abruptness of a toggled switch.

"*Christ*," Michael muttered.

"Nice show," Ryan agreed, but his voice was somber. "Michael, this isn't a game you want to play. Etsuko's I.D.'ed this Gharia fellow. He's a religious activist—"

Michael's palm sliced through the air. "I don't care who he is! The Indian constitution promises equal rights for women."

"It's a piece of paper, Michael." Etsuko's voice was softly sad. "In a far off city. Women like Rajban are subject to an older law."

"Not anymore. Muthaye said she would come up with a shelter for Rajban by today. If the bastards can't find her, they can't hurt her."

But if they did find her? Rajban was already a woman ruined, simply by being inside Michael's house.

He jumped as the lights flashed, and a soft alarm bonged through the residence. Locks clicked. The air-conditioning system huffed into silence. "Perimeter intrusion," the house informed him. "Michael Fielding, you will remain secured inside this residence pending arrival of Global Shear security. Arrival estimated at three minutes fifty seconds." It was the same feminine voice the house always used, yet it didn't sound like the house anymore.

"Where is Rajban?" Michael shouted.

"Identify the person in question?"

This was definitely not his house. "Rajban. A girl. She's been . . . she's stayed here for a day or so—"

Ryan's voice cut in: "The courtyard, Michael."

Michael dashed for the courtyard doors. His hand hit the latch, but it would not move. He tried to force it, but the door held.

Through the glass, he saw Rajban crouched on the path beside a freshly worked bed of earth, the little hoe in one hand. She gazed up at the courtyard wall. Michael looked, to see Gharia leaning over the top. It was eight feet of smooth concrete, but somehow he had climbed it, and from the Shastri courtyard, too. Now he leaned on his chest, the breast of his shirt smudged with dirt, his dark brows pulled together in an angry scowl. Michael had only a glimpse of him, before he dropped away out of sight.

Again Michael tried the latch, slamming it with all his weight while the house instructed him to "Stay away from all doors and windows. Retreat at once to the interior—"

"Who the hell am I talking to?" Michael interrupted.

"Easy," Ryan muttered. "Cool under fire, boy. You know the chant."

The house answered at the same time: "This is Security Chief Sankar. Mr. Fielding, please step away from the door. You must remove yourself from this exposed position immediately—"

Rajban had seen him. She was running toward him now. She threw herself on the door latch, while Michael tried again to force it from the inside. It would not budge. Rajban stared at him through the glass, her dark eyes wide, confusion and terror swimming in her unshed tears.

"Sankar!" Michael shouted. "Unlock this door. Let her inside *now*—"

"Mr. Fielding, please remain calm. The door will not open until the situation is secure. Be assured, we will be on-site momentarily."

Michael bit his lip, swearing silently to himself. "Is Gharia still out there, then? He's after this girl, you know. Not me."

"Negative, sir. Raman Gharia has fled the scene. He is presently being tracked by a vigil craft—"

The drone aircraft that watched the house. Of course. The security AI must have seen Gharia climbing the Shastri wall . . .

"Well, if Gharia's gone, then you can open the door. Sankar?"

A helicopter swept in, no more than fifty feet above the wall. Rajban looked up at it, and screamed. Michael could not hear her through the sound-proofed glass, but he could see the terror on her face. She pressed herself against the door, covering her head with the new sari Muthaye had given her while her clothing licked and shuddered in the rotor wash. First one man, then a second, descended from the helicopter, sliding down a cable to land in the courtyard garden.

"This probably qualifies as overkill," Ryan muttered.

"Sankar!" Michael shouted. "What the hell are you *doing?*"

No answer.

The helicopter pulled away. The two men on the ground were anonymous in their helmets and shimmering gray coveralls. The first one pulled a weapon from a thigh holster and trained it on Rajban. The second sprinted toward the wall where Gharia had appeared. Crashing through the half-dead plants, he launched himself at the concrete face, and to Michael's amazement, he actually reached the top, pulling himself up to gaze over the side, in a weird echo of Gharia's own posture. He stayed there only long enough to drop something over the wall—Oh, Mrs. Shastri was going to *love* this—then he slipped back down into the garden, landing in a crouch. A weapon had appeared in his hands, too.

"Net gun," Ryan said. "Launches a sticky entangler. Non-lethal, unless it scares you to death. Michael, I had no idea you were this well protected."

"They're bored," Michael growled.

"Do say."

"Explosives negative," Sankar informed him, through the voice of the house.

Now both net guns were trained on Rajban.

"Leave her alone," Michael warned. "Sankar, I swear—"

"Situation clear," Sankar announced.

The man by the wall stood up, sliding his weapon back into its holster. The other did the same. He slipped his visor up, revealing a delighted grin. Michael recognized Sankar's handsome face. "Quite an adventure, eh, Mr. Fielding?"

The door lock clicked. Michael slammed the latch down, yanking the door open, so that Rajban half fell into the living room. He started to reach for her, to help her up, but she scuttled away with a little moan of terror. He turned to Sankar, ready to vent his fury, but he found the security chief praising his man for a job well-done.

"Absolutely by the book!" Sankar was saying in a suitably masculine voice, quite a jolt after the feminine voice of the house. With his gaze, Sankar took in Michael too. "Mr. Fielding. This has turned out to be a minor incident, but we had no way of knowing that when the perimeter alarm sounded. It is essential that you remain inside in such situations, away from doors and windows. If explosives had come over the wall—"

"Then Rajban would have been killed," Michael said softly. "All I asked was that you unlock the door to let her in."

Rajban had gone to hide behind the sofa. Michael could hear her softly weeping. Sankar frowned at the noise, as if it did not fit into any scenario he had ever practiced. "This woman, she is not the housekeeper registered in our security files. Have you changed employees?"

"No. She's not an employee. She's a guest."

"A guest? All guests should be registered, Mr. Fielding. Without a profile, we have no way of discriminating friend from enemy." He said this matter-of-factly, without a hint of judgment. Well, Sankar was a modern man, educated in California, Michael recalled. What the boss did was the boss's business, no doubt.

Michael sighed, letting the edge of his anger slip away. "You're right," he conceded. Global Shear security protocol was strict and effective. "So take her profile now. She's a waif, just a little girl, without home or family. And that's all she is, Mr. Sankar. I want you to put that in your profile too."

(x)

Rajban plunged her hoe into the hard earth of the garden bed, prying up chunks of clay. Grief sat in her stomach like heavy black mud, but it was not grief for her husband. It was for herself. Now she was widowed. She had no home. She would have no sons.

Brother-in-law had sent her away.

So why had Gharia come after her?

She hacked at the earth, and thought about it. Gharia had been a frequent guest at Brother-in-law's table, where they discussed the *foreign issue*, and the *influence of non-believers*. At times they would grow very angry, but when the talk lapsed, Gharia's eyes often found their rest on Rajban's backside as she worked in the kitchen with Mother-in-law.

Mother-in-law would notice the direction of Gharia's gaze, and her words to Rajban would be angry.

Rajban remembered these things as she crumbled each chunk of clay in her hands. She picked up the hoe again and dug deeper.

The soil here was bad. There were no worms in it. No tiny bugs. It looked as sterile as the soil in Brother-in-law's courtyard. Even the weeds were yellow.

No matter.

She would use the magic soil. With love and prayers, its influence could be worked into the ground.

A winged shadow drifted slowly over Rajban's hands. She paused in her work, squinting against the noon sun. There! She spied it again: A tiny plane the color of the sky. It was very hard to see, yet if she looked long enough, she could always find it floating above the house.

The door latch clicked. "Rajban?"

Rajban smiled shyly when she saw the kind woman, Muthaye, looking out between the glass doors. "Namaste," she murmured softly. "You came back."

"Namaste," Muthaye echoed. "Will you come inside? The sun is high, and it is very hot."

Rajban obeyed. She stood on stiff legs, taking a moment to brush the soil from her sari.

Inside, she was startled to discover other women. They were four, sitting in a half-circle on the carpet. They were not fine women, like Muthaye. Their saris were worn and their faces lined. All of them were older than Rajban. She felt sure they were all mothers, and she felt ashamed.

Twice in her first year of marriage she had thought herself pregnant, but her hopes were shattered by a late, painful, and heavy flow of blood—as if a baby had been started and then had died.

Rajban remembered the midwife who had come to visit on the day she arrived in her husband's household. This midwife had not looked like the village health aides Rajban had seen at her father's farm. This one was young and finely dressed, and she wore an eye veil, like Michael. "She will make your womb healthy," Mother-in-law declared. "So healthy you will bear only sons." Rajban had bit her lips to keep from wailing in pain as cold, gloved hands groped inside her. She had not felt healthy afterwards. Her abdomen and her crotch had ached for days—and she had never conceived a baby. Or maybe . . . she had conceived only girls?

Muthaye had joined the circle of women. Now she smiled at Rajban. "Please won't you sit?" She patted a spot at her side that would close the circle. Rajban did as she was asked, though she would have been happier to disappear into the kitchen. She sat with her hands folded neatly in her lap while Muthaye told a story that did not sound like it could be true.

"My mother was an illiterate country woman," Muthaye began. Her gaze sought Rajban. "That means she was like you. She could not read or write or speak any language but the one she was born to. At fourteen she was married to a young man only a little more educated than she, the third son of a cruel and selfish family. It was a great struggle for my grandfather to gather the large dowry demanded by her husband's family. Still, he paid it, though he was forced to mortgage his land. Several months later there came a terrible storm. The land was flooded, the household of my mother's husband was destroyed, and along with many others in the village, he died of disease. When afterwards my mother gave birth to a daughter, she was driven out of the family. She returned to her father's house, but he refused to receive her, so she went without food and shelter, and her baby girl died.

"My mother became angry.

"She remembered that in the year of her marriage, she had met an agent from the women's cooperative. She went to that agent now, and was given a job sewing embroidered scarves. She earned enough to feed herself, but she wanted more. With the help of the women's cooperative, she taught herself to read. She received a small loan—only $200—but it was enough to buy books and start her own lending library. When the loan was paid back she took out another, and eventually she started a school just for girls. In time she married again—"

There was a murmur of surprise from the circle.

"—the son of a long-time member of the women's cooperative. No dowry was paid—"

Again, a whisper of astonishment arose from the gathered women.

"—for dowry is evil and illegal. She still runs her school, and through it she has earned more money for her family than she might have ever brought as dowry. She is middle-class, Rajban. Yet when she was fifteen, she was just like you."

Rajban stared down at the lines of dirt that lay across her palms, knowing it wasn't true. "She had a baby."

Muthaye's tone became more strict: "It is not unexpected that a husband dying of AIDS gave you his disease instead of a child. That does not mean you will never have a child—or another husband."

"My brother-in-law will not allow it."

"You do not belong to him anymore."

Rajban considered this. She turned it over and over in her mind, wondering if it was true. At the same time, she listened to the other women talk about themselves. These women were all learning to read. Three of them had businesses. One made sandals. Another drove a zip. The last cleaned houses. The fourth member of their group was building a fruit stand. All of them had started their businesses with small loans from Muthaye.

"Not from me," Muthaye corrected. "These are loans from the Southern Banking Association."

The loans were for a few hundred dollars at a time, enough to buy the tools and supplies that would let them work. Together, the women ensured that each one of them made their weekly payments. If any failed to do so, all would lose their credit. This was the "microcredit program" administered by Muthaye. Three of the women in this lending circle had been involved for several years. One for only a few months.

"A lending circle should have five women," Muthaye explained. "The fifth lady of this group has moved away to join her son in Bangalore, so there is a place for you here. I have told you the story of my mother. This can be your story too."

Rajban bowed her head. Her heart fluttered, like a bird, seeking to escape its cage for the peaceful serenity of the sun-seared sky. She stared at her hands and whispered, "I don't know how."

One of the older women patted her mud-stained hand. She asked if Rajban could sew or cook. If she could keep a house clean or carry a heavy weight. Rajban didn't know how to answer. Her mother had raised her to do the things women do. All these things she had done, but surely no one would pay her to do them?

"Is there anything you are so good at?" Muthaye asked. "Is there a kind of work that blossoms like a flower in your hands?"

Rajban caught her breath. She glanced out at the garden. "I have a bag of magic soil that makes a garden strong and happy."

This brought a shower of laughter from the women. But why? Hadn't Rajban believed all their tales? And yet they laughed. Their kindly faces had all become the face of her Mother-in-law, laughing, laughing, and endlessly scolding her, *Stupid girl!*

She felt a touch on her hand, and the vision vanished, but even Muthaye's warm eyes could not chase away the pain.

"Magic is the comfort of old-fashioned women," Muthaye told her. "A modern woman has no need of it. Think on what we've talked about. Think of a business you might like to do. Think hard, for you must be settled before the AIDS treatment can begin."

(xi)

Word of the morning's misadventures got around quickly. It was still early when Michael stepped from a zip into the shade of the portico at Global Shear's district headquarters. The five story office cube was newly-built, situated halfway up a shallow, rocky rise dividing two of the original villages. A temple occupied the high ground, while a pig farmer kept his animals in a dusty pen on one side of the landscaped grounds. Laborers shacks made up the rest of the neighborhood.

A nervous community-relations officer greeted Michael even before he entered the building. "Shall we issue a public statement, Mr. Fielding?"

"Not unless someone asks."

"There *have* been several inquiries about the helicopter."

"Then state the truth. Intruder alarms went off and security responded. Play it down though, and add that we're reviewing our procedures to see if our response might be tempered in the future."

"Yes sir."

Glass doors slipped open, and Michael stepped into the air-conditioned paradise of the public lobby. The receptionist looked up, and smiled. "An exciting morning, Mr. Fielding! That helicopter raid must have shaken the dust off anyone still doubting our diligence."

"So I hear."

He met more compliments on the elevator ride to the fifth floor, but the tenor changed when he entered his corner office, where Karen Hampton waited for him, her image resident in an active wall screen. "A most interesting report appeared in my queue this morning. Talk to me, Michael. What the hell is going on?"

Michael sat down in the chair behind his desk, swiveling to face her. Nothing to do but tell the truth. He explained the situation, but she did not look relieved.

"Michael. I can't believe you've involved yourself with this girl. Do I have to remind you that trust is the most important asset we are building in Four Villages? I don't give a damn how innocent your actions are, stop for a minute and ask yourself how this must look to those people whom you are there to serve—not to exploit. If you can't find her a shelter, than *buy* her one. For the sake of your reputation and the company's good name, rent this young woman her own house and then stay far away from her."

"What if Gharia comes after her?"

"This isn't our business—"

"Karen, it might be. I've checked the census figures, and there's a growing imbalance in the sex ratio here. There are far fewer young women than men. Rajban may be a widow, and she may be ill, but Gharia's not exactly a kid. She could still be the best prospect he has."

"If that's so, why did her family get rid of her, instead of marrying her off?"

"I don't know. Maybe they didn't want to pay a dowry. Maybe they don't give a damn. Maybe they're strict Hindus and don't believe in remarriage for women."

"Listen to yourself! There are cultural complexities here that you haven't begun to grasp. This is not why you're in Four Villages."

"We're here to build a stable, diverse, and functional economy, and that can't exist where there is slavery. I won't send Rajban back into slavery."

"I'm not asking you to do that. Just get her out of your house. I want you in this job, Michael. I really do. Show me my confidence is not misplaced."

Michael called in the personnel officer, and she promised to hunt around for an available residence, though she wasn't hopeful. "There are very few rentals in town, and most landlords will deal only with a certain class of clientele. I might be able to obtain a room, or perhaps a shanty, but that would almost certainly bring about the eviction of a current resident."

"We don't want that. Do what you can."

The day failed to improve. Near noon, Michael looked up from his desk to see Pallava Sen, his second-in-command, coming through the open doorway, a half-page of neon yellow paper in his hand.

"Michael, we have a problem."

Leaning back in his chair, Michael slipped off his shades, laying them carefully on the desk. "How bad a problem?"

Pallava rolled his eyes, as if casting a quick prayer up to the gods. With his portly figure and balding head, he looked like a youthful version of the little Buddhas sold in Japanese tourist markets. "Not so bad at the moment, but with admirable potential to get much worse."

"Wonderful."

Pallava handed him the yellow paper. "These have appeared all over the town. They are being read aloud, too, so the illiterate will be informed."

Michael scowled at the notice. It was written in Hindi.

Pallava settled into the guest chair, a grim smile on his face. "It is written as a news report, by the Traditional Council of Elders. You've heard of them?"

"No."

"Neither has anyone else. They do not say whose elders they are, but they do tell us some interesting things. Here—" He leaned forward, pointing at the headline. "That Global Shear has poisoned the people of this district."

Michael had been so fully set to hear how he had kidnapped

and raped a good Hindu woman, that it took him a moment to shift modes. ". . . poisoned?"

"The argument follows. It says that independent testing of well water throughout the district has revealed severe pesticide contamination. The wells have been regularly tested, and for many years they have produced only clean, unpolluted water. Now they are suddenly contaminated? The only plausible explanation is that the groundwater was deliberately poisoned."

"That's ridiculous."

"Oh, there's more." He leaned back, lacing his fingers together in a nervous, unsettled bridge. "The notice does not name specific chemicals, but it claims those present will suppress the birth rate of the district's women, and in many cases will cause monstrous birth defects leading to early miscarriage. This may be one reason so few girls have been born this past year. Girls are weaker than boys. They die more easily."

He said this last in a deadpan voice that made Michael's eyes narrow. "The notice says that?" he asked cautiously. "Or is that your interpretation?"

Pallava's face hardened. In the same low, flat voice, he answered, "*I* would not say that. I have a wife who, I am proud to say, is stronger and smarter than I am. I have two brilliant daughters, a sister, a mother, a grandmother. We are not all that way, Michael."

Michael felt his cheeks heat. "I know. I'm sorry."

Pallava shrugged. "You understand the implication? That Global Shear is using cheap birth control?"

Michael nodded.

"The article is also circulating as an internet message."

"Christ."

"And Shiva. It has not, mercifully, appeared yet on cable TV."

"We need to dispatch crews to field-sample some wells."

"I have already sent them."

"Good. Get me the results as soon as possible." He drummed his desk. "Better test some crop samples too. The harvest is just coming in on the demonstration farm. Check that, especially. *Dammit!* We have to counter these accusations today—and on cable TV too."

It was an hour later when Pallava Sen walked back into Michael's office, collapsing once more into the visitor's chair. Global Shear had used paper, internet, cable TV, messengers, and paid gossip mongers to vehemently deny the allegations of the Traditional Elders, and to announce their intention to immediately investigate the condition of the well water.

Pallava didn't speak right away. He frowned, his brow wrinkling in lines that made him look old.

"How bad is it now?" Michael asked.

Pallava's sigh was long and heartfelt. "Mega-bad. Giga-bad. It seems the slander was at least partly right. We've fast-tested a sample of wells from across the district and everyone of them shows extensive pesticide contamination." He shook his head. "This is not something that could have happened overnight, not even if it was deliberately done, which I don't believe. We are looking at the results of years—probably decades—of seepage into the water table. It's quite obvious the water quality reports we've been using have been falsified. Deliberately falsified."

Michael breathed slowly, trying to calm the fierce pounding of his heart. *Don't panic, but don't hide from the truth either. The first thing to do is get a handle on the problem.* "Let's be specific here. We're talking drinking water?"

"Drinking, agricultural." Pallava spread his hands helplessly. "It's all the same thing, and judging from the spot samples, we have to assume there is pesticide contamination in every well in the district." His hands laced together as he stared at a spot beyond Michael's shoulder. "The Ikeda rice crop is contaminated too. The sample we tested came out so bad the stuff can't be legally used even for animal feed."

"Christ."

"And Shiva too."

No pesticides had been used on the Ikeda rice. That was, after all, a major benefit of genetically-engineered crops—natural insect and disease resistance could be spliced in—but Ikeda rice had not been designed to flush itself free of chemical contamination.

No more assumptions, Michael swore. "Tell me now if Global Shear had anything to do with developing the phony reports."

Pallava straightened, his eyes wide with surprise. He had been in on the operation here from the opening day. "No! No, of course not. Global Shear had nothing to do with preparing the reports. Water quality monitoring has been a government function. Our mistake was relying on the test results we received."

"Why would anybody want to fake these reports?"

Pallava shrugged. "There are many possible reasons. The wells were a government project. To find fault with them would not be patriotic. To find them dirty must mean the money spent to build them was wasted, or that those who built them didn't do sufficient background work, or that more money would be needed to clean the water, and where is that supposed to come from? And will those who built the wells be punished? Those who built the wells also report on their functions, so you see, it's not so hard to understand how it could happen. It's not the first time."

"And still, it's our mistake for trusting the data without testing it."

"Yes. Ultimately, it will come back to that."

"Michael?"

It was Jaya's voice, issuing from the shades he'd left lying on the desk. She spoke softly, as if he were a sleeping child, and she, reluctant to wake him. Her priority-link let her open a line at any time.

Michael grabbed the shades and slipped them on. "Jaya! How are you? How's the baby?" He transferred the link to his portal screen, and Jaya's image replaced the document he'd been working on. She was as lovely as any magazine model and not for the first time, Michael thought of Sheo with a twinge of envy.

"We're all fine," Jaya assured him. Then she hesitated. "Michael, I've been talking to Ryan."

He grunted, sinking back into his chair. "You've heard about Rajban, then."

"Yes. I think it's sweet, what you're trying to do for her." Jaya touched her ruby-red lips. What a perfect alliance she had made with the colorful, symbiotic bacteria living in her cells—yet most people, upon hearing the source of the color, would respond in revulsion: *Yuck. I would never do that.*

It took practice, to keep the mind open to new possibilities.

"Sheo told me about the reaction of the nurses to Ela's birth," Jaya said. "I didn't notice, really. They were very kind to me. The older woman, though, was concerned that I have a son next time. She told me she had been trained in these things."

Michael scowled. "What things?"

"That's what I asked. It seems there is a uterine implant on the market, which can be used to selectively abort female embryos. It isn't legal, but the nurse was quite casual about it. She offered to set me up with one before I left the hospital, for a small fee of course. Sheo thought you might like to know this."

Michael grimaced. "Sheo was right."

A uterine implant was better than infanticide—Michael even found himself admiring the ingenuity of such a device—but what of the imbalance it would generate? He remembered Gharia, and the look of wrath on his face. "How long do you suppose this has been going on?"

Jaya shrugged. "In one form or another, for hundreds of years."

"Though it's gotten easier now."

"Yes."

But who would bear the cost?

Tensions in Four Villages were not readily visible, yet Michael had sensed them anyway, in the whispering of the nurses on the maternity ward, in the heat of Rajban's fever, in Kanwal's cheerful lament over dowry and women and net access. The people here were experiencing a strange, sideways tearing of their culture, like raw cotton being combed apart, the pieces on their way to a new order, while still clinging helplessly to the old.

"This fellow Gharia is supposed to be a religious activist," Michael said. "I'm starting to wonder if it's only coincidence that this attack on Global Shear followed so closely on his visit this morning."

"Rajban is just one little girl," Jaya reminded him.

True, but a fuse was small, compared to the explosives it ignited.

Jaya might have read his mind. "Michael, please be careful. These things have a way of getting out of hand."

(xii)

After a day spent researching a bid on the Victoria Glen project, Cody found she could not sleep. So at 3AM she pulled on her VR helmet and joined her mother on a stroll in the Paris sunshine. That is, Annette strolled, through tourist crowds along a river walk, beneath a grove of ancient trees. Cody felt as if she were floating, a balloon gliding at her mother's side.

"Of all the uses of VR, I like this best," Cody said. "Being able to step out of the awful three AM hour, when everything's so dark and cold and hopeless—step right out into gorgeous sunshine. It's like slipping free of your fate, flipping a finger at the cosmos. Ha!"

Annette laughed. Cody was looking out of her shades, and so she couldn't see her mother's face, but she could feel her presence. It was a strange, tickling feeling, as if she might see her after all if she turned just a little bit more . . .

Cody had not lived with her mother since leaving Victoria Glen for boarding school, and still, Annette had been an indefatigable presence in her life, through phone calls and email and brief visits several times a year as they both worked toward their degrees. It had been so hard. Cody felt scared even now when she remembered the loneliness, the resentment she had felt for so many years living on the charity of a corporate scholarship, in a private school where almost everyone else had money and a home and a real family. But even at her worst moments, Cody had never doubted Annette's love.

Now Annette was forty nine, a data analyst on vacation in Paris with her husband of many years. She had helped him raise his son and one of their own. "Doing it right this time," she'd joked with Cody. It had only hurt a little.

"So, girl. You've been up to something, haven't you? Hurry up and tell me before Jim gets back."

"Up to something?" Cody echoed, disquiet stirring near her heart.

"Something's put you in a mood," Annette said. Up ahead, Jim was waiting by a flower stand. Annette waved to him. "Are you working yourself up for a fight?"

"Oh." Cody had promised herself she would not mention Victoria Glen. Her mother didn't like to think about those days. She didn't even like to acknowledge that time had ever been real. And still, Cody found herself confessing. "I went back to Victoria Glen—"

"Cody!"

"In VR," she added, hoping to appease her mother's scathing tone. "I'm bidding on a job there. I spent all day developing the proposal. I guess I'm wound a little tight."

"Why *there*, Cody?" Annette sighed. "I know you're doing well. You're not desperate for the job. Are you?"

"No."

"Then why go back there?"

"I don't know. Or . . . maybe I do know. I—"

Annette stepped into a bookstore, leaving Jim waiting beside the flowers. Cody watched her hands touch the spines of a row of English-language guidebooks. They were strong, long-fingered hands, golden as teak, each nail painted in milk chocolate brown. "Cody, do you know the greatest difference between you and me?"

Cody laughed. It was the only reaction she could think of. "Oh, you're smarter than I am."

"No. I'm more ruthless. I have never let the past own me. If I don't like it, I cut it out. I throw it away. It's not an easy thing to do, but it's needful. I don't think about Victoria Glen, and I don't muse over the boy who was your father, and I don't apologize to anybody for letting Prescott Academy take you away. Holding on to all that would have made my soul so heavy I couldn't get up in the morning. I have to live lightly. I have to do all that I can with what I have in my hands right now." She looked up at the bookstore door. Jim had just come in.

Annette's voice grew softer. "Brace yourself for a mother-lecture," she warned. "Cody, you need to learn to live lightly too. You don't have anything to make up for. Let the past go. Let it slip away, and find your joy here, today."

But what if the past is looking for you? Rising in your life like a flooding river, climbing past your ankles, past your knees and your thighs, flowing into your secret places, nesting in your womb?

Cody let the link close, plunging herself back into the darkness of her VR helmet. Not absolutely dark. A call-waiting light glowed amber in the corner of her vision.

When had that come on?

She tapped her glove, calling up a link ID.

Confirmed identity: Michael Fielding.

"Oh God." She felt as if a heat lance had plunged through her, diving in a beam between heart and stomach and out the middle of her back. *Michael.* "Why now, baby?" she whispered. All the lines of force that guided her life seemed to be intersecting tonight.

She laid her palm against her flat belly. Was there a baby there? Still a single cell, moving toward her womb, and the judgment she had built-in. She'd blamed herself for the loss of that first pregnancy, but had it been her fault? Or had she been poisoned oh so long ago, in Victoria Glen?

She bowed her head, laughing, crying—some strange mix of the two, her guts feeling like jelly. "Baby, *why* are calling tonight?"

Easy to find out.

She wiped her eyes on the hem of her shirt. She drew a deep breath to steady herself. Where did he live now, anyway? Hong Kong, wasn't it? She'd gotten a card from him last Christmas.

Her finger curled. She tapped her data glove.

Link.

Just like that, he was there, his head and shoulders drifting in an ill-defined space only an arm's reach in front of her. He looked surprised to see her. "Cody?"

She smiled. "Come on, baby, I don't look that old."

He blushed. Bless him. "Old? Not at all. Hey, it's been awhile. And I know it's an outrageous hour. I meant to leave a message, but then I thought I'd query your status, and you were awake—"

"How are you, Michael?" she asked. He had always talked too much when he was nervous.

"Oh, I'm good. The job, though . . . I've got a situation here. I'm working in southern India. Did I tell you that?"

"No."

That flustered him further. A rosy blush heated his bronze complexion. He looked down at his desk a moment, then grinned. "I sound like I've got a few too many cross links in the old wetware, don't I?"

"It happens to the best of us."

It was on her lips to tell him what she'd remembered in the VR last night, yet she couldn't do it. It had been her decision to end their marriage. In the long dark months after the abortion she had watched their union rot, until she could kick it over with one cold clutch of words, *There's nothing left. I'm leaving.*

How could she tell him now, "Oops. Sorry. I made a mistake"?

"How's your schedule?" he asked. "Are you busy right now?"

"At three AM?"

His brows rose over a crooked smile. "Well, yeah. Sorry. I wouldn't be bothering you, but we've just stumbled over a critical ground water problem—and a possible political stew, to make things exciting." Quickly, he explained the details. "I called you first. You're the best. And basically, you're a pushover."

Don't smile at me like that, she thought. And breathe, girl.

Thank God this wasn't a full-sensory link. She didn't want to smell him, or feel the heat off his body. That smile was like a light shining into her soul . . .

She asked, "Are you looking for a professional reference?"

"If you think that's what I need. I was wondering though, if you could handle it?"

"An operation that size?" She shook her head, uncomfortable with the idea. "Green Stomp has only done domestic work. It would take time for us to hire the extra personnel, and mobilize." *And besides, there's another job I need to do.* "You'd be better off with a local outfit. I could ask around for recommendations."

He nodded, but he looked tense and unhappy. "I really need a favor, Cody. Could you do a VR consultation now? I mean right now. This afternoon . . . oh hell. This morning, where you are. I need a specialist to survey the wells. I need solid answers for the people who live here. It's a bad situation, and it could get out of hand so easily, especially . . ."

She didn't like the awkward guilt lurking in his eyes. "What Michael?"

He told her about Rajban. Cody listened, unable to completely suppress a dark spear of suspicion, of jealousy, but when he finished, she shook her head at her own tumbled existence, knowing she had thrown away something precious, for all the wrong reasons. It was all she could do not to cry.

(xiii)

Cody's workday had been Michael's night. While he slept, she studied the test results from the sample wells. While he dreamed, she ordered select strains of genetically engineered bacteria from New Delhi, along with case upon case of the nutrient broth that would stimulate them to rapidly reproduce. Near 3AM the frozen vials and sealed boxes arrived in Four Villages, after a quick trip on a southbound jet. When Michael called into the office first thing in the morning, Pallava Sen reported that everything was in place to run a demonstration treatment on a well at Kanwal's farm.

"Great! I'll be there in half an hour." It was already eight o'clock.

It was a vibrant morning. Rajban was in the courtyard, working at the soil with the little hoe she'd found. The ground around her was wet, and the air steamy. The eastern sky had turned itself into a fluffy Christian postcard. Columns of light from the hidden sun poured down between tearing rain clouds, like radiance leaking from the face of God. In a patch of blue sky between the towering cumulus, two tiny white cloud scraps drifted on the edge of visibility. *Angels,* Michael thought. They looked like angels, gliding in slow, raptor circles on the threshold of heaven.

Was this how myths got started?

Rajban looked up at him as he approached. He pantomimed eating food. She smiled tolerantly, then went back to her work. Michael frowned, troubled at her lack of appetite. Then Cody's glyph winked on in the corner of his shades and he forgot to worry. He tapped a full link. "Good morning!" It felt so right to be working with Cody again.

"Or good night," Cody answered, her voice husky and tired. "I'm going to catch a few hours sleep before the demo . . . Is that your waif? She looks like a little girl."

"She is a little girl. And she hasn't been eating much. Muthaye was here yesterday, but she didn't leave any messages. I'm a little concerned, Cody. It's past time her AIDS treatment was started."

Rajban's work had slowed; Michael guessed she was listening to him. What did she imagine he talked about? He shook his head. She looked so lost, a little girl caught on an island in the midst of a rising river, her spot of land steadily shrinking around her.

"She hides inside her work," Michael mused. "Just like we do."

The house pre-empted any reply. "Mr. Fielding, please step inside immediately." The French doors swung open as the injunction was repeated in Hindi. Rajban scrambled to her feet. "Air surveillance has identified the intruder Raman Gharia approaching the premises," the house explained. "Please return immediately to the safety of the interior."

"Michael, what is it?" Cody asked.

"A local troublemaker, that's all." He beckoned to Rajban. They went inside, and the doors swung shut behind them.

"Hark, give me a street view," Michael said.

A window opened in his shades. He looked out on the lane, and saw Gharia approaching in the company of a portly older man with salt and pepper hair neatly combed about a face so dignified it was almost comical, as if he were possessed by dignity, as if it held him together, so that if he ever let it go, his body would crumble to helpless dust. A Traditional Elder? Michael wondered.

A link came in from Sankar. "Security forces are on their way, Mr. Fielding. Please stay inside."

"Sankar, I trust you won't be sending helicopter shock troops this time?"

"Uh, no sir. As per our discussion, we will be striving for an *appropriate* response."

"Thank you." In their discussion, he had also insisted he have voice override on any house functions. He wasn't going to be locked up again.

The house announced visitors. "A Mr. Gharia and Mr. Rao to see you, Mr. Fielding."

Michael glanced at Rajban. Her chest fluttered in short little pants. Her eyes were wide. "Hark. Ask her if she knows this Mr. Rao."

The house translated his question to Hindi. Rajban closed her eyes, and nodded.

Michael strode toward the door.

"Michael, what are you doing?" Cody's voice was sharp and high, reminding him of another time. *It's all gone. Can't you see that?*

"Mr. Fielding," Sankar objected. "Perhaps you have not seen my report. These two men are deeply involved—"

"I only want to have a civil discussion with them." And learn what it would take to get them to leave Rajban alone. "Hark, open the door."

The door swung open to reveal Gharia and Rao, shoulder

to shoulder in the alcove. Gharia looked up in surprise, then, "Namaste," he muttered. Rao echoed it, and introduced himself. Michael was unsurprised to learn that this was Rajban's brother in law, the head of the household, the one who had rejected her after her husband died.

"You look at me with anger," Rao said, his voice deep, his dignity so heavy it seemed to suck the heat out of the air, "when I am the one who has been shamed. Return the woman you hold, pay a dowry for her shame, and I will not involve the police."

Behind his back, Michael could hear the house whispering a string of Hindi as it translated Rao's words for Rajban. He drew himself up a little straighter. "She is not my prisoner."

The house uttered a brief line in Hindi. Rao waited for it to finish, then: "She is my brother's widow. Perhaps you don't understand what that means, Mr. Fielding. You are a foreigner, and your modern culture holds little respect for a woman's dignity. Upon my brother's death, I was prepared to allow his wife to live in my household for the rest of her life, despite the burden this would place on me. Rajban rejected my generosity. She desired to marry again. My wife also counseled this would be best, but I am an old man, and I believe in the old ways. A widow should be given respect!" He sighed. "Sometimes though, a woman will not have respect. The immorality of the world infected this woman. Carnal desire drove her into the street."

Michael felt his body grow hard with a barely contained fury. "That's not how she told the story." Rajban hadn't even known her husband was dead until Gharia's visit.

Gharia glared at him. Michael watched his hands.

Rao alone remained unruffled, glued together by dignity. "I am learning we must all bend with the times," he announced. "I have found a new husband for Rajban. If you will pay the dowry and the medical expenses of her rehabilitation as the penalty of your shame, I will allow this marriage to go forward."

"What an evil old mercenary," Cody growled, while Michael traded stares with Gharia. It was quite obvious who the intended husband was to be. "Tell him to shove off, Michael. She's just a little girl."

Rao could not hear her, and so he continued laying out his terms. "If you do not pay the dowry, I will return the woman to my household. With the help of my wife and son, we may yet protect her from the weakness of the flesh, for as long as she is living."

"Which won't be long," Cody said savagely, "when Rao refuses to buy treatment for her AIDS."

"She's staying here," Michael said.

"Then I will summon the police."

"She's staying here! It's what she wants."

"Have you asked her that?" Gharia demanded. "No woman wants to be a childless whore."

"You dirty son-of-a—"

Michael broke off, startled by a wash of cold air at his back. He turned to see Rajban, her face veiled by the hem of the sari Muthaye had given her. Her eyes were wide and frightened as she squeezed past Michael. "Rajban, wait!" She slipped past Rao too, out of the alcove and into the street. Michael stared after her in astonishment, but Rao, he didn't even look at her. She might have been a shadow.

"Jesus, Michael!" Cody shouted. "Don't let her go."

Rao nodded in satisfaction. "I will send a servant with the bride price."

Gharia was smiling. His gaze slid past Michael on a film of oily satisfaction. As if to himself, he murmured, "Every woman desires respect."

"Michael, stop her!"

"Rajban! Don't go." She would not understand his words, but surely she would ken the meaning?

Rajban looked at him, with doubt in her eyes, and fear, and a deep sadness that seemed to resonate through millennia of suffering.

"Rajban, please stay."

Her gaze fell, and docilely she turned to follow Rao, who had not even bothered to look behind him.

"Michael! Damn you. Go after her. Stop her."

"Cody, she's made her own decision. I can't grab her and force her back into the house."

"For God's sake, Michael, why not? For once in your life, go out and grab somebody. Stop her. Don't let her make the decision that will wreck her life. Michael, she's hurting so badly, she's in no condition to decide."

To his astonishment, he could hear her weeping. "Cody?"

Her glyph winked out, as she cut the link.

(xiv)

Something had changed in the house, though Michael couldn't decide exactly what. All the furniture remained in place; the lighting was just the same. Mrs. Nandy had not been by, so the mud-stains remained on the couch, and Rajban's bag of soil—half empty now—still sat by the glass doors. Maybe the house was colder.

He sent a call to Cody, but she didn't answer, and he declined to leave a message on the server.

So Rajban had left! So what? Why did Cody have to act like it was the end of the world? Rajban had *chosen* to leave. She had walked freely out the door.

Michael wished she had not, but wishing couldn't change the decision she had made.

He wondered what her reasoning had been. Perhaps she preferred whatever small life Rao might offer her, to the strangeness she had glimpsed here. Illiteracy was a barrier that kept her from a knowledge of the wider world. Access to information was another hurdle. So she had returned to the life she knew. It was probably as simple as that.

Rao's messenger arrived at the door after only a few minutes. Michael listened to the price he quoted, then he put a call through to his bank, adjusted the worth on a cash card, and handed it over, letting the house record the transaction. He had promised to pay for Rajban's AIDS treatment, after all. And she was better off with her family, wasn't she?

He told himself it had all been a misunderstanding.

On the long walk back to the house of her brother in law, Rajban could feel the sickness growing inside her. It was a debilitating weakness, a pollution in her muscles, dirt in her joints. By the time she reached the house she was dazed and exhausted, with a thirst that made her tongue swell. As she crossed the threshold behind the men, Mother-in-law glared, first at Gharia, then at Rajban. She asked Rao if it had been agreed that a dowry should be paid. Rao shrugged. He sat at a table, ignoring everyone, even Gharia, who stood by looking confused and a little angry. "We wait," Rao said.

Inside the house the air was very still, a puddle of heat trapped under the ancient, seeping walls. Mother-in-law turned on Rajban. "No water. No!" she said, cutting her off from the plastic cube with its spigot, that sat upon hollow concrete blocks and held the day's supply of water. "Out! You have work. There is work, you stupid girl."

Rajban felt dizzied by the swirling motion of Mother-in-law's hands. She stumbled back a step.

"Won't you let her drink?" Gharia asked softly.

Rajban cast him a resentful glance. Oh yes. He had an interest in her now. Or he imagined he did. Michael's house had told her what was said on the doorstep. She blushed in shame again, remembering the words Rao had spoken.

He had painted her with those words. He had painted her past. *Dirty whore*. Her polluted body testified to it. And why else would all this have happened to her? What Rao said had felt just like the truth. Michael would not want to look at her now that he knew, and Muthaye could never come to visit her again—but Rao had offered her sanctuary.

Of course there would be no dowry. She thought it strange that Gharia didn't understand this. Rao scowled at him. Then he scowled at Mother-in-law, standing guard by the water cube. "Women's business," he growled.

"Get out!" the old woman screeched at Rajban, now that she was sure she had permission. "No one has done your work for you, foolish girl." Under the assault of her flailing hands, Rajban stumbled into the courtyard. She looked around. The courtyard seemed strange, as if she had dreamed this place and the life she had lived here.

Heat steamed from the moist ground. The plants were wilted in their containers. She shared their thirst, and, using the dirty wash water stored in a small barrel by the door, she set out to allay it.

Michael took a zip to the office, to find Pallava Sen waiting for him in the lobby. "Good morning, Michael! Our bioremediation consultant called a few minutes ago to say she will not be able to attend today."

"Cody called?" Michael's voice cracked with the force of his surprise.

"Yes. Of course I've been consulting with her throughout the night, so I'll have no problem directing the media gig."

They matched strides through the security sensors. Armored doors opened for them. An elevator stood waiting on the other side. "Be assured, everything is in place," Pallava continued, as the doors closed and the elevator rose. "We have technicians from New Delhi to handle the bacterial cultures. Several media teams are already at the airport, and within a few hours an international task force will be here to examine the complaints against us, and our counter-charges of fraud against the local water commission."

They stepped out into the carpeted hallway on the top floor, greeted by the scent of fresh coffee. "When will the water purification units be here?" Michael asked.

"The first shipment is due to arrive within the hour. They'll be set up in stations throughout the district. People will be able to withdraw five gallons at a time—enough for drinking, anyway."

"Excellent." At least people could start drinking clean water now, today, for the first time since . . .

He sighed. Probably for the first time ever.

Someone had left a steaming cup of coffee on the desk. "Pallava, thank you. I know you've been up most of the night with this situation. It sounds as if you have things well under control." Then, because he couldn't help himself, he added, "When you talked to Cody just now, did she . . . sound all right?"

Pallava frowned, his eyes narrowing suspiciously. "She sounded tired, but then she has worked through the night as well. There's no need to worry, Michael. Let her rest. I can handle the gig."

"That's not what I meant. Pallava, I know you can do it. I want you to handle the press conference too. It's your scene now."

Rajban crouched in the shade just outside the kitchen door, patting dirty water on her cheeks and breast. Inside, Gharia and Rao were talking heatedly. Gharia was saying, "Fielding will pay. You'll see. He wants the woman to have medicine so that—"

Gharia broke off in mid-sentence. Startled, Rajban glanced

over her shoulder to see if someone had spied her, resting in the shade. No one looked out the door. Instead, she heard a stranger speaking from inside the house, crowing about the cleverness of Rao's demands. This was the messenger sent to collect the dowry.

"Give the money to my son," Mother-in-law interrupted, her old voice tight and frightened, as if she feared a rebuke for her boldness, but couldn't help herself nonetheless.

Rajban peeked around the edge of the doorway, to see Rao still seated at the table, Gharia still standing. Both he and the messenger stared hungrily at the cash card Rao twirled in his hands. Then Rao's long fingers closed over the card, hiding it from sight. His face was fleshy, and yet it was the hardest face Rajban had ever seen. "You may both go now."

Gharia looked confused. "We need to discuss the finances, the wedding, and—"

"There will be no wedding," Rao announced. "My brother's widow must be subjected to no further shame."

Rajban slipped back behind the wall. The garden looked so queer, as if she had never seen it quite so clearly before. Inside, Gharia's voice was rising in indignant anger, but Rajban did not listen to the words, knowing that nothing he might say could change her fate.

Pallava Sen had hardly left when Muthaye's glyph winked on in the corner of Michael's shades. He tapped his glove, transferring the call to a wall screen. Muthaye snapped into existence. She stood in Michael's living room, her stern face framed by a printed sari, which she had pulled over her head like a scarf. In her hand, she held Rajban's half-empty bag of soil.

Michael's gaze caught on it. "Rajban has gone."

Muthaye's lips pursed petulantly. "I am at the house, Michael. I can see that. Where has she gone?"

Michael felt inexplicably guilty as he made his explanation. He did not feel any better as he watched Muthaye's expression darken. Her eyes rolled up, beseeching the heavens for patience, perhaps. Then she spoke: "Mr. Fielding, I would be interested to someday engage you in a discussion of free will. What does it really mean? You tell me that Rajban *chose* to leave with this Rao character, her brother-in-law who treated her as less than human even as you looked on. Mr. Fielding, can you tell me why she *freely chose* to go with him?"

Michael scowled, feeling unfairly impeached, by Muthaye and by Cody too. "I suppose she felt torn from her roots. Most people are, by nature, afraid of change."

Muthaye's scowl deepened. "Rajban did not suffer a failure of nerve, Mr. Fielding."

"I didn't say—"

"No, of course. You wouldn't say such a thing. You are a kind person, Michael, and obviously you've done well in life. It's only natural that you believe opportunity is omnipresent, that we all rise or sink according to our talents and our drive—but the world is more complex than that. Talent is meaningless when we are schooled in the belief that change is wrong, when we are taught that we are worthy of nothing more than the ironbound existence fate has given us. Believe me, Rajban has been well-schooled in her worthlessness. She knows that she lives at the sufferance of her husband's family. Obedience and acceptance have been drilled into her from babyhood. To expect her to freely *decide* to defy her brother-in-law would be like expecting a drug addict to freely decide to stay sober at a crack party. There is no difference.

"And it is partly my fault too, for I laughed yesterday when she suggested this soil had a magic." Muthaye lifted the stained cloth bag. "Perhaps it does. I have talked to a horticultural specialist and he is intrigued. He tells me there may be valuable microorganisms in this dirt. I will have it tested, and I will not laugh at naive optimism ever again."

"Muthaye—"

She raised her palm. "Michael, I apologize for lecturing you, but you must begin to see that to dream is itself a learned skill."

Stop her! For once in your life . . .

Michael sighed. "I gave Rao money to pay for the AIDS treatment." That was something, at least.

Although from the way Muthaye glared at him, it might have been worse than nothing. He scowled, irritated now. "Was that wrong too?"

"There will be no treatment."

Michael felt his patience snap. Really, he'd had enough. "You don't know that. She was to be married again—"

"Did Gharia pay the dowry?"

"No, but it was understood—"

"I expect none of you understood the same thing. You each heard only what you could tolerate. Understand this, Michael. Rajban is the childless wife of a dead man. Rao can gain nothing by letting her marry. He will refuse her the AIDS treatment and keep the money for himself. Mark my words: If we do not find Rajban and get her out of her brother-in-law's house, then she will die there, most likely in a matter of days."

Cody linked into the Terrace on a full sensory connection. The private VR chat room had been designed as a flagstoned California patio, embedded in a garden of pepper trees and azaleas. Everyone had a personal animation stored on the server, an active, three-dimensional image of themselves that reflected their habitual postures and gestures, so they would seem to be present, even when they weren't fully linked through a VR suit.

Cody's image looked a good deal younger than it ought to—a sharp reminder of how many years had gone by since she'd visited the Terrace. The last time had been during those nebulous months between the abortion and the divorce. Not the best of days, and returning now made her feel a bit queasy.

Still, she had come with a purpose. She set about it, sending a glyph to Etsuko, Ryan, and Jaya, asking them to come if they could—and within a minute, they were all represented. Etsuko was involved in a meeting, so she sent only a passive image of herself to record the chat: an alabaster statue dressed in formal kimono. Her flirtatious eyes and the cant of her head as she looked down from a pedestal gave an impression of sharp and regal attention.

Ryan and Jaya were able to interact in real time. Their images lounged in the French patio chairs, behind steaming cups of coffee. Jaya had a half-smile on her face. Ryan looked uncertain. He and Michael were very close, Cody knew, and questions of loyalty were probably stirring in his mind.

She drew a deep breath. "Thank you for coming. Jaya, Michael told me about your newest daughter. Congratulations."

"That was an adventure!" Jaya said. "I don't know what I would have done without Michael. He's a wonderful man."

Cody felt herself stiffen. "He is a good man, but he made a mistake this morning when he let Rajban return to her husband's family."

"The girl who's been staying with him?" Ryan asked. "But that's good, isn't it?"

"No," Michael said.

Cody turned, to find Michael's image standing a few steps to the side.

"Cody's right. I made a mistake. I didn't want to believe this was an abusive situation."

"I'm afraid for her," Cody said. "Michael, we need to find her as soon as we can. I came here to ask the Terrace for help. I know I have not been part of this group for many years, but I still trust you all more than anyone, and you're already familiar with Rajban. Will you help? I've rented two drone planes. I know you're busy, but if you could rotate shifts every few minutes, the three of you might be able to guide one plane, while I inhabit the other. We don't know where she lives, but we know some things about her."

Michael said, "I'm opening up the Global Shear census data. That'll speed things up. When we do find her, Muthaye and I will go after her on the ground."

Inside the house there were oranges on the table, and clean water, and sweetened tea, but no one invited Rajban in. She stole a half-ripe orange off one of the trees. Its rind was swirled with green and the flesh was grimly tart, but she ate it anyway, her back to the house. She wondered at herself. She had never stolen fruit before. In truth, she did not feel like the same person.

The orange peels went into her heap of magic soil.

Muthaye had laughed at the idea that it might be magic.

Rajban picked up a damp clump. It was soft and warm, and smelled of fertility. If magic had a smell, this would be it, yet Muthaye had laughed at the idea.

Rajban rocked back and forth, thinking about it, and about Muthaye's mother and her dead baby girl. It was better the baby had died. A girl without a father would only know hardship, and still it must have been a terribly painful thing. For a moment, she held the baby in her arms, acutely aware of its soft breath and warm skin, its milky smell. When she thought about it dying, grief pushed behind her eyes.

Muthaye's mother had married again . . . and had another daughter. Not a son, but the school she owned earned money, so perhaps she could afford a daughter.

She was just like you, Rajban.

What did that mean? Rajban did not feel at all like the same person. There was an anger inside her that had never been there before. It felt like a seed planted under her heart, and it was swelling, filling with all the possibilities she had seen or heard of in the last two days.

Her fists clenched as the seed sprouted in a burst of growth, rooting deep down in her gut and flowering in her brain, thriving on the magic soil of new ideas.

Cody was a point of awareness gliding over the alleys and lanes of Four Villages. Linked to the GS census, the town became a terrain of information. Addresses flashed past, accompanied by statistics on each building and the families that owned them—occupation, education, income, propensity for paying taxes. At the same time the drone's guidance program spun a tiny camera lens, recording the people in the streets, sending their images to the GS census, where a search function matched them against information on file, spitting back identifications in less than a second.

No way this search could be legal. There had to be privacy strictures on the use of the GS census data.

What did privacy mean anymore?

It didn't matter. Not now. Cody only wanted to find the combination of bits that would mean Rajban.

Rajban was a non-entity. She did not appear anywhere in the census—and that was a clue in itself.

Some heads-of-household refused to answer the census questions, forcing the field agent to guess at their names and family members. Michael had used that fact in his search parameters. It was likely such a house was in a fundamentalist neighborhood and that it had an intensely cultivated private courtyard, where a young wife could be hidden from an agent's prying eyes . . . but not from the eyes of a drone aircraft.

The plane was powered by micropumps that adjusted its internal air pressure, allowing it to sink and rise and glide through the heated air. The pumps were powered by solar cells on the plane's dorsal surface, backed up by tiny batteries built into its frame. It could stay aloft for months, maybe for years. Its only drawback was that it was slow.

Cody's fingernails had dug crescent impressions in her data glove by the time the drone cruised over the first household on Michael's list. A woman was hanging laundry in the shade, but she was older than Rajban, with two children playing near her feet. At the next house the courtyard was empty, and the garden it contained was yellow and sickly. Cody tapped her glove, sending the plane on.

Recorded names and faces slid past her, until finally, the camera picked out a familiar face. "*Gharia.*" The GS census confirmed her guess.

Cody ordered the drone lower. It hovered over the street as Gharia stumbled along, head down, each sandaled foot ramming into the mud like a crutch, while chickens scurried to get out of his way and children ran indoors, or behind their mothers until he passed. Rage and helplessness were twisted into his posture. Cody's heart rate tripled, knowing something terrible had happened.

The drone's shadow was a cross in the mud. Gharia saw it and pulled up short. He looked up, while Cody let the plane sink lower.

She had expected to hate him, but now, seeing the pain and confusion in his eyes, she could feel only a desperate empathy. The old ways were dissolving everywhere. Her own tangled expectations neatly echoed his.

Then Gharia crouched. Still staring at the plane, he groped blindly, clawing a fistful of mud from the street. Cody's eyes widened as he jumped to his feet and flung the mud at the plane. Just a little extra weight could upset the plane's delicate balance. She started to order it *up*, but the guidance AI responded first, activating micropumps that forced air out of the fuselage. The plane shot out of reach, and Gharia became a little man.

He threw his head back. He opened his mouth in a scream she could not hear. His shoulders heaved as he looked around for some object upon which to vent his rage. He found it in the white cart of a water station being set up at the end of the street. The startled technician stumbled back several steps as Gharia attacked the cart, rocking it, kicking at it, but it was too heavy to turn over. Even the plastic frame would be very hard to dent.

After a minute of frantic effort, Gharia gave up. Chin held high, he walked away through a crowd of bemused spectators, as if nothing had happened.

Cody touched her belly, wondering if there was life growing in there, and if it was a boy or a girl—if it would die, or live.

What difference is there, between me and this unhappy man?

Both of them had let antique expectations twist the balance of their lives.

A winged shadow passed over the courtyard. Rajban looked up from where she crouched in the shade of the mandarin tree. Her hands left off their work of pulling tiny weed seedlings from the mossy soil. Squinting against the glare, she searched the sky. There. It was the little airplane that had flown over Michael's house, blue like the sky and very hard to see. More like a thought than any solid thing.

She reached to touch the necklace her mother had given her, before remembering it was gone. The life she'd lived before was fading, and she was not the same person anymore.

When she first came to her husband's house this thriving mandarin tree had been ill. The soil in which it was rooted had been unclean, until she tended it, until she prayed the magic into existence. A worm had hatched from the barren dirt, and the mandarin tree had been reborn, no longer the same tree as before.

Rajban felt that way: As if she had been fed some potent magic that opened her eyes to undreamed possibilities. Perhaps Muthaye's mother had felt this way too?

Rajban rose unsteadily to her feet. The heat of her fever was like a slow funeral fire, made worse because she had been allowed no water. Her mouth felt like ashes. No matter. Like Muthaye's mother, she was ready to step away from this empty round of life.

Michael waited with Muthaye in the cramped passenger seat of an air-conditioned zip. The driver had parked his vehicle between two market stalls set up under a spreading banyan tree. Young men lounged in the shade, eating flavored ice. Michael idly watched three tiny screens playing at once in his shades. Two were the feeds from the searching drones. The third was the bioremediation demonstration out at Kanwal's farm.

There was Kanwal, hungrily watching Pallava explain the activity of the technicians gathered around the well. Kanwal's ambitions were an energy, waiting to be shaped.

"Michael!"

Cody's tense voice startled him. His gaze swept the other two screens, and he caught sight of Rajban, gazing upward, her golden face washed in the harsh light of the noon sun.

"Michael, we've found her."

He whooped in triumph. "She looks all right!"

Muthaye squeezed his arm. "Why is she outside at noon? It's so terribly hot. Look at her cheeks. Look how flushed they are. We must hurry." She leaned forward, to tell the address to the driver of the zip.

The driver's eyes widened. Then he laughed in good humor. "I no go there. Too many of the politics there. Don't like any new way. Throw mud my zip."

Muthaye sighed. "He's right. It's a bad neighborhood. Michael, you won't be welcome there."

"If it's that kind of neighborhood, you won't be welcome either. You'll be as foreign as me."

A ghost of a smile turned her lips. "Maybe not quite so, but—"

"I can't send a security team in, you understand? This isn't company business, and I've already stretched my authority by using the census. But I can go after her myself."

"We can both go after her," Muthaye said. She used a cash card to pay the driver. "I only hope she is willing to leave."

The silent drone floated above the courtyard. From this post, Cody looked down and saw that something had changed. Rajban had moved out of the shade of the little potted tree. She stood in the sunshine now, her back straight, no sign of timidity in her posture. Her gaze was fixed on the house. She seemed in possession of herself and it made her a different person. The timorous girl from Michael's garden was gone.

Cody swallowed against a dry throat. Clearly, Rajban intended something. Cody feared what it might be. A woman who has been cornered and condemned all her life should not protest, but Rajban's obedience had been corrupted—by the whisperings of Muthaye, by her glimpse of a different life.

Cody felt as if she watched herself, ready to burst in the close confines of Victoria Glen. She wanted to cry out to Rajban, tell her to wait, not to take any risks . . . but the plane had no audio.

Rajban stepped toward the house with a clean, determined stride.

Cody ordered the drone to follow. The micropumps labored and the plane sank, but with excruciating slowness. It was only halfway down when Rajban disappeared inside.

Muthaye hid her face with a sari. She walked a step behind Michael but no one was fooled. Change had risen in a slow flood over Four Villages, dissolving so many of the old ways, but here was an island. The people of Rao's neighborhood had resisted the waters, throwing up walls of hoary tradition to turn the flood away. It was as if history had run backward here. Girls received less schooling every year, they were married at younger and younger ages, they bore more children . . . or at least they bore more sons.

The sex selection implant was an aspect of modernity that had worked its way inside the fundamentalist quarter. It was a breach in the walls that must ultimately bring them tumbling down . . . but not on this day.

Michael walked at a fast, deliberate pace, following the directions whispered to him by Jaya as she watched from the second drone aircraft. He felt the stares of unemployed men, and of hordes of boys munching on sweets and flavored ice. Tension curled around him like a bow wave.

A link came in from his chief of security. "Mr. Fielding, I don't like this at all. Let me send some people in."

"No," Michael muttered, keeping his voice low, trying not to move his lips. "Sankar, you send your people in here, you're going to touch off a riot. You know it."

The brand of fundamentalism didn't matter, and it didn't even need a religious affiliation. Michael had encountered the same irrational situation as a boy when he'd gotten off the bus at the wrong stop, finding himself in a housing project where the presence of a prosperous mixed-race kid was felt like a slap against the hip-hop culture.

Fundamentalism was so frightening because it taught the mind to *not* think. Such belief systems cramped people's horizons, sabotaging rational thought, while virulently opposing all competitive ideas.

Michael heard Muthaye gasp. He turned, just as a clump of mud hit him in the cheek. A pack of boys hanging out at the entrance of a TV theater erupted in wild laughter. "Keep walking," Muthaye muttered through gritted teeth. Mud had splashed across her face. Her sari was dirtied. More clumps came flying after them. Michael wanted to take her arm, but that would only make things worse. Boys jeered. They made kissy noises at Muthaye. A few massaged their crotch as she passed.

Jaya was watching over them from the drone. "Turn here," she said, her voice tight. "There is hardly anyone in the alley to your left. All right, now go right—walk faster, some of the boys are following you—keep going, keep going. Turn again! Left. There. Now you're out of their sight."

"How much farther?" Muthaye whispered into the open line. Michael glanced back over his shoulder, but the boys were not in sight.

Mother-in-law looked up as Rajban stepped across the threshold. Surprise and anger mingled in her wrinkled face as she scurried to guard the water cube. Rao pretended not to notice. *Women's business.*

Rajban drew a deep breath. The little airplane had been a sign, pure as the searing sky, that the time had come to follow Muthaye's mother into another life. So, without looking at Mother-in-law again, she walked past her. She kept her face calm, but inside her soul was trembling.

Rajban passed the table. She approached the door. Only then did Rao admit her existence. "Stop." His voice ever stern. "Get back to your work."

Her insides felt soft and hot as she told herself she did not hear him. She took another step, then another, the concrete floor warm and hard against her toes.

"I said stop."

The doorway was only five steps away now, a blazing rectangle, like a portal to another existence. Rajban walked toward it, her steps made light by the tumbling rhythm of her heart.

Rao stepped in front of her, and the light from the doorway went out.

Rajban made no effort to slip around him. Instead she reached for her sari and pulled it farther over her head, so that it partly concealed her face. Then she stood motionless, in silent protest.

At last.

The drone dropped to the level of the doorway. Through the cameras, Cody gazed into the house—and could not believe what she was seeing.

Rajban was walking out. She was heading straight for the door. Cody watched her pass the flustered old woman, and the table where Rao sat. It seemed certain she would reach the door, when abruptly, Rao rose to his feet. In two steps he stood in front of Rajban, blocking her exodus. Rajban stopped.

For several seconds nothing more happened. Rajban stood in calm serenity, refusing to yield, or to struggle. It had the flavor of a Ghandian protest, an appeal to the soul of the oppressor. Rao did not seem to like the taste of guilt. Outrage convulsed across his face. Then Cody saw a decision congeal.

Warmth fled her gut. What could she do? She was half a world away.

"Michael," she whispered. "It would be good if you were here now."

"Two or three more minutes," Jaya said. "That's all."

It was too much.

Cody ordered the drone forward. The autopilot guided it through the door, its wingtips whispering scant millimeters from the frame.

She could not defend Rajban, but she could let Rao know that Rajban was no longer alone.

Rajban kept her head down, knowing what would happen, but so much had changed inside her she could not turn back. Her heart beat faster, and still the expected blow failed to arrive.

Cautiously, she raised her eyes—to encounter a sheen of unexpected blue. The little airplane! It hovered at her shoulder like a dream image, so out of place did it seem in the hot, cloistered room. Brother-in-law stared at it as if he faced his conscience.

The tiny plane had summoned Rajban with its color like the searing sky. Wordlessly it now advised her, *Time to go*.

So she straightened her shoulders and stepped to the side, circling Rao until the doorway stood before her again. She walked toward it, through it, on unsteady legs, out into the mud of the street. The little airplane cruised past her, floating slowly back up into the blue. Brother-in-law started shouting . . . at Mother-in-law? Rajban didn't stay to find out. She stumbled away from the house, not caring where her feet might take her.

"Rajban!"

She turned, startled to hear her name. "Michael?"

The street was crowded with women moving in small, protective groups. Hard-eyed men lounged beside the shop fronts across the street, watching the women, or haggling over the price of goods, or sipping sweetened teas. Flies buzzed above the steaming mud.

"Rajban."

Michael emerged from the crowd, with Muthaye close behind him. She called out Rajban's name, then, "Namaste."

"Namaste," Rajban whispered.

Muthaye took her arm. Above her veil, her eyes were furious. "Come with us?"

Rajban nodded. Some of the men around them had begun to mutter. Some of the women stopped to stare. Muthaye ignored them. She stepped down the street, her head held high, and after they'd walked for a few minutes, she tossed back her sari and let the sunlight fall upon her face.

(xv)

Cody relinquished control of the drone, leaving it to return like a homing pigeon to the rental office. She lifted off her VR helmet, to find herself seated in her darkened living room, the lights of Denver and its suburbs gleaming beyond the window. She felt so scared she thought she might throw up.

There was a ticking bomb inside her.

She imagined a fertilized egg descending through one of her fallopian tubes, its single cell dividing again and again as it grew into a tiny bundle of cells that would become implanted against the wall of her womb. With a few hormonal triggers this nascent life form would change her physiology, so that her body would serve its growth. Quite a heady power for an unthinking cluster of cells, but as it reordered its environment, it would begin to shed evidence of its identity. Very early in gestation the uterine implant would classify it: Desirable, or Undesirable, and would act accordingly.

Cody laid her hand against her lower abdomen. She imagined she could feel him inside her, a bundle of cells with the potential to become a little boy. She remembered Gharia standing in the street, looking up at her with utter confusion, with helpless rage. He had tried too hard to hold onto the past and the world had gotten away from him.

Live lightly.

She felt as if she could hardly breathe. Her shoulders heaved as she struggled to satisfy her lungs. Air in, air out, but none of it absorbed. She felt as if she might drown, trapped in the close confines of her apartment. So she found her shades and called a cab.

If we are lucky, life shows us what we need to see.

Cody snorted. It was one of the many inspirational aphorisms drilled into her at Prescott Academy. And how had that particular pearl of wisdom concluded? Ah yes.

If we are brave, we dare to look.

Cody was not feeling terribly brave right now, and that was why she was running away. The cab took her to the airport, and from there an air taxi took her north. Upon landing, she picked up a rental car, arriving at Project 270 just before dawn.

An ocean of cold air had settled over the land. Though she wore boots and blue jeans, a thermal shirt and a heavy jacket, she still felt the bite of the coming winter as she stumbled through the darkness. A flash of her company badge soothed the security system. Ben would not be by for two or three hours, so she made her way alone to the upper gate, where she found the card slot by feel. The gate unlatched and she slipped inside.

The sky was a grand sweep of glittering stars, and in their light she could just make out the slope of the land. A few house lights gleamed far, far away across the river. Leaving the ATV in the garage, she set out down the long slope of the meadow, stumbling over clumps of sod, and seedling trees. The meadow grasses were heavy with dew, and when their seed heads brushed her thighs they shed freezing jackets of water onto her jeans, so that in less than a minute she was soaked through. She kept walking, listening to her socks squish, until she reached the bluff above the river bank.

The sky was turning pearly, and already birds were stirring in a lazy warm-up song. At the foot of the bluff, a doe hurried along the narrow beach, while the river itself grumbled in a slow, muddy exhalation that went on and on and on, a sigh lasting forever. Cody shivered in the cold. *Can't run any farther*.

It was time to discover what she had done, get the truth of it.

So many chronic problems came from not facing the truth.

She slipped her shades out of her jacket pocket and put them on. They were smart enough to know when they were being used. A menu appeared against the backdrop of the river. Tapping her data glove, she swiftly dropped the highlight down to "U." Only one listing appeared under that letter: UTERINE IMPLANT.

"Upload status report," she whispered. "And display."

Even then, fear held her back. She let her gaze fix on the river, its surface silvery in the rising light. Steam curled over it, phantom tendrils possessed of an alien motion, curling, stretching, writhing in a slow agony lovely to watch.

Lines of white type overlay the prospect. For several seconds Cody pretended not to see them. Then she drew a deep breath, and forced her gaze to fix on the words:

Status: No pregnancy detected.

Action: None.

She stared at the report for several seconds before she could make sense of it.

No baby. That made it easy . . . didn't it?

Her body did not feel the same. Somehow it had become hollow, forlorn. She stared at the water, wondering how something that had never existed could have felt so real.

The doe gave up its stroll on the beach to climb the embankment, stirring ahead of it a flight of blackbirds that spun away, trilling and peeping, noisy leaves tumbled on a ghostly wind. Cody remembered the painful confusion on Gharia's face as he stood in the street, looking up at her. She had seen herself in his eyes, asking *why?*

A figment of mist curled apart and she laughed softly, at herself and at the strained script she had tried to write for her life.

Gharia had wanted a scripted life too, except half the cast had vanished.

It was the same all over the world. Virtually every culture encouraged loyalty to social roles . . . but why was it done that way? Because there was some innate human need to eliminate chance? Or because it saved conflict, and therefore the energy of the group? Even as it wasted intellect and human potential . . .

The world was evolving. Energy was abundant now, and maybe, the time had come to let the old ways go, and to nurture a social structure that would unlock the spectrum of potential in everyone.

Starting here, Cody thought. She looked again at the menu, where Uterine Implant remained highlighted. "Shut it down," she whispered.

The letters thinned, indicating an inactive status.

Cody started to slip off the shades, but she was stopped by the sudden appearance of Michael's glyph within an urgent red circle, meaning *Please please please talk to me Now*.

Her throat had begun to ache in the cold air, but she tapped her data glove anyway, accepting the link. Michael's glyph expanded until it became his image. He stood in the open air beyond the bluff, remote from her, though she could see every detail of his face. "Michael? Has something happened to Rajban?"

"Rajban's all right." He squinted at her. "I can't see you."

"I just have shades."

His scowl was ferocious. "Then I borrowed this VR suit for nothing." She waited for him to get over it. After a moment his body relaxed. He turned, to look down at the silvery path of the river. "We did the right thing, Cody. Rajban is set now, in a house with two other women. She'll probably do garden work. You know the bag of soil she carried? Turns out to be a natural bioremediation culture, a community of microorganisms fine-tuned for the pollutants particular to the soil around Four Villages. Muthaye thinks it might be possible for Rajban to sell live cultures, or at least to use it to enhance her own business."

"That's good. I'm glad." She felt a fresh flush of wonder at the adaptiveness, the insistence of life. She toed a clod of exposed soil on the bluff. Contamination had been rampant in this land too, but it had been chased away, broken down in a series of simple steps by microorganisms too small to be seen. The scars of the past were being erased.

"Where are you?" Michael asked. "It's beautiful here."

"At a project site. It is pretty, but it's also very cold. I should head back to the car."

He stiffened. "If you're thinking of running away from me again, Cody, I might have some objection to that. It's been suggested to me that I give in too easily to other people's choices . . . when I know those choices are bad."

Her fingers drummed nervously against her thigh. A Canada goose paddled into sight, leaving a V wake unfurling behind it. "I really said that, didn't I?"

"Cody, I never wanted you to leave. You chose to go. Rajban chose to go. Should I have forced either one of you to stay?"

The goose had been joined by another. Cody's hands felt like insensate slabs of ice. "I don't know."

"If we each can't be free to decide for ourselves—"

"I have used the same uterine implant you discovered in Four Villages, only it was my choice, and I wanted a daughter." She said it very quickly, the words tumbling over one another. "I've shut it off now, and . . . I'm not pregnant."

He stared at her. His stunned expression might have been funny if she didn't feel so scared. "Say something, Michael."

"I . . . wish I was there with you."

She closed her eyes, feeling some of the chill go out of the dawn.

(xvi)

Michael finished the day in his office, facing Karen Hampton on the wall screen. Outside, the sun was a red globule embedded in brown haze. Its rays cast an aging glow across his desk as he leaned forward—tense, eager, and a little scared—the same way he'd felt on his first flight out of the US.

He knew it was likely Karen would fire him. He didn't want

it to happen, but that wasn't the source of his fear. He had done only what was needful, because trust comes first. So it wasn't Karen he feared. It was himself. He had lost some of his tolerance for the foibles and foolishness of human culture. He had learned to say *No*. It was a terrible, necessary weapon, and that he possessed it left him elated, and afraid.

Karen stared at him for several seconds with eyes that might have been made of glass. "You have a unique conception of the responsibilities of a regional director."

Michael nodded. "It's been a unique day."

He watched the lines of her mouth harden. "Michael, you're in Four Villages because I felt it was an ideal setting for your creativity, your energy, and your ambition, but you seem to have forgotten your purpose. You are there to grow an economy, *not* to rescue damsels in distress."

Michael no longer saw a clear distinction between the two. "Damsels are part of the economy, Karen. *Everyone* matters and you know it. The more inclusive the system is, the more we all benefit."

"How does offending a significant segment of the population expand the system?"

"Because doing anything else would break it. You said it yourself. Trust comes first. If people can't trust us to support them in their enterprises, then we've lost. If we come to be known as cowards, then we fail. I'm not here to fail."

Four Villages was a microcosm of the world and it faced formidable problems—poverty, over-population, illiteracy, environmental degradation, and perhaps worst of all, the poison of old ideas—but none of these challenges was insurmountable. Michael swore it to himself. *Nothing* was insurmountable. Terrible mistakes would be made, that was inevitable, but the worst mistake would be to pull back, to give up, to give in to the dead past.

"It's fear of change that's holding us back."

Change was coming anyway. The old world was being washed away, and soon there would be no paths left to follow. Then everyone would need to find their own way, like fishes or sleek eels, tracking ever-shifting currents, trailing elusive scents, nosing into the new possibilities of undreamed of futures.

Karen shook her head. "I love your thinking, Michael, but the hard fact is, this project is floundering."

Michael smiled, as the sun's last gleam finally vanished from the horizon. "No, Karen. It's just learning to swim."

Goddesses was published online by SciFi.com in July and August 2000. It won the 2000 Nebula Award for Best Novella.

From Mythic Island Press LLC

Fantasy and Science Fiction by

LINDA NAGATA

Stories of the Puzzle Lands

The Dread Hammer – Book 1

A tale of love, war, murder, marriage, & fate

Hepen the Watcher – Book 2

A tale of exile, rebellion, fidelity, & fire

The Nanotech Succession:

Tech-Heaven *(Prequel)*

The Bohr Maker *(winner of the Locus Award for Best First Novel)*

Deception Well

Vast

Other Story Worlds:

Goddesses & Other Stories *(a short fiction collection including the 2000 Nebula Award winner for Best Novella)*

Limit of Vision

Memory

Skye-Object 3270a *(young adult)*

Made in the USA
Columbia, SC
20 November 2017